Buffy the Vampire Slayer™

Buffy the Vampire Slayer
  (movie tie-in)
The Harvest
Halloween Rain
Coyote Moon
Night of the Living Rerun
Blooded
Visitors
Unnatural Selection
The Power of Persuasion
Deep Water
Here Be Monsters
Ghoul Trouble
Doomsday Deck
Sweet Sixteen
Crossings
Little Things

The Angel Chronicles, Vol. 1
The Angel Chronicles, Vol. 2
The Angel Chronicles, Vol. 3
The Xander Years, Vol. 1
The Xander Years, Vol. 2
The Willow Files, Vol. 1
The Willow Files, Vol. 2
How I Survived My Summer Vacation,
  Vol. 1
The Faith Trials, Vol. 1
Tales of the Slayer, Vol. 1
Tales of the Slayer, Vol. 2
The Journals of Rupert Giles, Vol. 1
The Cordelia Collection, Vol. 1
The Lost Slayer serial novel
    Part 1: Prophecies
    Part 2: Dark Times
    Part 3: King of the Dead
    Part 4: Original Sins

Child of the Hunt
Return to Chaos
The Gatekeeper Trilogy
  Book 1: Out of the Madhouse
  Book 2: Ghost Roads
  Book 3: Sons of Entropy
Obsidian Fate
Immortal
Sins of the Father
Resurrecting Ravana
Prime Evil
The Evil That Men Do
Paleo

Spike and Dru: Pretty Maids
  All in a Row
Revenant
The Book of Fours
The Unseen Trilogy (Buffy/Angel)
    Book 1: The Burning
    Book 2: Door to Alternity
    Book 3: Long Way Home
Tempted Champions
Oz: Into the Wild
The Wisdom of War
These Our Actors

The Watcher's Guide, Vol. 1: The Official Companion to the Hit Show
The Watcher's Guide, Vol. 2: The Official Companion to the Hit Show
The Postcards
The Essential Angel Posterbook
The Sunnydale High Yearbook
Pop Quiz: Buffy the Vampire Slayer
The Monster Book
The Script Book, Season One, Vol. 1
The Script Book, Season One, Vol. 2
The Script Book, Season Two, Vol. 1
The Script Book, Season Two, Vol. 2
The Script Book, Season Two, Vol. 3
The Script Book, Season Two, Vol. 4
The Musical Script Book: Once More, With Feeling

Available from POCKET BOOKS

Angel™

Available from Pocket Books

Buffy
the Vampire Slayer™
ANGEL™

monster island

**By Christopher Golden
and Thomas E. Sniegoski**

POCKET
BOOKS

New York   London   Toronto   Sydney   Singapore

First Pocket Books edition March 2003

Text copyright © 2003 by Twentieth Century Fox Film Corporation
All rights reserved

POCKET BOOKS
An imprint of Simon & Schuster
Africa House
64–78 Kingsway
London
WC2B 6AH

www.simonsays.co.uk

The text of this book was set in New Caledonia.

Printed in the United Kingdom by The Bath Press, Bath

10 9 8 7 6 5 4 3 2 1

A CIP catalogue record for this book is available from the British Library

ISBN 0-7434-6776-0

For Allie Costa, superstar
—C. G.

For Lily Grace, Alessandra Duanan, and Ryan Michael,
the Island's newest little monsters
—T. E. S.

ACKNOWLEDGMENTS

As always, the authors would like to thank Lisa Clancy and Lisa Gribbin at Simon Pulse. Special thanks are also due to Allie Costa for research assistance and unflagging enthusiasm, and to LeeAnne Sniegoski for cleaning up the mess. And . . .

Thanks, as always, to my wife, Connie (the woman who makes it all possible), and to our children: Nicholas, Daniel, and Lily. I love you all. And thanks to my comrade-in-pens, Tom Sniegoski. It's more fun with two in the sandbox.

In addition, thanks are due to: Mom and Peter, Erin and Eileen and Jake, Jamie and Gina and Kasey, the Russo family, the Benson family, Jose and Lisa, Meg Bibeau, Bob Tomko, Rick Hautala, Paula Carlson, Nancy Carlson, Ashleigh Bergh, Sally Partington, Rob Francis, the folks at Eclipse 2002, the

ACKNOWLEDGMENTS

Wicked Street Team, JavaDoc and the Yahoo crew, John McIlveen, Vanessa, and everyone else who has chimed in along the way.

—C. G.

All my gratitude to LeeAnne and Mulder. I'm not quite sure what I'd do without you two knuckleheads in my life, but I'm sure it wouldn't be half as interesting. And to Chris Golden, the best dang collaborator a guy could hope for. Thank you, sir, may I have another!

Special thanks are also due to: Mom and Dad, Dave Kraus (a monster in his own right), Tim Cole and the crew, Paul Griffin, David Carroll, Bob and Pat, Jon and Flo, Eric Powell (READ THE GOON!), Don Kramer, Greg Skopis, Meloney Crawford Chadwick, Ken Curtis, Mike and Anne Murray, and Bill Oppenhiem. Thanks for everything.

—T. E. S.

PROLOGUE

Cambodia

Demon bones and the scribblings of madmen.

That was the life of Harry Doyle. As an ethnodemonologist she spent her days sifting through the remains of ancient civilizations and far more recent demonic settlements, and her nights playing Jane Goodall anthropology girl amongst the monstrous tribes of the world. In places an ordinary human woman would be torn to shreds by a thousand species of hellbeast, Harry was offered a warm welcome and safe passage. Even some of the most vicious breeds respected her for her courteous and contemplative approach to her study of their kind.

Right about now, though, Harry Doyle needed a break. A party, even. A couple of shots of tequila and a reason to laugh. Music to dance to.

Anything but another steamy day, sweat streaming down her face, streaked with dirt from the pit she and her team had dug in the middle of the jungle. The insects were worse than any demon she had ever come across. Hell, she had been married to a Brachen and, after their divorce, had nearly married an Ano-Movic demon. Mosquitoes were about the most infernal creatures she had ever seen. Pretty much proof of the existence of evil.

"Damn it," she snapped, slapping at one of the insects on the back of her neck.

Not all demons were evil. That was the first thing she taught members of her team when they came on board. Or, at least, the human ones. It was the most important lesson she herself had ever learned, and the most important she could teach them. After all, if they were going to work for her, they were also going to have to work with demons.

Harry felt another bug alight on her cheek and brushed it away. Frustrated, she headed back to her pack to retrieve her repellant. She passed Al Gray and Jasvig, a wisp-thin Fawquilla demon. They smiled and waved, and Al tried to act nonchalant. Harry waved back, resolving to tease the big man mercilessly later about his flir-tation with Jasvig. She thought it was sort of sweet, actually. They were cute together. Harry herself found nothing attractive about the deep purple, almost skeletal Fawquilla tribe, but she had to work only with Jasvig and her brother Vist-yiq.

But later, there would definitely be teasing. It wouldn't be tequila shots and wild dancing, but in the middle of the Cambodian jungle, a girl had to take her pleasures where she found them.

At her pack, she sprayed on some more insect repellant, then quickly returned to the site. Al and Jasvig were no longer on break, and when she returned to the dig, they were hard at work once more. Harry stood back and surveyed the project. Vist-yiq was calling out instructions to the team, who were digging carefully around the Rhajadhow temple that had been unearthed there.

Of all the digs she had participated in, as a student or as the team leader, this was by far the most exciting. Volumes of the occult history of the world, compendia of demon lore—even the oldest such books she had ever been able to get her hands on—all of them offered the suggestion that the Rhajadhow might have been entirely mythical, never really having existed at all. There were records of sightings of the species before the Mahkesh Wars, but then afterward, nothing. Nothing at all.

But now Harry had found proof. More than proof. Not only had they discovered wall etchings inside and weapons that matched the descriptions in the ancient volumes of Rhajadhow blades, but she had instantly connected the temple with human places of worship in the region, both Hindu and Buddhist. One only had to look at the line of carved stone heads that rose on pillars near the entrance, or at the hideously grotesque, massive faces that loomed out from the stone spire that jutted from the top of the structure, to realize that places like the temple of Angkor Thom—perhaps a hundred miles distant—owed a great debt to Rhajadhow architecture.

Once this demonic temple was completely unearthed and she was able to document it, get it photographed and mapped, even filmed, there wasn't an occult scholar in the world who would be able to deny that she had made the first truly vital contribution to ethnodemonology of the twenty-first century.

A tiny smile played at the edges of her lips. *Maybe sweat and dirt and a few mosquitoes are a small price to pay,* she thought.

"Okay, fine," she whispered to herself. "But I'd still kill for a shot of tequila and a wedge of lime."

With a sigh she leaned her head back and looked up through the trees, trying to gauge the time by the color of the sky and the slant of light against the leaves. Midafternoon—still far too early to quit. But even though she herself was not doing the digging, just looking at the members of her team who were made her hotter and more exhausted. Harry knew that the sooner they finished the dig the better. The Cambodian government had not been too much of a nuisance yet, but she figured it was only a matter of time, particularly once they realized there was something of value in the ground out here.

But there were probably only a few more weeks of digging before the entire temple was unearthed and they had already uncovered enough so they could enter all of the rooms, save several ritual chambers that had caved in, probably hundreds of years past. Harry watched Al and Victor Kelso and the others on her team. She glanced at Vist-yiq, who was digging out a window on the side of the temple, sweat pouring off his purplish-black torso. Her first thought was that maybe she had been hasty in thinking she could never find his species attractive. He was a powerfully built creature, that was for sure, the males of the species being so unlike the females.

Her second thought was that there had been enough digging for today.

Harry called to Vist-yiq in his native tongue, which she knew she spoke well enough for a human but also knew probably sounded crude to him. He had been tearing through the dirt bare-handed, his talons better than any shovel, and now he glanced up at her. Harry started to walk over to the edge of the pit, several of the team members glancing up at her curiously.

Vist-yiq wiped his hands on his pants and strode to the bottom of a ladder that leaned against the wall, looking up at her. "Yes, Harry? Is there a problem?"

"No problem," she said, smiling and thinking wistfully of music and dancing. "But why don't we cut out the digging early today?

Give everyone a break. We can work on the mapping and photo survey and leave off the backbreaking stuff till tomorrow."

The demon grinned, showing yellowed fangs, and ran his talons through his thick, matted hair. "The team will be pleased."

"Good," Harry replied. "Do we have any tea left?"

"Lots," Vist-yiq said simply.

No lemon, Harry thought. *No ice. No tequila, either. But it'll have to do.*

Vist-yiq turned to relay the news to the rest of the team. In that same moment, something shrieked behind Harry. It lunged past her, swift and deadly, covered in copper fur. It landed on Vist-yiq's back. Its maw opened impossibly wide, revealing rows of teeth like daggers. It clamped its jaws down on Vist-yiq's neck and tore his head off with a snapping of bone and a rending of flesh, sounds that echoed across the dig, insinuating themselves in the space before the screaming began.

They were under attack.

Harry turned back toward her tent. There were weapons in it and she thought if she could only reach them, she might be able to drive the marauding demons off.

In her path was a hideous thing with a flat, triangular head and filth dripping from what appeared to be armor plating that covered its body. It had vestigial legs and slithered on its belly, long arms reaching for her. "Yesss," it hissed. "You are the one. Harry Doyle." The thing grinned, and Harry wanted to vomit. "A pleassssure to make your acquaintansssss."

The horror of its words knocked the breath out of her, and Harry stared at it wide-eyed.

These demons weren't marauders. This thing knew her name. They had come for *her.*

CHAPTER ONE

Sunnydale

Buffy Summers closed her eyes, took a deep breath, and wished she were anywhere else. She didn't tap her heels together three times, though. That was just dumb.

When she opened her eyes, nothing had changed. Not that she had expected it to, of course, but deep in her heart she wondered if maybe there wasn't something to that heel-tapping business after all.

The soles of her shoes clung to the sticky, warped wooden floors as she walked into Willy's, the notorious watering hole for those of a not-so-natural nature. The oppressive stink of stale beer, cigarette smoke, and other things she really did not care to think about lingered in the air, and Buffy wrinkled her nose in distaste.

Yet it was not just Willy's that she wanted to be away from. It was so much more than that. In the time since she had . . . come back, she had begun to see the world through new eyes. It was still difficult for her to really digest the truth, but the previous spring she had actually *died*. She had been dead for months. And in that time, she had been at peace.

Her friends had resurrected her. Ever since, the whole world had seemed just as gray and dingy as the interior of Willy's. Still, here she was. Alive. And now she had work to do.

Buffy stood in the middle of the poorly lit bar, gazing around at the tables and the clientele. Willy's was not very busy tonight, a smattering of demons and wanna-be sorcerers—and even a few ordinary humans—scattered about the room, drinks in front of them. From the corners of their eyes, they watched her, some with fear and others with hatred, even a few with open curiosity. Those were the ones who had no idea who she was.

The Slayer. The Chosen One. The one girl in all the world gifted with the power to combat the forces of darkness. She'd heard the line so many times when she had first discovered her destiny that it seemed hollow to her now. And it had been a long time since she had thought of her duties and her abilities as a *gift*.

Tension brewed in the air as she stood there, letting all the demons and demon/human half-breeds soak up her presence, and she wondered how they would react if they knew how she felt these days about being the Chosen One.

A table in the far corner caught her attention. There were three of them, two men and a woman. Most of the ordinary humans who spent time at Willy's were lowlife barflies who didn't care who they drank with, or those who'd tinkered with the supernatural before. This trio appeared at first glance to be so normal that Buffy wondered what they were doing there.

7

Then one of the men nervously licked his lips with a tongue that was impossibly long, bright pink in color, and forked at the end.

So much for normal, Buffy thought as she watched them. The one with the tongue was some kind of half-breed, and she assumed the other two were as well. The trio grew increasingly agitated by her attention, and at last stood as if suddenly remembering a previous engagement. They left the premises through a fire exit at the back of the bar.

Buffy considered going after them. Someone had been hunting and killing demon/human half-breeds in Sunnydale in the past week, with three dead already that she knew of. That was her job—slaying supernatural beings. But whoever was killing these half-breeds was not interested in figuring out first if they were actually evil. One of the guys, a Dakini-Swedish mix, had been an accountant, for God's sake.

When you started killing the demon accountants, something was really wrong with the world.

But Buffy could not go chasing after Tongue Boy and his amigos at the moment. Not only could she not muster the enthusiasm, but she was not about to provide personal security for every part-demon who passed through Sunnydale. Nope, she was going to have to take a more direct route. That meant information about the dark underbelly of Sunnydale.

And that, more often than not, meant Willy. Bartender, proprietor, snitchy weasel of the dark underbelly.

Willy stood behind the wooden bar, a variety of liquors in fancy bottles at his back, and worked furiously at drying a beer mug with a towel Buffy guessed might once have been white. He smiled nervously, avoiding eye contact, and continued to work at the mug. She'd done this so many times before that it took everything she could muster not to turn away and leave, to forget about the murdered half-breed demons and return home—to go to bed, to dream—to escape this world and remember the peace that had been taken from her.

Paradise. The memory lingered like the stab of a knife. It pissed her off. The problem was, her friends had thought she was trapped in some dark dimension, suffering eternal torment. They had thought they were doing her a favor by using sorcery to pull her out of that place. But they were wrong. Terribly wrong. Still, she could not take out her anger and frustration and despair on them.

Which meant she had to take it out on someone else.

"Willy," Buffy said. "Look at me."

He glanced up as she stepped to the bar. A pale smile twitched at the edges of his mouth. "Buffy. Hi. Been a while. Thought you might'a forgot about us or something." He laughed anxiously, still rubbing the towel against the drink glass.

"You're not that lucky," she said, her ire on the rise. "But if you want to change your luck, maybe we can skip right past the beating to what I need to know."

"Okay, okay." Willy set the mug down, convinced that it was finally dry, and slung the dirty towel over his shoulder. He held up his hands and gestured for her to keep her voice down. "I'll tell you everything I know, just don't call any more attention to yourself than you already have." He looked past her to make sure that none of his clientele was paying close attention. "Business has picked up a little since you haven't been around much. I don't need you to start spookin' the regulars."

He put a coaster in front of her that advertised something called a Shoggoth's Spritzer, as if he expected her to order a drink. Buffy sighed and slid onto a stool, playing along.

"What'll it be?" Willy asked her. "On the house."

9

She wasn't the least bit thirsty and, even if she had been, she doubted she ever would have accepted this sleazeball's charity.

"I'll just have a few of these," she said as she reached for a bowl of cheese balls that sat just a little ways down the bar.

Her fingertips touched one of the cheese balls, and they shrieked. Black spindly legs emerged from the sides of their yellowy-orange bodies and they scrambled over the side of the bowl and across the bar-top.

"Son of a—I am so sorry," Willy said, staring at her with a gaze both penitent and fearful. "They were supposed to be dead. I can't believe they sold me the live ones again. Here, have some of these."

He snatched away the now empty bowl and replaced it with one full of what appeared to be pretzels. But then again, one never could tell. Buffy wrinkled her nose and pushed the pretzels away, watching for telltale signs of movement within the new bowl.

"Me, having questions. You? Having answers."

"Sure, sure," Willy said, again glancing nervously around at his customers. "Whatever you want."

"Someone's killing half-breeds. If they keep it up, I figure that'll end up being most of your customers dead. The kind of dead when they can't still come in and pay their tab. What do you know?"

"Not much," he said as he used the dirty towel to wipe down the bar to her left. "But you're right. Things picked up when you did your disappearing act, but these killings have seriously cut into my business. Look at it in here, it's a freakin' cemetery."

A demon dressed in a powder blue leisure suit, its white shirt opened at its throat to reveal pale green mottled flesh and a gold chain as thick as a suspension cable, sidled up to the bar beside her. It gazed at her with eyes covered by a milky, nicti-tating membrane that moved aside when it blinked to reveal moist, bloodred orbs.

Willy seemed to panic. "What'll you have, pal?" he asked the demon. But it refused to answer his question.

Buffy attempted to ignore the horrible creature, looking just about everywhere other than those nasty scarlet eyes. But it was staring at her. And smiling.

"Come here often?" the leisure-suited demon asked her.

"More often than I care to," she muttered beneath her breath as she attempted to read the label on a skull-shaped bottle across from her.

The demon laughed. It sounded wet, as if there were some-thing it should spit out just at the back of its throat.

"Hey, barkeep," it gurgled to Willy, "you'd better call the cops, 'cause this little firecracker just stole my heart."

Buffy tried to stay calm; she really did. She tried to ignore the monster and hoped it would eventually be bored by her unre-sponsiveness and return to its table in a really dark corner at the back of the bar.

But then it touched her.

It was like somebody had taken that nasty jelly stuff from inside the can of a processed ham and slapped it down on top of her hand. She reacted out of utter revulsion, snapping an elbow up into the demon's squishy face and then flipping it off the barstool beside her to land upon the floor.

"Touch me again, it's your own personal apocalypse."

Behind the bar, Willy rubbed his forehead like he had suddenly come down with a really bad headache. The demon thrashed about where it had fallen, and its body seemed to expand. The sound of polyester ripping and seams bursting filled the barroom as the creature grew to more than twice its size. Black, razor-sharp protrusions emerged from along the limbs that jutted from its gelatinous body.

"Gonna make you pay for that, girly-girl," it growled as it rose slowly from the floor to tower over her.

Buffy realized that any thoughts of leaving Willy's without violence were simply wishful thinking. She should have known better.

"How about a drink and some free potato skins, huh?" Willy asked the demon, voice erupting with mock enthusiasm in an attempt to defuse the situation. "We'll call this a little misunderstanding and get on with our night."

The creature flexed its bulbous mass as it prepared to defend its wounded ego, and Buffy heard Willy muttering something behind the bar about insurance premiums. The disgusting thing lunged at her, but Buffy was ready. She leaped high over its quivering, thundering mass to land in a crouch behind it. Like some amorphous blob of Jell-O, the thing had completely enveloped her empty barstool. Now it searched its own globby mass for some sign of her, apparently assuming it had absorbed her as well.

Buffy reached toward the demon from behind, careful not to cut herself on its nasty spines, and took hold of the cable-like gold chain still around its neck. With a jerk she twisted the chain tight, cutting off the demon's oxygen. Whatever its body was made of, it still had a mouth and a nose in the front. She hoped that meant it still needed to breathe.

Score one for the Slayer.

The oxygen-deprived demon gasped and clutched at its throat. Its body shivered in undulating waves as it struggled to breathe.

"Now that I've got your attention, Mr. Suave," Buffy said, twisting the chain a little tighter, amazed at how thin the demon's neck had become, "how about you promise to retire your oh-so-promising career as a pickup artist, and I let your neck return to its normal size."

"He don't look so good, Slayer," Willy warned from behind the bar. Nervously, he poured himself a shot. "He's turning green."

"Turning . . . what do you call the color he was before?" Buffy asked as she let go of the chain. The demon sucked in a heaping lungful of air and dropped to its knees, where it gazed up at her with gratitude.

The scream came from outside, tearing into the bar through the open fire door that led to the back alley. It was the kind of sound that made the tiny hairs on the back of Buffy's neck stand at attention. The first wail was followed by another, equally unnerving, but this one was dramatically cut short. The sudden silence inside the bar seemed to close in around the Slayer.

Buffy rushed across the barroom. Many of the demons she passed on her way flinched as she ran by. The fire door in back stood partially open—left that way by the half-breeds who had taken off at the sight of her. Buffy pushed through it and found herself outside in a winding alleyway that separated the backsides of two city blocks. The largest of the buildings just along the alley was a huge brick structure that had stood empty for ages. Windows were shattered, some of them boarded, and the brick still bore the faint ghost of a painted logo for the family-run furniture business that had flourished in Sunnydale once upon a time.

The alley stank like a toilet, the stench made all the more fragrant by the unusually humid weather that the region had been enduring the past few weeks. The air was so thick and foul, she could practically taste it, and it made her want to throw up.

Hell. She'd been in paradise once. But this was hell.

Another scream ripped through the oppressive night and it spurred her to move faster. As she rounded a corner she nearly ran headlong into a barrel-chested demon in black jeans and a white muscle T-shirt.

Buffy stepped back into a battle stance, ready for anything, and studied the face of the demon. It grinned, showing off a smile that looked like a visit to a cutlery store. With its leathery brown skin and those nasty jagged teeth, the monster reminded her of a crocodile.

"Where's that nutty Australian guy when you really need him?" she muttered beneath her breath.

Her gaze ticked past the reptilian creature. Farther along the alley a quartet of hideous creatures, demons of various species, were lashing out with hard kicks and swinging brutal weapons, putting a serious hurt on someone or something curled into a ball upon the alley floor.

"Four on one. That doesn't look too fair."

Croc-boy shrugged. "What in life really is?" it replied, leaning down to grab at her.

Buffy snapped her fist forward, putting her weight into it, and gave it a hard shot in the face. There was an explosion of blood and teeth and a sound like tree branches snapping. The crocodile demon moaned in pain, eyes wide in surprise as it stumbled back away from her.

The Slayer sighed. "Nothing I hate more than philosophical demons."

The croc started to choke on something—*probably teeth,* she thought—and she took the opportunity to glance around for something that would pierce the thing's thick, armor-plated hide. Buffy spotted a wooden pallet leaning against the factory wall and she snapped a side kick at it, shattering it into pieces. Keeping an eye on Croc-boy, she picked up a jagged piece of the wood from the ground. It wasn't a fancy crossbow or an antique sword, but it would do in a pinch.

The croc-demon threw itself at her with a ferocious roar, its jagged maw looking like the front of a Halloween pumpkin. She sidestepped its lunge—but the demon was faster than she'd anticipated. It stopped abruptly and spun to lash out with a solid blow to her face. Her head snapped back and to the side and the bitter taste of blood flowed into her mouth.

Buffy didn't care for that in the least.

The demon lunged in closer and threw another punch—one that could very easily have sent Buffy's head into orbit if she allowed it to connect. The Slayer tilted her head out of the way and felt a breeze as its fist passed dangerously close to her cheek. Croc-boy gaped stupidly at her, apparently stunned that its punch did not find its destination. It seemed even more surprised when she gripped its massive, tree limb–like arm and savagely bent it in a direction it was clearly not meant to turn.

The whip crack sound of breaking bones and the bellow of pain that came from the demon were strangely satisfying. Croc-boy cradled its broken arm to his chest.

"Don't be such a baby," Buffy said, snapping a high kick to its throat, cutting off its wails of pain. She snatched up her piece of wood from the ground and plunged it through the tough, scaly hide of the demon's chest.

Buffy stepped aside as the monster crashed to the ground like a felled oak. Another night, in a better mood, she might have muttered, "Timber." But not tonight.

Not when there were four other demons twenty yards away, still intent upon their victim, as though her presence did not bother them at all. Only when she started cautiously toward them did they look up. One was a Fyarl, with the hooves and ram horns and bony protrusions that went along with that. One was a Polgara, judging by the massive spike that jutted from its wrist. She thought the third was a Vahrall, but she didn't have a clue what the fourth one was.

Nasty-looking bugger, though. Yellow skin, like something diseased.

What the hell are they all doing together? Buffy thought. Most of the demon breeds kept pretty much to themselves—at least in her experience. These things working side by side like some street gang . . . it baffled her.

"So," she said, with a razor-edged, humorless smile, "which one of you is Justin?"

"Pretty fancy moves against one enemy, Slayer," hissed the Fyarl. "But how will you fare against us all?"

A Fyarl that speaks English. Curiouser and curiouser, she thought. Buffy crouched and snatched up another jagged shaft of wood from the broken pallet. "Only one way to find out."

With a cacophonous roar of demon voices, they all charged her at once. The Vahrall reached her first, the other three stepping back as if to allow it first dibs. The eye symbol of its tribe, nastily carved into the mottled flesh of its forehead, bore down on her as it attacked. Its large hands reached for her neck.

"So what's your story?" she asked, slapping its clawed hands away. "Night out with the boys, things got a little out of hand?" She drove the piece of wood into its left eye and gave it a nasty twist for good measure. There was a wet squelching sound, and black ichor spurted out onto her fingers.

"You should've stayed home," Buffy said.

But the demon wasn't listening. It cried out in agony and reared back away from her, its hands feebly attempting to remove the splintered board from its eye socket. A moment later it fell to the ground, twitched, and was still.

The Polgara snarled and circled, looking for an opening. The towering Fyarl eyed her warily now and took a step back, but the thing with the pus-yellow skin only hissed, crouched low, and lunged for her, its slitted eyes gleaming madly.

"We are legion," it whispered as razor-sharp claws extruded from the tips of its fingers, lashing out as though to rip the flesh from her bones.

Buffy ducked beneath the swipe of the claws and lunged up to drive an upturned palm into the creature's jaundiced face. It stumbled back from the blow, stunned.

The Polgara had been lingering, waiting for an opening. Now it charged in at her, the long, deadly spike that protruded from its left arm slashing swordlike down at her. Buffy's entire body was raging with the adrenaline that surged through her now, and it was as though the warrior part of her had taken over. She moved fluidly, almost without thinking, and with a roundhouse kick to the side of its misshapen skull, she stopped the Polgara cold.

As the Polgara stumbled to one side, dazed, she gripped it by the wrist. "Mind if I borrow this?" Careful not to injure herself, Buffy snapped the bonelike protrusion off at the base. The demon screamed in agony.

"Oh, stop whining. I'm gonna give it right back."

With a grunt of effort, she drove the point of the organic blade through the Polgara's throat, killing it with its own weapon. Buffy hefted the swordlike appendage in one hand.

"Much nicer than splintery pieces of wood," she said with a smile, liking its feel and weight. "Lightweight but durable."

The jaundiced demon had recovered from the kick to its face and came at her now, a chittering noise like a swarm of locusts escaping from its thin-lipped mouth.

"Gotta say, yellow? Even pukey yellow? Just not a color that makes me tremble with fear."

Buffy thrust the Polgara's spike forward, using a fencing move that Giles had taught her in her early days as the Slayer. The demon dodged and lashed out at her, its claws raking across her wrist, causing her to drop the Polgara appendage.

"You are but one of the obstacles we will surpass on our way to supremacy," it growled.

Buffy drove her fist into the creature's abdomen. "Is there a direct route to supremacy, or do you need to transfer to another bus?" She jumped up into a high, spinning kick, but the demon ducked, her kick passing over its head without connection.

"Would you mind standing still?" she asked, perturbed. "How am I supposed to kick your ass if you keep moving around?"

From ten feet away—a safe, spectator-type distance—the Fyarl roared its displeasure. "Kill her, you idiot! She's only one! A human! Kill her and you shall have an army to command!"

Buffy smirked as she shot a glance at the Fyarl. "Big words coming from a guy who hasn't gotten closer than five feet from me."

The putrid yellow demon tackled her, driving her hard to the alley floor. She could hear the Fyarl leader still urging it on as it attempted to pin her arms down.

"Surrender, Slayer," the demon growled, bearing down upon her. "You can never hope to defeat us. Bare your throat to my claws and I will send you to the afterlife swiftly."

Up close, its skin looked and felt like rotten lemon peel. She held on to its wrists, keeping its claws at bay. To her horror, she saw that it had started to drool, a thick bead of saliva growing, on the verge of falling down from its mouth onto her.

"Thanks," she said, bringing her head up sharply to slam it into the monster's looming face. "The thought of your drool landing on me was a pretty big incentive." Lemonhead was stunned, but she head-butted it again for good measure.

The monster went limp, and she rolled it from atop her.

She sprang to her feet to see that that the Fyarl leader was beginning to back from the alley, trying to hide its obvious cowardice.

"This isn't over," it warned her. "The day is coming, Slayer. The day when all the tainted halflings will be destroyed, and the human race will be buried beneath an onslaught unlike any this world has ever seen. All will bow and bleed for their betters!"

Buffy shook her head, frowning, and took a single step toward it. "Could you take that from 'tainted halflings'? I'm not sure I caught the rest."

The Fyarl spun on one hoof and began to run. "The day is coming, Slayer!" it shrieked again, as if the vaguely ominous threat might make its departure appear less craven.

She started to go after the loudmouthed demon but remembered the screams that had brought her here. Buffy turned to see a body sprawled in front of the open side entrance to the abandoned furniture factory. Even through the dark splashes of blood—turned black by the shadows of the alley—and in spite of the beating he had taken, she recognized the corpse as that of the long-tongued half-breed who had fled from Willy's minutes before.

Buffy had considered going after him and his friends, asking them what they were afraid of. A twitch of guilt went through her. If she had followed them . . . but she did not allow her mind to follow that path. A dark resignation swept over her now. There was no way for her to have known the killers would strike now, here, and getting answers out of Willy had been a higher priority than some skittish half-breed demons.

An image swam into her mind, of the anxious, even frightened, faces of the one with the tongue and his comrades, and Buffy had to wonder if they had fled from her because they'd thought she might be the one that was doing these killings. She was the Slayer, after all. Maybe they had been afraid she was adhering to a stricter definition of the job description.

Troubled, she squatted beside the body and checked its neck for a pulse. Not that she expected to find one. As she suspected, the half-breed was dead. Her hand came away stained with its blood, and she wiped it on her pants leg.

The heavy factory door creaked as it swayed, coaxed by the muggy evening wind. A faint smell wafted out from the darkness within the factory, and Buffy peered inside, curious about the source. She knew the smell; it had become quite common to her since she had picked up the mantle of the Chosen One.

A baker knew the smell of yeast and freshly baked bread; a hairstylist the fried-egg smell of a perm, a florist the array of aromas from various flowers and plants.

The Slayer knew the smell of death.

Buffy rose from beside the corpse and cautiously stepped through the doorway into the embrace of darkness. It was cooler inside than out. She waited momentarily for her eyes to adjust. Gradually the shapes became more distinguishable, and she was able to discern the nightmarish scene laid out before her. She wished that she had never come inside.

Half-breeds, by the look of them—male, female, young, and old: murdered horribly, savagely, without mercy.

It looked as though they had been living here. She remembered how the three had reacted when she first came into the bar. They had been scared, not wanting to be noticed. Even if they had not feared that she might be the one doing the killing, they would not have wanted anyone to discover them here.

But someone had.

From behind an overturned barrel, a tiny hand, still clutching a filthy rag doll, could be seen. Buffy quickly looked away.

When she had first heard about the murders, she had been unable to summon up a great deal of concern. Since returning from the dead she was finding it difficult to care about her *own* species, never mind demons.

But this was different. These were innocents. Seeing them like this shook something up inside of her. Something that she realized had been badly in need of a shake-up. Numb as she had been, Buffy Summers felt something, now, and with a shuddering sigh, she recognized a second emotion coming right on top of the first. Buffy was horrified. And at the same time, she was grateful for the feeling.

The grisly tableau splayed out before her had awoken something within her.

Buffy stepped from the abandoned factory, now turned charnel house, and out into the night. No matter how she tried, she could not erase the image of the child's hand clutching the doll from her mind.

It stayed with her well into the night.

CHAPTER TWO

Rupert Giles sipped at a steaming cup of Darjeeling tea and studied the Magic Box's receipts for the last month. Business was good—unusually so. There had been an increase in sales of more than thirty percent during the last month, but an incessant nag of a voice somewhere at the back of his mind wondered *why?*

He set his cup down upon the saucer and picked up the stack of inventory sheets to peruse. Giles remembered that Anya had mentioned that certain magickal herbs and powders had been in great demand of late, but for the life of him couldn't remember which ones.

There was a light knock at the door, and he glanced at his wristwatch to check the time. "Rather late for visitors," he muttered, rising to his feet to answer.

When he opened the door, Buffy marched headlong into

his apartment, not even glancing at him. A deep frown furrowed her brow. "We have to do something about this," she declared.

Giles smiled slightly. "Do come in."

She spun around to face Giles, focusing on him for the first time. "I don't know what's going on out there, but it's pretty nasty."

Giles closed the door and regarded her curiously, his amusement dissipating as he realized just how troubled Buffy was. "Perhaps you ought to take it from the top? Did your patrol tonight provide some revelation regarding these half-breed killings?"

"Revelation? That's one way to put it," she said, a disturbing expression on her face. Buffy went to the sofa and sat down, while Giles took a chair opposite her.

"I stopped by Willy's. Obvious choice, right? One-stop shopping for all your local Gossip o' Darkness needs. Got hit on by a disco-era Jell-O demon. Scared off some half-breeds. They ran out the back."

Buffy grew very quiet and pulled her legs up beneath her on the sofa, and Giles thought he saw her shudder. "Buffy?" he asked. "What is it? What's happened?"

And she told him. Giles listened to her tale of screams from the alley behind Willy's, of her fight with a quartet of demons whose alliance was highly unusual, and of her discovery afterward.

"I've seen a lot of things, doing what I do," Buffy said, glancing up to meet his gaze. "But this was awful, Giles. It was a massacre. Just . . ." She shook herself. "It's gotten under my skin."

"Of course it has," he said softly. He removed his glasses for a moment and massaged the bridge of his nose, leaning back into his chair. "Logic suggests these four were responsible, but the Fyarl's boasts make me certain there's more to it. And what did the other, the yellow one—probably a Grazniczh, by the way—say to you?"

"'We are legion,'" Buffy repeated, looking at him gravely.

Giles nodded. "So there are more who are part of this . . . crusade of slaughter. And they're obviously organized."

"I don't get it," Buffy said. "Most of these demon breeds are like high school kids, sticking with their little cliques, not hanging out with anyone who doesn't belong. Does this make any sense to you?"

Giles slipped his glasses back on. "No. No, it doesn't. A Fyarl demon can barely get along with its own species never mind a Polgara and a Vahrall. Demon 'breeds,' as you say, have historically been stratified into a caste system that was brutally definitive. Some of them mix, of course. But the majority keep to themselves. In the past there were large-scale wars between various species and tribes of demons, sometimes decimating entire regions."

"When they weren't decimating humans," Buffy muttered.

Giles nodded. "True. Though the truth is that in ages past, demons spent a good deal more time fighting amongst themselves than trying to conquer humanity. By the time they realized they weren't the dominant life-form on the planet, it was too late. This world was already overrun by human civilization."

Buffy let out a short, humorless laugh. "So we're the problem. That's a twisted take on things."

"From the demonic perspective, we are indeed the problem. The evolution of humanity led to our usurping their control over this world. That's a large part of the reason they hate demon/human half-breeds. Think of it, Buffy: They're the offspring of a full-blooded demon who dared to mate with a human being. Historically, half-breeds have been beneath notice. Now, it appears that someone has taken special notice of them, with the most horrible intentions."

"Well, no wonder they were hiding," Buffy replied, laying her head back against the sofa. "I mean, this demon Gestapo comes to town, of course the half-breeds are gonna hide out. I just wish we'd known what was happening before the Romper-Stompers figured out where they were hiding."

Giles stared at her, barely hearing the latter portion of her comments. *Hiding,* he thought. *And the others—the Gestapo, as Buffy called them—were hunting for them.*

"Um, hello? Wakey-wakey, Giles," Buffy said.

He shook his head. "Quite." The Watcher placed his glasses back upon the bridge of his nose and reached for the inventory sheets on the coffee table. Quickly he scanned the sheets to identify the items that had been selling with increased frequency from the store: Slippery Elm, Poke Root, Eye of Fire Newt, Dracoena Draco, Dove Hearts.

"Damn, what a fool I've been!" Giles snapped angrily. He tossed the papers back onto the coffee table.

"What's up?" Buffy asked, leaning over to take a look.

"The Magic Box has of late had a run on particular items. Business has been very good," he said, frustrated. "You'd think I'd have noticed that these things that have been in such great demand are ingredients used to erect a ward that will mask the presence of supernatural beings from locator spells."

"The half-breeds trying to hide." Buffy glanced at him, then picked up the pages herself and began leafing through. "And let me guess. I bet there's an increase in the stuff used for locator spells as well. My Gestapo buddies trying to find them."

Giles could only muster a tired nod. "I should have noticed."

"You would've. Eventually," Buffy offered, trying to placate him.

But even though he believed she was correct, that he would have noticed eventually—he had begun to look into it this very night—he still could not shake the suspicion that lives might have been saved if he had noticed earlier.

"So what now?" Buffy asked. "There are probably more half-breeds out there, and we have no idea how many demons have joined the extermination squad."

"The first thing we'll do is remove these ingredients from the shelves, making them inaccessible. Hopefully that will at least prevent some of those in jeopardy from being found."

Buffy nodded, a grim sort of anticipation lighting up her face. "Good. And then I start hunting the hunters. Make sure the demonic Hitler youth don't hurt anyone else."

Two days and nights went by with no further conflict or revelations regarding the killings of half-breeds in Sunnydale. Buffy had patrolled both nights and had succeeded only in dusting a vampire drifter who had just come to town. Tourists. Buffy hated them. Beyond that, it had been quiet.

Quiet bothered her. Something more was brewing. She was certain of it.

When she walked into the Magic Box that afternoon, her best friend, Willow Rosenberg, was seated at a table with her girlfriend, Tara Maclay, searching through a leather-bound book that was faded, its binding cracked and pages yellowed. The two witches looked up and greeted her amiably.

"Hey guys," Buffy replied.

Behind the counter, Giles was sighing heavily and glancing heavenward while Anya stomped a foot in protest.

"It's just not fair, Giles!" Anya whined.

Buffy strode up to the table where Willow and Tara sat. "What's today's trauma?"

Willow grinned and rolled her eyes, tucking a lock of her red hair behind one ear. Tara shifted awkwardly, uncomfortable with gossiping. There was a kind of tired wisdom in Tara that Buffy had always admired.

"This thing Giles did, taking some of the inventory off the shelves?" Tara began. "Anya's mad."

"Sales, pretty much plummeting back to their old pitiful level," Willow added.

Buffy raised an eyebrow. "Ouch."

Once upon a time—for centuries, actually—Anya had been a vengeance demon. When her demonic power had been taken from her, she had been forced to make her way in a modern world and deal with human emotions that were completely foreign to her. Somehow, she had managed it. Buffy and Willow's friend Xander Harris had helped. In a twist neither of the young women could have predicted, Anya and Xander had fallen in love. But, then again, neither Buffy nor Xander would have predicted Willow falling in love with Tara either.

Anya did her best to contribute to the group, more out of her feelings for Xander than anything else. When Giles had opened the magick shop, it had simply fallen into place that Anya would work for him there. She relished the business end of it, separating people from their money, and had proven so good at it that often enough Giles left the running of the shop to her.

It was inevitable, as far as Buffy was concerned, that this would sometimes lead to conflict.

"Would somebody please lock the door?" Anya called, turning away from Giles and beginning to count the day's receipts out of the cash register. "We're closed, in case nobody bothers to look at a clock."

Giles threw up his hands and went about arranging, by height, a selection of urns in a counter display. "Anya, it isn't forever. Only until we determine what's going on here. It would be irresponsible of us to continue to sell—"

Anya snapped a hard look at him. "I know. It's just . . . I don't know if I can bear to watch another customer walk out of here without leaving all their hard-earned money behind. It's so . . . so depressing."

That seemed to be the end of it for the moment. Anya went back to counting receipts, and Giles could not seem to find an arrangement for the urns that satisfied his sense of aesthetics.

Buffy smiled softly and crouched down beside Tara at the table. "So, what else is up?" she asked in a whisper. "Besides Anya's inconsolable grief, I mean."

Willow nodded enthusiastically. "Tara and I are the research girls. We've been going through these dusty-musties looking for stuff on the half-breeds. We were thinking maybe there'd be a record of other crusades against them." She then looked to Tara, and the two of them beamed at each other. "I think we are making excellent progress."

"If you do say so yourself," Tara replied archly, looking at her girlfriend with her trademark sweet, lopsided grin.

"And I do!" Willow declared. Then she shot a conspiratorial glance at Buffy. "Even though we really don't have squat."

Tara looked sheepishly back into the open book before her. "Well, we haven't found anything that could help yet, but—"

"But we *did* learn that Fyarl demons have a bizarre aversion to asparagus," Willow interjected, nodding proudly.

"That'll be helpful," Buffy told them both with a faux earnest nod. "Next time I catch up to the cowardly Fyarl-lion, I can kill him with an asparagus."

"Sorry," said Willow, "we're reading as fast as we can, but there's not even a hint in here about this stuff. For so long it seems like half-breeds were just beneath notice. The demon world's dirty little secret."

With a sigh, Buffy moved across from her and slumped into a chair. "That's okay. Something's bound to rear its ugly head sooner or later."

"Did I hear someone call my name?"

Xander stepped out of the back room, carrying a large box. "You guys really shouldn't be talking about me when I'm not around."

Buffy smiled at him. Xander Harris had been her best guy-friend since she had moved to Sunnydale, and Willow's best friend pretty much since birth. Though he had fought alongside her hundreds of times, Buffy never failed to be amazed by him. Despite the fact that his girlfriend was a former vengeance demon, Xander was really the only ordinary one among them. No Watcher-training, no witchcraft, no history of supernatural powers. Xander was just Xander.

And he brightened any room he entered.

"Hey," Buffy called to him as he set the box down on the floor. "You're awfully chipper tonight."

"Actually, still 'Xander.' I knew a kid named Chipper growing up, though. Bad teeth. Rotten baseball player." Xander glanced around, realized that no one was following his line of rambling, and then shrugged as he looked back to Buffy. "See, I'm like 'invisible boy.' I'm gonna get myself a flute and hide out in the ceiling of the high school music room. Or, I would, except we blew up the high school."

Buffy laughed softly. "You like to bring that up, don't you?"

"How many people can say that?" Xander asked. "It was a milestone."

"Not to mention a felony!" Willow piped up.

The three of them shared a moment of recognition, a little lightning bolt that connected them to the past and one another. Tara had glanced up and smiled, but was looking at her book again. Giles had at last moved on to pricing the urns, and Anya was still counting register receipts.

"What's in there?" Buffy asked Xander, motioning with her chin to the box on the floor.

Xander crouched and began to pry it open. "Something that I hope will pull my sweetie from the depths of despair."

Anya lifted her head to see what Xander was doing.

He pulled back the flaps of the box and reached inside. "Look, An," he said, removing a fetish doll from the box. Its body was crafted from some kind of dried, human-shaped root; the hair adorning its head was bright orange grass. He shook it at Anya enthusiastically. "A whole box full of crazy chotchkes that you can mark up and sell for three times their value, what do ya say?"

They all looked up abruptly as the door to the Magic Box opened and three figures stepped into the store, clad in black trench coats and hats, their features masked by the upturned collars of their coats.

"I thought I told somebody to lock the door!" Anya wailed from her place of misery at the cash register.

One of the figures turned to the door, found the lock, and clicked it into place.

"At least somebody listens to me around here," she grumbled.

"Excuse me," Giles began, coming around from behind the counter. "Perhaps you've misunderstood. The store is closed for the night."

The three silent figures came farther into the store, their movements cautious, tentative. Buffy felt a ripple of alarm go through her, and she rose from her seat. One of the three reached up to remove the hat from its head, revealing cruel, demonic features and skin the color of drying blood. The demon studied them with malicious intent and then smiled.

"Yeah, look, sorry about that," the blood-hued demon said, waving one hand in the air. "It's just that it's urgent. Maybe you can help us out and we'll get out of your hair in a wink."

A nasty vibe was rolling off the three newcomers in waves, but Giles did not seem overly alarmed, so Buffy hesitated to start something. It was possible these guys really were customers. It was a magick shop, after all. The store drew all sorts of walk-in business.

The Watcher strode to the middle of the store, only a few feet from Buffy, but his eyes were on the demon that had spoken. "You're of the Tok'mundar Clan, aren't you?"

The bloodred demon narrowed his cruel eyes. "What of it?"

"Nothing at all," Giles said politely. "It's only that I'd thought I'd read that your clan never left Malaysia."

The Tok'mundar glared at the Watcher. "Maybe you'd better double-check your sources, then, huh?"

"Maybe I'd better," Giles agreed. "In any case, we *are* closed, but if you know what it is you're looking for, perhaps I can help you."

The other two trench-coated demons reached up to remove their hats as well, and Buffy saw that they were very obviously not Tok'mundar. The Slayer eyed them warily. From the sound of things, the Tok'mundar were an isolationist species of demon. The idea of it traveling with other breeds ought to have surprised her. The truth was, however, that she had half-expected it. The arrival of these three couldn't have been a coincidence. Someone was marshaling full-blooded demons of all species into a kind of extermination squad to hunt half-breeds. If Buffy had not been certain of it before, she was now.

The Tok'mundar admired its surroundings. "My, this place certainly seems to have everything. Don't you agree, Belnick?"

The demon beside it was looking around as well. A long, trunklike appendage hung from the center of its face and it twitched as the demon sniffed at the air.

"It certainly does," Belnick answered, a throaty, rumbling voice emitting from the end of its formidable proboscis.

The third demon, an insectoid whose eight mirrorlike eyes reflected multiple images of the store and all its contents, nodded its head in agreement. "Everything," it said, its voice tinny and hissing with a bizarre static.

The Tok'mundar let his hat drop to the floor. "Yes, well, we'll have to do some more casual shopping another day. For the moment, we're in urgent need of certain herbs and powders, ingredients for a spell used to cancel out magicks that would attempt to hide the inferior from us. I have a feeling you know exactly what I'm talking about."

"Oh, you've got to be kidding me!" Anya muttered behind the register. "There we go! Another sale out the window!"

Giles stepped toward the demonic customer with an air of authority about him. But an air of authority wasn't going to keep him from getting hurt, and Buffy moved in close behind him, her gaze ticking from one of the grotesque creatures to the other, warily awaiting an attack.

"I think I do," Giles told the Tok'mundar. "Sadly, however, we've had a run on such items recently. Fresh out, I'm afraid."

"You're lying," spat the red-skinned demon. He pointed to the monstrosity with the elephantine trunk. "He has the scent."

The demon called Belnick let loose a low grunt of amusement and pointed to the twitching appendage in the center of his face. "The nose knows," he said.

"Buffy?" Willow said warily, as she, Tara, and Xander all began to move toward the center of the shop to back Giles up.

The Slayer held up a hand to warn them back, but the moment her focus had shifted away from him, the Tok'mundar charged. The blood-hued demon bared his razor-sharp teeth and charged her with a rumbling growl. Buffy pivoted on her left foot and threw a right hook that would have dropped the demon in his tracks if it had connected. But the Tok'mundar was faster than she had expected and easily dodged the blow, lashing out with an attack of its own, striking her hard in the side of the face.

"Find the ingredients," the demon instructed his lackeys. "I'll deal with the Slayer."

Belnick and the insectoid demon spread out to go around her. Buffy would have liked to stop them, to protect the others, but her friends had been in fights before, and for the moment, she had to finish up with the Tok'mundar.

The blood-hued demon started toward her. Buffy did not give him time to close the distance. She launched a high kick to the side of his head, but he dodged out of the way, then threw several fast punches. She managed to block them, but only just. His movements were a blur of motion, his attacks seeming wild and yet very much on target. The way he flailed, it was a fighting technique that she had never encountered before.

Great. Demon-Fu, she thought.

"I'm disappointed, Slayer," the demon said, coming at her, swinging wildly. "I expected more." The Tok'mundar extended his arm, claws shooting out to grasp the soft flesh of her throat.

"And y'know? I'm all broken up about it." Buffy bent backward, the monster's clutches rewarded with nothing but air.

She shot forward and slammed an elbow in his face, then followed through with an uppercut to his gut. "I'll try to be impressive the next time I kick your ass."

The demon staggered back and wiped greenish blood from the nostril slit in his skull-like face. He launched a powerful snap kick at the center of her chest, knocking her backward and to the floor.

The Tok'mundar grinned. "Now that's more like it."

Willow tensed as the two demons came down into the store, taking advantage of Buffy's preoccupation with the Tok'mundar. The one with the elephant trunk was Belnick, or at least that's what the leader had called him. The other, the one that looked a lot like a giant bug, was just disgusting.

Belnick pointed a stubby black finger at the door that led into the rear of the store. "Back there," he told the insectoid demon with its mirrorlike eyes.

Anya was behind the counter, and now she snatched a battle-ax and a sword from the wall and tossed them to Giles and Xander, admonishing them not to damage the weapons, they were merchandise. Giles and Xander ran to intercept the demons. Belnick lay back his head and let loose a thunderous blast of noise from his trunk as he and the insectoid faced their attackers. Willow doubted the guys would be able to take these two demons on alone. She glanced to her left, where Tara stood holding her hand, looking back at Willow anxiously.

"How do you want to d-do this?" Tara asked.

Willow squeezed her hand. "We keep them from getting what they came for."

"A spell of obstruction?" Tara asked.

Willow nodded. Tara smiled confidently, and Willow felt a pang of warmth spread to her heart. With this girl by her side she truly believed there was nothing the two of them could not accomplish.

"The subject?" Tara asked, looking about the store for something that could provide them with the obstruction needed.

"How about that nifty old display case with all those heavy burial jars in it?"

Tara nodded in agreement and closed her eyes. Willow did the same, and they both began to chant in unison. The air around them became charged with a preternatural power, crackling with electricity. The witches extended their arms, and the power that they had harnessed slipped from their fingertips to enwrap the display in arcane energies.

Willow breathed in and out as the power coursed through her. Magick had become second nature to her, like breathing or watching cartoons on Saturday morning. It was an amazing feeling, one that she could never imagine living without. In that way, it was very much like being in love with Tara.

The towering display case lifted up from the floor as if weightless and sailed across the room to crash down in front of the storeroom door, blocking it.

"That oughta do it," Willow said, looking to her partner, a flush of magickal exertion upon her cheeks.

"Good one, guys!" Buffy yelled from across the store as she avoided the Tok'mundar demon's relentless attack.

Willow and Tara turned their attention to the other demonic attackers. Belnick grabbed Xander by the front of his shirt and hurled him across the room, where he struck the counter and crumbled to the ground. Giles already lay on the ground, cradling the back of his head and trying to rise, obviously disoriented. But Belnick had forgotten the Watcher for the moment. His focus was on Xander.

Anya scrambled out from behind the counter to check on her boyfriend as Belnick bore down on them.

Instinctively Willow and Tara began to utter a spell of defense, their voices intertwining. The air began to crackle around them, and a sudden wind whipped at their hair and clothes.

The insectoid leaped at them, landing right in front of Willow, and she let out a cry. In its mirrored eyes she could see many reflections of her own face, and Tara's, both frightened.

"There will be no more spellssssss," it hissed, and a thick, milky fluid vomited from its mouth in a powerful stream, knocking them to the floor. The substance covered them, stuck to them, and dried quickly, rendering them completely immobile.

Anya hated this.

How was she supposed to run a business and make lots of money if demons and monsters kept coming into her establishment, beating up her boyfriend and his friends, and wrecking the place? It was a question that enraged her. If she still had her demonic powers, she'd show these vandals some serious vengeance. One thing was for sure, she was going to have to have a talk with Giles about the insurance rates on the Magic Box. They were sky high already, and this wasn't going to help.

Xander moaned as she cradled his head in her lap. She had dragged him behind the counter to keep him out of harm's way. Or out of the way of any further harm, at least.

"It's okay, dear," she said lovingly, patting his face. "We can hide back here until everything blows over and there's no chance of you being damaged again."

Xander lifted his head from her lap. "Buffy?" he asked. Anya pushed him back down into her lap.

"Buffy's doing what Buffy does. Willow and Tara are dealing with the buggy looking guy, and Giles is unconscious again. You just stay here and don't die and everything will be all right."

Xander struggled to stand as she attempted to keep him with her. "We gotta help them," he said as he pushed away her hands and stood up from behind the counter.

Belnick was waiting for him. As Xander stood, it trumpeted with that disgusting trunklike thing again. Anya flinched as it reached for Xander.

"There you are!" she heard the demon say.

"Xander!" Anya screamed as she watched him be pulled over the counter.

Anya stood and saw that the store was in turmoil. Everywhere she looked she saw merchandise being destroyed—potential dollars going out the window. Something had to be done or there wouldn't be anything left of the store for her to work at—never mind the fact that Xander and all her friends' lives were at stake.

She knelt back down behind the counter and slid open a drawer in the display case used for merchandise layaway. She remembered that one of the store's regulars had recently put a down payment on a particular item that she realized might come in handy right around now. She fished around inside the drawer, beneath the fertility charms and bags of cured wombat brains, until she found what she was looking for. Carefully, Anya withdrew the golden short sword, the jewels in its encrusted hilt twinkling in the florescent light overhead. A price tag dangled from around the blade, and she hoped that the weapon would not be damaged.

Heaven forbid they had to give the down payment back.

Buffy took a step backward, infuriated that the Tok'mundar had her on the defensive. She should have finished off the ugly s.o.b. by now. And from what she'd been able to tell in the chaos, the other two were working as a team, and very effectively. They were strong, and organized, and had turned their differences into strengths, not weaknesses. The Tok'mundar demon in particular was stronger than it looked, and faster, but if she didn't finish it soon, the other two were going to start killing her friends.

The Tok'mundar snarled at her and reached inside its trench coat to produce a vicious-looking dagger, then lunged forward with the blade.

"Not fair," Buffy said as she retreated even farther into the store.

"Anything that'll get the job done, Slayer," the demon replied, slashing toward her face, but Buffy blocked the blow, then snapped a sidekick into his gut, driving him back.

Hah! she thought. But the feeling of triumph was short-lived. One little kick wasn't going to finish it.

The Tok'mundar held the twelve-inch dagger before its face and let the blade glint menacingly in the store light. "Give in, and I'll make it quick. You're not going to like what the future has in store for your kind, anyway."

When it lunged again, Buffy grabbed the demon's wrist, turning the blade away from her, and brought her leg up to kick him in the face three times in quick succession. Every impact gave her satisfaction. The Tok'mundar snarled and broke her grip, taking a step backward, wiping a hand across its bloody mouth.

"Hey, Buffy!"

The Slayer glanced over her shoulder and saw Anya holding a beautiful, gilt-edged sword inscribed with arcane runes. With a grunt of effort, Anya flung the sword toward her as though it were a boomerang. It spun across the room.

Buffy snatched it out of the air with unerring precision.

"Don't break it," Anya called as Buffy gripped the jewel-encrusted hilt. "It's a relic. And it retails for twenty-seven hundred dollars."

Buffy turned back to the Tok'mundar. The demon had been dazed by her previous attack, and grabbing the sword had given it a moment to recover. But the Slayer was confident that recovery was going to be brief. She brandished the sword in front of her. The Tok'mundar glanced once at its own weapon and then back to hers.

"Anything that'll get the job done," she said with a smile.

And the Slayer attacked.

One word—not even a word, really—filled Xander Harris's mind as he struggled with Belnick, turning his face from right to left in an attempt to keep the damp, sticky trunk of the demon from touching him.

Eeeew!

He knew it was an infantile response, that he should be focused on staying alive—keeping them all alive—but Belnick's moist proboscis was the most disgusting thing he had ever encountered in his time with the Scooby gang. *Well, okay, with the possible exception of Mr. Pfister, the maggot demon.*

The mouth at the end of the demon's trunk bit into the soft flesh of Xander's cheek, and he screamed out in shock and pain. Xander reacted with a sudden and well-placed knee to the groin, which proved quite effective. Belnick howled and staggered backward. Xander pushed the creature away to catch his breath.

Across the store he spotted Anya throwing an antique sword across the shop, and saw Buffy catch it. *Okay*, he thought. *We can do this.*

But then his heart skipped a beat as he watched the spidery demon skitter across the room toward his girlfriend. *Skittering,* he thought, repulsed. *I hate things that skitter.*

Xander moved to intercept the creepy-crawly, but felt the arms of Jumbo the elephant demon drape around his neck.

"You're not going anywhere," Belnick rumbled.

"That's it." Xander grunted, trying with all his might to throw the demon off of him. "No more peanuts for you."

But as he grappled with Belnick, Xander saw that the spidery demon was almost on Anya, and she had not even noticed its approach. He screamed her name, and she called out to him in fear for his safety, unaware of the danger she was in. Xander felt a horrible rage and despair building inside of him. Belnick was too strong. There was nothing he could do but watch as the insectoid demon grabbed Anya by the shoulders and vomited on her.

Xander almost puked.

That was even more disgusting than Belnick's sticky trunk. The insectoid demon's spew shot from its maw in torrents, knocking Anya to the floor with the force of its expulsion. Again Xander screamed her name, terrified what the stuff might do to her. He had to get to her.

Belnick lifted him off his feet and threw him across the store.

Xander collided with a display case and fell to the ground in a shower of broken glass, his head spinning. *Gotta get up,* he thought as, through blurred vision, he watched the demon with the oh-so-disgusting nose come for him again. *Gotta get to Anya.*

His hand struck something, and he looked behind him to see the box that he had brought out of the storeroom earlier. Belnick thundered toward him, already reaching for him. Xander reached into the box, praying there was something among all the chotchkes that he could use as a weapon.

The hideous Belnick roared as it came to a stop before him and reached its massive hands for him. Xander's hand clutched something in the box and drew it out. It was the same red-haired fetish doll he had pulled out before, and he stared at it with an odd mixture of disgust and horror.

Belnick wrapped thick sausage fingers around his neck and hauled him up off the ground. Xander's feet dangled below him.

"What the hell you got there?" the demon asked. "Looks like freakin' Carrot Top."

Xander's eyes locked on the mouth at the end of the creature's trunk. The sheer wrongness of it made him shudder in revulsion, but then he saw his opportunity. Xander clutched the fetish doll in his hand and, as the monster drew him closer, he thrust the dried-root doll into the opening at the end of the trunk. There was some resistance at first, but he forced it, and buried the doll—and his hand up to the wrist—deep inside the creature's trunk.

Belnick staggered, eyes bulging, and dropped Xander roughly to the floor. The demon thrashed around the store, clutching at his face as though he couldn't breathe.

Death by Carrot Top, Xander pondered. *Talk about humiliating.*

Through its eight eyes, Myga saw Belnick staggering, clutching at his proboscis. It was a shame, really. Myga liked Belnick. But the insectoid demon knew that their purpose here was far more important than one life, and so he skittered again toward the door that led into the rear of the shop. Myga hoped that Belnick's death thrashing would distract the humans long enough for it to finally get what they had come for.

Myga could feel it all going wrong. This was supposed to be an easy snatch-and-grab. They had heard that the owner of the Magic Box had started holding out on the substances and items they needed. Human filth had obviously realized what was happening and had done it to protect the half-breeds. They were to take from him what he would not sell, and teach him a lesson in the meantime. But they had never expected this kind of opposition.

Myga grabbed hold of the display unit the witches had blocked the doorway with and strained to slide it aside. The display case fell away with a crash, and Myga stood before the door.

All the insectoid demon needed to do was find the withheld ingredients and then it could return to the commander. It would have to leave its comrades behind.

Simple enough, Myga thought.

But there was someone standing in the doorway, blocking his path. A man with hair so blond, it was almost white, and a smile as cruel as any Myga had ever seen.

"Well, well, aren't you a big, ugly wanker," the man said.

Something was wrong with this man, Myga sensed. Myga felt afraid. The demon cleared its throat to ready another blast of its liquid webbing.

"There'll be none of that," the man snarled, and he grabbed Myga's throat in a viselike grip that prevented the demon from spewing.

The man's face underwent a disturbing change, his features becoming more demonic, teeth elongating into fangs. Then Myga knew why the man had made him so uneasy. But it was too late. This new enemy, the lowest of the low, was dipping his head toward its neck.

Not a man, Myga thought in a panic as the creature's jagged canines broke through the thick carapace that covered his throat and began to tear at his flesh.

Not a man at all—Vampire.

Buffy drove the breathless and bloody Tok'mundar demon to the floor with one hand and held the antique, bejeweled sword half an inch over its throat. She had broken one of its arms, and the fight seemed to have gone out of it. "You? Pretty much done," she told it. "So now we're gonna play a little game. It's called 'Don't Lose Your Head.' That means I ask those burning questions, and if you don't answer 'em, well, pretty sure you get where this is headed. No pun intended."

The demon glanced over at the dagger it had dropped. It was not far away, but Buffy dared not move to kick it farther. The demon was too strong and too fast. No way was she letting it get up again.

"Ask away, Slayer," the Tok'mundar said. "But you're running out of time. Myga's webbing hardens quickly. It must be getting difficult for your friends wrapped up inside it to breathe right around now."

Buffy slammed the demon's head against the ground and glanced back. Xander was ripping Anya free of the thick webbing, but Willow and Tara . . .

The Tok'mundar bucked beneath her, stretching out one hand to snatch the dagger up from the floor. Buffy swore loudly, knowing that every second was another second closer to suffocation for her friends. Her sword was right over the demon's neck, but she did not want to kill it. She wanted answers.

With an angry shout she brought the hilt of the sword down on its skull, but too late. The Tok'mundar had the dagger and was even now twisting the blade toward her.

No. Not toward me.

"No questions," it said. "For purity!"

Buffy watched in horror and amazement as the demon drew the blade across its own throat and green ichor sprayed out, warm where it spattered her face.

It was too late for answers from this one. Buffy leaped up and started to run to Willow and Tara. She spotted Giles in one of the aisles, sitting up, disoriented, and rubbing the back of his head. If she could free the witches in time, everyone would be all right.

They have to be all right!

Out of the corner of her eye she spotted a huge shape about

to fall upon her and she dodged, only to have it land with a dry crack on the floor beside her. Buffy stared down at the insectoid demon, its eight mirror eyes looking up at her, and wondered why it looked so wrong. Then she understood, and her stomach did a sick twist. Its neck had been snapped, the head turned around the wrong way.

"Little present for you, Slayer."

Buffy looked up to see Spike leaning against the counter, an arrogant smile on his face. She was glad he had arrived when he did, but at the same time she wanted to dust him right then and there.

"You moron. You killed our last chance to get some answers." Spike flinched at her tone and looked grumpy, but Buffy ignored him, rushing to Willow and Tara.

Buffy used the sword to cut through the solidifying webbing, which had grown rubbery and hugged tightly to the contours of her friends' bodies, crushing their chests, stealing their breath. As she cut away hanks of the foul-smelling stuff, she could hear muffled sounds coming from beneath it and breathed a sigh of relief.

Willow and Tara gasped for air as Buffy tore away the shroudlike covering about their heads.

"You guys okay?" Buffy asked, still fearful for them.

"Fine," Tara said, taking in deep lungfuls of air.

Willow nodded. "Ditto with the fine. Just . . . big headache."

Buffy gazed around the room to see that Giles was up and about. He rubbed at the side of his head where he had been struck as he examined the inert form of the demon they had called Belnick.

"We'll get no information from this one either, I'm afraid," the Watcher said tiredly.

In front of the counter, Xander was holding Anya in his

arms, speaking to her softly. Now he held up his hand. "That'd be my doing—and trust me when I say anyone with the urge to shake my hand for a job well done should just . . . not."

Still leaning on the counter, Spike cleared his throat to get their attention. "When you're all done with the bizarre little mixture of whining and self-congratulations, let me know.

"Could be I've got the answers you're lookin' for."

CHAPTER THREE

Los Angeles

Calvin Symms placed the bag of groceries down upon the kitchen table, careful not to disrupt the decorative bowl of plastic fruit on display there. He studied the apple for a moment, trying to decide whether he could ever have been fooled into thinking that it was genuine. The color was off, and the fact that it was covered in dust did little to convince him of its reality.

"Did you have enough money?" Mrs. Green asked as she slowly made her way from the small living room into the kitchen, leaning heavily upon her wooden cane.

The whole place smelled like cat. And mothballs.

"Plenty," he answered, even though she had been around three dollars short. Calvin was only thirteen, and not exactly flush with cash, but he didn't mind picking up the difference.

Mrs. Green had been good to him since his parents died, almost like what he imagined having a grandmother would be like.

"Now I want you to keep the change," the old woman said with a smile, fussing with her white hair where it was tied into a bun. "Save up and buy yourself something nice."

"I will, ma'am," Calvin replied as he began to put away the groceries.

Every Wednesday he came to visit Rhondella Green, to sit, have some cookies with a glass of milk—and then to do her shopping for the week. It was the least that Calvin could do after all that she had done. After his parents had been taken, a lot of the folks in the neighborhood—Mrs. Green more than almost anyone—had gone out of their way to make sure that he grew up right. This was just one of the ways he was saying thank you to those who had always been there for him.

Mrs. Green shuffled over to the kitchen table in her pink slippers and peered into the shopping bag. "Did you put the cat food away yet, Calvin?" she asked, poking around in the bag. Her eyesight had been getting pretty bad over the last few months, but she would not admit it.

"No, ma'am. It's still in there." Calvin moved up beside her, and Mrs. Green stepped aside. He reached to the bottom of the bag and removed six cans of Feline Favorites Cat Food—all of them tuna flavored. Tuna was all Mrs. Green's finicky tiger cat would eat.

"Do you want me to feed Chauncy for you?" he asked. Calvin set one can on the counter and stowed the others in a cabinet to the right of the sink.

"You know how that cat gets around his suppertime," Mrs. Green said with a sweetly indulgent laugh. "Nasty's what he is." She began to make weird kissing sounds to call the cat to his dinner.

Calvin opened the can with the electric can opener. If anything would bring Chauncy running, it would be that sound. But other than the whine of the can opener, the apartment was silent. No scratch of cat claws on the floor. Half a minute went by, and Chauncy had not appeared.

Weird, Calvin thought.

"Now where is that cat?" Mrs. Green wondered aloud. She looked beneath the table and then shuffled into the living room.

"Oh, dear. Mr. Denton was up to see me earlier—I hope Chauncy didn't get out of the house on me."

Panic was beginning to creep into the woman's voice as she called for the cat again. Still, Chauncy did not appear. Calvin set the now open can of food down upon the counter. "I'll go check the hall for him. If he's not there, I'll go check the alley out back—that's where I found him the last time."

He went to the door.

"You're a good boy, Calvin Symms," Mrs. Green said, leaning on her cane in the doorway of the living room.

Calvin smiled as he closed the door behind him. "I'll be back as soon as I can."

Chauncy was not in any of his usual hiding places in the building. It looked like the cat had found its way out to the back alley again. Calvin didn't like the alley, especially at night. Though he would never admit it to any of his friends or to the people in the neighborhood who had looked after him the last nine years, he was afraid of the dark.

Still, Mrs. Green would be frantic with worry if he didn't get Chauncy back to her. Calvin could not stand to see her agitated. He made his way to a bolted door at the rear of the first floor of the apartment building. He slid the bolt across, tentatively gripped the antique iron knob, and turned. Calvin pulled open the door and hesitated a moment as he peered out into the night beyond it.

The weather was humid, and the aromas of the neighborhood hung heavy in the alley. It was nights like these when he often thought about his mother and father and the fate that had befallen them—a fate that had come from the dark to take away their lives.

"Chauncy," he called out into the alley. "Where are you, kitty cat?" There was a bright half-moon in the sky tonight, and it wasn't as dark out there as it could have been. "C'mon, you pain in the ass cat—ain't you hungry for your supper?"

He carefully descended the three creaking wooden steps to the alley floor. Looming out of the darkness just in front of him was a large wooden box with a cover where the tenants could leave their bags of garbage for pickup at the end of the week. The closer he got to it, the stronger it smelled. He didn't know how the cat could even go near it, the stink was so rank, but then again, he wasn't a cat. To the feline nose, this may have smelled like a twelve-course banquet.

Something moved in the darkness on the other side of the trash bin, and his heart skipped a beat. Calvin took in a large gulp of the putrid air.

He'd only been six when the monsters had murdered his parents. He would have been killed as well if it hadn't been for Charles Gunn. Gunn and his crew had heard his screams and had actually come to his aid. Saved his skin. But they had been too late to save Calvin's parents from the darkness.

Calvin attempted to crane his neck around the box, wanting nothing more than to just find Chauncy and get back inside.

Gunn had taken a special interest in him. He and Luce and Pico and the other guys in the crew had watched out for Calvin for years, made sure he continued to go to school, that he always had a roof over his head and a full belly. Made sure he never felt like he was alone. It was also Gunn who had told him all about the monsters that had killed his mom and dad.

Vampires.

There were two of them crouched behind the trash bin as if they had been waiting for him. Their eyes glinted yellow in the moonlight, and he felt the blood in his veins turn to ice.

"Hey, Calvin," one of them hissed.

He spun around and started to run back toward the building, the door still yawning open in the dark.

It knows my name, he thought wildly. *The vampire knows my name.*

Gunn had told him that there were certain rules the blood drinkers had to follow, and one of those rules was that they had to be invited into someone's home before they could come in.

As one of his sneakered feet touched the first step, Calvin prayed that nobody inside the building had ever been that stupid—or lonely. The sound of his heart beating throbbed in his ears as he reached for the door. He was going to make it— he *had* to make it. How pathetic would it be to have escaped the vampire's hunger all those years ago only to fall prey to it now?

They grabbed him from behind—hands clutching his arms painfully, tugging at his clothing—and yanked him backward. The door seemed to grow smaller as he was pulled into the alley, deeper into the darkness. *Nice and dark,* he thought wildly. *They like it like that. That's where they'll drink my blood.*

He fought them, but they were too strong. Images of the monsters feeding on his parents flashed through his frenzied mind. Calvin had only been a little boy, but he remembered nonetheless, remembered his mother, eyes frozen wide in shock, one of the pale-skinned vampires latched on to her throat.

Mom, he thought now, a silent plea, as though she might come to save him. But there was no one left to save him. No one in the world.

"Somebody wants to talk to you, Calvin," one of the vampires whispered in his ear now as they dragged him through the alley. He flinched as he was struck again by the horror of this creature knowing his name.

They dragged him to the end of the alley and across the street, where long ago a block of houses had stood. All that remained now was a vacant lot, a kind of graveyard for discarded junk—old cars, washing machines, refrigerators, televisions—rusted and broken things discarded all over the weed-covered expanse of the unused land.

There was a car parked in the middle of the lot; a nice car, not the burnt-out shell of something left there after a joyride. A black Cadillac with tinted windows. Calvin didn't notice the figure squatted down beside the driver's side door until the man abruptly stood, and he could see Mrs. Green's cat in his arms. For a few seconds he could not breathe. Not at all.

The vampires dragged him across the street toward the man, who looked up from gently stroking the cat's fur to smile a welcome. "Hello, Cal," the man said. "How's it going?"

Calvin could only stare, slowly shaking his head in denial. *It's not possible,* he thought. But of course that was idiot talk. For the man was standing right there in front of him.

Dad, Calvin thought. *Oh, Jesus . . . Dad.*

He stared at his father's neck. Where there should have been a gaping wound—the place where the fangs of an overexcited vampire had torn the skin—there was only smooth, unblemished flesh.

"It can't be," he whispered aloud as the monsters let him go and he dropped to his knees before his father.

"It *is*, Calvin," Raymond Symms said, stroking the tiger cat's side, making it purr. "It's me."

Then his father smiled and his face *changed*, and everything became horribly clear. The smile was wrong, as if his father's mouth was crammed with far too many teeth. The face was hideous, a distortion of the man he had been. But he wasn't a man anymore.

Raymond Symms was a vampire.

Dad, Calvin thought again.

"What's the matter, boy?" his father asked him. "You look like you've seen a ghost."

Not a ghost, Calvin thought as he gazed up into his father's feral, animal eyes.

Much worse.

Angel's brow furrowed in concentration as he studied the daunting task before him. He was deeply troubled, yet despite his focused efforts he could not seem to formulate any solution to the problem that faced him now. With a deep sigh, he glanced over at Cordelia, who was diligently organizing a large stack of multicolored case folders at the hotel's front desk across the lobby from him.

"What's an eight-letter word for decapitated?" Angel asked her.

"Gee, I don't know," Cordy replied, a touch of annoyance in her voice. "Why don't you ask Wesley that one too?" It was the same response she'd given him the last five times he'd asked her for assistance.

"Can't," he answered as he reclined on the circular sofa in the hotel's lobby and crossed his legs. "Wes said he'd stake me if I bothered him again." Angel scratched the side of his head with a pencil and studied the empty boxes of the crossword puzzle with great intensity, as if this would cause the missing letters to miraculously appear.

"Well, if you bother *me* again," Cordelia said, carrying the folders to a file cabinet, "I'll go him one better and make you help me with these closed-case files."

Angel sighed and tossed the newspaper onto the sofa. He stood and strolled to the front desk and studied Cordelia closely. "Are you sure you haven't had a vision? Maybe a Sloth demon that you forgot to mention or a nest of Phra Phum that might have tied one on and gotten out of hand?"

Cordelia stuffed the folders in the back of the file cabinet drawer and slid it closed. "Sorry, chief," she said with a shake of her head, "no visions in the fifteen minutes since the *last* time you asked me, but hey, keep checking in. You never know."

Things had been remarkably quiet of late, and the staff of Angel Investigations was having an opportunity to decompress, to relax, to catch up on things that should have been done ages ago.

Angel was bored to tears.

He walked away from the front desk and briefly considered returning to his puzzle, but decided against it. He needed something a bit more visceral to pass time away during this dead period between cases. For a moment he grew excited by the prospect of cleaning and sharpening the weapons in his arsenal—best to be prepared for anything—but then was disappointed when he remembered he had done exactly that the day before.

He was startled from his reverie by Wesley's voice calling to him from the office in back. Angel felt a weight lifted from him as he responded. The lull had been fine while it lasted, but now was the time for action.

Wesley came from his office clutching an open book in his hands, a leather-bound tome that looked ancient. Angel reasoned that the former Watcher had probably deciphered another prophecy about the coming of a great, supernatural evil that could very well threaten the fabric of reality—or something equally dangerous and interesting.

"What's up, Wes?" Angel asked.

Eyes still glued to the ancient text, Wesley began to laugh. "Were you aware that the 'Song of Azog-Thoth' from the *Book of Abominations* is a limerick very much in the same tradition as 'There Once Was a Man from Nantucket?'"

Wesley giggled like an eighth grader, his mouth moving soundlessly as he continued to read the demonic text.

"It's really quite funny," he added as he at last glanced up from his book, eyes twinkling with mirth. When he spoke again, it was in a sly, conspiratorial whisper so that Cordelia would not hear. "It's rather off-color, but if you want me to translate for you—"

"What are you boys whispering about?" Cordelia asked from the front desk.

"Nothing," Angel replied, casting a quick glance her way. He shook his head and ran a hand through his dark hair. He turned back to Wesley. "Maybe later," he said, his hopes of something to do, some powerful evil to vanquish, sailing out to sea with the man from Nantucket.

Wesley seemed slightly miffed, but obviously still very amused by his discovery. He turned his back on Angel to return to his office. "Very well, then. Your loss."

"Hey, Wes?" Angel called. "Got a question for you."

One eyebrow raised, Wesley put a finger into the book to hold his page and looked up at Angel curiously.

"What's an eight-letter word for decapitated?" Angel asked, poking his hands into the front pockets of his dark pants.

Wesley thought for a moment and seemed about to respond when Fred interrupted from the top of the stairs, dressed in an oversized bathrobe, her hair a complete mess. She began to say something, but instead was rocked by a powerful sneeze. Her eyes were red, and she wiped at her nose with a tissue.

"Gesundheit, Fred," Wesley said.

"Thanks," she said with a pitiful shake of her head, looking even more forlorn than usual. She had only recently returned to this world after a five-year stay in an alternate dimension, and already she'd fallen victim to the common cold.

Fred reached the bottom of the steps and glanced at Angel. "Headless," she said.

Angel frowned. "Huh?"

"Headless," Wesley answered. "That's your answer. I presume you were trumped by attempting to find a synonym for 'decapitated' in its past tense verb form, as in 'the horseman decapitated Ichabod Crane.' But in its descriptive form, a synonym would be 'headless.'"

The vampire grinned broadly and nodded. "Headless." He happily returned to the sofa and his newspaper, leaving his friends to their own affairs.

"And how are we feeling today, Fred?" Wesley asked.

"Fine, just fine," Fred replied, attempting to smile but failing miserably. She had come farther into the lobby of the former hotel and now she leaned against the reception desk, trying in vain to smooth her bedraggled hair.

"Well, you look like a wreck," Cordelia said bluntly, glancing up from her case files. "You shouldn't even be out of bed."

"No, no, I'm feeling better. Maybe not a hundred percent," Fred declared—and then her face contorted and she let loose a thundering sneeze. "But I should be fit as a fiddle in no time."

Cordelia came out from behind the counter. "Okay, but until then, Doctor Cordy prescribes a big bowl of chicken soup and an industrial-sized box of tissues." She took Fred by the shoulders and began to steer her back the way she had come. "C'mon, let's get you upstairs and back into bed."

As the women started up the steps, Wesley retreated to his office once again, and Angel focused on his newspaper. He had decided that the crossword puzzle was going to be his salvation. Never had he even had the desire to complete an entire crossword puzzle before. But now it was his goal—every block filled. It would be an exercise not in physical might, but in the power of the brain.

Headless, he thought, staring at the crossword. *This might take a while.*

He had just begun to read the next clue when Gunn charged in through the double doors, face etched with such gravity that Angel knew something was terribly wrong. *Finally,* he thought, dropping the crossword puzzle.

"What is it?" Angel asked eagerly as Gunn descended the steps into the lobby.

Cordelia and Fred had stopped halfway up the stairs, and now Wesley emerged once more from his office.

"Got a call on my cell as I was on my way here," Gunn said, tension in his voice revealing how tightly he was wound. "There's this kid, Calvin Symms. Me and my crew kind of look after him—ever since the vamps got his parents." He shook his head in frustration. "Damn, this ain't right. Not after what he went through. Calvin's got potential. You can just feel it when you talk to him. My sister always said the kid was going places."

Wesley moved closer to the center of the lobby, where Gunn now stood. "What happened to him?"

Gunn scowled. "Someone saw him get taken earlier tonight, an old woman he visits sometimes. She thinks it was vamps that got him."

Angel tossed the newspaper onto the sofa and strode toward the arsenal. "Time's wastin', people," he said. "Let's move on this."

Gunn stepped in front of him, blocking his way. "Angel, this isn't your responsibility. It's a neighborhood thing. I only came in 'cause I was already on the way. Thought maybe I could borrow a couple of weapons."

"You can," Angel said amiably. "It's just that we're going to help you carry them."

His words were punctuated by a loud sneeze from Fred. Angel turned to look at her. "Fred," he said, "I don't want to leave you here not feeling well and all, but we're gonna need stealth and quiet tonight, so there isn't much choice. You can hold the fort?"

She stifled another sneeze and, with a weak smile, gave him the thumbs-up.

"Angel, this isn't your fight," Gunn reiterated as Wesley and Cordelia joined them at the center of the lobby.

With a hand propped on one out-thrust hip, Cordelia stared at them both. "You know, in spite of how incredibly busy we are with all the business that's *not* rolling in, somehow I think we can lend a hand."

"You're one of us, Gunn," Wesley said, reaching out to lay a hand on his shoulder in camaraderie. "Your fight is our fight."

Angel moved around Gunn and went to the weapons cabinet. He pulled open the two doors and perused his selections before deciding on a small battle-ax. He hefted the weapon and admired the sharp edge that he had put on the blade the previous day in a fit of complete boredom. "Shall we?" he asked, the crossword puzzle already forgotten.

• • •

"Cookie?" Raymond Symms asked, offering his son the bag.

Calvin studied the face of the creature sitting across from him on the lime green sofa. At first glance, it certainly did look like his father, but the more that he stared, the more it became obvious that this was just some kind of inhuman thing. It looked like his dad, sure. Was wearing his body, so why shouldn't it. But this was not his father.

"No, thanks."

Raymond set the bag of cookies aside and studied his son. "How you been doing in school?"

He asked it the way a father would, concern in his eyes, paying attention. Calvin shuddered. The vampire had asked the question like he really wanted to know, like it was the most normal conversation in the world for them to be having. But how normal could it be when the monsters had just snatched him up off the street, when they were in a room with half a dozen other vampires who were just standing around the apartment. The vamps were watching, and they nodded at the question as if the answer were important to them as well.

After a short ride in the Cadillac, they had brought him to a rundown apartment building on the corner of First. He knew of the building; it was notorious for the kind of criminal activity that made even the police stay away. As he was pulled from the back of the car and carried into the building, Calvin had been surprised by how quiet it was inside. In addition to the silence, the thing about this place that had stood out to him right away was the smell. The stink. It wasn't all that far removed from the stench that came from the trash bin back in the alley of Mrs. Green's apartment. It was the smell of rot.

Decay.

Calvin figured he knew why the building was so quiet, but he did not want to think about it any further than that.

"Talk to me, Cal," said the vampire with Raymond Symms's face. "I'm your father."

Calvin sneered at him. "You're not my father. My mother and father died nine years ago."

For a long moment Raymond stared impassively at him. Then he reached into the bag, took out a cookie, and bit into it. He chewed thoughtfully a moment before he replied. "Has it been that long?" he asked through a mouthful of chocolate chips.

Then he leaned forward and clasped his hands together before him, almost as though he were praying. "I know how hard it must have been for you, Cal, all these years without me or your mother around. I'm sorry for that and I want to make it up to you."

Calvin couldn't believe what he was hearing. Had the vampire snatched him from the alley only to apologize for not being in his life? He was confused now. Gunn had explained it to him, and the rest of the crew had hammered it into his mind over the years. Vamps weren't really the people they looked like. Just bodies. Walking dead folks with demons inside them. But this thing had his father's memories, some of his mannerisms. Could it still have some of the man's feelings as well? It didn't seem likely, but just thinking about it unnerved him.

"If you're here, where's Mom?" Calvin asked. "Is she like you?"

Raymond's expression became pained. "Afraid not, Cal," he said, suddenly showing a great interest in his fingernails. "You're probably not aware of this, but your mother was a bit of a problem. She was the reason all the nasty stuff happened in the first place."

Calvin squirmed in his seat and felt the eyes of the other vampires in the apartment hungrily upon him, like a cat waiting for a mouse to run from its hiding place, waiting to pounce. They lurked in the shadows of the abandoned apartment, watching him.

"I don't understand. What did Ma have to do with—vampires?"

The thing his father had become bit at a fingernail and spit something onto the floor. "It wasn't your mother who had to deal with the vampires, it was me."

Raymond looked up at him with an icy, piercing stare, and Calvin felt a shiver pass from the nape of his neck down his spine.

"I was employed by a couple of groups of vampires to provide them with . . . nourishment. It was a good job; it paid well. Remember, I had a family to support."

Calvin felt sick. He'd always believed that his father had been in construction—and had done odd jobs around the neighborhood to make ends meet.

"You found people for them to kill?" Calvin asked in a whisper, making no attempt to hide his absolute disgust and horror.

"Well, yeah," Raymond said, leaning back in his seat upon the couch. He frowned as though he had no idea what it was about that concept that would upset Calvin. "Most of the time they were criminals, drug addicts, homeless—you know, the dregs who wouldn't be missed. Better them than us, right? You, me, your mother, the good people of our neighborhood."

One question seared through Calvin's mind, and he asked it without taking the time to consider if he could bear to hear the answer: "Did . . . did Ma know? Did she know what you did?"

His father's face shifted to something horrific and unnatural before he answered. "Not at first, but then she found out. I tried to explain to her—I begged her to keep her big mouth shut. Told her that it would be better for everybody."

Raymond shook his head and snarled. "She didn't listen. Your mother told some people, ended up getting some of my employers killed. That was stupid, Calvin. These weren't guys you could screw around with."

Calvin felt as though he couldn't breathe, the reality of what he had always known of his family, of his past, crumbling from beneath him to expose a yawning abyss below, waiting to swallow him up.

"They wanted revenge for what your mother had done, eye for an eye stuff."

"But . . . but they turned you into one of them."

His father shrugged. "What can I say? They liked me, they liked the job that I did for them, and I couldn't do it for them if I was dead, could I? They wanted you dead, too, but I stood up for you—pulled some strings."

Raymond smiled, and Calvin felt as though he was going to throw up.

"Look, I know I haven't been the world's best dad, but I want that to change."

Calvin slowly shook his head from side to side. His fear and horror had kept him numb, kept him still, but now anger threatened to overwhelm those other emotions. "I don't want anything from you."

Raymond slid off the couch onto his knees and moved toward him. Calvin sank deeper into his chair as the thing that had once been his father came closer.

"Don't be like that, Cal," Raymond said, a hint of disappointment in his voice. "The higher-ups in this organization said that I could turn you, that I've earned the right." The vampire smiled proudly. "Your old man has become pretty important over the last few years."

Raymond's eyebrows danced up and down mischievously. "Somebody's going to be in charge of a major push into this neighborhood, and I could really use somebody I could trust as my right-hand guy."

Calvin gazed into his twisted features and came to the sickening and devastating realization that Gunn and his crew had been wrong. This man had not been changed by the bite of the vampire. Physically, yes, but not in his heart. He had not been turned into a soulless beast when his blood was drained from his body. Raymond Symms had been a monster long before that.

"I . . . ," he began, but faltered when he saw the excitement on his father's face.

"Yeah, Calvin? What do you have to say to your old man?"

"I think I'd rather die," he said, glaring hatefully at the creature who knelt beside him.

Raymond's head bowed sadly, as if the words had been a physical blow that had slapped him down hard. Slowly he raised his head. Then, with a smile, Raymond reached out and rubbed the top of Calvin's head with affection. "That's funny," he growled. "What you just said? It's exactly what your mother said to me when I asked her to stay quiet. And you know what I said to her, Cal, when she said she'd rather die? Know what I said?

"I said 'no problem.'"

From a concealing pool of shadows across the street, Angel studied the building closely. Gunn, Cordelia, and Wesley stood arrayed with him, and behind them were four other people, fighters who belonged to what had once been Gunn's crew. Young people from the neighborhood whose lives had been scarred by vampires or demons, who had joined Gunn's crusade against the forces of darkness. Monster hunters, all of them. Gunn ran with Angel now, but his old crew was still together, still fighting the good fight. Sometimes there was tension between the crew and Gunn, but tonight they were all here for the same reason.

They were all here for Calvin.

"How many?" Angel asked, staring at the building.

"Six plus the kid," said Caesar, a part of the crew who went back a long way with Gunn. "But there're probably more inside. Nobody's seen any sign of the tenants in over a day. We were checking the place out when we saw them bring Calvin in."

Angel glanced to his left. Gunn was staring at the darkened apartment building, concern etched upon his strong features. "It's your call. We can wait for sunrise, when they'll be sleeping and vulnerable, or we can go in now."

Gunn looked at him, his expression hard. "There's a good chance the kid's already dead—but then, maybe he ain't." He adjusted the leather strap holding a sword and scabbard across his back. "Always was a sucker for the slim chances."

Gunn turned to face the four members of his old crew. They were still loyal to him even though others thought him a traitor for working with Angel. The way these four looked at him—the way they listened—Angel was certain they would have marched through Hell itself if Gunn asked it of them. Or maybe it was only that it was Calvin in trouble up there, and they all felt responsible for him. Gunn had explained that much.

"You guys go around back," Gunn told them. "We'll take the front."

Like trained combat soldiers, Gunn's men disappeared into the night.

"Sneaky little buggers, aren't they?" Cordelia commented as she watched them merge with the shadows.

"Let's try to be equally stealthy, shall we?" Wesley suggested as he removed a short sword from somewhere inside his jacket.

"Are you ready for this?" Angel asked Gunn.

Without answering, Gunn bolted from concealment and ran toward the building's front entrance. He was first through the open door into the lobby, with Angel close behind—Cordelia and Wesley bringing up the rear. The lobby was dark, the only illumination thrown by the two emergency lights. There was a smell in the air that didn't give Angel the most optimistic feeling. The place reeked of death.

They approached one of the two doors on the first floor. The foul aroma from apartment 1A was almost overwhelming. "We should check the apartments," Angel said, looking back to them. "No stone left unturned."

He reached for the doorknob, but stopped short as the knob began to turn all on its own.

"Angel?" Cordelia whispered, taking a step back and warily preparing to defend herself. "Did you knock first to see if anyone was home—or dead?"

They both stepped back, and he raised his battle-ax. The door creaked in protest as it slowly opened. Angel was ready, prepared to bring the killing blade of his ax down upon any foe.

A figure appeared in the doorway; an elderly woman in a flowered housecoat. She grabbed at her sagging bosom and gasped when she saw them. "Oh my," she said, her wrinkled hand upon her chest.

Cordelia held her stake down beside her leg as inconspicuously as possible. "We're sorry, ma'am," she said. "We weren't sure anybody was home."

Angel arched an eyebrow, a wry smile playing at the edges of his mouth, but he did not lower his weapon. Wesley and Gunn joined them at the woman's door.

"Have you noticed anything strange going on in your building?" Gunn asked.

She smiled. Her teeth were remarkably white. "You kiddin' me? Every day's a freak show around here."

They were interrupted by a scuffling noise followed by two heavy thumps from somewhere in the building. It could have been a lot of things, but given the circumstances, Angel figured it had to be a struggle.

"People knocking on doors all night, screamin' and carryin' on until all hours. Don't they know that people need their sleep?"

Angel turned his attention back to the elderly woman.

"But Raymond, he had some story about needin' to use the phone—that his car broke down and he was tryin' to get to the hospital to visit his sick mother."

The commotion was growing louder.

"Angel, we really should go," Gunn said tersely.

The old woman continued. "Bypass surgery," she said, scratching her hip. "He said she was having bypass surgery." The old woman shook her head as if disappointed in herself. "Never should have let him inside."

"No," Angel said. "I guess you shouldn't have."

Then he swung the ax, decapitating the old woman. Wesley and Gunn shouted in alarm, and Cordelia actually tried to stop him. Even as her head tumbled toward the ground, the old woman—the vampire—exploded in a burst of cinder and ash.

The others stared at the dust as it drifted to the floor.

"She was a—" Cordelia began. Then she whacked Angel on the arm. "Why didn't you say something?"

"You two seemed to be getting on so well," Angel replied. "I didn't want to ruin it."

"Cutting off her head isn't ruining it?" Cordelia asked. Then she sighed. "Okay, vampire, but still. She reminded me of Mrs. Kunkel. My piano teacher."

Angel raised an eyebrow, but Cordelia was just staring at the open doorway from which the vampire had emerged.

"I hated piano lessons, but Mrs. Kunkel baked the best peanut butter cookies."

Gunn couldn't wait any longer. If his crew was in danger, he had to do everything in his power to keep them safe. With Wesley by his side, he moved toward the stairs. They peered up into a pool of solid darkness.

"Nobody thought to bring a flashlight, I guess."

Wesley said nothing, looking at his weapon and hefting its weight in his hand. Behind them, Angel cleared his throat.

"Didn't think so," Gunn said, placing his foot on the first step.

As if summoned by that step, the vampires emerged from the darkness above in a hissing wave.

"Here they come!" Gunn managed before the first of the blood drinkers reached him, launching itself down the stairs at him.

The vampires swept down at them, driving them back into the lobby. The stench of freshly spilled blood flowed from them, some of their clothes spattered with gore, and Gunn feared for the fate of Calvin and the others of his old crew who had come along.

But not me.

Gunn pulled his sword from the scabbard on his back and lashed out at the feral attackers. He would use his fear as he always had, honing it to a fine rage that gave him the strength to continue his fight.

The broadsword sliced through the neck of the vampire closest to him. With a high-pitched shriek, it exploded to dust and he shielded his eyes from the floating remains before he attacked again.

To his left, he caught sight of Wesley as he dispatched one of their attackers with a cold efficiency, again reminding Gunn how truly deadly the sometimes effete former Watcher could be.

Cordelia and Angel worked back-to-back, vampires falling all over themselves as if eager to be destroyed by the pair.

Gunn hacked his way back toward the stairs, determined to discover whether his people were still alive—he had to be sure. He stopped cold as he saw what had emerged from the darkness: Calvin, in the grip of a leering vampire.

"Gunn!" Calvin screamed, thrashing in the leech's grip, and the battle came to an abrupt halt.

Then it all clicked into place. Gunn heard the old woman's voice as she muttered about how she never should have let *Raymond* in. Raymond Symms. Calvin's father was supposed to be dead and gone, but here he was. Dead all right, but not quite gone.

"You know I'll do it, Gunn," Raymond said, his clawed fingers digging into the soft flesh of the young man's throat. With Calvin pressed against him, the vampire began to descend the stairs while his followers moved aside to let him pass.

Calvin looked both terrified and ashamed. "I'm sorry, Gunn," he said in a soft voice. There was blood on his throat where the vampire's claws had nicked him.

"Why don't you and your two pals put them weapons down and we'll see if we can all keep Calvin alive," Raymond said as he continued his slow descent.

Though it made him crazy to do so, Gunn did as he was told, fearing for the boy. Wesley and Cordelia did the same.

And then the vampire's words hit him. *Two?* he thought. Gunn quickly chanced a look around the lobby and realized that Angel was no longer with them. Cordelia glanced at him and he saw that she had noticed as well.

Raymond offered up a smug grin as he set foot in the lobby, and Gunn smiled back.

"What you smiling for, *Charles?*" the vampire asked. "Hope you don't think this is gonna end any way but ugly."

Gunn shook his head and prepared for the inevitable. "Nope, in fact I'm countin' on it."

Angel leaped from the shadows behind Raymond Symms, coming *down* from the second floor, his coat billowing about him like the wings of a gigantic bat.

Gunn raced for Raymond and tore Calvin away from him, pulling the kid out of harm's way. "Ugly all right."

Ax in hand, Angel hurled himself at his enemies. He felt his features change, his brow thicken, his teeth sharpen in anticipation of battle.

He had seen the vampire emerge from the darkness with the boy and had known what would follow. With the open front door behind him, he had left the building unnoticed and raced around to the back, returning via the fire escape. On the second floor he had found Gunn's men with their throats torn out. It looked as though they had been surprised, but there was also evidence of a struggle, and he reasoned that they had managed to dust a few before finally succumbing to the vampires' greater numbers.

Angel landed in a crouch just behind Raymond Symms. Symms and two other vampires turned to confront him. In a single swift motion Angel backhanded the vampire on his left and swung the ax up to decapitate the one on the right. *Six-letter word for decapitated,* he thought. *Dusted.*

Before Symms could react, Angel kicked the boss vampire to the floor and beheaded his other lackey. Through a drifting cloud of vampire remains, Angel watched as Symms rose to face him. Gunn had already snatched Calvin away, and even now Cordelia and Wesley retrieved their weapons to continue the fight.

Angel leaped at the startled vampire leader, grabbed him by the front of his jacket, and threw him up against the wall. Ax in hand, he swung the sharpened blade toward the vampire's exposed neck. Symms dodged, and the ax blade buried itself deep in the plaster wall. The vampire boss lashed out with a hard kick, knocking Angel backward.

Like something from an obscene nightmare, the vampire scrambled on all fours back up the stairs and into the darkness to escape. Angel swore under his breath and, still clutching the ax, started to follow.

There was a scream of terrible heartache from the lobby, and he turned to see the kid, Calvin, struggling in Gunn's arms.

"I got you, Cal," he heard Gunn say, trying to calm him. "It's cool. Don't you worry about a thing. I'm here to protect you."

The child looked up at Angel with eyes overflowing with emotion. "Please," he whispered, "please don't do it."

Angel was confused.

"Please don't kill him," Calvin pleaded, his body trembling as he broke down and cried. "Please don't kill my dad."

CHAPTER FOUR

Sunnydale

"Tonight?" Buffy asked. "You say this is happening tonight?"

Spike sat at the table where Willow and Tara had been researching, chair pushed back, black motorcycle boots up on top of the table. Giles wouldn't let him smoke in the store, but he had a silver lighter in his hand and was flicking the top open and then clicking it closed. The repetition was growing annoying.

"Do I stutter?" the vampire asked, frowning. "Look, Slayer, gotta say I'm not feeling the gratitude I was expecting. Thought I'd get at least a thank-you out of it, maybe a massage. I did play bloody cavalry a few minutes back, or doesn't your memory go back that far?"

Buffy glanced around the Magic Box. Anya had the first aid

kit open on the counter and was disinfecting a number of cuts and scrapes on Xander's arms and forehead. Willow and Tara were helping Giles put things to rights in the store as best they could, picking up fallen merchandise. Willow had offered to use magick to repair the large unit they had used to block the door into the back room, but Giles had firmly declined. Magick was not meant to be used merely for convenience.

Though Buffy thought she saw a wistfulness in his eyes. If it wouldn't have made him a hypocrite, she suspected he would have loved to have some help cleaning up the mess.

Spike was right. If he had not arrived when he had, things might have been much worse. That did not mean Buffy had to like it.

She put her hands down on the table and leaned toward him. "Put your feet down. This isn't your crypt."

Spike complied, a twinkle of mischief in his eyes.

"Now start again."

The vampire shrugged. "Simple enough. Before I retired to my luxurious granite flat at sunup this morning, I had a bit of a chat with a friend. Told me about these major doings, someone trying to organize full-blooded demons, wiping out half-breeds. Not that I care much for half-breeds in general, or any other sort of demon. But the full-bloods get my hackles up, right? Look down their noses at a bloke like me. Snotty bastards."

Xander, newly bandaged, clicked the first aid kit shut and walked toward the table. "Color me ignorant. I get half-breed, as in dictionary definitions of the word. But I thought the only pure demons were the Great Old Goofballs, or whatever. Pure demons like the big ol' mayor-snake we charbroiled when we blew up the high school."

As he swept broken bits of crystal into a dustpan, Giles paused and glanced over at them. "Certainly a pure demon, one of the original beasts that roamed the earth, would agree with you, Xander. But there are thousands of varieties of demon that have been recorded over the millennia, some that have arrived on this plane from a dark dimension, and others that originated here and have evolved over time. They're not as ancient as the Old Ones . . . hence the name . . . and many have been affected by this plane over the ages, becoming more humanoid. In truth, most demon breeds probably have some human blood in their geneology, though they'd be loathe to admit it."

Anya snickered, and everyone glanced over at her. "You can say that again," she said. "This one time, I told D'Hoffryn . . ." Her words trailed off, and she blinked. "Never mind. Demon humor. But pure demons and full-bloods are far from the same thing."

Buffy noticed Willow using a little spell to repair some of the burial urns that had shattered, then casting a guilty glance over at Giles, who had not noticed. Tara was focused on the conversation, however.

"So, in the hierarchy . . . or pecking order . . . or whatever," Tara said haltingly, then shook her head as if to clear her thoughts. "Anyway, there are pure demons like the Old Ones, then all these gazillion full-blood species, and then half-breeds?"

"And then vampires," Spike sneered, flicking the lighter in his hand closed again as he sat forward in the chair. "Arrogant sods look at us as bottom-feeders."

Buffy stared at him. "I'm not seeing the irony."

Spike frowned. "Look, you want my information or not?"

"I do. I'm just trying to understand your motivation. I'm guessing you just want to make sure that after the Gestapo demons get done with the half-breeds, they don't come after you bottom-feeders."

Once more the vampire leaned back in his chair. Everyone in the room was focused on him now, and Buffy had always thought that was just how Spike liked it. He grinned.

"Got me there, Slayer. Didn't stay alive all this time by being stupid. But it isn't just me. Clem's in trouble. He's in hiding until the demon stormtroopers leave town."

Buffy shook her head. "Sorry. Small aneurysm there. Who is Clem?"

"Oh, he'd be so hurt if he heard you say that. You remember Clem. My mate with the floppy puppy ears and the taste for kittens and card games."

"Right. Him." Buffy shivered. Clem was pitiful looking, a demon version of those dogs with the scrunchy necks and the most ridiculous-looking ears she had ever seen. He wasn't menacing at all, and she had a hard time thinking he got a lot of dates, even with demon girls.

"Clem's good people."

"And probably owes you money from poker," Xander pointed out.

"There's that," Spike allowed. Then he glanced around at all of them. Other than Xander, everyone else had gone back to the job of cleaning up the shop. Spike seemed somewhat miffed as he turned his gaze back to Buffy. "Look, you want the details or not?"

"I'm waiting for them. You're babbling," she replied calmly.

"Oh, hell, you're an infuriating girl." The vampire sighed as he rolled his eyes upward. "All right, here it is. This little army— Gestapo demons, you called 'em? They're holding a recruitment drive tonight. From the sound of things it's gonna be a hell of a party, and it isn't the only one. Apparently they're havin' them all over. Word is, the Sunnydale shindig's got demons coming in from northern California, all the way up to Canada."

"Why here?" Willow asked, pausing now to sidle up beside Xander. "I mean, duh. Buffy Summers. Slayer."

Spike nodded. "Yeah, that's what I wondered." He glanced back at Buffy and locked eyes with her. "From what I can tell, they don't care."

A little shudder went through Buffy, a tic of annoyance that she wished she could dismiss. It wasn't ego, exactly, but she had grown used to the fact that to most demons, she was like the bogeyman, the thing monster mothers whispered to their children about to make them behave. It bothered her that whoever was behind this militant demon organization, they might not be intimidated by her at all.

"So where is it? The big demon pep rally? Where are the Gestapo doing their recruiting?" she demanded.

As silently as she was able, Buffy scaled the chain-link fence that surrounded the devastated ruins of what had once been Sunnydale High School. Spike, Willow, and Tara were already on the other side. Xander and Anya had stayed with Giles to continue putting the store back together. Also, Buffy had thought that if Spike was right about the size of this gathering, it was best to keep the infiltration group small. Spike, Willow, and Tara were all more than capable of defending themselves, and the witches' magick might be necessary to keep them from being discovered, if it came to that.

Once Buffy was on the ground, the four of them moved swiftly and quietly across the grass, keeping low, until they were in the shadow of the stadium where the Sunnydale Razorbacks had once played football. It had suffered little damage in the explosion of the school, but town engineers had questioned its structural integrity and so the stadium had been closed. The local papers reported that further studies would be made and it might be reopened eventually. Buffy thought the place would stay closed, at least until a new school was built. She suspected that the town council wanted to keep people away from the ruins of the school, to discourage the curious from poking around in there.

Walls might collapse. Someone could cut themselves or fall through a weakened floor. Or something could come up out of the Hellmouth and eat them. So, for now, the stadium was just as off-limits as the corpse of Sunnydale High.

They paused to get their bearings. Spike scouted ahead a few yards while Buffy, Willow, and Tara surveyed the overgrown lawn across which they had just run. *No sign of pursuit,* Buffy thought. *That's something.*

"Confession?" Willow whispered, glancing up at the stadium. "I kinda figured when the school was destroyed, the bumps-in-the-night would stop coming here. But it seems like we don't go a month without having to come back and, y'know, do battle with the nasties. They really oughta just tear down the stadium and bulldoze what's left of the school."

"And build what?" Buffy asked. "We're right on top of the Hellmouth. No matter what they build here, still gonna be an evil magnet."

Tara chuckled softly. "Yeah. Why do you think Spike keeps coming back?"

Buffy and Willow exchanged a look, but the Slayer said nothing. She turned to see that Spike was motioning to them, beckoning them over. The three young women crept along the wall of the stadium, passing a gated entrance that had been closed off with heavy chains. Spike was at the corner of the building and when he turned to look at them, his eyes seemed to gleam cruelly in the moonlight. "Have a butcher's at that," he whispered, almost excited.

The Slayer frowned. "Butcher's? What the hell does that—"

"*Look,*" Spike muttered. "Have a peek round the corner."

The vampire drew back so Buffy could press herself against the stadium wall, and she slid forward to peer around the other side. Her stomach gave a sick twist as she saw what had gotten Spike so riled. The entire property was fenced in, but someone had opened the fence. The high school parking lot was over-flowing with cars, trucks, and vans, and much of the land around the ruins was also filled with vehicles.

Buffy drew back, eyes wide, and motioned for Willow and Tara to have a look. When the witches had done so, the four of them stared at one another for several moments.

"Am I the only one here who doesn't like the odds?" Tara asked quietly.

"Of course not," Buffy told her. "But they're not going to stop us."

"Sod that," Spike hissed. "They probably packed 'em eight to a car like teenagers sneaking into the drive-in. You can't really think we've any option here but running like hell."

"No, Buffy's right," Willow said. "This is way, way, and did I mention way bigger than we could have ever expected. But we need to get a look at what we're dealing with. Numbers. Species. And see if we can overhear anything of value."

Buffy smiled at her. "Just what I was going to say. If I'd have said it."

Willow grinned and nodded. "Solidarity, sister."

The Slayer glanced at Spike. "So, if you want to run like hell, feel free. We're going in."

Spike glared viciously at her for several moments, then swore under his breath. He shook his head and then silently stalked back to the chained-up entrance gate. Once there, he turned on Willow. "If it comes to it, Red, you make us invisible right quick.

Got it? Otherwise we'll never get out of here," he whispered. Then he pointed at the chain on the gate. "And whip up a spell for this. Anything else'll be too noisy."

Willow obliged, and they managed to slip into the dark interior of the stadium in almost total silence. They were on the opposite side of the structure from the main entrance—the one facing the parking lot—but still, they moved as quietly as possible up a set of stairs that took them high into the bleachers.

There were hundreds of them.

Buffy swore under her breath. She spotted dozens of demon breeds she recognized and many, many others she did not. They had to maintain silence—she would not risk giving herself and the others away—or she would have revealed to Willow the horror that was swirling in her mind now. Even after seeing the parking lot, it had not truly struck home to her. Even knowing someone must have paid off the Sunnydale authorities to look the other way while this convention of terrors was held here, the enormity of it had eluded her.

No more.

There were so many of them—a small army—and if they decided to tear Sunnydale apart, house by house and board by board, she did not think that she could stop them. Even with the help of her friends. If she had to fight them all at once, it was going to take some major mojo to bring them all down or drive them off. She was going to have to gather up a posse of her own, and ideas began firing off in her mind so quickly that at first she was not listening to what was being said down on the football field.

The demons had gathered in loose clutches, many by species, those not yet indoctrinated into this organization still suspicious of one another. In the Razorbacks' former end zone was a phalanx of different demons. Buffy spotted the Fyarl that had fled from her behind Willy's. But the one who was speaking was taller than the rest, a demon in battle armor with ram's horns who strode back and forth as he addressed those gathered there. *Clearly, the guy in charge,* Buffy thought. She didn't know the name, but she recognized the species; back when Faith had first come to town, Buffy had gone up against a demon called Lagos. This one was the same breed.

"Tonight!" the ram-horned demon shouted. "Tonight this field will run with the blood of many tribes."

I don't like the sound of that, Buffy thought, and she glanced at Willow and Tara before looking back down to the field.

Mr. Ram's head had stopped pacing and was glaring out at the demons before him. Buffy thought there were probably three hundred or more, but she did not want to count. Did not really want to know the true tally.

"General Axtius has issued his commands!" the demon roared. "Those of you who are tested this night and found worthy will depart first thing tomorrow morning for Los Angeles, to join the Coalition for Purity!"

Buffy had to cover her mouth to keep from laughing. She glanced to her left and saw Spike roll his eyes. *Coalition for Purity.* They sounded like some ridiculously ignorant, racist group like the Aryan Brotherhood or something.

Her amusement disappeared when she realized that was exactly what they were.

Mr. Ram's-head wasn't finished. "Those who are tested, and found *wanting,* however," he said, drawing out the last two words as he scanned those on the field before him, "will never leave this place. The worthy will execute the unworthy. Purity and strength are our twin goals.

"One by one you shall be judged. I will be proud to present

those who are worthy to General Axtius in Los Angeles tomorrow evening. We have a long war ahead of us, my brothers and sisters. This is but the first stage. But the day will come when we will have purified this entire world and eliminated the scourge of the tainted, the half-breeds, the abominations."

The words echoed in Buffy's mind. She felt nauseated listening to the rambling of this creature, but the basic facts had not escaped her. A lot of the demons down in the stadium were going to die tonight, but given what they had come here for, she did not feel any particular compulsion to try to save them. They knew what they were doing. Only monsters with evil intentions would have shown up here tonight.

And the ones who survived? They were leaving Sunnydale. Clem and the other half-breeds who had managed to hide would be safe . . . for now. But this recruitment was just the tip of the iceberg. A real demon army was gathering unlike anything she had heard of in modern times. Whoever this Axtius was, he had some big plans, and it looked like he might have the power to pull it off. *And what if Axtius isn't even the top of the totem pole?* she thought. Spike had said these meetings were happening all over.

One thing at a time, Buffy. The army that was being recruited was going to gather in Los Angeles the next night. Buffy had been thinking about doing her own recruiting to combat this problem, but now she realized that instead of having the cavalry come to her, it was going to be her playing cavalry.

The Slayer tapped Willow on the shoulder, then beckoned to Spike. Slowly, silently, they began to slip back the way they had come. Miraculously, they managed to get out to the street unnoticed. Buffy had to get to a phone.

She had to warn Angel.

The four of them headed back to the Magic Box, speaking very little. Buffy was turning the whole thing over in her head, and there seemed only one acceptable course of action. She didn't like it, there were a lot of complications, a lot of personality clashes that might result, but there was no choice, really.

They were going to have to go to Los Angeles.

She did not notice the ambulance in front of the Magic Box until Willow whispered her name. Then the Slayer looked up, saw the police car and the ambulance with its spinning red lights on the roof throwing ghoulish colors across the front of the building. She ran full-tilt for the Magic Box, with Willow, Tara, and Spike barely keeping up.

Buffy pushed through the front door, nearly knocking over a policeman who stood just inside, taking a statement from a pale, disheveled Giles.

The look in Giles's eyes made her heart sink. "More of them?" she asked as Spike and the witches came into the store behind her.

"More of what?" the policeman asked, obviously confused.

"Thieves," Giles said quickly, covering. "We had someone try to force the rear door the night before last."

The cop scribbled on a notepad. "You didn't mention that before."

"I'm a bit preoccupied with tonight's events, I'm afraid," Giles said snappishly.

But Buffy wasn't listening to her Watcher anymore. Her eyes had gone to the two paramedics, and to the bloody, pallid figure on top of the gurney they were rolling toward her. Anya was unconscious, her face badly bruised, and a brace had been placed on one of her arms. Xander walked along beside her, looking as though he was afraid she would shatter at any moment.

"Xander," she said softly.

He looked up at her. Spike hung back, but Willow and Tara rushed over to him. The paramedics went up the steps and took the gurney between Giles and the policeman, then headed out the door.

"They must have sent two teams to get the stuff, just in case," Willow said. "Oh Xander, I'm so sorry. Is she going to be all right?"

He shrugged, unable to meet any of their eyes. "They think she probably has a concussion. Her arm was really hurting, but they said it doesn't look like it's broken. She came around for a minute. Told me not to worry, that she'd be okay. Her eyes were kind of glassy. She said she had to be all right because she was going to have my babies someday." His voice sounded hollow. "They banged her up pretty good."

Xander looked at Buffy. "They got what they came for. We . . . we tried to stop them. They would've killed us all if one of them hadn't recognized Anya from the . . . from the old days."

Then he moved past them, hurrying after the paramedics. Buffy assumed he would ride to the hospital with Anya.

"I don't get it," Tara whispered. "If they're leaving town, why do they still need the stuff for the spells?"

Buffy stared at the door as it closed behind Xander. "Why?" she echoed. "'Cause Sunnydale's only the beginning."

Los Angeles

It was Dollar Daiquiri Night at Caritas, and the place was more raucous than usual, the air filled with staccato eruptions of laughter and the clink of glasses. Lorne was the Host of Caritas, which meant he had seen this sort of thing hundreds of times, yet the turnout on Dollar Daiquiri Night never ceased to amaze him. He wasn't sure if it was the cheap booze or the cute little umbrellas, but DDN put derrieres in the seats, all right.

Usually he enjoyed the spectacle. For some reason, the very ordinariness of Dollar Daiquiri Night drew more human customers to Caritas. There was something Discovery Channel–fascinating about the hesitant little mating dance that so often went on between demon and human clientele curious about walking the wild side, swinging the other way for once. Put a few strawberry DQs in a mild-mannered accountant and he might very well take off for one of the local no-tell motels with a Tarvorg she-beast. Or a he-beast, for that matter.

Lorne had seen it all. That was one of the bohemian pleasures of being the Host. Different strokes for different folks, as the saying went. He had to keep an open mind. Otherwise he wouldn't be able to do the other part of his job, which was reading the emotional states and destinies of those who got up on the karaoke stage at Caritas to sing.

Open mind. That was almost funny. Tonight his mind felt anything but open. Lorne was deeply troubled and could not find it in himself to enjoy the crowd.

On the stage, a diminutive goblin with bloodstained teeth was singing Paul McCartney's "Live and Let Die" like he was the particularly ugly reincarnation of Anthony Newley. It should've been absurdly funny. Much of the audience seemed to think so, if the grins splashed across their faces were any measure.

But the patrons of Caritas, demon, human, or the ever popular "other," didn't see what Lorne saw. They did not know what he knew. They had no idea, for instance, that the goblin's wife of 371 years, with whom he had stolen and eaten countless human children, had been run down the day before by a speeding ice-cream truck, and the goblin was contemplating suicide because he simply could not live without her.

Not that a monster that regularly dined on innocent children would be a great loss, of course, but still, it was depressing stuff.

Worse than that, however, was that Lorne did not feel safe in Caritas.

That was not supposed to happen.

The club had been laden beneath magickal spells that prevented any supernatural creature from perpetrating violence within its walls. It was a sanctuary, a haven from the petty hatreds and turf wars that existed amongst the various demonic breeds and monstrous societies. No killing. No hunting. Just music, pub food, and drinks—sometimes drinks with pretty little umbrellas. Caritas was supposed to be a place to unwind, to take a breath, to get up on stage and sing your heart out, and then let the Host advise you on how to handle whatever life was throwing your way at the moment . . . or in the moments to come.

But Lorne wasn't in the mood to read karaoke singers. Even the good ones. He wasn't in the mood for daiquiris or suicidal goblins.

There was just too much death around.

In the past week he had noticed that several of his regulars had stopped coming in. Of course at first he took it personally, wondering if something about the club had put them off or if there was some new competition he did not know about. But then the whispers had begun to come back to him, and the night before, a werewolf who hung around Caritas pretty much whenever the moon wasn't full had gotten onstage to sing.

"New York, New York," it was. And while he sang his little lycanthropic heart out, Lorne *read* him.

His name was Hank Wagner. In the time he had been hanging out at Caritas he had gotten to know a lot of the other regulars. That day, the word had gotten around, but Lorne had not heard it until Hank-wolf started to sing and he had read it in the creature's mind.

Ling Shen—a Thuy-tak with a taste for tequila and Tom Jones—had been found massacred in her apartment.

A half-human troll named Maurice—Lorne hadn't known his name, only that he always drank George Dickel on the rocks and only sang Motown—had been thrown off the roof of a downtown shopping center.

Cacce-Olmai, son of a construction worker and a water spirit from Norway, loved Caritas but did not drink alcohol, so it was virgin piña coladas all the way. Cacce loved the modern pop—bubblegum girl singers and boy bands—but he never sang. Someone had caught him in the bathroom at the movies and burned him alive, boiling off his elemental power and leaving only a charred semihuman corpse.

After the werewolf finished singing, Lorne tried to talk to him about it, but Hank had no interest in sharing his grief. Wanting to be a good Host, Lorne gave him a couple of drinks on the house. But in the twenty-four hours since then he had not been able to shake the unease that he felt.

Now he stood in Caritas, watching the overwrought goblin finish up his tune and take a glowering bow, and Lorne found himself watching all of his customers much more closely. The pattern was obvious—all the dead folks were half-breeds—and he knew the killing might not be over. All day he had been meaning to go speak to Angel, but it was a big job, running a club like this, and something always seemed to pop up. It would have been easier if the broody ol' vampire-with-a-soul would just drop by, as he and his associates often did. But Lorne knew that he shouldn't wait any longer. Tonight, after Caritas closed, he would give Angel a call.

He knew the vampire would be awake.

As his gaze ticked around the room, Lorne wondered who among them might be next and he sifted the minds of those who got up to sing for malign intent.

But it was the ones who didn't sing that really made him nervous.

Once upon a time, the warehouse had housed the soundstages for a cult favorite television series. The producer was a thrall, a human slave, to Mistress Giuliana, a Cylirric succubus who had the idiot convinced she was a muse. As if muses had more than two breasts.

It mattered not to Axtius. The important thing was that Giuliana had persuaded the producer to give the Coalition for Purity access to the empty soundstages for as long as they needed a base in Los Angeles.

And if the guard who worked the gate wondered about the hideousness of the people who came and went onto the lot around the soundstages, the human fool kept silent. One of his lieutenants had told Axtius that the guard had been informed that a horror film was being made on the lot, so no matter what the man saw, he would likely keep telling himself that.

Humans had a wondrous ability to deny the truth of things that were right in front of them. Selective perception, he had heard it called. Axtius called it stupidity, but at the moment it was working in favor of the Coalition's long-term goals, so he was grateful for it.

An army of darkness was assembling beneath their very noses, and the residents of Los Angeles paid it no mind at all.

There was but one small item of business that Axtius wanted to take care of before he continued with the recruitment and then began the process of eliminating all sanctuaries for half-breeds within the region that had been assigned to him—the entire Pacific time zone.

The limousine's tires hummed on the street as it rolled into Santa Monica. Axtius sat in the back, tapping a cellular phone against his leather-sheathed knee. He hated moving from place to place, always felt that it was time wasted, time that would have been better spent with strategy, or violence. But all of his lieutenants were engaged at the moment, and nothing more was scheduled until the recruits from the Hellmouth arrived tomorrow night.

No, tonight there was but one task at hand.

The driver of the limousine was another of Giuliana's thralls. He wanted to be a screenwriter and thought that she could make it happen for him. *If he only knew that she plans to suck his imagination dry, and then eat his brains, licking the inside of his skull clean with a forked tongue. . . .*

The guard at the gate stood up straight when Axtius's limousine went through. He knew who was in charge, even if he had never been told. The gate closed behind the limo, and the driver navigated the vehicle to a spot that had once belonged to the television producer.

The driver said nothing. He never spoke unless Axtius asked him a question. That was best. The general did not want to kill him until he had outlived his usefulness.

Axtius stepped out of the limousine, heavy boots thudding on the pavement. His leather armor creaked as he moved, though he kept it well oiled. The Brachen demon moved to the driver's window. In it he could see a reflection of his own proud features, of blue skin and the hundreds of sharp spines that jutted from his face. *A warrior born.* Axtius knew that this was the crusade he had been waiting for his entire life.

With sharp talons, he tapped on the glass.

The window rolled down. "Y-yes, sir?"

"Do not leave. You may sleep in the vehicle, but do not move from this spot."

"Yes, sir."

Axtius turned with a click of his boot heels and strode over to the tall, broad door that led onto the soundstage. The doors reminded him of Spanish cities in centuries past, when doors were made to accommodate merchants with carts or warriors on horseback.

Within the soundstage his soldiers awaited. They grew restless, he knew, but they would have work to do very soon. The entirety of the empty warehouse was filled with cots and bedrolls. Cooking areas were set up on each soundstage. Only one of the soundstages was filled, but more recruits were coming soon.

Most of the soldiers—those who were not sleeping—stood at attention as Axtius passed. He did not stop them. Their obeisance was good for discipline. They must respect him. Fear him. He was their commander.

On the other side of the soundstage, Axtius pushed through another large door and out onto the back lot, which was empty save for several large trailers that had once been occupied by the stars of the foolish television show. Television numbed the brains of humans, and so Axtius appreciated its effects. Television was the ally of any who were enemies of humanity.

The second trailer had a single door. In front of it stood his two most trusted lieutenants, for he would not have given this assignment to anyone else. It was too . . . sensitive. On the left was a thin, dangerous little flesh-eater named Guhl-iban.

He could survive only a diet of human viscera and bone marrow. On the right was Haborym, a towering female who had been a fire deity in her homeland. Flames flickered from her eyes.

Both of them snapped to attention as he approached.

"General Axtius," Guhl-iban said in the rasping growl that served him as a voice. "The filth is confined, as you ordered. He gave us quite a chase."

Haborym let out a long breath, and tendrils of fire spurted from her nose. When she spoke, her voice crackled like wood in a furnace. "Would've been a lot easier to bring you just his head."

Slowly, Axtius turned his head to regard her. So tall was the blazing-eyed demoness that he had to look up to meet her gaze. When he did, Haborym quickly looked away, cowed.

"I did not ask for just his head," Axtius sneered.

"No, General. You did not."

There was the proper amount of apology in her tone, and yet . . . Axtius did not like the fact that she had questioned him. It suggested that Haborym and Guhl-iban might have even discussed amongst themselves their curiosity about why Axtius had allowed this one half-breed to live.

That would simply not do.

"Never question me," he told them, barely containing the fury within him. He could not afford to lose these two at the moment. They were too valuable to the Coalition, seasoned warriors.

But he would have to tread carefully.

With a snarl he threw open the door to the trailer and climbed up the three metal steps. Axtius drew the door shut behind him. Neither of his lieutenants turned to watch him now, but both of them had ears.

Axtius turned to peer into the gloom of the trailer, its interior lit only by the moonlight streaming through the blinds over the windows. In a chair was a scrawny Jashak with its long, scaly neck and a head shaped like a crescent moon. Even for a demon it was a freak.

The Jashak whimpered as Axtius walked toward it. It was bound to a chair and gagged and it squirmed as he crouched in front of it, eyes wide with terror. There were gashes on its flesh, bright pink blood staining its clothes.

"You look like a demon," Axtius mused. He inhaled deeply. "You even smell like a demon."

His enormous hand shot out, and he gripped the Jashak's throat, hearing the creak of his own leather armor and the rasp of his calloused palm against its scaly neck.

"But you're not a demon," he snarled. "You know this, do you not? You are an abomination."

The Jashak nodded slowly, carefully, crescent-head bobbing on its long neck. It no longer tried to mumble words through its gag. Axtius reached out and slid one talon beneath the gag, and the Jashak began to cry acrid-smelling tears.

"I am going to remove this. I will ask you a question. You will answer, and you will whisper. If you do this, you may yet live. Do you understand?"

Again, the Jashak nodded. Axtius slipped the gag down from its mouth.

"Please," the half-breed pleaded in a tiny whisper.

Axtius clutched its malformed head between his huge hands. Had he wished, he could have crushed its skull between his hands as though it were a tiny bird. He bent over and stared into its eyes, leaning close enough that the sharp spines on his face poked through the Jashak's flesh. It hissed in pain, but said nothing more.

"Where is Francis Doyle?" Axtius demanded, his own voice a low, dangerous whisper.

The Jashak blinked. Clearly it had not expected this question. "Doyle?" it asked in a whisper.

Axtius pressed its face between his hands, and the Jashak moaned, alarm lighting up its eyes.

"Where is Francis Doyle?" Axtius whispered again.

The Jashak swallowed hard. With its long neck, the action was unmistakable. More acrid tears slipped down its cheeks. It looked terrified by this question.

"You know him," Axtius said.

It nodded.

"Then tell me. Where. He. Is."

With another whimper, the Jashak bit its lip and sobbed. "Doyle . . . Doyle's dead."

Axtius froze. His nostrils flared, and he felt a heat rage inside him unlike anything he had ever felt before. This could not be. Not after all this time, all of his preparation.

It cannot be, he thought.

And yet the Jashak was too terrified to lie.

Axtius could not tell if what he felt was fury or grief, or perhaps some combination of the two. But he knew it could not be allowed to fester. With a hiss he clutched the Jashak's head in his hands and pushed his own face forward, the needles jutting from his skull puncturing the Jashak in dozens of places. The two were eye to eye, which was the only thing that saved the Jashak from being blinded by those needles.

"How?" Axtius growled low. "Tell me how."

CHAPTER FIVE

"Oh, thank you," Fred said with surprise as Wesley appeared before her with a steaming bowl of soup.

"It's chicken with stars," he explained, carefully setting the bowl on the front desk counter. "I was hoping we had chicken noodle, but alas, only stars."

Fred shoved the crumpled tissue she had been using to dab at her runny nose into her pants pocket and picked up the spoon. "Stars are fine, Wesley. It's sweet of you." She smiled as she took a spoonful of the steaming broth. It felt good as it traveled down her scratchy throat. "A few more gallons of this and I should be right as rain."

Wesley stood with his arms clasped behind his back, watching her with an expectant smile, as though she might suddenly leap to her feet in the full bloom of health.

"Feeling better already," she assured him.

This seemed to satisfy the former Watcher. "Happy to hear it," he said, starting back toward his office. "If you should need anything else, please don't hesitate to ask."

Fred had another spoonful of soup and waved. Wesley returned the wave, smiling nervously, and at last ducked inside his office. A warm feeling of contentment that she had not felt in ages passed through her. It was good to be back, surrounded by people who really seemed to care—not only about her, but about so much more.

Across the lobby she watched as Angel, Gunn, and Cordelia returned the tools of their trade to the weapons cabinet. They had come back from their mission while she was in the shower. She had not actually intended to be in there for so long, but ever since she had returned from Pylea—from five long years in that brutal, alternate dimension—the steaming water of a shower had the tendency to hold her captive. She often found herself losing track of the time. The shower had helped clear some of her cold's congestion, too, making her feel a little bit more human, and she'd quickly dressed and come downstairs to find that the others were already back. She was supposed to have been manning the phones, and hoped they wouldn't be too upset with her.

Cordelia was the first to finish at the weapons cabinet and now she walked over toward Fred, stretching herself out with a small, catlike yawn. She smiled. "Chicken noodle?"

"Chicken with stars. Wesley made it for me," Fred explained with a shy grin.

"The making of soup," Cordelia said appreciatively. "In some circles, you two would be engaged now."

"Really?" Flustered, Fred dropped the spoon into the bowl. Broth splashed over the desktop. "So much has changed since I was away, sometimes I don't think I'll ever catch up."

Cordelia strode over to her, a sympathetic expression on her face. "That was an attempt at humor, Fred. You remember humor? One of the things that's obviously still missing in your life since coming back from Pylea."

"Sorry, Cordelia," Fred said with an embarrassed shrug. "Nothing much to laugh about there, so I'm a little bit out of practice." She retrieved the tissue from her pocket and began to wipe up some of the soup spatter. "Though there was the time this guy had a Messarian Blood Fish? I'm not sure how he did it, but he got it stuck on his—"

"What are these?" Cordelia interrupted. She had picked up two pink message slips and was looking them over.

"Oh," Fred said, startled. How could she have forgotten? First she had abandoned the phones, now she had forgotten to give them their messages. If she wasn't careful, they'd be showing her the street for not pulling her weight. "Those calls came for Angel right after you guys left. He sounded pretty upset."

"He always does," Cordelia said with a scowl. She held up the messages and waved them at Angel. "Hey, boss man, messages."

Fred ate some more of her chicken with stars as Angel and Gunn closed the weapons cabinet and walked over to the reception area.

"Man, poor Calvin. That's gonna seriously screw with his head," Gunn said to Angel, the two of them in the midst of a conversation. "Your own dad wanting to turn you into blood-sucking evil to make up for being a crappy father? It's like a whole Darth Vader–Luke Skywalker thing."

"But without Ewoks," Angel said. "I hated the Ewoks."

Cordelia handed the messages to Angel. "Speaking of ugly, nasty little monsters, Charlie Nickels called."

Fred had a final spoonful of her intended cure but found it cold. She pushed the bowl away and studied Angel. "Mr. Nickels seemed very upset," she warned.

"He's always upset," Angel said, reading the messages and then placing them on the counter.

"He . . . he made me cross my heart and swear on the soul of Liza Minnelli that I'd tell you to call him just as soon as you got in."

Angel rolled his eyes.

"Charlie Nickels," Gunn said, obviously amused, "he's that shriveled-up little dude who wants you to—"

"That's him," Angel said shortly, cutting him off. "And I'm not calling him back. I don't care how much help he was on the Kraus case."

Fred was confused. "Um, who is he? Mr. Nickels, I mean."

"Charlie Nickels," Cordelia began. "Big-time informant for Angel Investigations. You want info on the underbelly's underbelly, Chuck Nickels is the guy to talk to."

"Then why doesn't Angel want to talk to him?" she asked.

"Well, that's where it gets interesting," Cordelia said with a mischievous grin. Angel glowered at her as if to silence her, but Cordelia went on. "Nickels also happens to be an enormous fan of musical theater and is trying to put together an all-demon production of *The Music Man*."

"That sounds like fun!" Fred said brightly. "Except . . . demons and . . . singing." She was trying to picture it in her mind, but stopped because it was kind of scary.

"He wants Angel in his show." Cordelia stifled a laugh and walked back to her desk. She glanced at the vampire. "You're a superstar!"

"Go ahead," Angel spat. "Laugh it up. I'm still not calling him back."

Gunn was grinning broadly and trying to cover it up with a hand. Fred had never seen him this way before. Usually he was always so tough, so streetwise. It was kind of nice to know that the life he led hadn't been able to kill his sense of humor.

He had a sweet smile.

"Well, I'm outta here," Gunn said, composing himself, his demeanor already reverting to the tough-guy image. He slapped the counter with his hand, turned to leave—and stopped dead in his tracks.

They all looked up in surprise. A lanky, tough-looking teenage boy stood just inside the front doors of the hotel. No one had heard him enter, but now Gunn was striding toward him.

"Calvin," Gunn said, obviously surprised. "Thought I told you to wait for me back at the—"

The teenager stalked forward, meeting Gunn in the middle of the lobby, anger on his handsome features. "I know what you told me," he said, getting right up into Gunn's face. "And I ain't goin' for that."

Gunn frowned. "What's the matter with you? This ain't the place to be talking about your business." He put his hand on the kid's shoulder. "Let's go back to the neighborhood and we can—"

"My business?" Calvin said. "I thought it was *our* business." Calvin swept Gunn's hand away from his shoulder. "We'll talk right here."

Fred felt awkward, as though none of them should be there to hear this exchange. She wanted to leave, go back to her room, but that would be even more awkward. This was obviously the kid they had gone out to rescue. Apparently it had gone as planned. She had assumed Gunn would leave Calvin with his crew again once they found him, and maybe that was what he had done, but now Calvin had come to them.

Gunn's posture was tense. Fred was sure he wasn't used to being spoken to this way, but he held his tongue and let the boy say his piece.

"You say you'll look out for me, and then you just take off," Calvin said. Fred thought he sounded more hurt than angry.

"I meant what I said," Gunn replied. He seemed uncomfortable having that conversation in front of the others, and Fred felt bad for him. Gunn glanced back at Angel, then returned his attention to Calvin. "When I leave you with my boys, it's like—"

Calvin shook his head. "Not the same. Look, ain't like I'm some scared little kid or something, but . . . but this thing with my father, it's not done. He's still around."

Angel broke in then, and though he spoke quietly, his voice carried across the stillness of the lobby like the crack of a bullwhip. "He's still around because you stopped me from going after him."

Calvin glanced guiltily at the ground. "I . . . know that. An' I know he ain't really my Pops. But part of him . . . part of him has to be for him to know the stuff he knows, to talk to me the way he talked to me."

Cordelia crossed the lobby to stand by Calvin, and stared at him sympathetically. "That's not true, Calvin. You've got to get it into your head. That thing has no soul. Your father is dead, hard as it is to understand that. The thing in him is like a parasite, living inside—"

"I know all that!" Calvin protested, waving her away.

"Doesn't *sound* like you do, Cal," Gunn said quietly. "Even though I've been telling you the same damn thing for years."

Calvin swallowed hard and looked up at Gunn. "It's just . . . I love all those guys. You know, Gunn. They're my family. But I feel safest with you. I wanna stick with you."

Gunn turned his head as if he wanted to gauge the feelings of the others.

Fred quickly snatched the phone messages from the counter. "So, Angel, do you want me to call Mr. Nickels back and tell him you're busy?"

Angel offered Gunn an almost imperceptible nod and then reached out to take the messages from Fred. "No," he said grimly. "I'll take care of it."

Gunn put an arm around Calvin and walked him over to a more private corner of the lobby, the two of them speaking together now, too quietly for the others to hear.

"That's a big boy, don't be afraid of Charlie," Cordelia told Angel from her desk. "Tell him, *Music Man,* no. *Phantom of the Opera,* maybe."

Angel shot her a look and started to move away, but was stopped when the doors swung open and their second visitor of the night appeared in the hotel lobby. It was Krevlornswath of the Deathwok Clan, whom Fred had first met in Pylea, and whom she now knew merely as Lorne, the Host at the demon karaoke bar called Caritas.

Lorne's green flesh and horns clashed horribly with his florescent orange suit, but somehow he made it work. Fred thought it was just confidence. Lorne had oodles.

"Lorne," Angel said, turning his attention from Cordelia to the demon nightclub owner, clearly relieved to be able to postpone calling Charlie Nickels a little bit longer.

Fred suspected that this wasn't a social call. There was a look on the demon's face that told her something was definitely up, the green of his skin seeming a little paler than usual.

"What's up?" Angel asked, catching on to the same vibe as she. He was crumpling the phone messages in his hand.

Lorne removed his fedora and descended the steps to the lobby. "I think there's big trouble in River City, gang," he said, nervously looking about.

Angel stared at him. "Great. Quoting from *Music Man.* Charlie's gotten to you. I'm not—"

Lorne gave him a grim look. "Not why I'm here, buckaroo."

Wesley had come out of his office yet again—so much for him getting anything done tonight—and he and Cordelia moved to Angel's side, as if they sensed trouble and it had drawn them together. Fred had felt it upon first moving into the hotel as though she had stepped into the midst of a family to which she did not belong. But they welcomed her and tried to make her feel at home, and already she had begun to think that maybe in time she *could* belong here. It was all very exciting.

Lorne spotted Gunn with Calvin in the far corner. "Good," he said, "all present and accounted for. I think we're going to need the whole cavalry to deal with this can of worms." He made a face, as if the idea of a can of worms was somehow distasteful to him.

"What's the matter, Lorne? What's happened?" Wesley asked, crossing his arms.

"Half-breed, half-off Tuesdays is the matter. One of my biggest nights is about to go the way of the dinosaur if somebody doesn't stop killing my customers."

The demon host noticed Fred sitting at the front desk. "Hey, sweetcakes," he said with a delicate wave. "How's she been doing getting reacquainted with this wacky, big blue marble we call Earth?" he asked the others, lowering his voice as though she would not be able to hear him.

"Fred's fine," Angel assured him. "Get to the point, Lorne. Somebody's killing half-breeds at Caritas?"

Lorne looked as though he'd been slapped. "Heaven forbid,

slugger. Any more death and destruction at my place and I'll be renting the space out to senior citizens for bingo nights. The halfies are being offed out on the mean streets. Quite a few of them, if I'm reading my auras correctly. Some of my regulars stopped showing up, and there've been whispers, not to mention lots of folks karaokeing the blues. And if the tingling in my horns is any indication, we got a serious problem here."

The hotel lobby fell silent for a moment as they each tried to make sense of Lorne's words. Fred felt her nose begin to run and reached for a Kleenex. When the telephone rang she let out a high-pitched squeak of surprise and, silence broken, everyone turned to watch her answer the phone.

"Angel Investigations. How may I help you?"

The others continued to watch her as she listened to the voice on the other end of the phone. "Just a minute, please."

She offered the phone to Angel. "It's for you."

Angel frowned and sighed deeply, glancing around self-consciously at the others. Fred realized that he must have assumed it was Charlie Nickels calling again.

"Tell him I'm busy and I have no interest in *The Music Man*."

"Oh, you should. What I wouldn't give for a crack at Harold Hill . . . ," Lorne said wistfully.

Fred shook her head vigorously, putting her hand over the receiver. "It's not Mr. Nickels," she said, voice low. "It's Buffy—and she says it's very important."

Sunnydale

"Hey," Buffy said with every ounce of cheeriness she could muster. She knew she was about to drop the proverbial ugly ball into Angel's lap. "Hope I didn't cut into your Must See TV time or anything."

"Not at all," Angel replied.

No matter what had transpired between them, it was good to hear his voice, even on the phone all the way from La-La Land. So far away, yet so very close.

"Besides, sweeps are over. It's all reruns now."

There was an uneasy pause, a hesitation on both ends. There were always so many things Buffy wanted to say to him and yet knew she never would, and she believed that Angel felt the same.

"Are you all right?" Angel asked. "Fred said—"

"Fred?" Buffy asked. "Her name is Fred?"

"Winifred. She's new."

With the phone held to her ear, Buffy glanced around the Magic Box. Her friends were helping Giles put things back in order after the latest in what seemed like scheduled attacks upon the shop. Though they thought they were being sly and disinterested, Buffy could see them glancing her way out of the corners of their eyes, gauging her reaction as she spoke with the one true love of her life. Buffy turned away from them.

"Winifred," she said, images of what a person with that name would look like flashing through her mind. "That's a nice, matronly, I'm-going-to-make-bread-from-scratch kind of name. Is she matronly? Not that she *sounded* matronly—but really, what exactly does matronly sound like? Does she bake—"

"You're babbling," Angel interrupted, cutting her babble off at the pass. He had always been good at that. "That's a sign of things being not so good. Tell me what's wrong."

Buffy sighed and switched the phone from one ear to the other. "The last couple of weeks we've been having a little local trouble with half-breed demons turning up dead—and I don't think it's going to stay local long."

"Isn't it amazing how similar L.A. and Sunnydale are?" Angel asked. "Country mouse, meet city mouse. You've got sunshine, we've got sunshine, you've got demon half-breed murders and guess what? So do we."

"That's what I was afraid of," Buffy said, glancing over to Willow and Tara. The two witches were standing in front of what, up until a few moments ago, was an overturned bookcase. A multicolored energy now swirled around the lovers' heads as the toppled books flew up from the floor and back onto their shelves.

"They call themselves the Coalition for Purity and they're putting together an army," Buffy told Angel. "I spied on a recruitment drive tonight, heard them talking. When they're done taking their pick of the litter from here, they're coming your way. Tomorrow. The demon running tonight's shindig was a Lagos, but he's not the boss. He was talking about a 'General Axtius.' A big bad name if I ever heard one. Ring any bells?"

For a moment there was silence on the other end of the phone line. "No," Angel said at length, "but I'll start looking into it. Thanks for the heads up. I'll let you know how things turn out."

"You won't have to. From the sound of things, the Sunnydale contingent is just part of it. This thing's huge. I'm coming in. We're all coming in."

Buffy knew that Angel would be far from thrilled by the prospect of the Scoobies on his turf, but this thing was too big for her to worry about her ex getting all territorial. Once again there was a long pause on the other end of the line.

"I don't think that's necessary, Buffy," Angel said. "We're pretty capable down here. I can let you know if—"

"We're coming. To even the odds a little," she said firmly. "And even that might not be enough."

"I never could argue with you."

The Slayer smiled softly—an intimate smile Angel would have recognized had he seen it, though it would have broken his heart all over again. There was always a lingering melancholy between them now, a sadness for what might have been if the fates had seen it in their hearts to let them stay together. But their destinies were separate. Begrudgingly they had resigned themselves to that fact. It still hurt to speak to him, and worse to see him, but this was simply how it was meant to be. She hated it, but she had accepted it.

"See you soon," Buffy told him, then she hung up the phone.

She stepped out from behind the front counter at the Magic Box. Her friends were quiet, a bit of respect for her emotional tenderness.

"So how *is* the caped crusader?" Spike snarled as he sat, leaning his chair back on two legs.

"Your literary references never cease to amaze me, Spike," Buffy said, sidling up to the table.

The vampire scowled, but she ignored him. Willow and Tara took a break from cleaning up to join her at the table, sitting side by side in the last two unbroken chairs.

"We're in," Willow said without preamble, with a tone and expression that would brook no argument.

Not that Buffy wanted to argue. "Good," she replied. "I think we're going to need that hoodoo that you two do so well."

The witches smiled at one another as though at some private joke. Buffy decided not to ask.

Xander had been unusually quiet since he had returned from the hospital, where Anya was spending the night under observation. After she had been sedated and drifted off, he had returned to the Magic Box, eyes dark with anger and frustration. Now he moved away from the front window and approached them.

"I'll get Ahn settled back at the apartment and give work a call to let them know I'm going to be using a few of them accruing personal days."

He stood in the middle of the store, his hands clenched into fists. Despite the lightness of his tone, Buffy had learned long ago to tell when Xander's humor was being used to cover up some more tempestuous emotion. It was obvious that he was torn between leaving the woman he loved and extracting a little bit of payback on those who had hurt her.

"You don't have to come, Xander," Buffy said. "I understand if you want to stay with Anya. In fact, somebody needs to look after Dawn and—"

Spike let the front legs of the chair fall to the floor. "Don't fret 'bout that, Slayer. I'll look after Little Bit for you."

She gave the vampire a withering look. "Not this time. As much as it pains me to admit, if this is as big as I think, we're going to need all the strength we can muster. Looks like little Spikey gets let off the leash for a while."

"Sic 'em, boy," Willow added, almost under her breath.

The vampire rubbed his chin as if in deep thought. "Hmm . . . well, it's short notice, isn't it? Been planning to tidy up the crypt some." Spike threw up his hands, a sly smile on his cadaverous face. "But what the hell. Seeing as how you need me an' all . . ."

Buffy knew Spike was looking for an argument, or some acknowledgment of his value to their excursion. She turned her back on him, focusing again on Xander.

"I'm going, Buff," he said. "Thanks for the understanding and all, but what kind of boyfriend would I be if I didn't rain vengeance down on the uglies responsible for putting the hurt on my main squeeze?"

Giles had been sweeping up the remains of a display of

healing crystals that had been shattered in the latest melee. Now he cleared his throat to draw their attention.

"I'll stay with Dawn," he said casually, dumping the crystal remains into a barrel that had been brought from the back room to handle the store's damaged refuse. "And I'll keep an eye on Anya as well."

Buffy frowned, staring at him. "We're going to need you down there, Giles. I appreciate it, but—"

"Not at all," the Watcher said, placing his dustpan atop the counter. "You and Angel are perfectly capable of field strategy, should that become necessary. Willow and Tara have greater natural magickal ability than I. No, I would end up being rather redundant."

"Rupert Giles redundant?" Spike asked aloud. "The horror of it all."

"Shut up, Spike," they all said as one.

Giles removed his glasses and set them on the counter. "Thank you for that," he said with a smile. "Actually, we mustn't forget that regardless of the scope of the threat presented by this demon coalition, Sunnydale is still situated upon the Hellmouth. There may well be further Coalition activity here. If Axtius and his coconspirators were to try to recruit from other dimensions, they might attempt to take control of the Hellmouth and open it. And even if that isn't part of the plan at the moment, there will be the usual vampires and demons. Someone must remain behind and continue to patrol. If we were all to leave and they were to become aware that Sunnydale was unprotected . . ."

"Looting, pillaging, blood running in the streets, chewing gum in school," Xander observed with typical melodrama.

Giles raised an eyebrow, but chose to ignore him. "As I was saying, there are a great many reasons for me to remain here, not the least of which is the safety of Sunnydale itself. You'll do fine without me. And I'll be accessible by phone should you need my help with research."

Willow looked distressed. "But . . . you're the expert. We see demon species and think 'ugly and uglier,' but you know what they are, how to fight them—"

"All of which Wesley knows as well," Giles reminded them. "Not to mention Angel. And I suspect you're giving short shrift to the knowledge you have all acquired in the many hours of research you have done these last few years. Someone needs to stay to look after Dawn and check in on Anya now and again. Logic dictates it should be me."

Spike laughed. "Not that I want your company, Giles, but logic dictates it should be the boy. He's the weakest bloody link, after all."

Xander bristled and started across the room toward Spike. "We'll see who's the weakest link, chip-boy! I'm not a cloud of dust waiting to happen."

But Giles ignored them, focusing instead on Buffy. "Xander would spend every minute you were gone wishing he had accompanied you, furious and anxious and wanting to hit something," the Watcher said sagely. "You are the Slayer, Buffy. You must take the helm."

"Wesley doesn't have your intuition," Willow warned. "And I'm betting nowhere near your knowledge."

"Plus, we like you a whole lot better than Wesley," Xander added. "What if we get Wesley to come here and he could watch the Dawnster?"

Buffy paid no attention to her friends' continued protests. She could see that Giles had made up his mind. She walked over to the counter and gazed at him as though they were the only two people in the room. "Are you sure?"

"Completely," Giles responded. "I have faith in you, Buffy.

With the team you'll have assembled down there, you won't need me. This sort of thing was always what the Slayer was meant for. And in case you have forgotten"—he looked around at his store, still in disarray but starting to shape up—"I still have a business to run."

He smiled at her, and an understanding passed between them, an understanding that told her he was never too far away if she was truly in need of him.

"So it's settled," she said, hopping up to sit on the counter and gazing around the Magic Box at the others. "Have your permission slips signed by your parents and get them back to me right away."

Los Angeles

Angel stood at the top of the stairs leading down into the Ninth Level Pub and Grill and was filled with dread. Of all the places he might find the information he sought, this was the one that he had hoped to avoid.

He had hit the streets soon after his conversation with Buffy. He had needed to get out, to distract himself from the fact that he would soon be seeing her. The idea of working with her on a case again was a strange mixture of excitement and sheer torture. As he prowled the streets of downtown Los Angeles in search of a snitch with information, he wondered how long it would take after she had gone home to Sunnydale for him to stop missing her like they had parted only yesterday.

Ever since the early days of motion pictures, Angel had loved the movies. He had seen many thousands of them, but only some of them echoed. When he thought about Buffy, for instance, he often thought of the film *Excalibur*. After King

Arthur and his wife, Guinevere, were separated by horrible twists of fate, the king went to see her one final time before heading off to what he knew might be his final battle.

"I have often thought that in the hereafter of our lives, when we owe no more to the future, you will come to me and claim me as your husband," King Arthur said. "It is a dream I have."

Angel couldn't watch that movie anymore.

He and Buffy had accepted what fate had brought them. When this crisis was over, she would go home, and he would stay in Los Angeles, and that was the way things were going to be. Angel would say or do nothing that would make it more difficult for them. But whatever else fate wrought upon them, he would always love her.

The usual informants that could be bought with a few bucks and a menacing glare were nowhere to be found this night, almost as if they had gone into hiding. That made him all the more determined to flip over as many rocks as he could, just to see what crawled out from beneath. Was there a connection between the half-breed murders in Sunnydale, what Buffy had seen, and the Caritas murders? Probably, but it was best to back up assumptions, to not jump to any conclusions.

Angel was certain that his answers were out on the streets. They had done enough damage to Caritas recently that he wanted to help Lorne out as much as possible. Even if they were part of a larger organization, if Angel could figure out who was killing half-breeds and take them down, that would help Lorne. And hopefully it would lead him back to whoever was behind the Coalition for Purity that Buffy had mentioned—and what a stupid name that was!

The problem was that he kept coming up empty. Some of his snitches had gone underground, and those he did manage to question didn't know anything, or at least that's what they claimed. He had nothing else to go on—which was why he had ended up here.

The Ninth Level stank of spilled beer and demon sweat, and Angel wondered how long he would need to air his clothes before the clinging stench finally faded. Usually the place was much busier than this, and he had to wonder if recent events were having an adverse effect on business. Angel walked down the center aisle, his eyes scanning the denizens of the room, an odd mixture of demon and human clientele. He remembered Willy's up in Sunnydale, but this place made Willy's look like a Vegas nightclub.

As he was about to pass the bar, he caught the eye of the bartender, Sol, who was mixing a strawberry margarita for a demon whose internal organs seemed to be located on the outside.

"Is he in?" Angel asked.

"What do I look like, his freakin' secretary?" Sol growled, slamming the drink down in front of the inside-out monstrosity. "Have a look for yourself."

"I'll take that as a 'yes,'" Angel said.

"Hey," Sol called, handing the vampire a glass of red wine. "If you're going back there, save me a trip. Take him this."

Angel considered ignoring Sol, but the man had not meant anything by his brusqueness. He was probably just on edge because business was light and that would kill his tip income for the night. Angel took the glass from the bartender, careful not to spill its crimson contents, and continued on his way. In the back of the bar was a row of high-backed, wooden booths. In the last booth Angel found a twisted caricature of a human being, a creature who had once been on *Fortune*'s list of the top five most wealthy businessmen.

Once upon a time, Charlie Nickels had had it all: fame,

wealth, good looks. But he had grown bored with the natural, and begun to dabble with the supernatural. Attempting to amass the kind of power he had accumulated within the cutthroat world of business, Nickels had begun to throw his weight around and soon had found himself running afoul of some very powerful magickal adepts. They cursed him for his audacity and arrogance, taking it all away and leaving him with nothing. They took his fame, his wealth, and his good looks, leaving behind nothing more than a twisted mockery of a man.

When Angel reached the booth where Charlie conducted his business, he saw that Nickels was resting his misshapen head on his arms on the wooden tabletop—and he was crying. Angel cleared his throat, not wanting to intrude on the grotesque man's misery, but there were things he needed to know, and lives at stake.

Nickels slowly raised his head, tears running down his discolored face. "Angel," he said in a trembling whisper. "Thank God you've come." Nickels noticed the drink in his hand. "Is that for me?" he asked, suddenly not so sad, reaching for it with tiny, gnarled hands.

Angel gave him the wine and watched as he consumed half of the glass's contents in one loud gulp. Then Nickels gazed up at him, and the vampire realized he was not going to have to apologize for ignoring his calls. Charlie Nickels was not angry; he was grief-stricken.

"They killed him," Nickels said, his voice oozing with sadness.

"Who?" Angel asked. "Who did they kill?"

"Harold Hill," the ugly little man gurgled. "They killed my perfect Harold Hill."

Angel was about to ask whom Harold Hill was, but the name seemed strangely familiar—and then he remembered where he had heard it before. It was the character from *The Music Man* that Nickels had wanted Angel to play. Apparently he had gotten someone else for the role, and that someone was dead now. Angel had a suspicion that whomever Nickels had found to play the part had been a half-breed.

Nickels had another swig from his wine. "You were my first choice, but when you started dragging your feet I had to look elsewhere. His name was Titus Brant. He was half-Gigaw, half-human, and so, so talented. Titus first came to my attention in a little production called *Turn on Anything, You'll Get It*. He stole the show and my heart."

Nickels wiped fresh tears from his face and snorted loudly. "He would have made the character of Harold Hill come alive, Angel." The little man's face sagged as if the leathery skin would slide from his malformed skull. "But somebody killed him. They beat him to death and took away my Harold Hill."

Nickels downed the last of his wine and slid the glass over beside a stack of compact disk cases and a portable CD player. It was the first time that Angel could remember ever seeing Nickels not listening to his music.

"So he was a half-breed," Angel said. "Do you—"

"That term's a bit crass, don't you think?" Nickels chided him.

Angel gave him a hard look. "Yeah. Sorry. I don't suppose you can think of anyone who might have had a grudge against your friend?"

Nickels slowly shook his head. "He was so much more than a friend," the twisted man said dreamily. "He was my star."

"Charlie," Angel snapped, and Nickels looked up, eyes wide with hurt and perhaps a little fear as well. "Your 'star' isn't the only half-breed to be murdered lately. If the term isn't politically correct, you can protest later. Right now, anyone who's half-human and half-demon could be in danger and I'm trying to make them safe. You going to help me, or cry about your musical?"

Nickels gaped at him, then nodded vigorously. "I've heard some stuff, but it really didn't mean all that much to me then. Demons, half-breed or not, they're getting killed all the time. Heck, sometimes you're the one responsible. So when I started to hear about some disappearances, well, with putting the show together and all, I just didn't think much of it."

Angel stepped closer to the table. "Does the name Axtius ring any bells with you?"

The deformed little man snatched up his empty wineglass and ran a finger along the inside. "Sounds vaguely familiar," he said as he popped the gnarled, wine-coated finger inside his mouth and sucked on it. "Think I heard it in regard to some demon purity rally that was happening around here a few months back—" He waved his hand in the air as if attempting to stir something from the ether. "The Coalition for Purity, or some such nonsense," he said. "Buncha Nazis, if you ask me."

Angel felt an icy chill run down his spine. Here was the connection he'd been searching for.

Nickels leaned out of the booth and bellowed up the aisle, "Hey Sol, another Merlot back here. And make it snappy, it's an emergency."

Sol shouted something filthy in return about Charlie's mother and her sexual adventures in Hell.

"He just doesn't understand the depths of my pain," the ugly little man said. Yet despite his seeming detachment, Angel could tell he was more focused now. Nickels looked up at him, eyes suddenly hard but still filled with pain. "Do you think these demon-Nazis had something to do with

Titus's murder? This Axtius guy, did he kill the perfect Harold Hill and my dreams of becoming a producer?"

Angel slipped his hands into his coat pockets. "That's what I'm trying to find out." From inside one of the pockets he produced a roll of cash and began to peel off Nickels's usual fee. "Thanks for the information," he said, offering the folded bills to the man, "and I'm sorry for your loss."

Nickels waved the money away. "Keep it," he said with a phlegmy growl. "This one is on me—in honor of Titus."

Angel heard the sounds of heavy footfalls behind him and turned to see an angry Sol making his way to the back, a glass of wine in hand, grumbling obscenities beneath his breath.

"Make them pay, Angel," Charlie Nickels said as he began to go through the CD cases on the table. "Don't let them get away with depriving the world of the best darn production of *The Music Man* ever seen."

"I'll see what I can do," Angel said as he started to leave. "But I do have to say, I'm a little surprised by your reaction."

Nickels stopped his CD pawing and stared at him. "What? You don't think I have the right to be crushed by this?"

"Sure, you have the right," Angel said. "I'm just surprised, that's all." He shrugged. "What's the old stage adage—'The show must go on'?"

Angel turned away just as Sol arrived with the drink. "Go easy on him," Angel said as he passed. "He's had a rough night."

As he headed for the door, he could just about make out Charlie's gravelly voice asking Sol if he had any experience with musical theater. With a slight grin, Angel left the Ninth Level, ascending the steps to the warm Los Angeles night outside. He had decided to return to the hotel, to see if the others had had more luck than he had. He would like to have as much information as possible before Buffy and the others arrived.

Angel was about to cross the street to his car when he heard his name called from somewhere behind him. He turned in time to see a familiar thin-faced, orange-skinned demon cautiously emerge from an alley. *Amos,* Angel remembered. *His name is Amos.* The demon was dressed in a multicolored jogging suit. Amos started to wave crazily, urging Angel closer. The vampire was relieved. Amos had served as a snitch for him several times, though not always reliably. Still, beggars couldn't be choosers. Most of his informants were AWOL at the moment, and if Amos had information for him—

Tentatively, Angel approached.

The demon danced spastically from one sneakered foot to the other, glancing back down the alley from where he had emerged.

"What's going on, Amos?" Angel asked as he strolled closer. "You have something for me?"

The demon, whose eyes were bulbous and multifaceted like those of a fly, again looked down the alley and nervously began to speak.

"Told you I could find him," Angel heard the jittery demon say to someone he could not yet see. "Now how about you pay up." Amos held out his trembling hand awaiting his compensation, but what he received in payment, Angel was almost willing to bet had not been part of the original agreement.

A mace wielded by a leather-clad arm descended from the darkness of the alleyway, crashing down upon the half-breed's head and shattering his skull like an eggshell. Brain matter shot from his ears and mouth like some hellish waterspout. The demon crumpled, dead before his twitching body hit the ground, the stench from his voiding bowels suddenly filling the warm night air.

"I hear you've been looking for me," said Amos's murderer as he stepped from the concealing shadows of the alley.

Angel gazed at a formidable Brachen demon and somehow knew full well who he was. The way he carried himself, the look of cruelty in his yellowed eyes.

"What a coincidence," General Axtius said with a humorless grin as he tapped the head of his battle mace rhythmically in the palm of a leather-gloved hand. "'Cause I've been looking for you."

CHAPTER SIX

"Filth," the Brachen demon whispered with a snarl that made the needle spikes that jutted from its face twitch.

Its flesh was a rich blue, its mouth too wide and filled with jagged fangs. The only Brachen that Angel had been acquainted with had been his friend Doyle, who had used the visions given to him by the Powers That Be to help Angel in his role as a champion for the Powers. But Doyle had been half human and, as such, even when he wore the countenance of the demon, had never been as ugly or as big as this thing.

"Filth?" Angel echoed. "Kind of a harsh character judgment, given we just met, don't you think? I mean, let's sit down, have a cup of coffee, get to know me before you rush in with the name calling."

The Brachen looked disgusted by Angel's monologue, but the vampire wasn't talking just to hear his own voice; he was buying time to take the demon's measure. His attention went from the Brachen's face to the corpse at his feet to the huge, spiked mace he carried in his hand. The demon wore leather, but his outfit wasn't designed for motorcycle comfort or for fashion. It was armor.

"All this work," the Brachen muttered to itself as it stepped farther from the darkness toward him. "All this planning for nothing."

Angel stared at him. "You know, Axtius—it is Axtius, right?— I'm getting the idea you don't like me. Which is fine, 'cause you know we just met and I already don't like you either. But if there's something you think I did, it would be helpful to know exactly what that is."

The demon's upper lip curled back, exposing those jagged teeth in a grimace that could not have been called a smile. "You know my name. That is good. You will have something to scream while you are dying."

The mace in Axtius's hand began to glow, sparks of blue light crackling across its surface. Angel studied the weapon, and a chill went through him. "That's not the Pristagrix, by any chance?"

This time, the Brachen demon did smile. "Oh, yes."

"Can't be," Angel said with a shake of his head. "The Codex listed it as lost after the Mahkesh Wars."

Axtius growled low in his throat and hefted the mace. The tiny lightning sparks that danced around the weapon's spiked head glowed more brightly, and Angel could smell sulfur in the air, could hear the hum of energy from the Pristagrix.

"It's been found," Axtius told him.

The demon stepped toward him and Angel crouched slightly, mind awhirl as he tried to find some strategy to deal with his predicament. If the Pristagrix was half as powerful as the legends indicated, he would need something to defend himself. Some weapon or shield. But there in the darkened side street in front of the Ninth Level, he saw nothing that could help him. His best bet, he realized, would be to flee back into the club and hope that a brawl would start that might give him an advantage over Axtius.

The thought made Angel snarl. He put his game face on, muscles and bones shifting and teeth elongating to points, revealing the demon within, the face of the vampire.

There was no way he was going to run. Which meant he had to get the Pristagrix away from the Brachen.

"All right," Angel growled. "You're so pissed off? Come and get me."

Swifter than Angel would have expected, Axtius leaped at him, both hands gripped upon the shaft of the mace. The ancient, arcane weapon crackled with power as it came down toward Angel's head. The vampire did not move. His left hand shot out and gripped the Brachen's arm. The Pristagrix gave its wielder such power that just stopping that blow forced him to stagger to one side.

Angel launched a volley of blows at the Brachen's leather-clad abdomen, struck him once, twice, a third time. Axtius let go of the mace with his left hand and slapped the vampire away. Angel grunted in pain, head ringing from the blow.

He let loose a feral snarl and glared at his enemy—not at the Brachen himself, but at the mace. Its ancient power surged through anyone who wielded it, lent them power, and the Pristagrix itself was deadly. Translated from the demon tongue of those that had created it, its name meant Bone Breaker. It never missed its target.

If Angel did not get the mace away from Axtius, he was dead.

He lunged at Axtius, feinting that he was going for another

body blow—only an idiot would punch a Brachen in the face with those needles poking out of its flesh—and when the mace swept down again, Angel reached to try to wrest it from Axtius's grasp.

The demon spun, dodging Angel's lunge, and brought the Pristagrix down on his right shoulder. The impact was one of the most painful things Angel had ever experienced; bone splintered to shards, and he was knocked a dozen feet to crash into the outer wall of the Ninth Level. The spikes had torn his flesh and spattered his blood across the pavement and the wall. Pain became rage, and Angel somehow managed to stay on his feet. He snarled as he turned on Axtius again, right arm dangling useless at his side. "That's gonna cost you," Angel whispered through gritted teeth.

Axtius closed in again. "I've heard you're a Champion. That the Powers That Be selected you to be their warrior." The Brachen sniffed, needles quivering with every change of his facial expression. "Well, let me tell you something, vampire. There are a great many powers in the universe. And you aren't much of a champion. I am a commander of warriors. You . . . you are a filthy leech, lower than low. And now you will be crushed."

Angel lunged at him, but it was a feint. Axtius swung the mace down and Angel pulled back, lashed out with a kick to the demon's midsection that sent Axtius staggering back. Silently, grimly, Angel followed after him, reached out with his good arm, and grabbed hold of his enemy's weapon. But Axtius had not let go, and the Pristagrix gave him extraordinary strength. He tugged the mace back with such force that Angel was lifted off of his feet.

"Filth," Axtius muttered again. "For what you have done, your pain is just beginning."

He struck Angel's injured shoulder and the vampire winced. Axtius shook him off, drove him to the ground, and Angel kicked him again, this time in the knee. The Brachen demon did not seem to have felt it. Angel struck him several times in quick succession.

Then the mace crashed down on his left arm, crushing bone and tearing flesh, spilling more of his blood. Angel felt himself spun around by the blow, a haze of pain veiling his mind. Both arms broken, he tried to rise, and the mace struck his chest. Angel could hear his ribs snapping, felt shards of bone tearing organs inside him, and he collapsed to his knees, all the fight gone from him.

Angel looked up to see Axtius swing the Pristagrix at his face.

Then there was only darkness.

Consciousness returned to Angel in agonizing fragments. It began in his hands, a screaming pain that felt as if the skin of his palms had been stripped off and the muscles frayed, pulled too taut. With an instinctive twitch he tried to move them, tried to pull them close to cradle them, and excruciating pain drove up from his shoulders to the back of his head as though someone had shoved knitting needles into his brain.

His eyes snapped open, and he shouted in agony against a crude gag that had been tied over his mouth. He did not need to breathe, but to speak he was required to draw air into his body. Shattered ribs tore at his lungs, and he fell silent and still. He would not try to breathe again.

Above him the dark sky was limned with gold, the lights of Los Angeles, but despite that light and the thin cloud cover he could see a scattering of stars. They had never seemed so far away. Angel could smell the copper scent of his own blood, which had caked his clothing and dried there, stiffening his shirt.

Below his knees he could feel nothing and he tried to lift his head to make sure his legs had not been amputated. They were still there, but he grunted in surprise and dismay when he saw the enormous railroad spikes that had been driven through the thick meat of his lower calves. The tiny noise inflated his lungs, sharp bone pierced them, and his head swam with darkness.

Disoriented again, he slumped his head back.

Tar. He smelled tar. Tar paper, roof, that was it. And for some reason that triggered his mind, and memories flowed into his head, the vicious, arrogant Brachen demon and that damned mace. He was pinned—nailed—to the roof of some old warehouse or an abandoned tenement. Somewhere Axtius could be sure no one would respond if he managed to shout for help.

Every second he remained conscious the pain in his palms and his shoulders grew more excruciating. *Still*, he thought. *Just keep still.* And so he tried as best he could to remain completely motionless. Only his eyes twitched back and forth.

In his peripheral vision Angel saw something moving off to his left. He heard the creak of leather upon leather.

"Ah," Axtius said in a satisfied rasp, "you're awake. Good."

With a grunt and a shuffling of feet, the Brachen demon lay down beside him. Angel flinched, pain searing all through his body, jabbing into his brain again. For a moment, consciousness left him.

When his eyes fluttered open again, the gag had been removed and Axtius was beside him. Glancing left, Angel could just make out the Brachen demon lying on his back, arms crossed under his head, gazing upward at the heavens.

"Beautiful, isn't it?" Axtius asked.

In deference to his broken ribs, Angel gave voice to none of the savage retorts that came to mind.

"You would think, I suppose, that someone of my disposition

would be incapable of appreciating the extraordinary loveliness found in this world," Axtius continued. "But you would be wrong. The cityscape at night is stunning. The stars. All of it will be far more beautiful, of course, when viewed by conquerors rather than mere visitors. And yet, do you know what is even more beautiful than the night sky, vampire?

"The sunrise. It will simply take your breath away."

Angel flinched, craning his head slightly to try to get a better look at Axtius. His eyes fluttered and his nostrils flared and he fought unconsciousness again. For a moment he thought he had managed to hold the darkness off, but when his vision focused again he saw that Axtius stood right above him, staring down into his face.

How long? he thought anxiously. *Damn it, how long was I out? How long until dawn?*

"It will be a horrible death. An ancient one I spoke to about your kind told me that though the burning happens very quickly, it seems an eternity to the vampire as the sun scours flesh from bone and chars bone to ash," Axtius told him.

The demon gestured to the roof around Angel. "You can't see them, but I have painted wards here that will keep your friends away. Demon and human alike, of course. Yes, I know about you, Angelus. Scourge of the darkness. Your own kind despise you and no wonder. If vampires are the untouchable filth, the gutter rats of the night world, then you must indeed be the lowest of the low. Vampire with a soul. You are the ultimate half-breed. The final insult to purity.

"Even if vengeance did not demand your death, I would feel honor bound to destroy you."

Angel snarled, steeling himself against the pain in his chest. Ignoring the broken ribs that stabbed his lungs, he spoke at last. "Vengeance for *what?*" he demanded.

Axtius gaped stupidly at him, and then shook his head in disbelief. "Surely you cannot be that much of a fool. 'Vengeance for *what?*'" The demon shook his head, then his lips curled back and he spat on Angel's chest, his saliva smoking like acid where it touched Angel's jacket.

"Well, you must know. You cannot die without knowing," Axtius said to himself, before crouching down beside Angel. The smile on his face was repulsive and profoundly unnerving. "My son."

This time when Angel flinched, he welcomed the pain that now sang in his hands and chest and limbs.

"Doyle," he hissed. *Of course it's Doyle.* It was the only thing that made sense.

At the mention of the name, Axtius spat again. "Yes, *Doyle.* Francis Doyle, or so his cow of a mother called him. I never had the chance to give him a proper name. My greatest shame, the offspring I could never lay claim to."

Angel forced himself to smile. "A half-breed," he grunted, and the look of fury on the Brachen demon's face was worth the pain it caused him to speak.

"Yes. A half-breed," Axtius said. He stared up at the stars. "There was a time when I was drunk on the beauty to be found in this world. I had not yet realized that there was only ever going to be one way to embrace it. The beauty did not belong to us, for we were considered the hideous ugliness lurking in the shadows, the things that crawled out from beneath rocks. I have learned. I know better now.

"My son's existence filled me with revulsion, and yet I wanted an heir. I wanted someone to carry on when the darkness claimed me again. For years I sought a way, a spell that would make Francis Doyle the son I wished for rather than the disgusting thing he was."

Axtius marched toward him again and bent so that the needle tips of his face hovered half a foot above Angel's.

"I found it, vampire. The sorcery that would have done it. Drained the human half from my son and left him pure Brachen, all demon. At last I would have an heir. I am surrounded by those of like mind, demons with whom I share a singular goal to be executed in stages. The first is the elimination of all half-breeds, all creatures who defile the purity of the demon nation. Now I would be able to enter into the fray without the stigma of what I had done, what I had brought into this world.

"I was going to make him truly my son at last."

Axtius dropped to his knees, facial needles spiking into Angel's forehead, barely missing his eyes.

"Then *you* got him killed!" the Brachen roared, its fetid breath hot on Angel's face. "You and that bitch-whore human he married. You pushed him to aid a vile pack of half-breeds. Lost and weak, he tried to please you. And then he died. Because of you, he died! If I had known it earlier, I would have gone myself to slaughter that despicable woman he married, but that pleasure is no longer in my hands.

"You, though," Axtius spat the words. He stood up, glaring down at Angel. "You will suffer the fires of nine hells when the sun rises. I only wish I could wait here to listen to you plead and then hear you scream. But you are not the only abomination I must attend to."

The Brachen demon took a single step toward Angel, then pushed his heavy boot down upon Angel's shoulder where the bones were still little more than splinters. Red spikes of pain shot through Angel's head—he could see them on the backs of his eyelids—and he was unable to stifle the roar of agony that erupted from his throat, bringing only more pain.

The darkness swallowed him again.

• • •

He swam in it. The stars and the glow of the city lights against the sky. The pain now at a distance as though he had stepped away from it somehow. But in the darkness, a sound, a tinny bleating, a cellular phone. And then that voice, that cruel, hard voice like a diesel engine, returned.

Angel moved in and out of consciousness, vaguely aware of the world around him one moment, and drifting off to somewhere inside his mind the next.

But he heard.

". . . the island . . . transport . . . all who live upon that island must be exterminated . . . half-breeds and anyone who tries to protect them, even purebloods . . . cowards will have no place in the world we will make.

"Yes, yes. I'll be along shortly . . . garbage to be rid of . . . got a revolution to run . . ."

The words faded out.

The stars faded out.

The sky ticked on toward morning.

Cordelia's eyes burned. She had been sitting in front of the computer for hours and now she felt stiff and sore. A deep yawn snuck up on her, and she stretched and rubbed her eyes before looking at the screen again. The hotel was quiet, save for the creaks and pops that come along with any structure of such venerable age. Fred, recovering from her cold but still drained by it, had gone to bed long ago, and Gunn had gone home. Angel had not returned yet, but that was far from unusual. At the moment it was just Cordelia and Wesley, and with Wes in his office, translating a prophecy he'd found that seemed to indicate everyone in Las Vegas might soon turn into chickens, she might as well have been alone.

She moaned to herself and stretched again, then stared balefully at the screen. Given what had been happening with Caritas customers, she had been scanning police logs from the past few weeks, trying to find anything that might give her a clue. Though she had never liked the woman, this was one of those rare times she wished that Kate Lockley, Angel's old sparring partner from the LAPD, hadn't given up her badge and left town.

Seconds went by, and her vision blurred slightly.

"Oh, forget this," she muttered to herself. If she kept squinting at the screen she was going to need regular Botox treatments before she was thirty.

Cordelia shut the computer down and snatched up her purse. She strode across the darkened lobby toward Wesley's office to say good night. When she was halfway there, the phone rang. She snapped her head around to glare at the clock, as though it had been the offending instrument. A few minutes before midnight. Plenty of time for one more crisis. "I got it," she called to Wesley.

Through the sliver of his slightly open door she saw him look up and then wave his thanks. He barely seemed to have registered her, and certainly not the lateness of the hour.

"Angel Investigations."

There was a click and a hiss on the other end of the line, and she knew the call was coming from far away.

"Cordelia?" A woman's voice.

Cordelia frowned. "This is she."

"It's Harry."

Harry. Doyle's ex. Even though they had long since been divorced, Cordelia always felt a little guilty talking to Harry. At the end there, before he died, Cordelia had felt something for Doyle. They had kissed, and through that kiss Doyle had passed to her the precognitive visions the Powers had given him to aid Angel against the forces of darkness. Cordelia was grateful for that kiss and the memory of it, but she could not help wondering if, under different circumstances, the kiss might have gone to Harry.

So whenever she talked to Harry, she was a little nicer than need be. She couldn't help it. "Harry, hi!" she said excitedly, despite the seconds ticking toward midnight. "Wow, we were just talking about you. You still on that dig in Bali, or wherever?"

"Not exactly," Harry replied, her voice thin, sounding almost weak. Cordelia chalked it up to the connection and the distance.

"So what are you up to, then? How are you?"

"Not doing well. I'm . . . in the hospital, Cordelia. Is . . . is Angel there?"

Cordelia went cold. She froze, there in the lobby. "No, Harry. He's not. What happened? Do you need us there?"

She sensed something out of the corner of her eye and swept her gaze over to find that Wesley had risen and was now standing just outside his office door, watching her with concern furrowing his brow.

The phone line was silent for several seconds save for the crackling of the poor connection.

"I don't think so. I think . . . I think the trouble has passed here, at least for now. He probably thinks I'm dead, so that's all right."

"Who? Who thinks you're dead? What happened?"

Wesley came farther into the lobby. "That's Harry?" he asked.

Cordelia waved at him to shush.

Then she listened as Harry told her about a group of vicious demons that had visited her archaeological dig in Cambodia. They had beaten her so badly that had it not been for a member of her team who knew a certain amount of healing magick, Harry would have died. Cordelia felt sick to her stomach as Harry described the attack. "Harry, that's terrible. I'm sorry. Do you want us to look into it?"

"I've been looking into it," Harry replied. Now her voice began to echo on the line, each word trailed by a ghost of itself. "I was touch and go for a few days, Cordelia. I . . . almost didn't make it. Since then I've started to do research on him. On Axtius."

"Axtius," Cordelia repeated. "I know that name."

"A Brachen demon. He's Doyle's father. He . . . he sent them to kill me because he blamed me for somehow tainting his son, for making him more human than he already was."

A small, perverse chuckle whispered along the phone lines from Cambodia. "Funny, huh? I was the one who had wanted him to embrace his demonic heritage."

"A riot. Axtius sounds like a barrel of laughs. Listen, Harry, what can we do to help you? You want us to track this guy?" Cordelia reached for a pad of paper on the reception desk and wrote down the demon's name as best she could sound it out.

"No. Not for me. But you should, Cordelia. I called to warn you. Something . . . something enormous is happening. All over the world, actually, but right now it's really centered in North America. And Axtius is involved. He's there. As far as I can tell, he's right there in Los Angeles somewhere. If he goes looking for Doyle . . ."

"He'll find us," Cordelia whispered.

"Who?" Wesley asked, stepping up beside her now. He mimed the word silently. A shadow of stubble was on his chin, and Wesley ran a hand over it now, staring at her. "Who'll find us?"

"Hang on," she told Harry. Cordelia shot Wesley a sharp look. "Hello, lack-of-courtesy boy. Horses? Hold 'em."

With a scowl she told Harry to go on. Wesley gave her a properly scolded look and crossed his arms, regarding her silently. His impatience was obvious, but he did not speak again.

"Axtius is a pure Brachen," Harry said. "He was always a bastard, apparently, but not at the level he is now. I made some calls. In my demon studies over the years I've made a lot of connections. Almost all of them knew who Axtius was. That surprised me. And it scares me a little too. Axtius was recruited by something called the Coalition for Purity. Sounds stupid, I know, but don't let it fool you."

Cordelia sighed. "Oh, crap."

"What?"

"The Coalition. Axtius. You're right, Harry. They're already here. I knew I knew the name. Angel got a call from Buffy and . . . anyway, they're in L.A. And this guy is Doyle's father? That can't be good. Tell me everything you've got, Harry. I've got a feeling things are going to get seriously ugly."

"Doyle's father rose up in the ranks and now he's a highly regarded officer of this alliance. The Coalition's goals are frighteningly simple. First, they're massacring all the demons they can find who *aren't* pure. It's a Nazi-esque philosophy. They think the half-breeds weaken them just by existing. They want to restore purity to demon kind, not just to their individual tribes, but to all demon races. And after that . . ."

Harry's words trailed off.

"After that?" Cordelia prodded, though she was not at all certain she wanted to know the answer.

"After that," Harry repeated grimly. The line crackled ominously. "The whispers in the dark say that they're covertly building armies they'll use to invade the home dimensions of the various tribes that are members of the alliance, and put the Coalition in as rulers of those dimensions. From there, other tribes and dimensions will fall. Our world is just a staging area. And Cordelia, in the years I've been involved with this stuff, I've found that the whispers are almost always right."

"I don't get it," Cordelia said. "Axtius sowed his wild demony oats. He slept with a human woman, or Doyle never would have been born. What's he doing mixed up with all the Nazi badness?"

"Making up for the sins of his past," Harry replied. "Or at least I'd wager that's his take on it."

"What about the Nazi demons we dealt with last time? The ones we were fighting when Doyle—"

Died, she was going to say. But she did not have to. Cordelia knew the word would have hurt them both.

"That's the only good news," Harry said. "That clan is so bigoted that it would never ally itself with other tribes. They're not involved. If they did show up, the Coalition would see them as an enemy to be conquered, because they wouldn't participate in the alliance."

Cordelia rubbed her tired eyes. "See? Good news!" There was no humor in the words. Her mind was spinning, trying to figure out what all this meant for them. Axtius was here in L.A. on his genetic cleansing quest, on the road to making war on all the demon realms—civil war—before coming back to Earth to take over here. It was a huge conspiracy. The biggest. Too big to possibly work.

Unless it does.

That would really suck.

"So, if he's here, he might try looking up Doyle," Cordelia said suddenly. "Maybe to kill him. Erase the evidence. Did his muscle boys seem to know Doyle was dead?"

"I have no idea. But all of you should be looking over your shoulders."

Cordelia thanked her and took down a number where Harry could be reached should there be any news. "Let us know if there's anything we can do for you," Cordelia said.

"Just stay alive," Harry replied.

Cordelia turned to Wesley as she replied to Harry, staring at him. "Pretty much doing our best."

She hung up the phone. For a long moment she kept her hand on it, digesting what she had just been told. At length, she said to Wesley. "You got most of that from my half of the conversation?"

"Most of it. Better run it down again, though," the former Watcher said, his expression grave. "What I heard, I don't like the sound of at all."

"Trust me, you're not going to like the rest of it either."

They were interrupted by a thump on the front door. Cordelia and Wesley looked up as it swung open. Cordy was expecting Angel.

Buffy Summers walked into the hotel like she owned the place. She was dressed for travel and for combat, in jeans and black-laced boots, but had managed to pull off an understated silk blouse with the rest of the ensemble. It shouldn't have worked, but it did. Her hair was pulled back in a ponytail, and she effortlessly carried a huge duffel bag that she dropped on the floor the minute she reached the bottom of the steps.

"Cordelia," Buffy said pleasantly. "Hey, Wesley."

"Buffy," Wesley replied, inclining his head in greeting.

None of them seemed motivated to hug.

"Your timing's dead on," Cordelia told her. "I didn't think you'd be down until morning."

The Slayer frowned. Cordelia studied her. Buffy really had

changed. She had settled into the power she wielded, and looking at her it was as though the girl she had been had been chipped away from the outside, leaving only the Slayer behind. It seemed to Cordelia impossible that anyone could have looked at her and not seen the power in her. But, then, Cordelia knew what she was.

"I said we'd come as quickly as possible."

As if on cue, the doors to the hotel were shoved open again. Despite the gravity of the evening's events, Cordelia's heart felt lighter as she saw Willow and Xander come in, followed by Willow's girlfriend, Tara. She had been through a lot with Will and Xander, and though she'd only met Tara briefly, the witch seemed sweet in a geeky, absolutely-NO-fashion-sense sort of way. It occurred to Cordelia that none of them had met Fred yet, and she tried to imagine Tara and Fred trapped in a conversation made up of pauses and hesitations. *Shy and Shyer.*

"We're going to have a full house," Wesley observed.

"Hey, Elwood, we're getting the band back together!" Xander declared happily.

"As usual, I have no idea what you're talking about," Cordelia sighed. "And we don't have time to figure it out."

Buffy had been looking around the lobby as though she had never been there before. Now she turned, brow furrowed, to stare at Cordelia and Wesley. "You've got news?"

"Oh, yes," Wesley agreed. "And all of the bad variety."

Before Buffy could press him on the new developments, the door swung open one final time. Cordelia glanced up, and her heart skipped a beat as Spike strode into the hotel with a black bag over his shoulder and a cigarette clenched between his lips.

"Well," she said icily, "now the gang's all here." Her gaze ticked toward Buffy. "I know he's neutered now . . . the chip-thingy . . . you explained. But that doesn't mean he's welcome here."

"Hello to you, too, sweet thing," the vampire said, pursing his lips with repressed anger. He took a drag off his cigarette and blew a ring of smoke. "I'd appreciate it if you didn't talk about me like I wasn't in the room. Hurts my feelings, like."

Buffy did not even look at Spike. She kept her gaze on Cordelia, her expression grim. All business.

"Spike can't kill humans anymore. He *can* kill demons. We're going to need some demons killed. I'm not saying you need to think of him as part of the team. Think of him as a weapon we can use. He's a tool."

Tara, Willow, and Xander had come farther into the hotel and had put their bags down near the reception desk as though waiting for a bellboy, but now Xander came striding up, still smiling. "Hey, I've always thought of Spike as a tool," he noted.

Cordelia allowed herself the tiniest smile, then scowled again as she glanced at Spike. "Fine. But there's no smoking in the hotel."

Spike shrugged, dropped the burning cigarette onto the marble floor, and ground it out beneath his boot heel. He came down into the lobby, leaving the cigarette stub where he had dropped it.

"So let's hear it," Buffy prodded.

Willow and Tara leaned upon each other, and Xander stood with his arms crossed, waiting to hear what Cordelia had to say. Spike dropped down onto a sofa and stretched out as though he wasn't paying any attention at all.

"Cordelia, while you get everyone up to speed, I'm going to call Gunn and get him back down here," Wes said. "Then I'll wake Fred."

"No," Cordelia said quickly. "Let her sleep. She needs rest so she can get well. I'd say even without her we'll have enough manpower to find Angel."

"'Manpower'?" Willow asked. "I think I might resent that."

But Buffy was not amused. She stared at Cordelia. "Angel's missing?"

"Not exactly. But he needs to know what we know—and pretty much right now. Hence the finding of him."

"All right," Buffy agreed. "First, though, give with the update. Someone's raising an army of demons. Can't be good. What more do we know?"

"Well," Cordelia replied, "we know it's personal."

CHAPTER SEVEN

Buffy stared at Cordelia, trying to make sense of what she'd just heard. "So this Axtius guy is the demon daddy of a friend of yours," she said, mostly to herself to get her facts straight. "What kind of demon are we talking about here? Wouldn't happen to be one of those warm and squooshy-like-a-puppykind, by any chance?"

"Sorry," Cordelia said with a shake of her head. "Brachen demon. Blue face, prickly spines sticking out of it. Only puppy connection with this guy would be the one he just had for lunch."

Buffy wrinkled her nose as she pictured the cutest puppy she could imagine sliding down a demon's throat like a Jell-O shot. She pushed the disturbing image away. "Wouldn't happen to have any hints as to why Daddy's got such a mad on, would you?" she asked.

Cordelia began to answer, but Spike cut her off. "Probably doesn't care for the kinda company his kid's been keeping," the vampire muttered from his place on the lobby sofa. "If it were my loin sprout, I'd probably be a trifle ticked as well."

Xander rolled his eyes. "If it were your spawn, we'd be able to track it by the whining. Brr. Shudder. Images of baby Spike in my head, begone!"

Buffy shot the vampire a withering glare. "I'm not going to tell you again," she warned. Spike closed his eyes and put his head back against the wall, and Buffy turned to Cordelia with a strained smile usually reserved for embarrassed mothers with precocious children. "Sorry about that, long car ride and all, makes 'em a little cranky. Go on."

Cordelia barely seemed to have noticed the interruption, or Buffy's attempt at levity. Her gaze was distant, and when she spoke, the weight of grief hung heavy in her voice. "Doyle was a good friend to us," Cordelia said, "but he didn't talk all that much about his past—he was kind of secretive about the whole demon thing. Ashamed of it."

For a long moment, Cordelia was uncharacteristically silent. She stared at her hands where they rested atop the front desk. At length she sighed and glanced up again. "If Axtius is Doyle's father . . . well, you've gotta figure a dad like that would probably have thought Doyle was too much in touch with his human side—maybe that he became tainted by his human acquaintances."

Spike snorted laughter. "What I said, innit?"

This time, Buffy ignored him, her focus instead on Cordelia. Buffy was impressed. It appeared her former schoolmate had somehow become the unlikely backbone of Angel's little group. Buffy was sure that the old Cordelia still made appearances from time to time; it would take more than a stake to kill that kind of beast, but it was amazing to see how Cordelia had changed, how much she had grown as a person. Buffy sensed that Doyle had meant a great deal to her. For all that she knew, Cordelia—maybe more than any of them—had evolved since high school; seeing the other woman's genuine pain made Buffy realize how much.

It also gave her a sudden jolt, reminding her of the mortality of all those around her, those she cared about. She herself had died and had been brought back—a cruel irony that tortured her soul. But it was even worse to think that she had come back to a world where her mother and people like Kendra and Jenny Calendar had died, and where the battle they all waged might cost the lives of any of her friends at any time. A sick feeling spread through her gut, the realization that with the kind of life she led, the probability of future losses was almost inevitable.

She looked to the others gathered about her: Willow and Tara were whispering softly to each other, Xander seemed to have discovered something really interesting underneath one of his fingernails, and Spike was pretending he had gone to sleep. Buffy wondered if they were thinking it as well—that being part of her life, they all lived the risk of not seeing another tomorrow.

A wave of dread began to crest within her, but she squelched it, grinding it down beneath a steely reserve. It was not the time or place to think of such things. They would be fine, she would do everything in her power to make sure that they were safe. And besides, they were the good guys after all—that had to count for something.

The uncomfortable silence was broken as a young man entered the hotel arguing with a teenage boy perhaps a few years older than Dawn. It took Buffy a second to recognize Angel's associate Charles Gunn from their previous meeting—the teenager was a distraction.

"You just follow my lead; not a word of sass, you got it?" Gunn told the kid, who nodded begrudgingly. The man slid a hand over his shaved scalp with a frustrated sigh, then turned his attention to the others in the lobby. "Got here as soon as I could," he said. He gestured toward the teen. "Having a bit of a problem cutting the umbilical cord."

"It's quite all right, Gunn," Wesley said. "We were just discussing our next course of action."

As Wesley explained what little they had learned so far, Buffy eyed the kid with Gunn. She wasn't exactly keen on having a teenager around. If this thing was as big as they thought it was, it was going to get seriously nasty pretty quick. *Too bad I didn't bring Dawn along,* she thought. *The two could have kept each other out of trouble.* In her mind, Buffy heard the cartoon sound of screeching brakes and she quickly reviewed her last thought—handsome teenage boy from L.A. and cute, impressionable teenage girl from the suburbs. Buffy shuddered. *Maybe it's a good thing Dawn's home with Giles after all.*

Spike snapped awake from his pretend nap with a snarl on his face. "Look, we gonna stand around the Bat-cave all night or are we gonna get down to business?"

Wesley arched an eyebrow and regarded Spike coolly. "Maybe we should begin with you?"

Everybody glared at the vampire, and Spike threw his head back. "Bloody hell, you don't need a stake. This buncha heroes are gonna soddin' bore me to death."

Buffy saw Gunn stiffen as he glared at Spike. Gunn had grown up hunting vampires on the streets of Los Angeles. From what she had gathered, he still wasn't completely comfortable with the idea that he had made friends with one of them, no matter how benevolent Angel might be. The presence of Spike obviously did not sit well with him. Gunn started for the

English vampire, and Buffy stepped between them to defuse the situation. Although she hated to admit it, Spike was right: They did need to get moving. Every second counted.

"Pay no attention to him, Gunn. We're all on edge, that's all." She glanced around at her friends and saw that Willow, Tara, and Xander were watching her expectantly, waiting to figure out what the plan was. Buffy glanced back at Gunn, then at Wesley and Cordelia. "First things first. We find Angel. We're on your turf. What's the plan?"

Cordelia came out from behind the front desk. "I've already tried his cell phone with no success, but that doesn't necessarily mean anything." She cupped a hand to the side of her mouth as if giving away secret information. "The boy's a little slow on the uptake when it comes to technology."

Wesley stepped up, taking control of the moment. "While it's true the lack of an answer isn't uncommon, we can't discount the possibility that Angel's in danger. If Axtius discovers that his son is dead, it seems quite likely he'll find out how Doyle died. I think it's safe to assume he won't take the news well. Angel could be the target of potential vengeance." Wesley glanced at Cordelia. "And he isn't likely to be the only target. We need to locate him immediately."

Buffy was impressed. Cordelia was not the only one who had changed considerably in the time since Angel had set up shop in Los Angeles. Something was in Wesley's voice that she had never heard there before, a strength and confidence that lent him a new authority.

"We'll split into two teams and canvass all the areas and the sources we know Angel to frequent in his searches for information," Wesley said. "Hopefully, that's precisely what he's been doing tonight and he's just lost track of the time."

For a long moment the former Watcher looked around the

lobby at those gathered there, contemplating. Then he nodded to himself. "Willow, Tara, I'd like you to go to a club called Caritas. The Host there is a friend of ours who was the first to ask us to look into this. Some of his half-breed demon customers had turned up missing or dead. If Angel learned anything tonight, or had more questions, he might well have returned there. Even if Angel hasn't been by, there's a good chance that Lorne might have learned something new on his own."

"We're game. Just point us in the right direction and we're there," Willow said.

Tara nodded in agreement. "I've never done the whole hitting-the-mean-streets-of-L.A. thing before. It should be interesting."

"Excellent," Wesley continued. "Buffy, Spike, Gunn, and I will be doing a broader sweep of Angel's usual snitches. We'll begin at the docks and—"

"What team am I on?" the boy asked, stepping forward.

Wesley blinked, then shot a questioning look at Gunn, who shrugged his shoulders and looked away. Wes focused on Calvin again. "Yes, I'd thought about that. I'm afraid Cordelia's going to need you here, Calvin—"

"Exactly," Cordelia said quickly, giving Calvin her most sincere look. "There's still loads of research to be done on Axtius and his nasty playgroup and . . ." She looked around the room. Buffy could practically hear the gears working inside her head. "And Xander and I are going to need all the help we can get. Aren't we, Xander?"

Xander, who was sitting atop his duffel bag, looked as though he'd been slapped. "Hey, wait a minute," he said, starting to protest. "Research? I've graduated to the next level—haven't I?"

"She's right, Xander," Buffy said. "The more we learn about this guy and his Nazi buddies, the more damage we can do on his face later."

His shoulders slumped as he resigned himself to the assigned task. "Hitting the books with Cordy," he said with a shake of his head. "Just like old times."

The two of them made eye contact, and Buffy noticed something pass between them. "Sort of," Xander suddenly interjected, looking away from her, his movements spastic, almost falling off the bag where he sat. "Old times—but different."

"Okay, then," Cordelia said, obviously derailing that train of thought. "You guys find Angel, and we'll hold down the fort here while digging in the research coal mines."

Calvin wasn't at all pleased. He turned to Gunn, looking irked. "Gunn, what's up with this? I've been around your crew. I know about the monsters. My old man is—"

"Hold up, Cal," Gunn said harshly. "I told you to stay back in the neighborhood with my boys. You didn't want to do that, all right. I brought you. By rights, someone should stick you in a room somewhere, 'cause it's us keeping you safe right now. It's not like I'm saying you can't handle yourself. I know you can. I'm saying you want to hang with this group right now, in the middle of a crisis, you gotta play the part that gets assigned to you. If you're not helping, you're in the way. And we can't afford to have you in the way.

"Now, maybe you missed what just happened here. I'll let you in on it, since nobody seems to want to talk about it. You and Xander over there? You're gonna help Cordelia do research so we know what we're up against. Nothing's more important than that right now. But I'll go you one better. Wesley just said Cordelia's a potential target, or could be, if this Axtius dude had too much revenge in his coffee this morning. So you and Xander staying here with Cordelia, it ain't just about helping her research."

Buffy smiled at how well Gunn had handled the kid, but

when Calvin turned around, she let the smile drop. She didn't want him to see it. The kid marched over to Cordelia, then stopped in front of her, arms crossed.

"That right? You need me here to help in case there's trouble, this demon comes looking for you?"

Cordelia pointed at Xander. "I don't really want him to be my last line of defense."

"Hey!" Xander cried. When no one paid any attention, he raised his hand as though he were in school. "Hey!" he said again. When there was still no response, he merely sighed.

Buffy glanced at her watch. No more time for assuaging hurt feelings.

"All right, kids," she said, clapping her hands together. "Let's get moving. We've got to find Angel before things get seriously nasty."

"Good hunting," Cordelia said, steering Calvin away from the flow out the door and over to Xander.

Spike pulled a cigarette from a pack inside his shirtfront pocket and placed it in his mouth. "It's what I live for," he said as he lit the cigarette and headed to the door with the others.

Buffy was the last to leave, all the while resisting an urge to put her foot through the back of the vampire's skull.

The air was warm and humid. On the street outside Caritas there was a kind of unpleasant vibe to the atmosphere. And yet, as she and Tara hesitated at the top of the stairs leading down into the karaoke bar, Willow felt a sort of tranquility emanating from the place. There was respite to be had here, and peace. Strains of a familiar tune drifted up, but she could not place its name.

"'Morning Train,'" Tara said without needing to be asked. "Sheena Easton." She smiled and looked away, embarrassed. "I had the tape when I was little. It was one of my favorites."

Willow reached out and took her hand, giving it a gentle squeeze. "Between your Sheena Easton and my Juice Newton, I think we make the perfect pair. Girls with sappy moms."

They shared a knowing smile, then began their descent into Caritas. At the foot of the stairs, Willow gazed into the trendy nightclub. It was not what she had expected. The place was actually kind of nice, painted in soft, pastel colors with neon lighting dappled about.

They left the doorway and stepped farther into the club. From the looks of it, Caritas wasn't only for creatures that went bump in the night. Willow saw a healthy mixture of humans and not-so-humans sitting at tables around the room and sidled up to the bar. She had never seen so many creatures of the night crammed into one place that hadn't turned into an instant bloodbath. And she liked that. Not enough to karaoke, but still, it was nice.

A demon whose skin was covered in what Willow suspected were poisonous quills was up on stage and beginning his heartfelt rendition of "Ventura Highway"—when a thing with two heads lurched in front of them, blocking their way.

Willow reared back, bumping into Tara. The thing's heads moved like twin cobras. Enormous smiles, barely hiding razor-sharp grins, decorated both faces.

"Hi," Willow said nervously to one of the faces. "Oh, and, yep, big hello to you, too," she quickly added to the other, not wanting to be rude.

"Hey there," said one of the heads with a leering grin, its voice as unpleasant to Willow as the sound of breaking glass. In one of its multiple limbs it was holding a tall, frosted mug filled with a colorful tropical drink, umbrella and all.

"Could I interest you girls in something wet?" asked the other head as it shook the glass, making the ice within tinkle merrily. It bent its neck around Willow to check out Tara.

"No, thank you," Tara answered.

Willow held up her and Tara's hands still clasped together. "We're together," she said bravely, hoping the beastie would get the idea that they weren't interested.

The two-headed demon smiled. "So are we," the heads said in unison as it gave itself a high five.

Willow was about to suggest to Tara a spell that would induce stomach cramps in the thing, when a horned, green-skinned demon dressed in a bright orange suit moved through the crowd toward them.

"Is this two-headed palooka bothering you ladies?" the demon asked with a sly smile, throwing his arm around one of its necks. "Go on, you two knuckleheads, beat feet to the bar for your mozzarella sticks or I'm gonna be forced to call your wives."

"Aw, c'mon, Lorne," said one of the demon heads, looking visibly shaken. "You wouldn't do that, would ya?"

"Yah," said the other head, "we was about to score."

Lorne patted the demon's chest with a bright green hand, obviously not fooled by their double dose of macho. "Otto, Cosmo, let's just say since your rather sad and embarrassing performance with the Holy Order of the Sisters of Solitude last week—I've put your ball and chains on speed dial."

Willow watched with amusement as the demon's macho body language wilted before her eyes. "Maybe some other time, Red," said one sad face.

"Yah, some other time, Blondie," said the other. Defeated, the demon walked slowly toward the bar and its consolation prize of mozzarella sticks.

The Host of Caritas watched the demon go. "Poor Otto and Cosmo, just can't take a double negative as an answer," he said with a shake of his head.

"Thanks. And, not that I'm feeling defensive, but I wanna be clear on the scoring. Or, non. 'Cause there was no scoring to be had," Willow said firmly. "I'm Willow and this is Tara," she added, both of them holding out their hands to the demon in introduction.

"Couple'a cuties like you? I shoulda guessed. I've heard nothing but good things about you two," Lorne said with a sly wink as he kissed both their hands. "Hear you're proving to be quite the mojo sisters."

"Thanks," Willow said, feeling a blush spread on her cheeks, charmed by the demon. She pulled her smiling girlfriend closer to her.

The demon crooning "Ventura Highway" wrapped up with a teary-eyed finish, and the crowd went wild with applause. Lorne studied the demon on the stage for a moment and then motioned for them to follow. They moved around the tables toward what looked to be a private space in the back, and he gestured for them to sit.

"Can I get you girls anything from the bar?" he asked. "A zombie? Oh, or I know just the thing. How about a Black Magick?"

Willow was about to ask what was in a Black Magick when she remembered why they had come. "No, thank you," she said politely.

"Ditto," Tara answered, and the demon Lorne sat down across from them. "We're l-looking for Angel," she said. "Has he been in here tonight? Or, do you have any idea where he might be?"

Lorne stroked his cleft chin and shook his head sadly. "Wish I did, kittens," he responded. "He was in earlier to see if I had any more info about our current predicament, but left when I gave him bupkus."

A skull-faced wraith had taken the microphone and was singing a song from *South Pacific*.

"I've been reading the crowd all night and haven't found out anything more than we already know. There's an ill wind blowing out there, girls, and I hope our pal Angel hasn't been swept up into it."

"It's kinda important that we find him. Any ideas on where to start?"

Lorne thought for a moment, absently stroking his chin. "I do have an idea," he said tentatively. Then he gestured toward the stage. "Not sure how much the lovely Cordelia and her compatriots told you about me, but I'm a bit of a fortune-teller. Music's my crystal ball. Usually I try to give my customers a little guidance, a little clarity, shake some of the cobwebs out of their skulls. But sometimes I can get a glimpse of things to come, or your heart's desire. Especially when there's already magick in the air."

The Host smiled kindly at the witches. "And, let's face it, ladies, I'm already reading some pretty beautiful music from the two of you and you're not even singing."

Tara reached out and laid her hand on top of Willow's. It was warm, and any unease Willow was feeling about Angel's whereabouts quickly melted. Just having Tara's fingers twined with hers made her almost certain that everything was going to be just fine.

"Why don't you two fabulous hex girls go up on stage and belt out a little number for me—maybe mixing our mutual mojo will give me the extra kick I need to find our Barry Manilow–loving, wayward vampire with a soul."

"Angel likes Barry Manilow?" Willow questioned.

"Did I say Manilow?" Lorne asked in a bit of a nervous panic. "I meant Barry White. Yah, that's it." The demon smiled, pulled a silk handkerchief from inside his coat, and dabbed at his suddenly sweating brow. "Not to change the subject—but what do you say? Will you sing me a little somethin' and see where it takes us?"

Willow was in a panic. She had absolutely no musical ability, was embarrassed even to sing "Happy Birthday" with a group.

Taking advantage of Willow's hesitation, Tara spoke for them both. "It's worth a try."

Willow looked to her girlfriend, utter horror etched on her face. "But . . . but I . . ." She was speechless. "I don't sing."

Tara smiled, eyes twinkling mischievously. "You'll be fine," she said, reaching out to lightly stroke the side of Willow's face. "I'll do all the harmonies. It'll be fun. And who knows, maybe we'll find out where Angel is."

There seemed to be a lull between performers, nobody wanting to follow the wraith's *South Pacific* medley, when Tara stood and gently pulled her from her chair.

"I can't," Willow said in a panic, looking to Lorne. "I'd need the right song—and you probably don't have it."

The green-skinned demon tapped at the side of his skull with a long, delicate finger. "Actually, any song will do. But baring your hearts and souls, the right song sure helps. I'm betting we've got it in the mix, though."

Willow dug through her memories for songs that didn't have a chance of being in the karaoke machine's menu. There was one song that forced away all others from her mind, a song that summed up how she felt about the woman now clutching her hand.

Willow blurted out the title and watched in shock as Lorne broke out in an ear-to-ear grin.

"Bingo!" he said, pointing at the two of them as the floor dropped out from beneath her. "It's one of our most requested songs," the demon said, standing up from the table and moving toward the stage. "Let me plug it into the machine and we'll be good to go."

Lorne felt a tear begin to form in the corner of his eye. Never had he heard "Endless Love" sung with such passion and utter sincerity. *Puts Diana Ross to shame,* he thought as he began to read the raw emotions streaming from the two young witches in the midst of a duet. Tara was singing in a voice filled with love. This little chickadee was baring her soul to anyone who wanted to listen. She loved her Willow and wasn't afraid to show it. And Willow, for all her reticence—and despite an inability to carry a tune—matched her girlfriend's passion note for tortured note. She certainly had powerful feelings for Tara; so powerful, in fact, that it was almost frightening.

In the midst of his admiration for their song, as he was reading their emotional connection, Lorne was psychically battered by a series of rapid-fire images that practically knocked him from his seat. He grabbed hold of the edge of the table and let the staccato flashes of prescience bombard him.

The first image that exploded into his mind surprised him. It was of an island surrounded by a mist so thick that it was practically hidden. The island was inhabited, and he received flashes of the residents peering out from the darkness of the jungle. These weren't simple island people, either, but demons of all sizes and shapes.

Images of violence erupted before his mind's eye, and Lorne felt his heart quicken, his throat go dry. Demons in the midst of bloody battle. He could practically hear their war cries, their screams of pain as some were cut down in the frenzy of battle.

The lovebirds were nearing the end of their duet, and Lorne was feeling drained. These visions were horrible, just blind savagery that he could barely make sense of. This was nothing like his usual clairvoyance, but rather a dark bit of prescience, somehow both amplified and muddled by the innate magick of the witches. He was attempting to pull back, to tune out the precognitive flashes, when another series of images unfolded before him.

The Host gasped aloud at what he was seeing: Angel, staked out on a rooftop beneath the rising sun like something out of a John Ford cowboy flick, his skin beginning to blister and then burn. Angel was screaming as the rays of sun ignited the flesh of his body.

Lorne recoiled. The connection to the two witches—these two very powerful women—was so strong that he had to tear his mind away, to shatter the bond his abilities had formed with them, created by the music. He drove the horrible sights from his mind, all the while knowing he had to remember the details, the landmarks.

Angel's screams melded with the final notes of the witches' song, and Lorne collapsed on the tabletop. The crowd at Caritas was clapping wildly for Willow and Tara, none of them noticing their Host's momentary faintness and the lime green pallor of his face as he struggled to his feet. The two women kissed sweetly and bowed to their adoring audience.

Lorne glanced at his watch. The visions had drained him so badly that he could barely stand, but he knew he had to get to a phone—to call Cordelia.

The sun would be up soon.

Xander Harris felt as though he'd gone back in time. He carried the stack of ancient texts from Wesley's office out into the lobby, and the musty aroma carried him back—back to the library at Sunnydale High, where hitting the texts of ancient arcanum was as common as going to gym class or studying for an English literature test. *Well, okay, even more common than the studying. Ah, the good ol' days.*

"Where do you want these?" he asked Cordelia, who was sitting at her desk looking at files from some demonic database on her computer.

"Put them on the counter," she said, her eyes never leaving the screen. "As soon as I'm done here, we'll hit the books to see if there's any mention of our demon buddy Axtius. So far, I'm not getting much other than the fact that he's bad news—which we already kinda know."

It was so much like the past, yet so entirely different, Xander thought as he set the books down. Yes, this was Cordelia—of that, there was not a single doubt in his mind—but she had changed.

But then again, so had they all.

"So do you ever rent any of the rooms in this place?" he asked, making small talk, leaning back against the counter and taking in the hotel's surroundings. "Or is this strictly a cover— the secret hideout kind of thing?"

"Why?" Cordelia asked, signing off from the demonic database and turning toward him. "You looking for work? You could probably snag a bellboy job somewhere."

Maybe she hasn't changed much after all, he thought. "Always fancied myself more of a cabana boy," he said as she approached. "Not the assistant to the cabana boy, but, y'know, the whole cabana shebang."

She smiled, rolled her eyes, and removed the top book from the stack he had brought from Wesley's office. "Are you going to help me or are you going to stand around and dream of your future—rubbing suntan lotion on the backs of women with skin like old saddlebags?"

He clapped his hands together and rubbed them eagerly. "One thing I've always liked about our demony friends, there's very little rubbing of lotion involved. Where should I start?"

Cordelia handed him a legal pad. "Axtius is a Brachen demon," she said as she divided the books into two stacks. "Find me anything you can on the Brachens, whether you think it's important or not: likes, dislikes, turnoffs, turn-ons, favorite country-western singer—the works."

"Favorite Beatle?" he asked.

"That would be very helpful. But I've got ten bucks it's Ringo."

He studied her face as she gave him further instructions. She was so much more serious now, filled with a kind of drive that she had never exhibited while they were together back in high school. Watching her made him think about himself. Had he changed as dramatically? Was she noticing the kinds of things about him that he saw in her—or did she still think him the big-time goofball he had been when they were together?

"You're going to need a pen," Cordelia said as she glanced down on the countertop below her. She reached for the pen, coming very close to him, and he breathed in the smell of her. Again, he was transported back to times past. He looked into her eyes as she handed him the pen.

"Problem?" she asked.

"It's good to see you again, Cordy," he said, taking the offered writing tool. "Really."

"Likewise," she answered, and her face blossomed into a familiar smile that belonged to no other.

Calvin came around the corner, noisily chewing on a mouthful of corn chips he had found in the kitchen. "So how long did you guys go out for?" he asked, giving them an attractive view of the contents of his mouth.

"Excuse me?" Xander asked, startled by the question. What the heck was this kid talking about? Was it that obvious? He thought of Anya back at the apartment, recovering from her injuries, and suddenly felt incredibly guilty. "I have no idea what you're talking—"

"Long enough," Cordelia replied, while jotting down some notes from a book that looked like it had been bound in rhinoceros hide. "But that was a long time ago, wasn't it, Xander?" she said, looking up at him. "The bad old days in Sunnydale. We block them out."

He wasn't sure how to answer. But the look in her dark eyes said it all. She was fine with the past and all that had happened to them—both the good and the not so good. *It was a lifetime ago,* her eyes said. She was not the same person—and neither was he.

"Ancient history. Practically prehistoric," he said, taking a book from the stack closest to him. "That's the Brachen demon we're looking for?" he asked, attempting to change the subject.

"That's it," she said, going back to her own book.

Calvin continued to chew noisily, watching them. "I knew it," he said between chomps. "You two got that whole energy going on. Don't need radar to pick that up."

Xander threw down his pen, tired of the teen's attention. "Enlighten us, Dr. Phil, what can you see that gives away our sordid past?"

The boy smiled knowingly. "You know, that whole we-was-once-kickin'-it-and-now-we're-not thing. You got a lot more information about each other than just ordinary friends do. It's kind of hard to forget that stuff when you find yourselves just plain old friends again, know what I'm sayin'?"

Xander was silent, chancing a nervous glance at the woman with whom he'd once been . . . kickin' it.

Cordelia smiled. "Wow. They teach that kind of relationship psychology in nursery school these days?" She raised an eyebrow at Xander. "I'd say he wins the big teddy bear stuffed with shredded Styrofoam, what do you think?"

Calvin had shoved another large handful of corn chips into this mouth, waiting for his accolades.

"I think he needs to learn to chew with his mouth closed," Xander snapped, not caring in the least for the teenager's observations—no matter how astute they were.

The telephone began to ring. "Play nice, boys," Cordelia said as she left them to answer it.

The youth continued to eat, unfazed by Xander's obvious hostility. "I can't believe you let something that fine get away," Calvin said in a conspirator's whisper. "She dumped you, right?"

Xander clutched his pen tighter and opened the book before him. "Brachen demons," he muttered beneath his breath as he began to read. "It's all about the Brachen demons."

"Angel Investigations," he heard Cordelia say. "Hey, Willow," she said in greeting, "any luck finding—"

The conversation went cold behind him.

Xander turned to watch as Cordelia spoke to Willow. The look on her face told him something wasn't right. He was good like that, a skill that he had mastered over his years with the Scoobies.

Looks of absolute horror usually meant bad news.

CHAPTER EIGHT

"So what exactly are we looking for, here?" Buffy asked.

Gunn glanced at her, his gaze sizing her up as it did every time he looked her way. Buffy had a feeling Gunn did not know what to make of her. Everything he knew of Angel had come after her, so his knowledge of Buffy was more as Angel's ex than as Slayer. Certainly he must know what the Slayer was, but from what she understood, Gunn had learned to fight vampires and demons on the streets without the benefit of the history or the folklore. He knew what she was, but it didn't mean anything to him. There was something sort of refreshing about that.

"Between me, Wes, and Angel, we've got a lot of informants running around L.A. The one with consistently the best info, the most reliable, is Zeke. That's short for Ezekiel. He's homeless. The places we've checked are the ones we know he hangs at. Figured we'd start with the best."

They stood on the kind of Los Angeles street corner that figured so prominently in the E! channel's *Mysteries and Scandals* and the works of James Ellroy. Prostitutes lounged against buildings under blinking neon, and homeless men and women lingered in the shadows a stone's throw away. A couple of cars had slowed, drivers eyeing Buffy as though she might be on the menu. She had assured them with a gesture that she was not, but Spike thought it was hysterical.

The vampire trawled the sea of prostitutes, smiling and flirting, oozing the sort of danger he had once been capable of, and the hookers giggled and smiled at him, loving his accent. Even the older pros seemed to love him, seemed to sense that he was one of them, in a way, used to roaming the night world.

Wesley had moved off a ways to speak to a pair of homeless people Buffy thought might not be people at all. Not with the way they moved and the way their bodies were so fully covered.

"Homeless demons," Buffy observed quietly.

Gunn nodded. "Zeke, too."

"What kind?"

"What kind of what?"

"Of demon," Buffy said, raising an eyebrow.

"Oh. Don't know, exactly. I just know he ain't human. Funky-looking dude, but he's never steered us wrong."

There was a loud commotion, suddenly, and Buffy and Gunn turned to see a prostitute slap Spike across the face. The vampire only grinned at her and blew her a kiss. Down the block, though, Buffy could see a tall, muscle-bound figure heading along the sidewalk toward them, and she knew it was time to rein Spike in.

The Slayer strode quickly over to him, ignoring the looks she received from the hookers, and tapped him on the shoulder. Spike turned toward her, one eyebrow arched.

"What's the matter, Buffy? Want to get your licks in?"

"Nobody's getting any licks in," she said darkly. "Come over here. And don't stray."

The prostitutes laughed, and Spike glared at her a moment before he followed. When they reached the place where Gunn stood on the corner, the demon hunter smiled at Buffy.

"Gotta keep your dog on a short leash, huh?"

"Either that or get him fixed."

Gunn's expression became grave. "Way I heard it, he's been fixed. Wouldn't be enough, to my mind. Only one way to make sure that kinda dog doesn't bite."

"Standing right here," Spike snapped.

Eyes glinting with anger, Gunn rounded on him. "Not by my invitation. I don't even know what you're doing here. What I've heard, Angel's not gonna be too happy to see you, anyway. I don't see why nobody's given him your ashes in an urn, just to make him smile."

Spike's laugh was heavy with irony. He reached into his pocket and pulled out a pack of cigarettes, tapped one out, and put it between his lips, then lit it with a silver lighter. Lighter and pack went back into his jacket with sleight of hand worthy of the stage. Then Spike smiled at Gunn, but it was a predator's smile.

"Got it all figured out, have you, Homeboy Van Helsing?" the vampire purred. Then he took a long drag on the cigarette and blew out the smoke and the smile disappeared. "Funny, that bit is. You've got one of the nastiest vamps ever lived right under your nose, day in, day out, and instead of giving him the pointy end, you spend your time cleanin' up his messes, wipin' his nose for 'im."

Buffy started to get between them, but Gunn moved quickly, getting up into Spike's face, glaring at him. They were practically nose to nose.

"Maybe you oughta watch your mouth. While you're doing that, you don't want to be comparing yourself with Angel. You're always gonna come up short."

Spike drew on the cigarette again, the tip glowing red like the neon of the stores around them. "Too right," the vampire agreed. "Pains my ego to admit it, but in his day, well . . . let's just say Angel was the one we all looked up to, the one we all wanted to be like."

"I've heard the stories."

"Not the bloody same as bearing witness to the master at work in all his glory. He was really something," Spike sneered. "Should've seen it. Drove people mad just for laughs. Saw him drink a little girl dry one time and slip her back under her covers, nice as you please; made it look like she was just sleeping." He turned to Buffy. "Did something similar to Giles's old girlfriend, didn't he, Slayer?"

Buffy felt a surprising surge of anger rush through her, and she reached out with her right hand and poked a stiff finger at his chest, her fingernail pressing the exact spot where she would have punched a stake in. Spike blinked and stared at her.

"That's enough," she told him.

Gunn smiled now, and Spike sneered at him, nostrils flaring.

"Don't know why you keep him around," Gunn said. "I'd kill him just to shut him up, never mind the basic principle of him being a vampire."

Buffy felt some of her anger switching focus from Spike to Gunn. Her brow furrowed as she gave him a hard look. "He has his uses. And I have a hard time getting my mind around killing anything that can't fight back."

"Never bothered him," Gunn sniffed, his skin gleaming in the neon light, voice too low for anyone but Buffy and Spike to hear, though the prostitutes and a couple of guys passing by on the sidewalk all seemed very interested in the conversation. "Maybe I oughta just dust him myself."

Buffy lifted her chin and stepped in front of him. "That isn't up to you."

"Who says?"

"I do. But I'll make you a deal. He gets that chip out of his head, gets all fang-happy again, you'll be my first phone call."

Gunn nodded slowly. He stared at Buffy, then glanced at Spike before stalking off to where Wesley was still in conversation with the two homeless demons. Buffy watched him go, troubled. She had known that working with Angel's people was likely to cause its share of friction, and that bringing Spike along was not going to be popular. Now she was second-guessing herself. When they managed to track Angel down, she had a feeling his reaction to Spike's presence was going to be a lot harder to defuse than Gunn's.

"Knew you'd stand up for me, Slayer," Spike said, sidling up beside her so close that it made her skin crawl.

She shivered and stepped away, glaring at him. "I wasn't. I was standing up for myself. Defending the decision I make every day that goes by with you still walking the earth."

Spike had smoked his cigarette down to a nub and he dropped it and ground it out with his boot. Then he took another step closer to Buffy, arms stretched out at his sides, exposing his chest to her. "Go on, then. What're you waiting for?"

Buffy stared at him a long moment, feeling the weight of the stake that was held tight in a small sheath she wore clipped to the rear waistband of her pants. At length she turned away and strode toward Wesley and Gunn.

"That's my girl," Spike called after her. "'S'at out of pity, or just my boyish charm working its magic on you?"

She ignored him as if he had never spoken. Wesley glanced up as she approached. He said something to the homeless demons, and they slipped off into the alley and were lost in the shadows.

Buffy was impressed by the changes in him. The officious, uptight Watcher who'd always had one hand on the rule book had become a very different man. He had always been bright, his expertise in the supernatural formidable. But Wesley had never shown any sign of leadership ability, no confidence, and almost no physical prowess to speak of. The time that elapsed since he'd been fired by the Council had forged someone almost completely new. Or perhaps, just stripped away the veneer they had cast him in.

Now, though it was Angel's mission they were all participating in, it was really Wesley who called the shots, and he bore that responsibility with a quiet grace and dignity. He had become stronger in every way, and there was something imposing about him now. Wesley Wyndam-Pryce wasn't a joke anymore. He had the mind for this work, and for the first time, Buffy had begun to realize he had the edge as well.

They had spent a couple of hours already in the monstrous underworld of Los Angeles, and Buffy had seen the respect with which Wesley and Gunn were treated. Angel's little family had made themselves a force to be reckoned with, that much was clear.

"Anything?" Buffy asked, her gaze ticking from Wesley to Gunn. Spike had started flirting with prostitutes again, but Buffy ignored him.

"Only what we already knew, I'm afraid," Wesley said. "Angel has been here. He sought Zeke out himself, but apparently he had no better luck than we're having at finding him."

"Is Zeke a half-breed?" Buffy asked quickly, thinking they were unlikely to find him alive if he were.

"No. Pureblood," Wesley replied.

"I don't get this," Gunn said, frowning. "We've been following Angel's trail. Doesn't sound like his search was turning up anything, and now he's disappeared on us. Time line says he was at Charlie Nickels's place last. So where would he go from there?"

Buffy studied him. "Charlie . . ."

"The Ninth Level," Wesley clarified. "That seedy—"

"I remember," Buffy replied. That particular dive had been their first stop, but the shriveled little man who ran the place had been useless, telling them only that he and Angel had spoken, that Angel had mentioned Axtius, and that he was distraught over the murder of someone named Harold Hill, whoever that was. Angel thought it tied in with his present case.

Gunn was right, though. Of all the places they'd been, it seemed like The Ninth Level had been Angel's last stop. Buffy realized that she knew almost nothing about Angel's life here in Los Angeles, that she had learned more about his haunts and the people he called his friends in the last few hours than in all the time since they had been apart.

"This isn't my town," she told the two men. "Where *would* he go next?"

Wesley furrowed his brow in contemplation a moment, tapping idly at his temple. Then his eyebrows went up, and he looked at Gunn. "How are the killers getting around?"

"The sewers, you think?" Gunn asked.

"Could be." Wesley nodded. "If Angel suspected as much, he might've gone to talk to Abner."

Now Buffy was lost. "Who's Abner?"

Half an hour later, she had her answer. Wesley had led them to a construction area behind which was a large sewer grating, and then down inside. The smell was terrible, but not nearly as bad as she had imagined. Buffy did not have to ask how Wesley knew the sewers; she herself knew the maintenance and sewage tunnels underneath Sunnydale very well, both because many of the nocturnal demons holed up there and because Angel had often traveled those sunless routes when he was living there.

Spike grumbled discontentedly for most of the journey, and several times Wesley's memory proved faulty and they had to backtrack, but soon enough they came upon a junction where a blockade had been constructed to bar passage into a side tunnel.

"What's this, then?" Spike asked, staring at the barricade. "That's one enormous beaver, built this thing."

And it was somewhat reminiscent of a beaver's dam. The faux wall had been constructed of shopping carts and discarded clothing, plastic and paper bags, and possibly other refuse as well. There was a sort of passage through this obstruction that Buffy gauged as roughly four feet square, and Wesley had to duck down to move through it.

"Getting the idea the evil is drawn mainly to cities with big sewer systems," Buffy muttered, mostly to herself, as she crouched to follow him through.

It was darker on the other side. Most of the tunnels had sparse lighting to guide workers, but here there seemed only one dim light, just a little farther along this side juncture. Wesley had paused to gaze at Buffy and she saw the gleam of that distant light off the rim of his glasses.

"Or, perhaps," the former Watcher suggested, "certain architects designed the sewer systems of some cities to accommodate the demonic races."

Buffy nodded. "Never thought of that before. Guess I don't think of them as that organized."

"They're not, usually," Wesley replied. "Which makes it all the more troubling, and perilous, when they are."

With that, he turned and continued on along the dark tunnel. Buffy followed, with Gunn and Spike bringing up the rear. She expected them to bicker more, or for Gunn to attack the vampire, but the two merely glowered at each other and kept on in silence.

Thirty yards from the barricade, the tunnel curved slightly left and around that corner it dead-ended. Buffy stared speechlessly at the sight that greeted them there. The dead end itself was another barricade similar to the first. In front of it was a kind of nest, the sort of squat that she had heard homeless people had built all over the subway tunnels under New York City. There were bookshelves and ragged carpets, an iron pipe that served as a clothes rack, and a futon neatly made up with a stained Winnie the Pooh bedspread. A huge high-backed chair with the stuffing poking out of several tears finished the picture. Candles burned in dishes set on the concrete all around this bizarre apartment.

Skinned rats hung from long nails that had been driven into the wall.

"Damn it. He's not here," Wesley said, his voice echoing wetly off the damp sewer walls.

"Ah well, what a disappointment," Spike said, sighing. "Now can we please leave? 'S'not exactly the sort of Hollywood nightlife I was hoping for on this trip."

"You down here on vacation, paleface?" Gunn said, his teeth clenched. "'Cause Disneyland isn't on the agenda."

Buffy ignored them, her attention instead focused on a shuffling sound she heard from beyond the barricade. She raised a hand and shushed them, and Wesley glanced quizzically at her before he, too, heard the noises. They all stared at the opening in the obstruction, beyond which there was only darkness.

The shuffling noises stopped. There was a pause, and then a face loomed out of the darkness, a horrid, apelike visage with long, jagged fangs. The demon was hideous and cruel looking. From what Buffy could see in the gloom, the back of its head was covered with sharp quills as long as knitting needles. The Slayer shifted her stance to prepare for an attack.

The demon smiled. "Why, if it isn't Abner's friend Wesley! Hello, Wesley!"

Wesley grinned and strode forward into the odd abode. "Abner! Good to see you. Did you ever get around to reading that Steinbeck I loaned you?"

The enormous demon, which turned out to be shaped much like a gorilla, only larger, lumbered farther into the light, and Buffy saw that his entire back was covered with the savage-looking quills.

He shook Wesley's hand and nodded gravely. "Abner did read the Steinbeck, Wesley. He did. It made him sad. But good sad." The demon studied the former Watcher's hands, and then his expression changed, his eyes going wide with despair. "No books for Abner?"

"Not this time, I'm afraid," Wesley said with earnest regret.

Buffy stared at the two of them. This was Angel's world, then, good-natured, sewer-dwelling Quasimodo-esque demons and gnarled former humans with a taste for musical theater. *And I thought Sunnydale was strange,* she thought. She glanced at Gunn, who shifted impatiently. Spike simply gaped at Wesley talking to the big, sweet, porcupine-quilled demon and rolled his eyes.

"Actually," Buffy said, moving onto one of the carpets, into the flickering candlelight, "we're looking for Angel. Has he been down here tonight?"

Abner blinked and stared at her. He sniffed the air and

came a bit closer, then sniffed again. Shyly, he glanced at Wesley. "Pretty girl. Don't get lots of pretty girls down here."

"Can't imagine why," Spike muttered, hanging back.

The big demon rose up suddenly, glaring at him, the quills on his back standing straight up like a dog's hackles. "Vampires," Abner said, and he spat on the floor in disgust.

"He's got your number," Gunn noted.

Wesley cleared his throat to get Abner's attention. "It really is important that we locate Angel. The Slayer asked if you'd seen him."

Abner visibly flinched. The quills lay flat and tight against his body, and he stared at Buffy in abject terror, staggering back several steps as though he had been struck. "Slayer?" he cried. "You bring the Slayer after Abner?"

"No, no, I'm not after you," Buffy said quickly, her heart going out to the big, ugly lummox. "I'm a friend of Angel's. We're all"—she glanced at Spike—"he's got trouble, and we're here to help him."

The demon shook his head back and forth with such vehemence, Buffy wondered if he was going to hurt himself. "Abner hasn't seen Angel. Nope, nope. Not tonight. Not for weeks. Angel doesn't visit like he used to. Since his old place exploded."

His gaze ticked from Wesley to Gunn to Spike and back to Buffy. He smiled, and there was something profoundly unnerving about that anxious grin filled with tiny dagger teeth.

"Abner going now. Angel's friends make themselves at home. Might be gone a while."

With one final, nervous glance at Buffy, the demon slipped out through the rear partition of his sewer apartment and was gone with a damp shuffling of feet. Buffy felt badly that she had scared him off, but they got the information they had come for. Angel hadn't been down here, as far as Abner knew.

"So we're back to square diddly," she said, sighing.

Wesley nodded. "Let's see if the others have had any better luck." He withdrew a cellular phone from his pocket and punched a button, then stared at the face of it. "Damn. No signal. We'll have to get above ground."

As they traveled back toward the ladder that would lead them up into the construction site where they had made their descent, Gunn fell into step beside Buffy. For several seconds he simply matched her gait, and then he glanced sidelong at her. "Man, Abner wasn't wild about you, was he? Acted like you were the bogeyman."

Buffy said nothing. She felt badly enough about frightening the harmless demon without Gunn making her feel worse. But Spike was just behind them and had heard Gunn's words.

"Silly sod, you don't get it at all, do you? That's what happens when your knowledge of the bleedin' forces of darkness amounts to, 'Hey, look, that doesn't look quite right, let's kill it.'" The vampire paused, and Gunn actually glanced backward, waiting for his next words.

"Far as the bloody night folk are concerned, she *is* the bogeyman."

They passed several minutes in silence and soon came to the ladder. Down in the sewers, he had been unable to get a signal on his cell phone. But Wesley had climbed only halfway to the surface when the phone began to chirp.

For what seemed an eternity, Angel swam in and out of consciousness, glimmers of awareness punctuated by pain as his broken bones tried to knit themselves back together. During the periods when he was awake, Angel tried to push away the smell of the tar paper roof and the words Axtius had whispered to him. He focused on the spikes that had been driven through his legs and hands and kept him pinned to the roof. Carefully, slowly, he tried to work his limbs against the cold iron of these impalings. But the pain was excruciating, and each time he tried to tear one of his hands or legs free he would tumble into black unconsciousness once more.

Each time he came to he would gaze at the sky, searching for any signs of the coming dawn. And it *was* coming, that was certain. Soon. The brilliance had begun to bleed from the glow of the city lights as hints of the rising sun turned the sky from black to blue. Soon it would be time for one final effort to tear himself free, an effort that was sure to leave him unconscious even longer than before. How long, he did not know. But too long and it would kill him.

In the back of his mind, Angel knew that it was for naught. The heads of the spikes in his flesh were too broad. He would not be able to tear loose without leaving both his hands and the muscle mass of his lower legs behind, and that would be impossible.

Sunrise was coming.

He was going to die.

With a roar more of frustration than pain, he tightened his grip around the spikes in the palms of his hands and pulled. Lightning shards of agony shot through his broken shoulder and shattered ribs—undoing any healing they might have accomplished—and in the darkness of his mind it seemed fireworks blossomed. He could barely feel the wounds in his hands, so great was the other pain. Then he felt flesh and muscle in the palm of his right hand begin to tear, and he let loose a bellow of pain.

Unconsciousness claimed him once more.

Angel! Oh, no. We've got to get him inside! Angel!

His eyes flickered open again.

165

"Wakey wakey, big boy. You're in a tight spot, my tone-deaf amigo, and there's no time for lying down on the job."

The edges of Angel's mouth turned up just slightly. Despite the pain he was in, that voice made him smile. He managed to rotate his head partially to the right, but stopped as his eyes went out of focus. His last effort had left him completely drained. Any further movement might make him lose consciousness again, and from the look of the lightening sky, he could not afford that.

Lorne. Lorne was here. The Host of Caritas was the last person in the world he would expect to play cavalry, but Angel was not about to complain. His vision slowly cleared, and Angel saw two other figures standing with the green-skinned demon. *Willow.* A stray thought skittered around inside Angel's head, that her hair clashed with the bright orange silk suit Lorne was wearing. *Crazy thought . . .*

"Willow," Angel rasped.

"I'm here!" she called to him. "He's awake. He's talking— which is good news, right?"

A response came, the voice soft, and Angel frowned as he tried to see through the predawn gloom. The simple scrunching of his eyebrows made his head swim again, but though he could not see her he realized the other person who had arrived with Willow and Lorne was Tara, Willow's girlfriend. Angel liked her, shy, quiet, powerful.

Witches, he thought. *Axtius wouldn't have expected witches.*

Still disoriented, he stared at them and his spirits sank. Willow and Tara were not moving any closer. Why were they so far away, still? Didn't they see that the sunrise was almost here? What was Lorne doing, just standing there? They could pry up the spikes, just drag him . . .

The wards, he thought. *They're not powerful enough.*

And it was true. In the strange fog inside his mind he heard Willow swearing, talking to her lover and to herself in that sweet cadence that he had always been so fond of, fretting over the power of the wards.

". . . down below . . . ," he heard Tara say.

Then Lorne's voice. " . . . knock the roof out from under him. The magick shouldn't stop the collapse."

Willow. " . . . covered up until we can figure . . ."

Angel closed his eyes. Their voices did not seem to match the movement of their lips. His brain was enshrouded in mist, nothing was working right. There was one thing he knew, one thing he felt quite keenly, however.

His skin was prickling with the unseen heat of the sun. Dawn was still a short way off, but he could feel it, as though his flesh yearned to burn with the sunrise.

Lorne, Willow, and Tara could do nothing but bear witness.

The door at the back of the tenement building had been torn off its hinges. The wood cracked as Buffy walked over it, eyes frantically searching the dark for stairs that would take her up. The place stank worse than the sewers they had just come from. There was filth here, dank walls, leaking pipes, excrement, and worse, the scent of death. Her mind flashed back to the warehouse in Sunnydale where she had found a group of murdered half-breeds, and she realized that if she searched this place she was likely to find a similarly grotesque scene.

Angel, she thought, spotting the entrance to the stairs. As she ran for them she glanced at a window. Even through the grime that covered it, she saw that the gloom had lightened even further.

Never had she wished so deeply that morning would not come.

"No!" Wesley said firmly as he came in behind her.

Buffy glanced back and saw that he was speaking into his cell phone, not to her. Not that she would have stopped if he had been. Gunn and Spike came in behind Wesley. Buffy did not even slow down. She sprinted up the creaking steps, leaving them behind even as she heard the dwindling sounds of Wesley's phone conversation with Cordelia.

"No, stay there," Wesley insisted. "We were closer, it only made sense for us to . . . we're here now, yes . . . I'll call you back."

Buffy raced up five flights of stairs. The fifth-floor door to the roof had also been magickally torn from its hinges. It smoldered where it lay on the wood floor, not with fire, but with the sorcerous power that had been used to rip it down. The Slayer ran past it, up the dozen steps to the roof.

The sky was a beautiful indigo.

On the eastern horizon, golden light gleamed, threatening morning.

"Angel," Buffy whispered.

She took in the scene in an instant, frozen there on the tarpaper roof. Willow and Tara stood with a garishly dressed demon with horns and streaked blond hair. It had to be Lorne, she realized, the demon from that karaoke club Wesley had told her about, Caritas. Beyond them, Buffy saw Angel, arms and legs spread out, huge iron nails driven through each of them, crucifying him against the tenement roof. His head was turned slightly toward her, but there was no flash of recognition in his eyes. He looked drunk, or drugged; he looked completely helpless, and it made her waver for a moment, feeling as though the world had been pulled out from under her.

Buffy was aware of Wesley, Gunn, and Spike coming onto the roof behind her, even heard the click of metal on metal and recognized it as the sound of Spike's lighter as he fired up another cigarette. She smelled the smoke as he took his first drag. None of these things really registered. She was frozen, and the sun was going to come up.

Willow called to her.

Spike whistled appreciatively as he saw what had been done to Angel. "Now that's a nasty bit of work."

The Slayer whipped around to glare at him. Spike only raised an eyebrow and took another drag on his cigarette. Buffy spun again and, freed from the paralysis that her fear for Angel had wrought upon her, she felt herself propelled toward him. Her conscious mind had been overridden by the primitive need, the instinct to save him, and she raced across the tar paper roof toward him.

Out of the corner of her eye she saw Willow moving to intercept her, reaching out for her. Buffy did not even slow down. Tara called to her to stop.

A dozen feet away from Angel, the Slayer struck something, a barrier in midair. Her body danced as though electrified, and then she was thrown backward, twitching on the ground as the magick coursed through her. It hurt, but she had taken pain before, and far worse than that.

Buffy sprang to her feet and tried to see what it was that had stopped her. Whatever was keeping her from Angel it was invisible. She shot a glance at the witches and the lanky demon beyond them, who even now was walking nearer to Angel with his hands out as if sensing the perimeter of the barrier that prevented them from reaching him.

"What is it?" she demanded, knowing her voice was frantic, but not caring.

"Wards. Really, really powerful wards," Willow said, the regret plain on her face. "We've tried a few spells, but—"

"Try some more," Buffy snapped, turning away from her and staring at the roof beneath her feet. She saw them now, symbols and crude drawings in white paint, like runes and hieroglyphics all run together. They made a circle all around Angel.

They were going to kill him.

If Buffy couldn't get through, Angel would die.

The injured, barely conscious vampire moved, and the motion drew her eye. Buffy heard him groan in pain and saw him trying to tear his left hand free of the enormous nail that had been pounded through it. Much as she wanted him to stop, for a moment she prayed he would succeed. Instead, his eyelids fluttered and closed and his body went limp.

Willow and Tara began to chant in Latin. Buffy paid little attention to the spell, knowing they would do everything in their power. But on the sorcery grading scale, they weren't at the top yet. Buffy had to acknowledge that whoever had done this was likely more powerful than Willow and Tara.

Gunn loomed up beside Buffy. He stood at the perimeter of the scrawled wards staring at Angel. Wesley had knelt down to look at them, and he swore under his breath. "I can't translate this," he said. "Not in the next few minutes. Not before—"

His words died unspoken, but Buffy knew what he was going to say. *Not before the sun comes up.*

At her side, Gunn spoke in a low voice, his gaze never leaving Angel's prone form. "Maybe if we try together?"

Buffy glanced at him. Wesley had looked up as well, and now he stood and moved closer to Gunn.

"Let's do it," the Slayer said.

The three of them took a few steps back, exchanged a glance, and in unison they rushed the invisible barrier above the wards. Buffy threw herself at it with all her strength, tightening her body up in hopes that the impact would allow her to pass through.

Once more she struck the barrier, and pain seared her bones, shot through her body. She threw her head back, twitching uncontrollably as she crumbled to the ground again. Wesley and Gunn had both shouted in pain and they fell in a heap beside her, the echoes of their agony sweeping across the roof.

Aching, Buffy rose once more. A moment later, Gunn did the same. Wesley did not get up. He was unconscious.

The upper rim of the sun appeared over the Los Angeles cityscape to the east, the sky on the horizon a pale, perfect blue.

Buffy ran to Willow, staring at her, pleading. "Will?"

Willow shook her head, reaching out to clasp Tara's hand.

"We just can't break it, Buffy," Tara told the Slayer. "We've all tried to go through," she said, gesturing toward the green-skinned demon. *Lorne,* Buffy reminded herself.

Even as she focused on him, Lorne smiled and nodded to himself as he completed his walk around the magickal barrier.

"Hold tight, handsome," the demon called to Angel. "That outfit is ruined, but we may be able to save the rest of you."

Buffy rushed to him. "What do you mean?" she demanded, eyes ticking past him toward the sliver of blazing sun on the horizon. "What do you know?"

Lorne pushed her hands back and brushed the lapels of his jacket. "Simmer down, sister. I want to save the big lug as much as anyone. Took me a minute, but I've translated the scrawl around him. Terrible penmanship, by the way."

"Lorne, *sunrise!*" Willow prodded.

"Right," the demon said, nodding. "Anyway, whoever installed this baby cast a spell that would hold back anything. That is, any *living* thing. Demon, human, or otherwise. I guess—given who Angel is and what he does for a living—our bad guy never figured anyone *dead* would try to help him."

A shiver went through Buffy. The sky was light enough now that she could see the expressions on the faces of everyone on the roof as she turned to glare at Spike, who stood safely in the shadows just inside the door that led back downstairs. The tip of his cigarette glowed. He had obviously not been paying attention, but now he seemed to feel them all staring at him and he looked up.

"Spike," Buffy said tentatively.

He glanced at each of them. Buffy doubted he had listened to much of what had been said, but he put it all together right there.

"You're the only one who can do it," she told him.

Spike stared at her, glanced at the sunrise, then stared at her again. "Bollocks."

CHAPTER NINE

Sunnydale

Giles's eyes were burning. He pushed his fingers up under his glasses and rubbed at them. His entire body ached from being slouched in the cramped front seat of his car for the past four hours with only a bag of chocolate-chip cookies and a repeating crossbow for company. Now he stretched stiffly, joints popping in his neck and shoulders. The backs of his legs were so tight, it felt to him as though he had just woken from a coma, his muscles atrophied.

It angered him. As Buffy's Watcher, he kept himself fit in order to train with her and to aid her in the field. But now, as the sky began to lighten after an excruciatingly long and boring night, the promise of the morning on the eastern horizon, Rupert Giles felt old.

Once more he rotated his head, trying to work the stiffness out of his neck. He cradled the crossbow in his lap and glanced over his shoulder, but there was no sign of anyone on the street. The car was parked in the circle at the dead end of Fenton Road. Giles gazed out through the windshield at the darkened face of the duplex that occupied the lot at the far end of the circle, its lawn overgrown, its paint peeling, and nothing behind it but a small stretch of trees that—after an interruption for a row of power lines that marched behind this neighborhood—turned into Miller's Woods.

That morning the local paper had reported a spate of recent disappearances in the area around Fenton Road. The news story had not mentioned Fenton Road specifically, but the neighborhood in general. In less than a month a seventy-five-year-old retired house painter, a forty-two-year-old school-teacher, and two teenage girls had turned up missing within four blocks of one another. In each case, the first guess the police had made was that they had run off of their own will. The retired house painter had Alzheimer's disease and might have wandered. The schoolteacher might have been having an affair and left town with her lover. The teenagers might have responded to the bright lights and the siren call, the seductive promise of Los Angeles. Teenage girls did it all the time, ran off to L.A.

Those were reliable answers for the Sunnydale Police Department. They avoided more difficult questions.

But four people gone in three and a half weeks?

The newspaper had found that suspicious, and so had Giles once he had read the report. He had spent the early part of the night patrolling the neighborhood for vampire activity, for that was always his first guess. Unless there were indications other-wise, he presumed it was nothing more exotic than vampires.

When his patrol had turned up nothing, Giles had taken a different approach. With Dawn's help he had searched the real estate listings for homes for sale in the vicinity of the disappearances. There were five. But only one of them was for sale because of the death of its owner. At present, the duplex he had spent the past four hours staring at was in the possession of the bank. The owner had left no will and had no offspring.

For the moment, nobody owned this place.

The vampires would not have needed an invitation.

When he had first rolled up in his car and gotten a glimpse of the place, he had known this place was a vampire nest. It was perfect. The FOR SALE sign was gone. At the end of the street, set back in the trees, and with so many victims nearby. They would nest here for a time, hunting far and wide, and then when they sensed they might be bringing attention to themselves, they would move on.

He had to hope that they had not moved on just yet.

Not yet.

But as the night wore on and the black sky turned to indigo and then to dark blue, he began to fear that he had missed them. If they had left this nest and found another, more people would die before he could track them again.

A glimmer of gold burned the eastern horizon. Morning was near.

"Damn it," Giles whispered in the confines of the car.

His sleepy eyes still burned, and he rubbed at them beneath his glasses again. This time when he dropped his hand he caught a glimpse of something moving in the darkness behind the duplex.

He froze.

For several long seconds, his pulse racing, he sat completely still and ignored the protests of his neck and the muscles in the backs of his legs. Something else shifted in the dark behind the house and then they began to flit from the wood toward the back of the duplex. In the predawn light they were shadow silhouettes, but watching them like this, seeing them slink across the overgrown back lawn of that house like the predators they were, Giles found the vampires' arrival chilling.

One of them paused. Its dark shape stood up a bit straighter, and he was sure it had spotted the car in the circle. Would the vampire think he was visiting a neighbor, or would it be curious enough to have a look inside the car? The leech took several steps toward the car, and though it was still at least eighty yards away, Giles held his breath.

He'd dusted more than his fair share of the things in his time as a Watcher, but there were a lot of them. The Slayer was out of town, and it was down to him. Alone. The odds were dismal.

But the vampire glanced once at the sky and then retreated around the back of the house, following the other dark silhouettes into whatever entrance they had forced into the house. Giles breathed a little easier and sat up straighter. He bent over the repeating crossbow, checking the action again to make certain it would not jam. On the seat beside him was a bag filled with vials of holy water he could splash on them or shatter against their skulls.

But that was not his plan. His plan was simpler.

Giles glanced up at the sky. The blue was no longer quite so dark. The morning would arrive in earnest momentarily. Then he would do a walking circuit of the house and search for blacked-out windows. If he found them, he would shatter them. Inside, he would keep to the sunlight as best he could, and he would hunt them, using the sun as his ally.

That was one of the things he loved about living in southern

California. The weather back in England had made waiting for morning a nearly useless strategy in dealing with vampires.

He stared at the windows of the duplex, wondering if he would see that vampire looking out at his car.

There was a rap at his window. Giles jumped, his finger twitched, and the crossbow fired a bolt that thunked into the passenger door just below the window. His heartbeat triphammered in his chest, and he spun on the seat, ready to kick out should a vampire shatter the window to reach for him, assuming that the vampire from the house had gotten a good look at him after all and circled around.

He stared out his car window, mouth opened in a gasp of surprise. Then he took a deep, shuddering breath and let it out, rolling his eyes. He sat up and cranked his window down partway. "What are you two doing?" he hissed. "Get in the car."

Dawn gave him a sheepish grin and pushed the hair away from her face, but Anya only looked annoyed. As quickly as possible, he got them into the backseat of the car.

"Sorry," Dawn said. "Didn't mean to startle you."

"Startle me, hell!" Giles said, his gaze ticking back and forth between the new arrivals and the duplex. "You nearly gave me a heart attack. What do you two think you're doing skulking about out here?"

"We were worried about you," Dawn said, her eyebrows knitting in consternation, as though she ought to be the one getting angry. "You've been gone all night. I woke up at, like, four, and look, no Giles! Hmm. Maybe we should go make sure he hasn't been eaten, I say. Though, if you're gonna act like this, maybe you not being eaten isn't a point for celebration."

Giles ignored her, directing his pique at Anya. "You were supposed to keep an eye out for her. If Buffy had any idea—"

Anya glared at him. "Which she doesn't. And, anyway, don't listen to a word she says. *We* were not worried. *She* was worried. I was sleeping very soundly, thank you, and was very comfortable and warm just where I was. But when I realized she wasn't going to leave me alone, I figured it was time she was your problem again."

For a long moment Giles only gaped at her. Then he looked at Dawn and shook his head slowly. "Dawn, you know better. Buffy's taught you better than this. So have I. By putting yourself in jeopardy, you may have put me in jeopardy."

Anya raised her hand tentatively. "And hello? Me? Jeopardy. Also in peril of having bags under my eyes, which makes me cranky."

Giles raised an eyebrow and shot her a quizzical look. "What about the rest of the time?"

"I'm too tired to respond to that."

"Good." Giles turned his attention to Dawn. "I appreciate your concern, Dawn, but you knew I might not return until morning. You should have waited."

The girl glanced away guiltily. "I know. I just . . . I don't like Buffy being away. I mean, I know she could just as easily end up toast here, but at least when she's home I can pretend to myself that I might be able to help if things got really bad. But down in L.A. . . . I don't know. I just decided if things were gonna get hairy, I'd rather be here with you."

Giles knew he should chide her further—the two of them coming here had been a very bad idea—but he could not bring himself to do so. With their mother dead, Buffy had gathered her friends around her and given Dawn a kind of makeshift family, but anytime Buffy was not around, Dawn became a bit skittish. Her father might still be alive, but the way he behaved toward his daughters, Dawn must have felt as though if anything ever happened to Buffy, she would be completely alone.

No, not completely alone, he thought. *Not as long as I'm still drawing breath.* The truth was, he was touched by the girl's concern.

"All right." He shot Anya a hard look. "You stay in the car. With the doors locked. I'm going in at sunrise. If I'm not out twenty minutes later, go back to the Magic Box and wait for Buffy to check in."

Giles could see that the weight of these words hung heavily upon Dawn. Her expression had changed, her eyes somehow seemed darker. He suspected that she wanted to tell him not to go in there at all, to wait for Buffy to come back. But she was the sister of the Slayer, and she knew better. Dawn Summers knew the consequences of letting the vampires have free rein. And this was why Giles had remained behind, after all. Someone had to keep the darkness at bay in Sunnydale while Buffy was away.

The last of the night drained out of the sky above, and the three of them sat in silence in that car, waiting for the sunrise.

Los Angeles

Spike could feel the warmth of the rising sun on his flesh, as though his skin had suddenly begun to tighten. The dawn's light would hurt him, he would begin to smolder, but he knew from experience that he would not begin to truly burn until he was out in direct sunlight, unprotected. The sun was only a sliver on the horizon, above the Los Angeles skyline off to the east. If he was really going to do this, he had seconds to make an attempt at it or it would be too late and they would both burn.

The vampire narrowed his gaze and glanced around at these people, his companions, perhaps even his comrades, though they all hated him.

Well, possibly not all, he thought. Gunn and Wesley for sure. The demon lounge singer he didn't know. Willow and Tara were always infuriatingly polite, but he saw it in their eyes, every glance seeming to sear a brand into him. *Monster.* And he was, after all, and proud of it.

Buffy, though? The Slayer did not hate him. Spike was almost sure of that. He had seen something in her eyes when she looked at him, a kind of understanding; there was a connection between them that he was certain she felt as well. Truth was . . . no. He did not want to think about that. Not right now. What he wanted wasn't going to happen in Los Angeles, not with Angel around.

A sly smile spread across his features as he glanced across at Angel, pinned to the tar paper roof like he was part of somebody's butterfly collection.

Not with Angel around, he thought again.

But if Angel were not around, things might be different. How could anyone blame Spike, after all, for not risking his skin for the big, broody ponce? Once upon a time Angelus had shown him what it was to be a vampire, yet there had always been a bitter shadow over Spike's heart. He had always known that Drusilla fancied Angel, that he himself was a substitute. Then after Angel went soft, got his soul back and all, Drusilla had come round at last. What she had felt for Spike was as true as she knew how to be, he was convinced of that. But then the bastard had to come between them, had to muck it all up, drive a wedge between Spike and Dru that was never going to be fixed.

Spike was over it. Mostly. His passionate interest was being spent elsewhere these days. But his hatred for Angel was profound. The last thing in the world he wanted to do was save his life.

His face felt scalded by the brightening sky. He blinked away the morning light and found himself looking at Buffy again. None of them had said anything to him, despite the urgency of the moment. They stared at him, holding their breath, and he liked that. There was power in it. It was up to him whether Angel lived or died.

Spike was thinking died.

But then he saw the look in Buffy's eyes, a silent plea and a flash of bitter spite. His heart ached to see that expression on her face.

"Bloody hell," he muttered, dropping his cigarette and raising his long coat up over the top of his head. He shot the demon, Lorne, a hard look. "I get trapped in there, I'll haunt you the rest of your days."

"What?" Lorne replied, cocking an eyebrow. "From an ashtray?"

Spike scowled, glanced at the sun again, but then looked away, his eyes seared by the brightness. He could not afford another moment's hesitation. With the coat pulled over his head he ran across the roof, the image of Buffy's pleading eyes stuck in his head. The circle of scrawled symbols had created an invisible barrier, but when he reached those wards that had been painted on the roof, he tensed. He struck the barrier and for a moment he was caught there like an insect in a spider's web, suspended in that magickal field as pain raced through his bones.

Then he was through.

"Oh, now *that* hurt!" he shouted.

His face was momentarily exposed. The sunlight scorched his flesh. He heard it crackle like oil in a frying pain and he covered up again. His hands were smoldering, smoke beginning to rise from them. When he had glanced at it, the sun had risen slightly farther and the city was quickly shedding the lingering night, dawn's rays reaching toward the building upon which they stood.

This was a bad idea, he thought. But it was too late to turn back, and he could feel the weight of Buffy's expectant gaze on him, her fear for Angel. Spike tried to tell himself that in the midst of her overwhelming concern for her ex, the Slayer might spare just a fraction of that worry for him. But he did not let the hope linger.

Angel was still unconscious. Not even the searing heat of the morning light had woken him, though his skin had begun to char and to smolder. On Angel's left cheek, which faced the east, a patch of flesh the size of a quarter had begun to glow red like the embers of a fire. He was not going to be any help at all.

Covering himself as best he could with the jacket—which slid and slipped so that he had to grasp it and let it hang over him—he knelt and crouched over Angel's supine form. He could smell the other vampire's blood, but that scent was overridden completely by another—the aroma of his own flesh beginning to burn.

Spike swore under his breath, snarling as he reached out and tore out the heavy nails that pinned Angel's legs to the roof. The flesh had begun to heal around the nails, and when Spike ripped them free it tore open the wounds again. Angel's eyes snapped open, and he roared in pain, his face changing, becoming the feral countenance of the vampire. There was recognition in his eyes when he glanced at Spike, but it was blurred instantly by pain.

Angel's eyes began to smoke. He cried out again and closed them, tried to turn his head away from the lightening sky as best he could. Spike saw that his eyelids had started to burn.

Angel's face was charring badly. Tempted as he was, Spike dared not turn to check the sun's progress on the horizon.

Seconds. No more than ten. Then they were both done.

Spike let the coat fall away from his face. Keeping it in place—protecting himself—was too awkward for him to be able to hurry. He felt the flesh of his face begin to bubble and blister, the back of his neck to burn. His right arm caught on fire as he reached down to tear out the nails that held Angel's hands in place. He had to dig his fingers into the wounds at Angel's palms, and this time the other vampire did not even open his eyes.

Without warning the dawn broke full upon them, there on the roof. The wave of sunlight that had marched across the cityscape had finally reached them. Morning was here. The sun set upon them like napalm, and Spike felt his hair begin to burn, his body catching on fire, burning his clothes from the inside out.

Panic surged through him. *Burning. I'm burning!* His every instinct was to run, but he would not. Now that he'd started this, there was no way he was going to run away.

"Let's go, then, you big git," Spike snarled.

With supernatural strength he hauled Angel up off the ground and threw him over his shoulder. Spike could hear Buffy shouting at him, could hear Willow yelling that Angel was on fire. Did she think he was an idiot? That he couldn't see it? Couldn't smell it? Couldn't *feel* it?

They were both burning.

His mind shut down. He did not even notice the circle of magickal wards as he lunged across the roof, barely registering the pain as he passed through the sorcerous barrier again. Spike heard a voice screaming in agony, and it took him a moment to realize that the voice was his own.

Then the others were grabbing at him, covering Spike and Angel up with their jackets, hustling them through the door that led down into the blessed, cool shadows of the abandoned building, beating at the flames that had erupted from the flesh of the two vampires.

Spike looked up and saw Buffy staring at him, eyes moist with relief and gratitude, and he drifted into unconsciousness in a haze of pain and satisfaction.

Buffy stood in the open doorway of a large suite on the second floor of Angel's building, watching as Willow and Tara prepared herbal poultices to apply to the worst of the burns Angel and Spike had sustained. They were terrible to look at, their flesh blackened and scorched, areas of skin burned away with only crisp edges remaining. The hair of both vampires had been on fire and partially destroyed by the flames. It would grow back, Buffy knew. That was the simplest thing, the least painful, she knew. But somehow it unnerved her deeply.

They did not even look human, these two old friends, these two old enemies. More like mummies rescued from a museum fire. In places their clothes had been burned into their flesh, so that it was hard to tell where leather and denim ended and where skin began.

"They'll be all right," a soft voice said behind her.

Buffy turned to find Fred in the hallway carrying a tray laden with more herbs and bandages, as well as several sharp knives. The slim, mousy brunette had been quietly aiding Willow and Tara, finding all the ingredients they needed for their poultices, and generally worrying over Angel as much or more than any of the others. Buffy wondered if Fred was in love with Angel, or if— given what she had been told about his rescue of her from slavery in a terrible alternate dimension—she was simply devoted.

"Excuse me," Fred said timidly, eyes downcast.

The Slayer did not move from the doorway. She stared at the knives. "What are those for?"

A flash of surprising impatience crossed Fred's features as she glanced up. "I have to cut their clothes away or they'll never heal right."

A shudder went through Buffy. It was an unpleasant job. "Are you sure you don't want someone else to do that? I could—"

"I'll do it," Fred said, eyes downcast once more. "I took care of Angel before when he was really hurt. I can do it again."

Buffy hesitated, but only for a moment. When she stepped aside to let Fred enter the room, the other girl gave her a grateful glance and went in. For several moments longer Buffy watched Fred and the witches at work, then, finally able to admit to herself that there was nothing more she could do for Angel . . . or for Spike . . . at the moment, she turned and traced her steps back through the second floor of the hotel. It was a truly impressive building, a classic. With a few million dollars Angel could actually have renovated it and opened it up as a working hotel again. But that kind of thinking wasn't allowed. Fate had made certain that nothing so mundane as that would ever be possible for either of them. Still, Buffy admired the place, the huge sprawl of rooms, and wondered what Angel would ever do with all that space.

Downstairs in the lobby she found that everyone was still awake. They had all been up the entire night and the morning hours were passing quickly, but nobody seemed in a great rush to go to sleep except for the kid, Calvin, who had crashed on a sofa in the lobby. Xander and Gunn were sitting on the steps that led up to the front doors. Lorne sat on an antique chair, legs crossed, reading a magazine nearly as old as the chair. He reached up and scratched behind one of his horns, apparently not even noticing Buffy's descent of the stairs. Behind the reception desk, Cordelia and Wesley pored over stacks of dusty old books that made Buffy wonder if Giles wasn't merely bragging when he claimed some of his own volumes were one of a kind.

Cordelia glanced up as Buffy strode across the lobby toward the reception desk. "How is he?"

Buffy nodded once. "Still unconscious. Gonna be in boatloads of pain when they wake up. But Willow says they're out of danger. We don't have any reason to think they won't recover, but we don't know how long it will take."

"Burns like that?" Lorne piped up from behind his magazine. "Humans would be dead. But vampires as old as those two? Give 'em a day, maybe a day and a half, they'll be right as rain." He lowered the magazine, a smile on his face, but the smile faded into a look of disdain. "Or at least Angel will be. The other one's a twisted fella, ain't he? No healing that."

"Thanks," Buffy said, forcing a smile.

"My pleasure, sweetcakes."

The demon straightened the crease along one leg of his pants, then raised his magazine again. Buffy stared at the cover as though she could still see him through it, amazed that a guy with that complexion and those horns—never mind that fashion sense—could call her "sweetcakes" without her pounding him through a wall. But there was something charming about Lorne that she couldn't quite put her finger on.

"All right," Xander said, clapping his hands together as he and Gunn rose from the steps and crossed to where the others were gathering. "So what's the next move?"

"Sleep," Buffy replied. Her gaze ticked from one of them to the next, Cordelia, Wesley, Xander, and Gunn. "Everyone needs a few hours' rest or you're going to be useless to me. After that, while Angel and Spike are healing, we do a little research, find out what we can about this General Axtius, then we hit the streets again. Only this time instead of finding Angel, we'll be finding the prickly, blue-faced freakazoid who did this to him. I take Axtius down, get him to spill on the Coalition's plans, and we tear down their war effort before it goes any further."

The Slayer looked around again. "So, what do we know?"

Gunn frowned, his brown eyes narrowed to slits as he shook his head, one hand up to halt her. "Hold up," he said, glancing at Cordelia. "Who got char-grilled and made you boss? This is our city and our case. If somebody decided we're supposed to take orders from you, I sure didn't get the memo."

"Whoa, camel," Xander interjected. "Wait just a minute. Maybe you missed the part where your boss is upstairs playing dead for a while? Even if he wasn't, Buffy's the Slayer. Slay-er. Look it up. Maybe it's your case, but it's her *mission*."

Buffy could not believe they were arguing about this. She had known that Gunn was dubious about her status, the way the others all deferred to her. He had no idea what it really meant to be the Slayer, and that was fine, but she needed a team, and this kind of arguing wasn't going to help them.

"Listen, both of you—"

"Actually, Buffy, I agree with Gunn," Cordelia interrupted. She crossed her arms and defiantly thrust out one hip. "No offense to your massive ghost-busting ego, but this isn't your show. You're on our territory here, and whatever Xander may think, the person in charge of Angel Investigations is not Angel at all. It's Wesley. He used to be a Watcher—your Watcher, I might add—and he knows the scene in L.A. You don't."

Wesley was watching this exchange with a thoughtful expression on his face. Buffy was taken aback by the whole thing. She found herself wishing that Giles had come along after all, despite the fact that she felt a great deal of comfort knowing that he was home keeping an eye on Dawn and Anya. Giles was her Watcher. Even when he had been assigned to the job she had not thought of Wesley as the one in charge. She automatically would have deferred to Giles's suggestions, particularly when it came to the investigative angle on something. As the Slayer, she felt confident in her field strategy, but it was easy to fall back on Giles.

But Wesley?

Buffy saw the stern, questioning look on Gunn's face, the expectant expression on Cordelia's, and she turned to the former Watcher. "They're right," she said. "This is your territory. I'm not trying to go all diva on you. I just want to get things done."

Wesley took off his glasses and tapped them against his chin in contemplation. After a moment he raised an eyebrow in that way he had that made Buffy think of Mr. Spock.

"As do the rest of us," Wesley told her. "But I have no argument with your suggestions. You're the Slayer, Buffy, and an excellent strategist, despite your frequent self-deprecation. We can and should work together as a unit. Please, lead on. If I think you're taking a misstep, I'll be sure to let you know."

Cordelia smiled, apparently happy to have it settled. Gunn, on the other hand, was not ready to dismiss the issue quite so readily. "Superpowers don't give her L.A. street smarts," he said.

"True," Buffy agreed, meeting his dubious gaze. "I'll be relying on you for that."

Xander clapped his hands together. "Good. Then it's settled. Can there be bed now?"

Over in his antique chair, Lorne set down his magazine, stood, and stretched, yawning hugely. "Ahh," he said. "Now that we're all one big dysfunctional family again, the kid's got the right idea. A little lullaby, and I'm off to dreamland."

"Lorne," Buffy said, using the demon's name for the first time.

The Host of Caritas turned to regard her quizzically.

"You might not be safe without an escort. You're a pure-blood, but there's no way to tell if Axtius will be able to find out you helped Angel. Maybe you shouldn't go anywhere without an escort."

"I'll be fine at the club," the demon argued. "The mojo I've got on that place means no one can touch me there."

"She's more worried about between here and there," Cordelia put in. "Why not take a room upstairs for the night? I can help you find some sheets."

Buffy shot her a grateful look, appreciative that Cordelia had come to bat with the team spirit, despite Gunn's obvious reservations.

"Thanks, doll," Lorne said. He glanced nervously at the front doors. "I think I'll take you up on that."

While the demon was speaking, Buffy sensed movement behind and above her, and turned to see Willow and Tara coming down the stairs, their hands twined together.

"Well?" Cordelia asked, before they had even reached the lobby. "What's the verdict?"

Willow shrugged and made a tired effort at a smile. "We've done all we can."

"They just need to rest now, and heal," Tara added. "Angel regained consciousness for a minute, but he's out again now."

"Did he say anything?" Wesley asked, eyes narrowed with acute interest.

"He mumbled!" Willow said helpfully. "Sure, it was pretty much gibberish, but hey, progress."

Buffy took several steps toward her, glanced at Wesley, and then focused on Willow again. "What did Angel say exactly?"

Willow's eyebrows went up in that expression of hers that could mean so many things. In this case, Buffy read it as confusion. "He kept talking about 'Harry.' Somebody killing Harry, actually. Didn't say who Harry was, but kinda thinking he's in trouble."

"He's a she," Cordelia corrected. "And she was in trouble. She's in the hospital. Axtius sent some goons to kill her because she used to be married to Doyle."

Gunn gestured toward her. "Doyle, he's the guy used to help you all before Wes and me came along, right?"

Buffy saw a kind of shadow pass across Cordelia's features, some strong emotions revolving around this question that the other woman was not interested in sharing with the group.

"That's him," Cordelia said.

"Angel mentioned him a couple of times too," Willow offered. "Pretty disoriented—and who wouldn't be, with the broken bones and traumatic sunrise? But yep. Harry. Doyle. Axtius. Something about Axtius blaming him, I guess for Doyle dying. Unfortunately, not a lot more sense to be made out of it except—"

"What would Axtius want with the ex-wife of Angel's dead sidekick?" Lorne asked.

Xander walked up beside Cordelia. "Tell 'em," he said. Then he glanced over at Buffy, Willow, and Tara. "You're gonna love this one."

Cordelia shot him a dark look, but it passed in a moment. "Axtius is Doyle's father."

Patiently, Cordelia explained to them all about the phone call she had received from Harry. Axtius had tried to have the woman killed because he believed she had further tainted his son. At the time, Axtius had apparently not known Doyle was dead, but given Angel's fevered ramblings and the attempt at vengeance, it certainly seemed that the demon had learned of his son's death.

"Pardon the interruption," Lorne said. "But I'm a little fuzzy on the logic here."

"Wasn't Doyle half human?" Buffy asked.

The Host pointed at her. "That was my question."

"Half human, half Brachen demon," Cordelia confirmed.

"Yet his father is part of an effort to slaughter every half-breed demon in the world," Wesley said slowly, the horror evident in his voice.

"That doesn't make sense," Tara put in. "Why would he care if his son was dead, then?"

Willow frowned. "Maybe he still hoped he could 'fix' Doyle. Make him 'normal,' y'know?"

The witches exchanged a meaningful look, their twined fingers tightening together.

"Is that even possible?" Xander asked, glancing at Lorne.

"Don't look at me, sugar. I'm one-hundred-percent, grade-A me. Never wanted to be anything else. I've found *my* corner of the sky."

"It's all pretty twisted," Gunn said, slumping down onto one of the lobby's sofas. He glanced over at Calvin, who was still curled up, sound asleep. "Like this kid, his pops was a sleaze even before the vamps turned him. Would have been better off if Cal never knew what his old man was up to, what kind of man he was. Now he's gonna have to deal with that the rest of his life. Every time he looks in the mirror, he's gotta wonder if being flesh and blood with a lowlife like that means he's got it in his genes."

Xander laughed, but there was no humor in it. Buffy knew him well enough to hear the bitterness when he spoke.

"Hey, if I thought I was going to end up being like my father, I'd just give myself over to the next hungry pack of flesh-eatin' ghouls that came along!" The smile disappeared from his face, and he looked suddenly nauseated. "Bad enough living with that. No way I'll become it."

Lorne yawned again. "Trust me, amigo. No controlling it. My home life was nothing to write . . . well, home about. Auntie Em couldn't give a damn if I ever came back from over the rainbow. But there's no denying who I am has a lot to do with how I grew up."

"Thanks," Xander said, his voice oozing sarcasm. "I feel oh so much better."

"Hey," Tara said, "my father's a controlling fruity nut bar who made me believe most of my life that my mom and I were monsters. But I'm not going to let him decide what I am."

Buffy had listened to the whole exchange with a heavy heart. She gazed at Xander, and when she spoke, it was really Xander she was talking to. "We don't get to choose who our parents are. Pretty much sucks, but that's the crumbling cookie. My . . . my father usually doesn't seem to remember he has any children."

"Talk about messed-up fathers," Cordelia said, her voice a hush.

Curious, Buffy looked at her. She had always had the impression that Cordelia got along fine with her father. Willow was the only one who seemed to have what passed for a normal home life despite her mother being sort of odd, but Cordelia had always been second runner-up. Sure, her parents were wealthy and a little distant, and her father had screwed the government in taxes, but *still*.

Cordelia noticed Buffy looking at her and rolled her eyes.

"It's not a big deal or anything. Not real high on the trauma scale. It's just not a cruise on the fun ship when anytime a situation might require emotion—say, affection or frustration, things like that—the ol' head of the household just throws money instead."

Buffy was about to respond when Wesley beat her to it. "There are worse options," he said gravely, his voice low and rough, his eyes haunted as though he were gazing not at the room around him but at some dreadful memory that lingered ghostlike in his mind.

"Looks like you're the oddball, Will. You with the healthy home life."

"Actually," Cordelia added, "Fred's parents are really sweet."

"Somehow I could have guessed that," Buffy observed.

"So it's just the rest of us who'll never be able to escape the shadow of our childhood and will probably never be able to have a normal relationship because of it," Xander said, clearly relishing the cynicism.

"Hey!" Willow balked.

"I second that 'hey!'" Cordelia snapped.

"Oh, sure, hey all you want. But tell it to someone who hasn't borne witness to the Angel-Buffy, Xander-Willow, Xander-Buffy, Wesley-Cordelia, Cordelia-Xander, Willow-Oz, Tara-Willow merry-go-round o'love."

Nobody had anything at all to say to that. Silence reigned for several long moments before Tara cleared her throat and everyone glanced at her.

"Um, well, I just thought I should mention that before? Angel also said something about an island. That Axtius was going to destroy some island."

Wesley glanced over at Cordelia. "Could he be talking about—"

"Monster Island," she interrupted.

Buffy stared at them. "Say again?"

"That's what I call it," Cordelia explained. "There's this island off the coast, it's magickally hidden from human eyes. It's like a sanctuary for demons that want to escape persecution in the human world, or from other demons. Kinda the Betty Ford Clinic of the supernatural set. We were helping a clan of demons get to the island. They were trying to escape these other . . . anyway, that's when Doyle was killed. He died saving them."

Lorne seemed wide awake now. "And that's where Axtius is headed next with his own personal army. Not liking the sound of that. Sanctuary is supposed to be just that. Like Caritas."

Before Buffy could weigh in on the subject there was a fast rap on the front door of the hotel and then a lean, hairy figure pushed his way inside. The demon had thick red hair and a beard slightly darker. The eyes that peered out from all of that hair glowed yellow in the dimly lit lobby. It was thin, almost too bony, and there was hair on its hands as well.

"Help me," the demon rasped, so shrilly that Buffy winced at the sound in her ears. "Hide me. I'm being . . . they're *hunting* me."

The last few words were a pitiful wail, and then the demon sank to its knees on the steps. Cordelia and Tara went to comfort the thing and to find out more about its plight, but Buffy knew this was no coincidence. She turned to Wesley.

"This is getting worse fast. There are probably going to be more refugees. Maybe a lot of them."

"They won't be safe here," Wesley replied quickly.

"No. No way," Gunn said. "Once Axtius figures out Angel's still alive, this'll be his first stop."

"*If* he figures out Angel's still alive," Xander said. "I'm not gonna tell him. Are you gonna tell him?"

"We need somewhere safe to hide them. Somewhere protected," Willow said.

As one, they all turned to look at Lorne. The Host held up both hands. "Just hold on there, gang. Caritas is a temporary sanctuary only. That's part of my charter. The magicks that make it possible don't come from me, y'know. The club's supposed to stay as neutral as Switzerland. That doesn't mean I have to, but Caritas does. Plus, the protective capacity of the place isn't limitless, and even it were, the space in there isn't."

Cordelia strode over to them, leaving the pitifully weeping demon behind with Tara to comfort him. "I have a thought," she said. "Wesley, what about Elijah Carnegie?"

"Like the old magician?" Willow asked brightly. When Buffy glanced curiously at her, she smiled. "I love all those guys. The old stage magic acts like Thurston and Blackstone and Houdini. Carnegie the Great was later, but just as talented."

"Not 'like' the old magician," Wesley corrected. "This is Elijah Carnegie. He's an old friend of Angel's, long since retired. He owns a used bookstore here in town. It's where Angel acquired many of the books in his . . . our collection."

Willow's eyes widened. "Very cool."

"Elijah had a nasty visit this past Christmas," Cordelia said, her brows knitting as if the memory had upset her. "After that he put a spell on his shop that hides it and anything inside from supernatural detection."

"That's a start," Buffy said, her mind working furiously as she tried to figure out the best steps to take next. "All right. I meant what I said before. We all need a few hours' sleep or we'll be useless. If Axtius tracks our new guest before then"—Buffy nodded toward the sobbing, redheaded demon—"we'll just have to deal. At least then we'd know where Axtius is. Up at one. Back down here in the lobby by two. We'll all have work to do. This old magician's bookshop will work for a little while, but it sounds like Monster Island is the sanctuary we're looking for.

"Big problem is, Axtius is looking for it too. I have a feeling it's going to be up to us to keep him from destroying it."

Cordelia yawned. "Wonderful. How come all of my island adventures involve some demon's idea of paradise and not Barbados or the Virgin Islands?" As if having second thoughts about that last bit, she shot a dark look at Xander. "Not a word from you. It was a rhetorical question."

The Slayer sighed softly. "Look, I know I'm the last one anyone would expect to bring this up, but if this thing is as big as we think it is, we can use all the help we can get. I'm wondering what it would take to spring Faith from prison. Just for a while."

Gunn scratched the back of his head, and Cordelia studiously looked away. Wesley seemed uncomfortable.

"What?" Buffy asked. "Come on, I've got issues with her too. She stole my body for a while, remember? Endangered the people I love. Never mind all the stuff before that. But—"

"It's been done," Wesley interrupted.

Buffy paused and stared at him. "You mean she's out right now? Already?"

"No," Wesley corrected, his hands behind his back. "I mean we've broken her out before. As a result, she's in isolation for the time being. No visitors. No way to get to her. Not on short notice. Unless we have the magickal power to teleport in, get her, and teleport her out. . . ."

Everyone looked at Willow and Tara, who shook their heads regretfully.

"Okay," Buffy said, nodding. "It was just a thought. We'll make do."

They all began to disperse, preparing to sleep for a few

hours. None of them complained about the suggestion, and Buffy thought that was testament enough to how exhausted they all were.

"One last thing of interest," Wesley noted as he walked back into his office, pausing just inside the door. "Zeke, whom we were searching for earlier? He is the only part-time resident of the island that I know of. If we want to know more about the island, or get a warning to the demons there, he's the one we have to find."

"Go to sleep," Buffy said. "It's going to be a busy day."

A short time later, after all of them had retired to the rooms they had taken in the hotel—not one of them sleeping soundly save Calvin, who had not moved from his snoring sprawl in the lobby—a grunt of pain came from the room where Spike and Angel had been left to heal.

Inside that room, Angel's eyes flickered open. He gritted his teeth against the pain in his charred flesh and his now-knitting broken bones. And across from him, he saw a blackened corpse. The sight startled him at first, but then he recognized the familiar facial structure despite the burned skin, saw the tufts of white-blond hair growing anew on the seared scalp.

Spike, Angel thought. His nostrils flared and he let his eyes close again, jaw set angrily.

Son of a—

CHAPTER TEN

"*Buffy!*" Angel gasped, coming awake with a start as he pulled himself from a bizarre, pain-induced dream.

In the dream he had been standing before an enormous, red velvet curtain, backstage at some cavernous ancient theater. He was dressed in white—suit, vest, and shoes to match. There was a straw hat upon his head, and he sensed he was waiting to go on stage.

Go on for what? he had wondered, panic beginning to grow. Why was he dressed like this? What was he doing in a theater?

Buffy was standing to the side of the curtain holding a thick rope in hand. Standing behind her was a small gathering of people: Doyle was there, as were Charlie Nickels and Amos, whose head was still leaking a jelly-like material since being caved in with a mace. They were all smiling at him, giving him the thumbs-up. It was nice seeing Doyle again, and it hit him how much he missed his old friend.

"Are you ready?" Buffy had asked, and he had not been quite sure what she'd meant. But then it had dawned on him: It must have been Charlie Nickels's show—his *Music Man* production—even though he had never agreed to be in it. Angel had raised his hands in protest as Buffy pulled on the rope.

"Buffy, wait," he had said, and the curtain had begun to rise.

But instead of an auditorium crowded with demons and curious Broadway aficionados, when the curtain went up Angel found himself looking out over a city rooftop just as the sun began to rise.

"Buffy!" he'd screamed. Then the rays of sunlight touched his vampiric flesh and he began to burn.

In that moment, Angel woke, tearing himself from the grip of the dream and thrusting his consciousness up into a world of excruciating agony. The real-world pain was so savage that it took him several moments to discern reality from pain-induced fantasy.

"She's not here," said a strained voice from somewhere in the room.

And suddenly Angel recalled his last vague memory—a memory he hoped was fantasy.

Spike, he said to himself, wishing this was part of some truly nasty fever dream. *Anybody but Spike.*

"She was in 'bout a half hour ago," continued the raspy voice. "I made an attempt at small talk, but the ol' vocal cords still felt like pieces of overcooked bacon. Better now. Sure wish I had a fag, though. I'd kill for a bloody smoke."

Angel stared up at the hotel room's ceiling and quivered with repressed fury. He despised the filthy creature lying on a cot beside him. Spike was a painful reminder of a past he would rather not think about, emblematic of every disgusting, insidious thing he himself had ever done. It sickened Angel the way Spike relished cruelty above all else, and yet even worse was his knowledge that Spike came from his own vampiric bloodline, that if Angel had never blooded Drusilla, she would never have been able to turn Spike. The vampire would have died a gentle, bad poet centuries ago and not become . . . this.

Angel was responsible for Spike, in that way. That knowledge lingered in the back of his mind nearly all of the time, and it made him feel almost obligated to dust Spike himself. Right now, in particular, he felt the venomous hatred he had for Spike filling him. If he had been at all capable, Angel would have taken the opportunity to rise up from the bed and finally put an end to the vampire's life. But although he was healing, he was still badly burned and his body shrieked out in agony from the tips of his returning hair to the ends of his toes.

So he would not be killing Spike today. And he did not even want to think about the chip in the vampire's head, the one that supposedly made him docile, though no less obnoxious. Buffy had decided it would be wrong to kill Spike if he was incapable of harming humans now. Angel was not so sure.

"What are you doing, Spike?" he asked in a strained whisper. "Why are you here?"

"What? Not happy that the Big Bad's come to the city of Angel?" he asked. "Sorry, mate, but I'm part of the team now," Spike said with obvious amusement. "The Scoobies had an opening for a strong, silent vampire type, and it just so happens I fit the bill quite nicely," he growled, twisting the proverbial knife. "The benefits ain't much, but I do occasionally get the pleasure of killing some nasty beasties—and saving the world, there is that. . . ."

Spike's voice tapered off to a wheeze, and then he began to

cough. It sounded wet, loose. "Oh bloody hell, that hurts," he hissed, finally getting himself under control.

Angel wanted to laugh out loud, but knew that would hurt more than it was worth. This inhuman, bloodthirsty monster saving the world, now he'd heard it all. He thought of his own suffering since the Gypsy curse had returned his soul. What had Spike endured? he wondered. What did William the Bloody know about the misery he had caused—did he even care?

"C'mon, Spike," Angel said, trying to turn his head and look at the vampire. He winced as the blackened skin around his neck crackled like dry fall leaves. "What's your angle? You couldn't care less about helping the Slayer or saving the world. What's in it for you?"

Spike maneuvered himself on the cot so that he could see Angel. The vampire's skin was black and cracked, the pink of raw, healing flesh peeking out from beneath the fissures. He snarled, his teeth unusually bright in the blackened hole that was his mouth. "Now is that any way to talk to the bloke responsible for saving your crispy bacon? Wasn't for me you'd be so much Angel dust in the wind."

Angel grunted with satisfaction. It seemed as though he had struck a nerve. He continued to prod, enjoying any additional pain he could cause the vampire, taking his mind off his own discomfort in the process. "No offense," he said, "I appreciate the save and all, but I am starting to recognize a familiar pattern here."

"What are you going on about, then?" Spike asked in a pain-wracked hiss as he turned onto his back.

"Face it, Spike," Angel said, looking away from the horrific sight of the vampire beside him and fixing his gaze on the cracked ceiling. "Since you were turned, you always wanted to be me, and that chip inside your head has given you the opportunity to play at it again."

"Be like you?" Spike yelled. "You're out of your sodding mind. The sun's cooked your brain inside your skull like a pudding."

Angel painfully raised his hand, lifting a charred finger to make his point. "I was the scourge of Europe until I got my soul back. Then who tried to fill my shoes? From Venice to Prague to London, who left a trail of slaughter in his wake, not caring what kind of attention he drew to himself? William the Bloody."

He heard Spike shift uncomfortably. "Drusilla and I saw the opportunity to expand our horizons and have a bit of fun, we—"

"That's another thing," Angel said, lifting his second burned finger. "Drusilla. You were her substitute for what she could never have with me."

"I could never do enough for that one," Spike grumbled. "I was just as savage as you in those days, but Angelus always got the better press. How many families did a fellow have to massacre to get out from beneath your shadow, anyway?"

Angel lifted a third finger. "And now we have the chip in your head. Not quite like getting your soul back, but it'll do in a pinch, keeping you on the straight and narrow." He lowered his arm. "I don't know about you, but I find the similarities pretty unsettling."

It had started as a bit of perverse entertainment to distract him from his own pain, but the more Angel thought, the more he realized that there really was something to his theory.

"Bollocks!" Spike rasped, attempting to sit up straight. "I think living here in La-La Land has given you too much time to think, old man," Spike said. "Me wantin' to be you?" he spat, his body again wracked with a painful coughing fit. "Next thing you'll be telling me I'm mooning after the Slayer or some such, but you don't see me behaving like a bloody prat, pullin' a little Anne Rice heartache-and-angst special. If I wanted to be like you, I'd need to whine a bit more, now wouldn't I?"

Angel lay silent, the thought of Buffy and Spike together obscene.

"You want to know why I'm knocking about with the pep squad, Angel?" He lay back down and flipped onto his side, a shower of loose, charred skin raining onto the floor. "I'll tell you why."

Angel waited, perversely curious.

"Chip in me damned head makes me a tad defenseless against certain types, like the bloody Council of Watchers, for example." He leaned closer, and Angel could smell his breath. It smelled of raw meat. "Lurking in the Slayer's shadow makes me less of a target, and I'm willing to bide my time until I work out my little problem. Till then, I'm happy to play along, fightin' on the side of—no offense—the angels."

There was silence in the room as Angel pondered the situation. He knew what he had to do, much to his chagrin.

"I don't know if you're smarter than you look or dumber than I think," Angel rasped, every breath painful for him. "You're in a building filled with people who'd like to see you swept up in a dustpan. Right now you're relying on Buffy thinking you're more useful than dangerous. For the moment, I'm willing to go along with that. As long as Buffy's got you on a leash, maybe we have use for a sadistic little lapdog like you after all.

"But the minute you prove Buffy wrong, it's over for you, Spike. I look forward to the day. For now, I'll play along. But as soon as this is over, I want you out of my sight. Out of my city."

Spike glared at him a long moment, hatred and other, unnameable emotions burning in the eyes that looked out from the charred features.

"No worries, caped crusader," he growled, crossing his scorched fingers atop his chest. "L.A.'s got your stink all over it. 'M'not gonna stay a minute longer than Buffy wants me to."

Than Buffy wants me to. Angel shuddered. He did not like the sound of those words at all, nor Spike's tone. He wondered if there was even more to his theory than he had imagined, but he pushed the idea away. It was too sickening to spend another second thinking about.

"Just as long as we understand each other," Angel said.

"Oh, we always have," Spike replied knowingly. "We always have."

Angel felt incredibly tired. He closed his eyes and shortly drifted off to a dreamless sleep filled with darkness.

And his body continued to heal.

The bell hanging above the doorway tolled their arrival.

"Did anyone else feel that?" Tara asked in a breathless whisper as she stepped through the doorway of Cobwebs Antiquarian & Used Bookstore.

"Was it a kind of tickly tingle in your stomach that feels sorta like you're hungry, but you're not quite sure what you're hungry for?" Fred asked, one hand furiously rubbing her belly.

Cordelia watched as Willow's better half nodded in excited agreement, somehow knowing exactly what Fred was going on about.

"You think it might be for waffles," Tara said, "but by the time you get to the freezer—"

"It's not waffles at all, and you think it might be more along the lines of cake," Fred finished with an enormous grin.

"It felt just like that," Tara confirmed.

They were both nodding now, and Cordelia wondered if there was some kind of rite of passage that she had missed out on. The two girls had been talking like this nonstop since dropping Lorne off at Caritas. It was like Tara and Fred were wired into the same bizarre frequency, picking up the exact same signals and speaking in some long-forgotten native tongue.

Good thing Fred isn't a big ol' lesbian, Cordelia thought, shutting the bookshop door behind them, *or Willow might have been in for a little competition.*

"Did you feel anything, Cordelia?" Fred asked.

She knew they were probably making reference to the magickal spells set up around the shop by its proprietor. After a run-in with a particularly nasty Chinese demon, Elijah had laid down some spells to hide the store from supernatural threats. With their experience in the magickal arts, it was no wonder they were reacting to the spell's presence.

"Other than the need for the two of you to take a deep breath?" she said. "You guys haven't come up for air in over an hour."

Tara looked down at her feet, embarrassed. "Sorry," she said. "I get sorta nervous when I'm around new people—but I feel really comfortable with you and Fred and—y'know," she paused for a moment, crossing her arms self-consciously and gazing at them from behind a stray lock of hair. "Thanks for making me feel like part of the team and all," she said with a shy smile and a shrug of her shoulders.

"And thank you for being part of it," Fred said happily, and the two of them grinned at each other, members of the same bizarre sorority.

"Right, good," Cordelia said, moving to the store's unmanned front counter. "Now let's see what we can do about setting up a safe house for our soon to be growing half-breed refugee population, shall we?"

"Just look at all these books," she heard Fred say dreamily as she noticed the old-fashioned bell that sat on the counter beside an equally antique cash register. *For service, ring bell,* said the note taped to the countertop. Cordelia reached out and gently tapped it with the palm of her hand.

A surprisingly loud *ding* reverberated through the store, like the bells of Notre Dame, a far larger and more resonant ring than should have been possible from a bell of that size. Cordelia suspected there was magick at work.

"Wow!" Fred said, blocking her ears against the splitting peel. "How hard did you hit that thing?"

Tara just laughed, amused by the strangeness of the situation, and glanced about the store in wonder.

Cordelia was about to silence the annoying bell by shoving it deep inside her purse when a voice called out from somewhere at the back of the store. "Just a minute, please."

A door opened to the right of a glass showcase filled with rare editions, and an older man stepped out into the store. He was a big man, dressed in baggy slacks, dark shoes, and an overly large, maroon cardigan sweater, and he looked a bit like Santa Claus from one of those Rankin and Bass holiday specials. Elijah Carnegie came bustling up one of the aisles and the moment he saw Cordelia his expression changed from that of a courteous businessman to a warm smile of recognition and welcome.

"Hello, Ms. Chase," he effused as he took her hands in his and shook them warmly. "What a pleasant surprise! I haven't seen you since that business around the holidays," he said, rolling his eyes, making reference to the Chinese demon that had battled Angel in the store just a few days before Christmas.

Cordelia and Angel had come to pick up a present for Wesley and had run into a little trouble over an ancient Chinese text and the demon queen of Hell who thought it belonged to her. *The nerve!*

"Hey there, Elijah," she said fondly. "How's tricks?"

The old man stared for a moment, a quizzical expression on his bearded face. "What's that behind your ear?" he asked curiously, reaching over to the side of her head and miraculously producing an orchid. "A thing of beauty to compliment an even greater loveliness," he said, offering the flower to her with a gentlemanly bow.

Tara and Fred applauded as Cordelia took the flower.

Elijah turned his attention to the other young women. "I seem to be in the presence of a veritable garden of beauty tonight," he said with a smile.

"You bet you are," Cordelia said as she placed the orchid in her hair above her left ear. "Elijah Carnegie, meet my associate Fred Burkle, and our friend Tara Maclay."

"Delighted," he said, shaking hands with each. "To what do I owe the pleasure of your visit tonight?" he asked. "I can't imagine that three such beautiful young women are simply seeking the company of musty old books."

Laying it on pretty thick, old-timer, Cordelia mused with a smile. *You must have been something in your day, a real lady-killer,* she thought, gazing at the framed posters above the cash register that advertised performances by Carnegie the Great. "Sorry to say, Elijah," Cordelia told the magician, "as crazy as it sounds, we *are* here on business."

Elijah shook his head, clucking his distaste. "Shocking," he said with mock disapproval. "Truly shocking."

"Sure beats the heck out of spending your nights in a cold, dark cave in another dimension trying to keep a fire burning by feeding it chunks of dried moss that smell like dirty feet and . . ." Fred stopped when she realized that everybody was staring. "Sorry," she said with an embarrassed grin. "I'm still getting readjusted to socialization. It's just that all things considered, this isn't so bad."

Cordelia stepped in before the old man could become any more confused. "Angel Investigations was wondering if we could ask you a really big favor."

Elijah looked at her, his grandfatherly features becoming very serious. "And what would that be, Ms. Chase?" he asked in a soft, gentle voice, intelligence and decades of experience a mystery in his eyes.

She began to tell him about Axtius and his Coalition, about the vicious murders of half-breeds. Elijah revealed that he had already heard about the deaths from some of his customers and had even sold some texts of spells that would help hide someone who didn't want to be found.

"And speaking of hiding people," she continued, getting to the real reason for their visit. "Do you think we could stash some of the refugees here? Things are getting kind of hairy on the streets, and you have that really neat spell around the store." She flashed her most winning smile at the old man. "What do you say? It wouldn't be forever."

"Excuse me, dear," he said, moving past her to climb the single step that would take him behind the front counter. "Would any of you care for a hot drink—a cup of tea or instant coffee?" he asked. "I have a fresh hot pot of water back here, and it won't take but a minute." The old man held up a white plastic kettle.

Tara and Fred politely refused.

Cordelia leaned against the counter. "Thanks for the hospitality, Elijah, but we don't really have a moment. We need to know your answer pretty quick, yes or no."

"Of course you do, Cordelia," Elijah said. "I understand the importance of something so dire, and I'm well aware of the danger these poor souls are in." He set the kettle down on a shelf below the counter and brought a hand up nervously to stroke his snowy white beard.

Something seemed to be bothering the old magician, something that he did not care to voice.

"I think if we were to move some of the stock around out back, we should be able to make adequate room," he said, his fingers still combing through the hair on his face.

"So that's a yes?" Cordelia asked carefully, not wanting to say anything to change his mind.

Elijah smiled weakly. "Of course," he answered. "How could I turn my back on those in need—or refuse the request of three ladies as fetching as you?"

Fred clapped like she was trying to bring Tinkerbell back to life, and Tara beamed.

The old magician turned the OPEN sign on the door to CLOSED, made himself a cup of instant coffee in a mug with a picture of Hemingway on its side, and showed them to the storage room in the back. Stacks of boxes and crates rose up all over the room. They were amazed at the volume of stock that still hadn't found its way to the store's shelves.

"I'd swear they were breeding," he muttered under his breath as he maneuvered around a pile of rare texts to reach a clearing amongst the sea of boxes. He took a sip from his mug and set it on the floor near his feet. "If you ladies would be so kind as to step this way," he said, and motioned for them to stand beside him.

Elijah raised his arms, cleared his throat, and closed his eyes. "I think I can recall the spell we need," he said as his eyes feathered open. "Shall I give it a try?"

The magician muttered something under his breath that Cordelia's years of occult research allowed her to recognize as Latin. She could not speak or read the language, but she knew it when she heard it. The air became charged with a pulsing, electric energy. He pointed his hands toward the obstacles in the room, his voice suddenly booming. Tendrils of white energy shot from the old man's fingertips, ensnaring the multitude of boxes and stacked books. In what seemed to be the wink of an eye, the back stock of Cobwebs Antiquarian & Used Books was stacked neatly along the walls from floor to ceiling, clearing an enormous space in the center of the room.

Tara's eyes widened in appreciation. "Wow."

"Impressive," Cordelia said as the magician flexed his hands and blew on his fingertips.

"It is, isn't it," he said, looking about gravely.

"Look, Elijah," Cordelia said, again sensing his discomfort. "If you don't want to do this, no biggie. We'll find another way to—"

"Please understand, Cordelia," he said, touching her shoulder. "It's not that I don't want to help, it's just that—I'm afraid what might happen if the demons should come searching for their prey."

"What do you have to be afraid of, Mr. Carnegie?" Tara asked. "Anybody who can do the kind of magick I just saw shouldn't have any trouble defending himself against—"

"It's not the demons that I'm afraid of, young lady," he said, deadly serious. "It's the magick."

"Why would you be afraid of magick?" Fred asked.

Cordelia stepped in to help the old magician. "Elijah has a . . . an aversion to certain kinds of magick," she began, vaguely remembering something he had said when she first visited the store with Angel.

"Please," Elijah said, "let me explain." He looked at them, his eyes grave. "I am an addict," he said, lightly touching his chest, "not to narcotics, or alcohol, or gambling—magick is my drug." They were silent, letting him say his piece. "During my years as a stage magician, I became bored with simple sleight of hand—smoke and mirrors, if you will—and I began to delve into real magick. Into sorcery."

The old magician bent down to retrieve his Hemingway coffee mug. He looked at its contents dreamily, as if seeing something other than himself reflected there. "I became engrossed in it, learning all I could about magick and its myriad uses. I allowed it to consume me."

Elijah took a sip of coffee.

"Is . . . is that even possible?" Tara asked haltingly. "Can a . . . a person actually be addicted to magick?"

The old man slowly nodded. "It gets inside you, makes you think that you can't live without it. The magick makes you its slave. It took me close to ten years before I became its master again—and even then—" The old man paused, remembering a time obviously very painful to him. "Now I only do constructive magick," he said. "The kind of magick that would be needed for defense against these demons would probably eat me alive if I tried to control it again."

They were uncomfortably silent. Fred nervously played with her hair, and Tara looked as though she might be sick. From her expression, Cordelia thought it had probably never occurred to the young witch that the magick she and Willow wielded with such ease could actually end up hurting them.

Elijah broke the silence with a clap of his hands. "That's quite enough of that," he said. "I just remembered that earlier this week I uncovered a case of talismans that might come in handy," he said, ushering them to the door. "Why don't we go up front and I'll show them to you."

"What would you do?" Tara asked in a barely audible voice. They all turned to look at her. "If Axtius's men attacked here. What would you do?"

Cordelia looked at Elijah and saw the pain spread across his face.

"Let's just hope it never comes to that," he said, turning quickly and proceeding up the aisle.

The Slayer stood before the open weapons cabinet in the lobby of the former hotel and slowly withdrew a funky sword.

"Neat," she said, brandishing the elegant, curved blade of steel. She held the scimitar before her, testing its weight, eyes tracing the razor-sharp arc of its blade. A smaller blade of equal sharpness curled from the pommel in the opposite direction.

"Wonder if Giles could get me one of these," she mused, slicing at the air, imagining the horrible damage it could do to Axtius's minions.

"I'm sure if you're extra good and eat all your veggies, Santa Watcher will put it under the Christmas tree," Xander said from behind the front desk where he was still doing research.

"Hooray for Christmas," Buffy cheered, practicing some fencing moves. From the corner of her eye she could see Xander set down his pen and watch her. The expression on his face told her she must have been doing well.

She completed her routine by bringing the sword swiftly downward and stopping mid slash. She inhaled deeply and then slowly exhaled through pursed lips as she lowered the blade. Xander gaped at her from the front desk.

"Sorry," she said, relaxing and heading back to the weapons cabinet. "Feeling a little antsy. Needed to show off."

"No problem," Xander said with a casual shrug. "Do you want me to call out for something you can kill?" he asked, reaching for the phone. "It's L.A. I'm sure they deliver just about anything."

Buffy carefully replaced the blade. "No, I think I've got the old bloodlust under control for now, thanks," she said, eyeing a display of Japanese throwing stars.

"Or if you don't want take-out, you could always go upstairs and put Spike out of our misery—but that's up to you."

Xander looked tired, and she realized that despite her instructions to the contrary, none of them had gotten much rest since arriving in Los Angeles.

"I know how you feel," she said, moving away from the weapons cabinet. "But he does have his uses, even though it makes me feel all kinds of grubby to say it. Thinking about Spike makes my head hurt. Sometimes I'm sure he just comes along for the ride 'cause it's safer for him with us than against us. But then he does something like this, risking his own life to save Angel's."

Xander slid his hands into his back pockets, glanced at the hotel ceiling, and laughed nervously. "Yep. That Spike. He's an evil enigma, wrapped in a sadistic mystery, and served on a bed of lettuce. I know where you're coming from on this, Buff, I really do, but I'm still having a hard time accepting an undead mass murderer into our happy little family."

He turned away, shuffling toward one of the lobby couches. "I don't know," he said plopping down onto the sofa. "Maybe it's just me, but I say—I've always said—dust him. Just because he can't hurt anyone now doesn't forgive what he's done before. It's not like he's Angel, looking for redemption, trying to make up for the awful things his body did when it didn't have a soul in it. With Spike it's like somebody hit the 'off' button on his homicidal maniac mode. But what happens when it gets turned on again?"

"Then we'll dust him." Buffy held out her hand to silence him. "You have to trust me, Xander," she said. Buffy sat down on the plush sofa beside him. "A lot of what I do is about instinct, in my gut. And I know how I would feel if we just dusted Spike without finding out what that chip has *really* done to him. Maybe there's more to it than just him not being able to kill humans? Sometimes I wonder."

Xander sighed and started to look away. She squeezed his shoulder and forced him to look at her. He winced, and she looked deep into her friend's eyes in an attempt to convey the importance of what she was trying to get him to understand.

"I have to trust these instincts, Xander. 'Cause if I don't, I won't have anything."

He gave her a tired smile. "Guess that's not too much to ask for the girl who's saved the world from apocalypse a couple'a times," he said as she returned the smile. He wagged his finger at her. "Just don't go expecting this level of mature understanding all the time."

Buffy laughed, leaning into her friend, her heart suffused with such love for Xander and appreciation for her friends that for the first time in a very long time, for just a fraction of a moment, she was glad that they had brought her back from the dead. The world was hellish, the opposite of paradise, but there were glimmers of bliss and wonder in it that were a kind of heaven unto themselves.

"A touching moment amidst the sweeping drama of war," said a low, rasping voice.

Buffy looked to the stairway to see Spike carefully descending as if every movement brought him excruciating pain—which it probably did. Angel was right behind him, looking equally pained. Their flesh was still badly burned—red and raw in places where the skin had peeled away. Buffy had to wonder how it was possible for them to be wearing clothes—never mind the fact that they were up and around.

She rose from the lobby sofa and approached the stairs. "Should you two be up already?" she asked. "You still look a little—crispy."

"If I have to spend another minute with him in that room, I'll stake myself back out on that rooftop just to get away," Angel muttered, going around the slowly moving Spike.

"Like I asked for your bloody company," Spike said, reaching into a shirt pocket for cigarettes that weren't there. "Bollocks," he growled. "Anybody have a ciggy they could spare?"

"There's no smoking in the hotel," Angel said as he reached the lobby. "If you want to do it, you'll have to go outside. It should only take you a day or so to make the trip."

Spike snarled. "Pretty tough for a guy beaten within an inch of his life by a Brachen demon."

Angel carefully turned his body toward Spike, who was still making his way down the stairs. "You know I'm still feeling a great deal of anger about that, Spike," he growled. "Maybe I can take it out on you a while, release my frustration."

"Maybe you could try, Mr. Tall, Dark, and Char-Grilled—"

"It's really great to see that distance hasn't torn asunder that special bond you two share," Buffy said, hands on her hips.

"Kinda like one of those A T and T commercials," Xander said, joining them at the foot of the stairs. "Gets you right here," he said, punching the area over his heart. "How you been, Angel?"

"I've felt better," Angel responded. "But all in all, can't complain."

"Just me being curious," Buffy suddenly spoke up, "but how is this going to work with you two? Are we going to have to separate you in the middle of taking down Axtius, or do you think you can control yourselves?"

Angel glared at Spike, who had finally reached the bottom of the stairs. "We've got a tentative détente going. We'll take it day by day, since what's going on out there is more important right now than what's going on in here."

"That's right," Spike said as he scratched at his neck, flakes of charred flesh drifting to the floor like black snow.

Buffy wrinkled her nose with distaste.

"For today we've agreed, nothin' homicidal," Spike continued, pushing the burned pieces of skin around on the floor with the toe of his boot. Then he grinned, the expression cracking his blackened skin. "But who knows what tomorrow'll bring?"

"He ain't here now," said the enormous beast as it slowly emerged from beneath a blanket of refuse and rose to its full and impressive height outside the basement entrance to the abandoned bakery.

"But has Zeke returned?" Wesley asked the creature, which he recognized as some breed of troll. He casually removed a twenty-dollar bill from inside his wallet and showed it to the beast.

"How come these guys always got their hands out—or claws, or tentacles or whatever?" Gunn asked in disgust, to no one in particular. "They ain't hiring down at the DoubleMeat Palace anymore?"

"Gunn, please," Wesley said.

"Yeah," the troll answered, extending a large, spadelike hand covered in thick, yellowed callus. "Yeah, he's back. Got back earlier today."

Wesley pressed the bill into the center of the troll's hand and watched as the black clawed fingers closed around it.

"I watch the place for him while he's gone," the troll said, examining the twenty before it disappeared into a pocket somewhere beneath the filthy layers of clothes. "I keep the riffraff out, and he lets me crash here, gives me a little cash now and again, y'know what I'm saying?" the troll asked.

Wesley put his wallet away. "And where is Zeke now?" he asked.

The troll thought for a moment, scratching the top of his shaggy head with a clawed nail. "Not too sure," he said. "Was kind of worked up after he got in, said he had to find out some stuff about what's been happening since he was gone."

"I see," Wesley said with a satisfied nod of his head. "We'd like to wait for him," he told the troll, gesturing to Willow, Gunn, and Calvin beside him. "If that wouldn't be any bother."

The troll smiled, showing off a mouthful of teeth that would have driven the most stalwart dentist to the brink of madness. "That's cool," he said, reaching down to the floor to pull up a stained blanket. "Zeke's talked about you," he said, draping the blanket over his shoulders like a shawl. "Said you were all right for a human." The monster reached out and opened the door for them. "Go on in, make yourselves at home."

The cool, fetid smell of dampness and rotting wood wafted out of the basement to greet them.

"If you don't mind keeping an eye on the place for me," the troll said as he prepared to leave them, "I've got a date with a bottle of Jack Daniels that I'd hate to put off any longer." He patted the area where he had stashed the money Wesley had given him and jauntily strolled away with a friendly wave. "Nice talking with you folks," he said happily. "Tell Zeke I'll catch up with him later."

"Nice guy," Willow said casually, "for a stinky troll. Meeting him I'm beginning to have second thoughts about that trash those three billy goats gruff were talking."

Wesley gestured for Willow to enter Zeke's dwelling before him.

"Why did we have to bring her along?" he heard Calvin ask Gunn in a whisper. "Fred would have been a better choice."

217

"You think so?" Gunn asked as they moved through the door. "And why is that?"

Calvin didn't answer as he stepped into the dark basement. Wesley was beginning to suspect that the boy was developing a crush on a certain young lady recently rescued from an inter-dimensional demon realm.

"So this Zeke is like a friend of yours?" Willow asked him as she gazed about the low-ceilinged room.

Wesley noticed a lantern hanging on a nail beside the door and removed it. "Not so much a friend as an informant," he said, looking around for a way to light the lantern.

"Here, let me," Willow said, taking the lantern from him.

He watched as she lifted the glass cover. She muttered something softly beneath her breath and touched the exposed wick with her fingertip. There was a flash of blue, and the wick ignited, throwing off a warm glow. Wesley thanked her and set the lantern down atop a rickety, makeshift desk.

"Oh yeah," Calvin said, turning his nose up. "It's so much nicer in the light."

The wood of the support beams was charred a nasty black, the low ceiling stained with soot. The smoky smell of fire still lingered in the damp and musty air.

Gunn nudged the teenager roughly with his shoulder and scowled at him. "What'd I say now?" Calvin asked.

"Zeke is a Miquot demon," Wesley said, ignoring the teen. "A pariah from his clan for some reason or another. He lives here—in the city, part of the time—and on the island during the rest."

"You mean Monster Island?" Willow asked, raising her eyebrows and smiling.

"Though a tad overly dramatic, yes," he said. "*Monster Island.*" He carefully leaned back against the table behind him.

"Zeke was a contact of Angel's before I arrived at the agency—introduced by Doyle, I believe."

"You didn't know him—Doyle—did you, Wesley?" Willow asked.

He shook his head. "No, I didn't," he responded. He had had to deal with the specter of Doyle's death when he had first arrived at Angel Investigations. Angel and Cordelia had never said much about their fallen friend, but they didn't have to. The depth of their grief had been evident to him each and every day. "He'd been gone a few weeks when I began to work at the agency."

"He sounded like a cool guy," Gunn said, walking around the basement. "It must have been pretty rough for Angel and Cordelia." He squatted down in front of a plastic milk crate beside a mattress. The crate was filled with mildewed paperbacks, and he began to rummage through them. "Even today, they can't talk about him without getting all weird and stuff." He began to flip through a Louis L'Amour Western as Calvin joined him.

"I think it hurt much more than we will ever really know," Wesley said as he crossed his arms. Though the awkwardness about Doyle's death had diminished over time between himself and his coworkers, it had never quite gone away. Grief was like that, he knew, beginning as excruciating agony and fading over time to a dull twinge that was barely noticed until something triggered it again, opening old wounds. Wesley was concerned that this case would do exactly that, putting an uncomfortable distance between Angel and Cordelia—and those who had joined them after Doyle's death. He wondered if he should have a talk with Angel.

The eerie quiet of the room was violently shattered as the door into the basement dwelling was kicked open. Startled,

Wesley pushed away from the desk, his sudden movement tilting the rickety table and sending the lantern—their only source of light—crashing to the floor.

"Damn!" he hissed as the basement was plunged into inky blackness.

"Wesley?" Willow called out from somewhere nearby.

He could just about make out the shape of a hooded figure as it darted through the door and into the embrace of the darkness.

"You think you can ambush me in my own lair?" asked a gravelly voice. "You're welcome to try," it hissed, and then came a distinctive sound, one that Wesley recognized as that of flesh being peeled apart.

Suddenly he knew exactly what was happening and who it was they now faced. Zeke. And that sound . . . the Miquot had the ability to produce organic knife blades from the flesh of their forearms. Wesley dove through the ocean of black—

"Everybody down," he heard himself bellow as the hiss of a razor-sharp dagger passed his head. "Zeke, it's me!" he shouted. "Wesley!"

Abruptly the room was filled with an intense light, as if the sun had suddenly decided to come to life in the basement. Shielding his eyes, Wesley looked upon a glowing sphere that spun and sparked in the air above them. Willow had conjured an illumination spell.

The Miquot demon stood ready, and his ever-present hood had fallen away to reveal his crested, demonic countenance. He was poised to throw another of his arm blades at Gunn.

"It's Wesley," he said again, climbing to his feet, reaching out to the demon. "They're with me—please, put the blade down."

It took a moment, but a spark of recognition gradually replaced the look of fury in the demon's dark eyes, and he lowered his weapon.

"Friend Wesley," he said in a breathless whisper. "I thought you were one of them—the killers who have begun to hunt in the night."

The others slowly drew closer.

"No, but we come with news about those very same killers," Wesley said to Zeke as the Miquot went to the door, checking outside before closing it.

"The streets are stained with the blood of half-breeds," Zeke said. "What can you tell me of those who are responsible?"

"A Brachen, who happens to be the father of your old friend Doyle, is leading a coalition of bloodthirsty soldiers on a crusade to eradicate impure demon races."

"Doyle's father," the Miquot said with disbelief, staring off into space, his hand slowly pulling up the hood of his sweatshirt.

"We have information that leads us to believe that the inhabitants of your island—Questral—may be in grave danger."

"Questral?" Calvin piped up. "What's . . . oh, so that's its real name."

The demon swiftly moved past them toward the old mattress in the far corner. "Although I have just returned," Zeke said, "I must get back to the island at once to warn them." He produced a duffel bag from somewhere beneath the mattress and began to fill it with items from his living space. "If what you say is true, there is little time." There was a calm intensity in the demon's voice.

"Axtius has raised an army," Wesley said grimly. "The people of the island won't stand a chance against them."

The demon stopped his packing and gazed at him. "What choice do we have?" he asked.

"If you can stand a little company," Willow said, raising her hand to draw the glowing energy sphere back to her, "you won't be going back to the island alone."

CHAPTER ELEVEN

Angel was in pain. Nothing like what he had felt earlier, of course, but his whole body stung. Every time he moved, the still-healing burns sent sharp splinters into his flesh that went down bone deep. The only consolation he had for his pain was that he knew Spike would be feeling it too.

Wesley and Cordelia had taken off for what they were all calling Monster Island, with Spike, Willow, Xander, and Lorne in tow. Now Angel drove stiffly along the Los Angeles backstreets—the dangerous neighborhoods that most of the traffic avoided—heading for the warehouse Gunn's crew still used as their main base of operations. Some of the streetlights were out, and there wasn't much by way of typical L.A. neon in this neighborhood, but what illumination there was striated the hood and windshield of the convertible.

The lights washed over Buffy where she sat in the passenger

seat, casting a golden glow upon her face for a moment before throwing her into shadow once more, only to begin again. The effect gave her the look of some old-time Hollywood starlet, and she was just as radiant.

Just drive the car, Angel chided himself.

With a smile that pained him as the skin at the edges of his lips crackled, he forced his gaze back to the road. Fred was in the backseat, along with Tara. Though Angel had met Willow's girlfriend before, he still was not sure what to make of her. On the outside was a kind of vulnerability that made him want to protect her, a classic damsel in distress, and yet, he sensed something resonating inside her, a steely resolve that told him that when put to the test, she might well be as strong-willed as any of them.

Stronger, even.

The combination of Tara and Fred, in whom Angel had sensed a similar internal power upon first meeting her, was odd, to say the least. Fred would mutter something that seemed nonsensical to Angel and Buffy, up in front, but in back, Tara would smile and say, "I know" with a certain inflection that made Angel wonder if the two weren't communicating telepathically. Not that he thought they were, but the women seemed to have formed an instant bond.

The headlights in Angel's rearview mirror belonged to Gunn's truck. He and Calvin were following behind, more to keep the teenager away from the rest of them in case something should happen than because they couldn't have squeezed in together.

Angel turned left along a one-way street that was little more than an alley. His own headlights splashed across a Dumpster and a bunch of broken wooden palettes. A police car was pulled up to a loading dock on the left, but it was empty and dark.

"James Ellroy, eat your heart out," Buffy said.

"You read James Ellroy?" Angel asked, raising an eyebrow as he shot Buffy a sidelong glance.

"I might," she replied, not looking at him. After a moment, a sweet smile came to her face. "Okay. I saw *L.A. Confidential.* Watched the extras on the DVD."

"Not much time for reading in this line of work," Angel observed, trying to reassure her.

"No," Buffy sadly agreed. "No, there isn't."

They were quiet after that. Tara and Fred continued their shorthand conversation of half-sentences and knowing mutterings, but Buffy and Angel had nothing else to say to each other at the moment. The truth was they had nothing else to say to each other ever. Ever. Forever. Once they got beyond "good to see you" and "how are you?" their conversations seemed to trail off into the ether. Neither of them wanted to get into painful territory or to repeat the grave conclusions they had come to about why their destinies were simply not entwined.

But Angel still felt it, and he knew Buffy did too. They were good together. They fit. Together they were simply deadly.

"Here we are," Angel said as he pulled the convertible up to the curb at the rear of the warehouse where Gunn's crew hung out. He glanced at Buffy, then back at Tara. "Follow Gunn's lead on this. Most of the traps set out are for vampires, but his friends don't take kindly to uninvited visitors even when they're human."

"Real social butterflies, huh?" Buffy replied.

She didn't wait for an answer, just leaped out of the convertible without using the door. Fred and Tara followed quickly enough, and by the time Angel had opened and closed his door—figuring that someone ought to—Gunn and Calvin had parked the truck and caught up with them.

"How we doin'?" Gunn asked, looking from Angel to Buffy.

"Following your lead," Buffy replied.

Gunn nodded, turning to Calvin. "You stick with me."

Calvin blew air out of his mouth in a noise of dismissal. "Gunn, you been out of the neighborhood a while. They my boys too. No one's gonna come down on me."

The teenager started toward the back door of the warehouse, and Gunn reached out and snatched the back of his shirt, hauling him backward. "Maybe not on purpose, Calvin. But you go in that door right now, the rest of us'll be hosing your remains off the pavement."

The kid's eyes went wide. Angel tried not to smile.

"After you," Tara said, gesturing for Gunn to lead them.

Gunn shook his head in mock disgust at Calvin and headed off to the left, along the back of the warehouse, away from the booby-trapped doors. A huge metal fire escape was attached to the rear of the building but came down only to a place about a dozen feet above the ground. There were no streetlights on this stretch of road, or if there had been they had been broken. But Angel's night vision was better than a human's and he could see that up in the scaffolding of the fire escape there was another ladder, an extension ladder that had been painted black and was not a part of the original structure.

From his pocket Gunn withdrew a small flip phone. He punched in a sequence of numbers and clapped it to his ear. "It's Gunn," he said. "Sweet Christmas."

He closed the phone and slipped it back into his pocket. Angel watched him carefully, bemused, and when Gunn looked up he just had to ask, "Sweet Christmas?"

"Just something a guy from the neighborhood used to say. Guy we all looked up to," Gunn explained. "It's this week's password. 'Course they'll change it now when they realize you've all heard it."

"Password for what?" Fred asked.

Angel glanced over at her and saw her studying the face of the building, mystified. She clearly hadn't noticed the other ladder. Tara had moved up beside Buffy, understandably more comfortable beside a friend should danger present itself.

With a ratcheting of gears, the black-painted extension ladder began to lower itself toward the ground.

"Whoa," Calvin uttered.

"Gotta like it," Buffy observed. She glanced at Gunn. "Motor and chain for a garage door opener?"

Gunn looked surprised. "Yeah."

"You boys have a nice clubhouse. Can girls join?" the Slayer inquired.

"Not a lot of playing in this clubhouse," Gunn replied grimly. "But yeah, there's women in the crew too. Girls, even. We all got something to fight for."

"Do they ever feel like you abandoned them?" Tara asked. "Working with . . ."

Her words trailed off as though she had suddenly realized where her train of thought was taking her. Tara flushed a bit, but Buffy gave her an encouraging look.

Gunn glanced at Angel before answering. "I guess they do. Keep tryin' to tell them I got a chance to step up to the Majors, fight our fight on a whole other level. Sometimes I think they get it. Sometimes I know they don't."

The ladder touched down, the gears grinding to a halt. Gunn reached out to steady it and ushered Calvin up first. He glanced pointedly at Angel. "You go last. You know you make them skittish, especially with that nasty-ass sunburn."

Angel nodded and waited patiently as Gunn, Buffy, Fred, and Tara preceded him. When they had all scrambled up the extension ladder and were mounting the metal stairs of the real fire escape, the sound of the chain and the gears began again and the ladder began to rise. By reflex, Angel looked beneath him to make absolutely certain nothing had followed them up the ladder.

Only the shadows below.

When he reached the roof he was met with the mouth of a blowtorch, spitting blue fire at him with a hiss. He froze at the top of the fire escape. Beyond the blowtorch and the grim-faced, one-eyed, twentyish man holding it, he saw Buffy, Gunn, and the others all standing with Calvin and a couple of guys from Gunn's crew he recognized.

He chose to ignore the blowtorch, climbing the rest of the way to the roof, physically forcing One-Eye to either burn him or back off. The grim young man took several steps back, but still watched Angel warily. The vampire did not blame him; nearly every one among Gunn's crew—or what had once been Gunn's crew—had lost loved ones to vampires. It was only natural for them to be suspicious.

"So," Angel said, shooting Gunn a dark look, "if we're done with all the welding, why don't we see what we've got?"

Gunn glanced at the two men he had been speaking with, then gestured toward the door on top of the warehouse that led down inside the building. Tara and Fred followed Gunn and Calvin down the stairs. Angel hesitated a moment, but it appeared Mr. Blowtorch and his two friends were going to stay topside, so he and Buffy followed the others.

"Gunn's friends are a little jumpy," Buffy whispered to him as they went down through the metal-and-concrete stairwell.

"One way to put it," Angel agreed.

At the bottom there was a door that led onto the floor of the warehouse. Gunn rapped hard on it three times and waited for it to be opened. When it was, they all stepped into a vast, poorly lit section of the building where cars were being worked on and racks of weapons lined the walls. Various members of the crew were out on the floor working on various projects, and Angel spotted a young priest in a white collar amongst them. That was new, but he was not surprised. Faith was a powerful weapon against vampires, against evil. Why not recruit someone who could wield it?

From across the warehouse floor came a phalanx of half a dozen members of the crew, led by a diminutive, dangerous-looking Latina woman. She went immediately to Calvin and gave him a big hug, kissing him the way a mother or older sister might. But when she looked up from the teenager, she was all business. "Gunn," the woman said, "we expected you earlier."

"We got a lot going on, Lucinda."

The woman, Lucinda, glanced dubiously at Fred, Tara, and Buffy. Angel could read the doubt in her expression. He figured a woman her size ought to know better than to judge the value of a combatant by his or her appearance, but he chose to say nothing—particularly given the sneer on her face when she finally looked at him, carefully studying the places on his face and hands that were still burned from his close call with the sun.

"Yeah. So do we," Lucinda sniffed. Then she looked at Gunn. "Only reason we're going along with this is 'cause if it's as big as you say, it'll affect us all."

"That's for sure," Fred said, her voice low.

Lucinda glared at her, stepped over, and looked her up and down. "You this 'Vampire Slayer' I keep hearing about?"

Fred's eyes went wide, and then she looked at the ground. "Oh, gosh, no. Not me."

The woman glanced at Tara, but only for a moment before her gaze settled on Buffy.

"Yeah," Buffy said. "Me."

"You don't look like much," Lucinda said doubtfully.

Buffy defiantly locked eyes with her. "Neither do you."

For a long time they just stared at each other. Concerned, Angel glanced at Gunn to see if they should intervene, but Gunn gave an almost imperceptible shake of his head. At length, Lucinda smiled and nodded.

"All right, then. Why don't you all come have a look at our guest," Lucinda said, turning to lead them back the way she had come, across the floor of the warehouse, past all the others who worked on various projects there. "We've got some information out of him that might be helpful, and I think we're not too far away from getting the rest."

"You're already working on this?" asked Angel.

Lucinda only laughed.

Gunn glanced back at Angel. "They've *been* working on it. Had a little more luck than you did."

"Well, there's a lot more of them," Buffy said helpfully.

One of the other members of the crew, who had fallen behind, snorted in derision. "And we don't have to hide from the sun."

"There's that," Gunn agreed.

Angel said nothing. These people might not answer to Gunn anymore, but they had still developed into their own little anti-supernatural army, right there in the dark heart of Los Angeles. It was impressive, and a little unnerving.

Lucinda led them to a trailer truck that looked as though it hadn't run in years and had long since been abandoned. The crew had use for the trailer, apparently, for there was a pair of guards with axes standing beside the rear doors of the huge metal box.

"We checked all our sources," Lucinda said. "And we weren't real polite about it. Came up with this guy."

At a nod from the woman, one of the two guards unlocked the rear doors of the trailer and pulled them open. Inside, the place was empty save for a metal chair to which had been chained a Lei-Ach demon. Angel had not seen one in years.

"Hey," Buffy said. "I've seen this species before." She frowned, turning to Lucinda. "But they don't speak English. How did you get any information—"

"Bite me, you filthy bitch," the Lei-Ach demon snarled.

Tara actually flinched at the words. "Apparently this one's learned the language."

Buffy glared at it. "Reminds me why I killed them all the first time I ran into them."

The Lei-Ach, its face gray and leathery, mottled as if with disease, snaked out its long black tongue, and made obscene noises with it. Fred blushed slightly and looked away, but Angel studied it more closely. The Lei-Ach had been severely beaten. Its left leg was broken above the knee and was already badly swollen. There were severe burns on its chest and neck, and all of the fingers on its right hand had been shattered. They were mangled and bloody, edges of broken bone jutting out from the skin.

"Who did this to it?" Angel asked.

Lucinda raised an eyebrow. "I did. Why, you soft on these freaks?"

Angel studied the brutalized demon. "Given that they're mainly known for sucking the bone marrow out of their victims, I'm not inclined to care much. Just wondering if it was necessary."

"It's horrible," Tara spoke up.

Fred took a timid step forward, her gaze ticking from the tortured Lei-Ach to Lucinda. "Isn't there another way to do this?"

"Maybe," Lucinda admitted. "But none that I know, and we've got a time crunch, anyway, don't we?"

"What's wrong with you guys?" Calvin asked. He had been quiet since they had arrived, tagging along but not making a nuisance of himself. Now they all turned to look at him, and the kid had a grim, dark look on his face, his eyes narrowed. "It's a demon. You heard Angel. It kills people and eats their bone marrow. It's evil, and you're gonna cry over it?"

"Well, I wouldn't put it that way," Tara replied awkwardly.

"Nobody's crying," Fred said.

Gunn rapped his knuckles on the metal wall of the trailer. "It's a monster. And there's a whole army of 'em out there, with plans that include us only if we're on the menu. End of story."

"Can't argue with that logic," Buffy said.

"All right," Angel agreed. He turned to Lucinda. "So what have you learned?"

Lucinda stared in at the Lei-Ach demon, which began to curse loudly in its own language as well as in English.

"This general—Axtius? His assault team is ready. Demon troops just waiting to go. Even our friend here wasn't sure how many he's got," Lucinda said, gesturing at the bleeding, mangled Lei-Ach. "They're headed out to some island. Couldn't get much more than that. Gonna slaughter everyone there, and that's just their first stop."

Buffy glanced over at Angel and he saw a familiar gleam in her eye.

"Okay. Maybe we can't stop him going there. There's only a few of us and a whole lot of them. But we've gotta be able to slow him down so we can prepare the islanders. Any idea exactly how Axtius was planning to transport this huge army across the ocean?"

Lucinda's eyes darkened. "I asked. He wouldn't say."

"We need to know," Tara said. "Willow's out there. We have to buy her some time."

Lucinda put her hands on her hips and shot Tara a hard look. "Well, we could maybe find out, but I wouldn't wanna hurt your gentle sensitivities by damaging the marrow-sucking homicidal demon anymore."

Before Tara could respond, Calvin stormed toward the rear of the trailer. "Hell, let me do it!" the teenager snapped.

Gunn grabbed him and held him back. Angel saw the discomfort in Fred's eyes and in the way Tara stood, uncertain, knowing what had to be done but not wanting any part of it.

"Give me a minute," Angel said.

He stepped inside the trailer and reached back to close the doors behind him. Buffy grabbed the door, holding it open so that she could enter with him. Their eyes met, and Angel stepped aside to let her go first, then he shut the doors nearly all the way, letting only a small sliver of light in but blocking out any view of their friends and comrades.

The vitriolic demon laughed and swore at them.

Two minutes later it told them that Axtius had engaged a huge freighter called the *Marianne* to take his troops across to the island.

"So that's our next step," Buffy said quietly, gazing at Angel over the silent, sulking, bloody form of the chained demon. "We sink his boat. Could be fun."

Questral

The fishing boat rocked with the surf as its captain piloted it toward Monster Island. Zeke had assured them all that the man, whom they had been introduced to only as Captain Hobbs, was reliable. Apparently Hobbs was Zeke's regular ride out to the island, and his loyalty and ability to keep a secret had been proven many times over.

Night had fallen, but before dusk Spike had gone as deep belowdecks as he could get, unnerved apparently by the idea that should he suddenly be exposed to the sun, there would be nowhere for him to run. He had mentioned something about always having bad luck with boats, but he wouldn't elaborate and no one was really interested enough to push him to do so. Now that it was dark, the vampire had still not emerged, but nobody seemed terribly interested in waking him from his nap.

Cordelia and Wesley were deep in conversation with Zeke in the main cabin, but Willow had gotten queasy down there. All she wanted was some fresh air, the starlit sky above her, and the spray of the ocean as the fishing boat cut the waves.

Willow felt strange being away from Tara. As much as her girlfriend would have chided her for worrying, she could not dispel the anxiety that lingered in her mind. She didn't like being apart from Tara, especially in a situation like this. If they were going to face danger, Willow thought they should face it together. At least, that was how she would have explained it to Tara. The truth was slightly different. She didn't want Tara facing any danger at all, ever, but if it was unavoidable, Willow wanted to make sure she was there when it happened.

"Worried for your lady love?" a kind voice whispered beside her.

Lorne stood beside her, gazing at Willow with those gentle eyes, and she smiled at him and nodded. It would be no use, she sensed, attempting to shield her feelings from him; even without the singing, Lorne could see right inside people.

"She'll be all right," the green-skinned demon assured her. "She's got Angel, Gunn, and your Slayer friend with her. Not to worry. They'll take care of her."

Willow smiled. "I know. But I want to be the one taking care of her."

Xander had been talking to Hobbs, who had given him a turn at the helm of the boat, but when Willow wasn't looking he had joined her on deck.

"Gotta say, pretty sure your witchy woman can take care of herself," he said, smiling as he sat down on top of a cooler full of Hobbs's beer. "Sure, she's a sweet girl, but also, one tough cookie. A chocolate-chip cookie. Sweet. Tough. See where I'm going with the snack metaphor?"

"Completely," Willow agreed.

"Sounds to me like you're hungry," Lorne noted.

Willow laughed. "Xander's always hungry."

A moment passed when the three of them simply gazed out at the ocean, searching the dark horizon for some sign of the island that was their destination. Then Xander broke the silence.

"So, Mr. Greenjeans," he said to Lorne, "any thoughts on the whole train-the-islanders-to-defend-themselves scheme, other than that it seems to work perfectly well in old Western movies?"

Lorne raised an eyebrow. "Don't look at me, handsome. I'm still not quite sure how Angel sweet-talked me into this one."

"It wasn't Angel," Willow reminded him. "It was Cordelia. Besides, we're all here for a reason. Wesley has the book learnin'. Cordelia knows some of these people from saving their lives before, so that's gotta help. Zeke's our ambassador. I'm mojo girl. Spike's muscle, and maybe some nasty strategy the rest of us are too nice to think of."

"And if you left him behind, Gunn might have killed him," Lorne noted.

"Oh, the tears we would not have shed," Xander muttered.

Willow pointed to Lorne. "You're our semi-seer and all-pro demon language translator. And Xander's still got all that magickal military training bouncing around in the back of his head, so he's gotta have some soldier thinking going on there."

The demon's eyes widened, and he turned to look at Xander, the moonlight glinting off his horns. "Military?"

"Long story. Magick. Halloween. Army man memories. Complicated," Xander said. "But better than eating school mascots."

"Ooh-hoh, okay, amigo and amiga," Lorne said, holding up his hands with a smile. "My mind made absolutely no sense of that, but I get the feeling it doesn't want to."

Willow stood up and went to the prow, gazing off across the ocean but seeing nothing. "What about the island?" she asked. "I don't see anything on the horizon at all. It's magick, isn't it? A shielding spell."

"According to our new playmate, Ezekiel, that's exactly right," Lorne replied. "And there's a ward that influences boaters and anyone else out on the water to navigate around it without even realizing they're doing it. Kinda nifty, actually. Sometimes I think we'd all like to be that invisible, just for a little while."

There was sadness in his voice, but when Willow glanced at him, Lorne was gazing back intently.

"Not to tell you your business, Red, but I wouldn't be so quick to mark Wesley down only in the knowledge column if I were you. I've seen him kick some big nasty booty once or twice."

Xander snorted. "Wesley? This is Wesley you're talking about?"

Willow smiled. "No offense," she assured Lorne. "But back when Wesley was a watcher, he wasn't exactly all, y'know, Macho Man."

"Ah, another day, another Village People reference," Lorne said, eyes twinkling. "Now I can go to sleep happy tonight.

Seriously, though, don't count our bespectacled British friend out. He might not come off as much of an action hero, but he's got the chops, especially when Angel's not around to lead the charge."

The demon stood and stretched, yawning, apparently having no difficulty staying on his feet despite the pitching of the boat on the water. As Willow watched him, the night seemed to sparkle around the fishing boat, and the vessel shuddered as if snagged on something. Then the clear night was transformed into a thick, glistening mist.

"Did I ever mention how I hate magick?" Xander asked, clutching at his stomach, apparently nauseated from the passage through the sorcerous wards protecting the island.

Zeke bounded up onto the deck, his lemon skin strangely complementing the lime of Lorne's. The Miquot demon strode across the fishing boat so quickly that he had reached the prow before Wesley and Cordelia emerged from the cabin.

"There it is," Zeke said, his voice husky with emotion. "Questral."

"Questral?" Willow asked, as Xander and Lorne joined her and Zeke at the front of the boat, all of them admiring the view of the lights of the harbor ahead.

"My home," Zeke replied. He glanced at Willow, smiling. "You call it 'Monster Island.'"

There was very little talk amongst them as Hobbs navigated the boat through the waters of the harbor. Willow was filled with an almost childlike excitement, and her mind whirled with thoughts about Monster Island—Questral. Here was a civilization made up entirely of nonhumans. In the midst of the twenty-first century, off the coast of one of the largest cities in America, an entire island filled with demons of all breeds, a bizarre utopia, a melting pot of the kind that America had been meant to be once upon a time.

Benevolent demons, and perhaps some who were not so benevolent but who had surrendered their hatreds and enmities for the dream of peaceful coexistence. It was truly a marvel.

The fishing boat drew closer, and Willow could see more details. The village that spread out behind the harbor was a patchwork of architectural styles. There were dwellings that were similar to human houses clustered in one place, and a series of treetop structures that must have belonged to a specific demon tribe in another. To the north was a grouping of huts such as one might have found in Southeast Asia, and to the south what appeared to be enormous anthills jutting from the earth, undoubtedly the home of some underground species.

In the center of the harbor village, where all of these sorts of living arrangements seemed to have been gathered in an extraordinary, almost surreal town square, electric lampposts shared space with blazing torches. Willow imagined there must be at least a few shops and restaurants, supplying the denizens of Monster Island with goods and services.

Despite the horrifying enormity of all of this existing here— a kind of microcosm of all of the demonic species and subspecies that roamed the world in secret—she felt her heart swell with wonder.

Hobbs carefully brought them up alongside a dock, where Zeke leaped off and grabbed a mooring line to tie up the boat. Xander dropped to the dock and gave him a hand, tying off the aft of the vessel. Willow was transfixed by the view she'd had of the island as they came in, but now the harbor itself and some of the small, thatched buildings nearby kept her from seeing much more. She was particularly interested in those anthill-like dwellings, but knew that her curiosity had to be put on hold for now. They were here to help the islanders, not to study them.

"It's beautiful," Lorne said.

"It is," Cordelia agreed, as the rest of them began to climb down to join Xander and Zeke on the dock.

"Oh, sure," Xander added. "Until they eat us."

"Thank you for your uplifting outlook," Wesley chided him. "I for one find it all fascinating. I'm wondering, also, if that mountainous area beyond the main village is volcanic. There might be something we can do with that, defense-wise."

Willow had barely noticed the mountain—really more of a large hill—that loomed above the lush, tropical forest of Questral. Now she saw that Wesley was right. There was likely to be some way to put the terrain here to their advantage when Axtius's attack came. But they would need time.

It was good, though, that they were already thinking along those lines. Wesley was already thinking ahead, planning and strategizing. Willow found that she was having less trouble than she had expected thinking of him as the de facto leader of this expedition.

Her thoughts were interrupted by shouts from the end of the dock. A pair of small demons of the same species—each with six Kali-esque arms and four eyes that glowed red in the dark— were coming toward them, gesticulating wildly with their many upper limbs. A third hung back on the wharf. It threw back its head and loosed an ululating cry that Willow was certain was some kind of alarm.

"Goody, the Welcome Wagon," Xander said, sighing.

The two six-armed demons rushed forward, and Zeke stepped out in front to greet them. They were agitated and began to shout at him in a language that seemed all glottal stops and spitting. Zeke argued with them in a rough approximation of their own language, gesturing wildly toward Willow and the others.

"What are they?" Willow asked.

"Bazhripa," Lorne replied by her side. He touched her elbow politely so that he could slip by her.

"Lorne!" Cordelia called, only to find him already moving past her and Wesley to join Zeke in conversation with the two Bazhripa.

Meanwhile, the screaming of the third one had already begun to gather a large crowd. Willow felt a chill sweep through her as she watched their numbers increase, and for the first time since they landed she had a real sense that if things went poorly, they might well have put their lives in peril just coming here, however noble their intentions.

Amongst the gathering crowd she saw a multitude of varying demon breeds, things with horns and fins, with many eyes and no eyes. There were Durslar Beasts and Skench demons, a Vahrall or two, and so many other things that Willow recognized from research but couldn't put a name to. Serpentine things and tiny things that might have been porcupines if not that they were armed. They came in every color and size, and had horns and fangs, tusks and antlers.

There were monstrous things that looked as though they might have crawled out of the deepest ocean trench, skittering things that once had lurked beneath the beds of human children. So many breeds had gathered there.

And they all looked pissed.

The gathering of demons remained at the wharf's edge, horrified spectators to the unfolding drama of Zeke and Lorne trying to reason with the furious, six-armed Bazhripa. Willow and Xander moved closer to Cordelia.

"What are they saying? Any idea?" Willow asked.

Cordelia shot her a frustrated glance. "No clue. Can you whip up some hocus pocus, nice light show, maybe scare off the locals so we can have a calmer conversation here?"

Willow thought about it. It wouldn't have been difficult, but she doubted, somehow, that most of these creatures would be frightened by a little magick, and a little magick was all she could manage without hurting someone. "I don't think that's a good idea," she said.

"Decidedly not," Wesley agreed. "We've got to be very careful here. We need these people to trust us."

Cordelia grabbed Lorne by the arm. "Hey! Could we get a little info back here? What's going on?"

"What do you think?" Lorne sighed. "Zeke isn't exactly supposed to be bringing tourists to the island. Especially human tourists."

"Tourists?" Xander snapped. "They think we're here for the *fun* of it?"

"They don't want us here at all," Wesley said, "but they do need us. Zeke, can you and Lorne try to explain to them—"

"We're trying!" Zeke said, but the six-armed demons seemed only to become more agitated. On the wharf, many more had gathered. They were all jockeying for a decent view of the goings-on.

"Okay. Enough of this. We don't have time for screwing around," Cordelia said. She grabbed Lorne by the hand and shot a glance back at Willow. "Come with me."

Though the Bazhripa tried to stop her, Cordelia marched down the dock until she was face-to-face with the gathered islanders, Lorne and Willow alongside her.

"Translate," she said, tapping Lorne on the arm.

Then she smiled at the islanders, and Willow recognized that smile. It was her radiant Homecoming Queen candidate smile, the smile she probably had used for auditions when she first came down to L.A. in search of an acting career.

"Citizens of Questral Island," she said. "My associates and I wish you no harm. We come, unfortunately, with pretty darn bad news, but we are here as friends, to offer what help we can."

Lorne quickly translated what she had said, and the crowd quieted down instantly. Willow stood up straighter, trying to look as impressive as she could manage without any actual magick. The truth was she didn't feel very impressive, but she figured if Cordelia could act all regal, she could too. She'd done the talent show back in high school, after all, and okay, sure, she had run off the stage, but she could act for thirty seconds without fleeing. She hoped.

Wesley made his way up until he was just behind Cordelia. "She speaks true," he said. "We are friends. We wish to speak with the august Assemblage who govern your island on a matter most dire."

There was a pause. Some of the demons undoubtedly spoke English, unlike the Bazhripa who had at first accosted Zeke— and who now stood back warily, ready to attack if any of them should make even a threatening gesture.

Then from behind the crowd of demons who watched them, these vulnerable newcomers there on the dock, came a deep, rasping voice, like the creaking of ancient, rusted hinges.

"And who, may I ask, are you?"

Instantly a path appeared in the mass of demons. They scrambled aside as quickly as possible to make way for the being who approached the wharf now, whose terrible voice had carried across the land and the dock and out over the water.

"Dai'shu," Zeke whispered hurriedly as the tall demon stepped down onto the wharf. "Yill demon. He's a member of the Assemblage. And a sorcerer."

And a sorcerer. Willow turned that over in her head a moment as she studied the new arrival. Dai'shu wore robes so long, they dragged on the ground as he walked. His torso was impossibly long, his legs and arms somewhat truncated, and his face was grotesque, the skin tugged obscenely back by a crown of spines that jutted from his scalp backward. The Yill were apparently hairless, but these spines—eight or nine all told— jutted back from Dai'shu's bald pate in a strange approximation of windblown hair. There was something unspeakable about them, and Willow tried not to stare.

"My name is Wesley Wyndam-Pryce," the former Watcher said, stepping forward only to then move aside and bow toward Cordelia. "And this is Cordelia Chase, the Princess of Pylea."

A rumble of mutterings went through the crowd. Then a trio of demons who were humanoid save the hideousness of their features pushed out of the onlookers. One of them, a female who appeared to be the oldest, called out to Dai'shu.

"She is!" the female declared. "I recognize her. I know not if she's a princess, but she is Cordelia Chase. They saved my family, saved all my tribe!"

Dai'shu peered at Cordelia through slitted eyes. In the illumination cast by the torches and streetlamps of the harbor village it was difficult to tell, but Willow thought that his eyes might have been glowing a dim blue. With that hideous, stretched-out face bent forward to study them all, the sorcerer seemed to float along the dock toward Cordelia.

"Is this true, Princess of Pylea?"

Before Cordelia could reply, a loud groan could be heard from behind them on the dock. Willow whipped her head around in alarm only to see Spike standing shirtless on the deck of the fishing boat, angry burn scars still visible on his white flesh. He was obviously freshly woken from sleep. Rubbing at his eyes he glanced at the enormous gathering of demons and the tall, monstrous sorcerer who loomed over Cordelia.

Spike sniffed and looked down his nose at Dai'shu as if he had just smelled something awful. "What's all this, then?" he asked.

With a roar, the Bazhripa warriors rushed at the fishing boat in a fit of rage, screaming a single word in their guttural language. Up on the wharf the menagerie of demon clans and tribes began to shout, some of them fleeing back toward the village and others moving onto the dock. Dai'shu's eyes were wide, and his face became even more grotesque as he sneered at them.

Willow felt a powerful hand on her arm, and she was spun around to face Zeke, who held her tight, his features very cruel up close like that, the fin on his head a golden color in the moonlight.

"A vampire!" Zeke snarled. "He's a vampire?"

"Is that what they're yelling?" Willow asked.

"He's a vampire?" Zeke roared again.

Willow shrugged. "Yeah?"

"Damn you!" Zeke said. "Why did no one tell me? Vampires are banned from Questral upon penalty of death should anyone allow them. They are the *only* banned demonic race. They have no conscience and cannot be trusted. They're going to execute us all!"

"That's wishful thinking, buttercup," Lorne said. "They're not going to wait for anything so formal as an execution."

Wesley and Cordelia backed up, and Xander rushed forward so that they were all grouped together there on the dock as the demons rushed in to surround them, brandishing weapons and shouting threats and curses in a hundred languages.

"Oh crap," Xander whispered in Willow's ear.

Dai'shu began to float, eyes glowing a fiery blue, and he raised his hands and shouted an order to the crowd.

"Tear the intruders apart and bring me their eyes to eat."

CHAPTER TWELVE

Los Angeles

On board the ship *Marianne,* Angel reached from a concealing pool of darkness and yanked the two pureblood demons into
the inky shadows with nary a sound. Beside him in the dark corner, Buffy pulled one of the startled demons toward her and
snapped its neck with cold efficiency. Angel did the same to his
captive, and they lowered the corpses silently to the metal deck.

"Anyone else here seriously grossed out by that sound?"
Gunn asked from behind Angel.

"What sound?" Angel said in a whisper, checking fore and aft
before emerging from the patch of shadows and heading
toward a stairwell that led down into the ship's main cargo hold.

"I didn't hear any sound," Buffy whispered, falling in behind
Angel.

"Nice to know you can keep that special sense of humor even during these high pressure moments," Gunn muttered as he followed them down into the cool darkness of the ship's innards.

At the foot of the rusted metal stairs, Angel motioned for them to stop. He crouched, listening to the sounds of the ship: the faint creak of old iron and steel as the freighter languidly bobbed in dock, the skittering of rats along her decks, the muffled sounds of demons they had yet to encounter somewhere in the distance. Confident that it was safe to proceed, he motioned for them to follow him to another set of steps descending farther into the ship's bowels.

Before he had even begun the gesture, Buffy was past him, taking point. He smiled to himself. It had been too long since they had done something like this—something so dangerous—together. Usually he was the one to lead the way, to take the biggest risks, to call the shots. But no way was Buffy going to wait for him to do that. Nobody called the shots for Buffy Summers.

"This just keeps on getting bigger and badder, doesn't it?" she whispered as Gunn joined them in the hold.

Angel gazed about at the crates stacked around them inside the hold. Supplies for troops going to war, he imagined as his eyes scanned the lists of contents stenciled on the many boxes.

"It's all so well organized," he said softly, moving farther into the hold amongst the crates. "Also pretty disturbing that we haven't heard about any of it before now." He motioned to the crates and the ship around him. "Something like this takes time and planning. We should have had some idea—"

"Shoulda, coulda, woulda," Buffy whispered. "No sense in beating yourself up. We're here now, and we're going to stop it."

Gunn stepped up beside them, carefully removing his backpack. He knelt beside the pack and unzipped it, then cautiously reached inside and slowly withdrew its deadly contents.

"Where did you say your crew got that again?" Buffy asked him.

"It fell off the back of a truck," Gunn replied as he gently placed a large block of C4 plastic explosive on the deck.

Angel imagined that his own expression of disbelief matched the look on Buffy's face.

"No, really," Gunn said, removing the detonators and makeshift timer from the pack. "A box of the stuff fell off a construction truck at the beginning of the year. We've been saving it for a special occasion," he said with a big smile as he peeled away the plastic sheath covering the C4 and began to break off pieces of the explosive.

"Something tells me I'd hate to be in your neighborhood on the Fourth of July," Buffy said, watching the man as he began to set up the explosive charges for placement.

Angel walked slowly around the hold and stopped at the slightly curved wall of the ship. "Here," he said, looking at Gunn. He placed his hand against the cool metal seam, letting his fingers fall across the vertical line of rivets. He could almost feel the patient power of the ocean outside just waiting for its opportunity to enter. "Set the first charge here."

Gunn showed them each how to insert the detonators and set the simple digital timers. Then they placed the explosives where they would do the most damage to the belly of the ship and send it to the bottom of the harbor.

"Think we've left ourselves enough time?" Buffy asked as the three quickly walked to the stairs that would take them back above.

As Buffy and Gunn began to climb the stairs, Angel stopped and glanced over his shoulder at the red digital readouts. They had a little more than six minutes.

They reached the next level without incident and quietly

crept to the second stairwell that would take them above deck. They continued their stealthy climb, Angel thinking of Tara, Fred, and Calvin waiting in the car.

"Hope nobody's gone poking around and found the guards we . . . ," Buffy began in a hushed whisper.

"What was that?" Angel asked quietly. "I didn't catch the last part," he said as he followed Gunn into the darkness on deck—and froze.

Ten of Axtius's soldiers were waiting for them; each armed with a variety of bladed weapons. There were Vahralls and Yuits, and a Doselle with that breed's trademark fanged abdominal maw gaping open, drooling bloody spittle.

Gunn chuckled dryly as he eyed the demons and tensed for a fight. "She said she hoped no one found any of the guards we killed."

Side by side, Angel and Buffy settled into combat stances, and a wave of familiarity swept through Angel. He could feel his connection to her, the way they worked together so perfectly in battle.

"Seems like old times," Angel said.

Buffy nodded, but she pulled up the sleeve of her denim jacket and tapped at her wrist where a watch would have been if she had worn one. Time was growing dangerously short.

Calvin didn't want to admit it, but half of him wished he had stayed back in the neighborhood. He had never understood the concept of stress until he'd started hanging out with Gunn and his whacked new friends. Here he was hiding with shy-girl Tara and the totally hot Fred behind a forklift stacked with wooden pallets, waiting for Gunn, Angel, and Buffy to return.

He looked down at the battle-ax clutched in his hands. *A battle-ax,* he thought with amazement. Never in a million years had he imagined the world was as complicated and dangerous as this. Peeking out at the freighter *Marianne,* he silently wished that parents would stop lying to their children. Monsters were real, and if you weren't careful—they'd get you, sure as hell.

"What's taking them so long?" he hissed, squeezing the shaft of the ax in his grip. "Maybe we should—"

"Maybe we should relax and wait for them to return," Tara said in what he thought was supposed to be a calming voice. It would take a lot more than calming voices to bring him down tonight.

"They're late," he muttered.

"Not yet they aren't," Fred said, moving up beside him to catch a look at the ship. "Not for another five minutes or so."

She touched his arm and gave it a gentle squeeze, and for a moment he actually did feel a bit calmer—but then came the sounds of screeching brakes and racing truck engines. Two pickup trucks, their open backs loaded with the unmistakable shapes of demon soldiers, had come around the corner and were speeding down the wharf toward the *Marianne.*

"Reinforcements," Fred said as she moved around the forklift to get a better look. "The guys must have been discovered."

"We gotta do something," Calvin snapped, attempting to build up a reserve of courage that would enable him to actually use the weapon he clutched in his hands.

There was a sudden gust of frigid wind that didn't come from the ocean ahead of them, and Calvin turned to see that Tara had moved away from their place of concealment and was now standing in the open.

"What the hell are you doing?" he hissed, looking to Fred for backup.

"I think she's gonna buy us a little more time," Fred replied. Tara stood with her arms outstretched—her mouth was moving very fast, but Calvin couldn't hear the words. An even colder wind whipped about them, and he could have sworn that he saw flakes of snow floating about in the freezing air.

The first truck had come to a screeching halt in front of the gangplank. The witch extended her arms, and the chilling wind that had been swirling around her was propelled toward the first truckload of demons with what sounded like an animal's growl.

It was truly an amazing sight to behold. A mini snowstorm moved with lightning swiftness across the dock and enveloped the entire truck and all its riders with its freezing embrace. Calvin felt a smile of wonder begin to creep across his face as the vehicle's demonic occupants ceased to move, covered by layer upon layer of snow and ice—frozen solid by Tara's powerful magick.

"That was killer," Calvin exclaimed, turning to look at the witch. Then he frowned, concerned, for Tara was pale and she stumbled backward, holding her head. "Are you all right?" he asked as he ran to her side.

"I'm fine," she said in a breathless whisper. "Just a bit of a strain—that's all."

"I don't mean to be ungrateful and all," Fred suddenly said, "but remember there were two trucks."

Calvin glanced back to see the second truck rumbling toward its destination. Tara lowered her head as if nodding off to sleep. She seemed to stay that way for quite a while, and he was tempted to give her a good shake when she raised her head. This time he could hear the words that were coming from her mouth, but they were in a language that he couldn't begin to understand—and from the way they sounded, didn't want to understand. Even her voice sounded different, as if she were speaking in slow motion—underwater.

The second truck was nearly to the gangway that would lead its cargo of demon soldiers on board the *Marianne*. Fred had begun to do a little dance of nervousness, when Tara tossed back her head and screamed. Tendrils of crackling energy flowed from her fingertips toward the demonic soldiers. She slumped to the ground as the sorcerous attack reached its destination. It was as if some gigantic, invisible hand had landed among the demons in the back of the pickup like an angry child swatting aside his toys. The truck veered off to the left, speeding up. The demons roared in alarm, and some of them tried to jump off the bed of the pickup, but they weren't fast enough. The truck was hurled into the harbor, its passengers tumbling out as it crashed to the water.

Tara lay upon the ground, her breathing shallow, exhausted by the strain. "How . . . was that?" she asked, looking up at Calvin through a curtain of sandy blond hair, a tired smile on her face.

He was too stunned by the girl's display of supernatural might to think of a reply, and could only give her the thumbs-up. When he had first figured out that Tara and Willow were girlfriends, Calvin had been fascinated by the two of them. Not just because they were lesbians—he knew plenty of gay people—but because they were lovers *and* witches. He had the idea that there was something powerful about the combination. Now, though, he knew that he was only partially right. Tara and Willow were powerful together, sure, but even individually they were not women to be trifled with.

"I think I see them!" Fred cried.

Calvin moved to stand beside her and, straining his eyes, searched every dark nook and cranny of the freighter until he too saw Gunn and the others, surrounded by some of the nastiest, most monstrous-looking demons yet. "I see 'em too. But we're not the only ones."

• • •

Buffy was always amused by the way nearly every nasty freak and monster she dealt with figured he was going to be the one to tame her, to whip the Slayer. She had met plenty of human guys who had the same attitude toward women, but with demons it was not just limited to gender. Sure, some of them ran away at the merest mention of her name. But too many of them were loaded with so much swagger that they could not help puffing up their chests and thinking about how tough they were, how their reps were going to be made by taking her down.

She was a petite little blonde, how could she possibly be everything the legends said she was?

Idiots.

She launched herself at the ten demon soldiers, very aware of the explosive charges ticking inexorably forward in the hold below them. Buffy went after the two biggest baddies first. They were the ones grinning the widest as she came at them, and thusly the ones that she felt deserved to buy it first. *Victims of their own arrogance,* she thought as she drove a balled fist into the throat of the one on her left, who kind of looked like Babe the pig, only seven feet tall with razor-sharp teeth. She felt his windpipe disintegrate beneath the force of her blow, then yanked away his weapon—a metal staff with a nasty, serrated blade at the end—before his body hit the deck. The Slayer slashed out to her right with the bladed weapon and severed the cobralike head of another demon from its writhing, muscular neck.

Angel and Gunn were trading blows with a Fyarl and a Vahrall, but now all of the surviving demons stopped in their tracks, stunned by the speed with which their comrades had been slain. *Maybe there is something to that reputation after all,* she imagined them thinking now, all nervous.

"Not bad for a little girl, huh?" she said, with a sly smile that told them they were not long for this world.

"Can't let you have all the fun," Gunn said as he drove his fist into the stomach of a Yuit, causing it to pitch forward. A powerful uppercut finished the beast and sent it sprawling onto its back, out cold.

Angel had liberated a sword from one of the other attackers and was moving amongst the troops that remained, cutting a swathe of bloody death for them to follow. The Doselle lunged at him, the fanged maw in its belly gaping wide. The vampire drove the sword into that mouth and tugged the blade up, cracking bone as he sliced the demon in two.

"Let's hustle, kids," he called before hacking off the hand of another Yuit. He finished it with a thrust through the shaggy thing's black heart. "Not much time before the big event."

Buffy and Gunn joined Angel, their backs against the cold, rusted metal of the *Marianne*'s railing.

"How much time you think we got left?" Gunn asked as thunderous footsteps hammered on the deck of the ship and reinforcements began to arrive on either side of them.

"I'd have to say we're pretty much out," Angel replied, gazing fore and aft at Axtius's soldiers.

Buffy gestured toward the expanse of ocean behind them. "After you."

Angel smiled and mimicked her gesture. "No, no, I insist. Ladies first."

She could feel the shuddering vibrations through the floor of the deck as Axtius's men charged. "Always the gentleman," she said, hurling herself over the railing into oblivion.

Angel and Gunn followed right behind her. As the three of them dropped toward the surf below, an explosion rocked the night. The sound was deafening as the explosive charges blew, signaling the death knell for the ancient freighter. The force of the blast was so great that Buffy felt its breath, hot and hungry upon her back, before being enveloped in the chilling, watery embrace of the Pacific.

Questral

It was all about to hit the fan on the Island of Misfit Monsters. Xander looked around at the demons now encircling them. The chattering, multi-limbed Bazhripa were carrying on as if someone had taken away their hand moisturizer, snarling and spitting, thrusting their spears in the gang's general direction. Call it a bizarre sixth sense, but something told him things were not quite going according to plan.

"So what do you think?" he whispered in Willow's ear as the Assemblage's demon sorcerer, Dai'shu, hovered in the air above them, his eyes crackling with a funky blue energy. "Last one to the boat is a Bazhripa's uncle?"

"You might want to step back a bit," the witch said just before beginning an incantation. Her fingers sketched angrily at the air as if she were trying to poke out the eyes of some enemy Xander could not see.

He moved away and stumbled over one of Cordelia's feet.

"Oh great," she muttered, "a broken foot, just in time to run for my life."

Xander was about to reply when Willow bellowed the last of her spell. Her hair was whipped about her head in a sudden gust of wind, and a shock wave of supernatural force exploded from her, propelling the encroaching demons away, scattering them like tenpins.

Cordelia stepped quickly away, Wesley close behind. "Hello! Listen to me," she said, hands outstretched in the universal gesture for everybody to cool their jets. "Let's just everyone take a deep breath and count to ten—we had no idea that vampires are as offensive to you as they are to us."

"I'll show you how bloody offensive I can be," Spike snarled.

Xander turned to see Spike jump from the boat to the dock and rushed forward to cut him off, pushing him back toward the boat. "Maybe you should stay put until we get things straightened out with the locals."

The vampire made a move to get past him, but Xander blocked his way. "Back off, dustball. Maybe you don't understand what's going on right now," he said, looking into Spike's cold, undead eyes. "They want to kill us because of you. Is that sinking into your thick vampire skull?" he asked, thumping him back toward the boat with his chest.

The sky was filled with a sudden flash of blue light and the deafening crack of a thunderbolt. Xander whirled away from Spike to see the sorcerer Dai'shu swooping down toward Willow like some gigantic bat, his robes billowing out like ebony wings, and azure energy jumping from the ends of the spines covering his head. If he wasn't busy being terrified, Xander might have stopped to admire it.

"You say you've come to help against some all-powerful threat, yet you bring that vile, soulless thing to taint our home," Dai'shu's voice boomed as he hung in the air above them. "I think it is you who are the threat!"

The demon sorcerer extended one of his short, stubby arms, and a blast of blue lightning erupted from his fingertips to scorch the wooden pier, narrowly missing Willow, Cordelia, and Wesley.

Willow seemed to be cooking up another blast of mojo when Cordelia again took it upon herself to play peacemaker. *Heaven help us all,* Xander thought as he watched his former girlfriend stride toward the enraged demon sorcerer.

"Maybe we should . . . ," Xander began, but was stopped by a firm grip on his arm. He turned and glared at Spike.

"Hang on there, boy wonder," Spike said with a smirk. "Let's see how the pom-pom queen is at diplomacy."

Cordelia placed her hands on her hips and looked up into the crackling eyes of Dai'Shu. "Look, blue eyes, we didn't want to come here any more than you want us to be here," she said, tapping one booted foot on the still smoldering pier. "But there are a lot of lives at stake, and the Powers That Be have dumped a load of responsibility in our laps—which just so happens to include trying to keep you folks alive."

"You dare to address me in such a manner?" Dai'shu growled, the electricity dancing from spine to spine atop his head growing more intense.

"Listen up, Spanky," Cordelia said, gesturing for the demon to come down. "I know you're upset about the vampire being here—that it's some big taboo deal or something—but we didn't know. We're sorry. Get over it."

The demon reared back as if slapped, and a collective gasp went out from all those present.

It didn't take the demon long to react—but Xander doubted it was the kind of reaction Cordelia had been looking for.

"Insolent human!" the sorcerer shrieked as he raised both of his malformed arms. Crackling energy leaked from his fingertips as he pointed his glowing hands at Cordelia. "You shall be the first to suffer!"

"My, this is getting interesting," Spike muttered, his amusement plain in his voice.

Xander watched as Zeke, Willow, and Wesley all moved to shield Cordelia from Dai'shu. Lorne, the green-skinned lounge singer, actually stepped up as well, proving himself far more courageous than he had let on.

"Great Dai'shu, please," Zeke pleaded. "Show the ignorant humans mercy. They are nothing more than children beneath the superiority of the populace of our blessed home."

"They're just a bunch of big dumb animals, really," Lorne added.

Xander frowned. *So maybe Karaoke-Boy isn't going to be as helpful as I had hoped.*

Dai'shu waved his arms, the air shimmered with his magick, and Cordelia's protectors flew off in different directions, their bodies entwined in tendrils of writhing eldritch energy.

"First the Princess of Pylea will be punished for her insolence, and then the others shall follow," the Yill demon growled, his hands again crackling with sorcerous energy.

Xander cautiously looked for something, anything he could use as a weapon, but there was nothing handy. The others appeared unharmed, stunned by the magickal force, but still intact—at least for the moment.

"This is between me and hover-boy here," Cordelia said.

The Yill demon was snarling, and the electrical activity between the spines on his head was truly something to marvel at. It was obvious this guy had some anger issues, and Xander wondered how much was actually about the fact that they had brought a vampire to Questral.

He was about to join Cordelia, to at least be by her side as they were both blasted into charcoal briquettes, when a cry filled the air. "Stay your anger, Dai'shu," pleaded the female demon who had earlier vouched for Cordelia. She emerged from the outskirts of the crowd of demon spectators, joined by several of her tribe.

"My kind will not allow this," she said in defiance as they encircled Cordelia, clasping their hands. "The Princess is under our protection. We would rather die as a whole than see any harm come to her."

Dai'shu shrieked his rage, his short arms flailing in frustration as the mystical energies dancing around the spines of his head erupted in a bizarre display of paranormal fireworks.

"Then die you shall," the sorcerer growled, his hands beginning to glow brighter, and brighter still, as the magickal charge grew within them.

"I think he means it, guys," Cordelia said, tapping the female demon on the shoulder. "You might want to get away before he blows his top."

"Then we meet our end protecting one who defended us in the past," the demoness said, turning her chin up proudly. The others within the circle did the same, and Cordelia cringed, waiting to be crispy-fried.

It seemed to Xander that time had suddenly stood still. The anticipation of the moment hung thick in the almost tropical air of Questral. Nobody moved. Nobody even seemed to breathe as the sorcerer prepared to rain death down upon Cordelia and those who chose to protect her.

Then the throngs of demons began to murmur loudly, many bowing their heads in reverence as something made its way through the burgeoning crowds. The commotion distracted the Assemblage sorcerer as he turned to see the cause of the disruption.

Another demon, this one dressed in flowing robes of scarlet silk, emerged from the crowd, and Xander wondered who this latest addition to the party could be to cause such a ruckus. The demon was tall and carried himself in a regal way. His skin seemed to be carved from fine, white marble, his eyes large and solid black. His hair was long, combed back severely on its pale, skeletal skull.

The new arrival raised a long, spidery hand, the fingers covered in multiple rings, toward the sorcerer angrily hanging in the air. "Cease your tantrum, Dai'shu," the demon said, his voice calm and soothing. "I have heard the reasons why these visitors have come, and I wish to question them further."

Lorne seemed to deflate. "Oh honey, you're not a minute too soon."

Dai'shu immediately backed down, although he looked none too happy to be doing so. Xander left Spike at the boat and moved to stand with the others. "Who's the guy in red?" he whispered to Zeke, moving to stand behind the Miquot, whose yellow skin gleamed in the moonlight.

"That is the Sage, Ephraim—leader of the Assemblage. Though its members rule together, his is the final voice."

"Great sage," Dai'shu said, bowing to his leader, still floating in the air, "the invaders have flagrantly broken our most sacred law." The sorcerer gestured toward Spike with his stubby arms. "They have brought an abomination to our paradise, and for that they must be punished."

The Sage nodded his head, his enormous black eyes seeming to take in all that was around him. "I am well aware of the laws they have broken, sorcerer," he said clasping his long, bejeweled fingers before him. "But if what they say is true—if there is a terrible threat to our home—then we must be tolerant of their ignorance."

Dai'shu descended to the docks, making his way toward the Sage. "But surely—"

"I will hear no more, Dai'shu," the Sage proclaimed, his voice growing louder and more powerful.

The sorcerer seemed to shrink, bowing his head in acceptance. "As you say, Great Sage," Dai'shu capitulated, his voice tinged with displeasure.

The demons encircling Cordelia unclasped their hands and moved back into the crowd, each bowing to her as they passed. *Yep, things certainly have changed since high school,* Xander thought as the tension in the air of Monster Island dramatically diminished.

Ephraim turned to regard them, these people who had come unbidden to the shores of the island sanctuary. His eyes scanned each of them in turn, but settled, in the end, on Zeke. There were beads of sweat on the fin on top of the Miquot's head.

"Ezekiel of the Miquot Clan," Ephraim began, his voice like distant thunder, filling the air. "You are welcome here. Your judgment in bringing strangers to this island, bringing humans here, shall be debated at another time. Until such time as the issue of their presence is resolved, you will continue to act as our ambassador."

Zeke nodded respectfully.

"Now, tell me, who speaks for these visitors?"

Wesley and Cordelia stepped forward. "I speak for us, Great Sage," Wesley stated with a bow of his head. "And I wish to reiterate how sorry we are to have broken your laws."

Cordelia nodded in agreement. "It's kind of ironic," she said in explanation. "We didn't even really want to bring him." She shielded her mouth with her hand. "Between you and me, I think he's a big pain in the butt."

"I heard that," Spike said, striding away from the boat.

This seemed to get the Sage's attention. He turned his large black eyes to Spike, and the vampire froze in his tracks.

"If the terrible warning you have brought to us is true," the Sage said, turning his attention back to the gang, "then it must be discussed amongst the Assemblage. Only then will we decide whether to accept your aid."

"Sounds like a plan," Lorne said, looking around, obviously relieved by the turn of events.

"Meanwhile, however," the Sage began again, "if you are to remain here"—he focused again on Spike and pointed a long, gnarled finger covered with multiple adornments—"The vampire must be placed in custody."

Cordelia shrugged. "Okay by me," she said, seeking the approval of the others. "Chain him up like a dog. Torture him if you want. You won't hear us complaining."

"Now just a bloody minute," Spike snarled again, moving toward them. "I've got just as much right to be here as—"

Xander intercepted the vampire and pushed him back toward the vessel. "If you act up, we're back to square one here," he said, attempting to be the voice of reason.

"I'm here to help these stupid gits," Spike spat. "Just like you are."

"Exactly," Xander said soothingly. "But if you don't do what they want, they're going to kick us off the island—and worse, all these people are going to die."

"Way I'm feeling, I'm not sure I really care one way or the other."

"Okay. We could just let them kill you," Xander said.

Spike thought for a moment. "There's that," he said, eyeing the gathering of very angry-looking demon folk behind him.

"What's it going to be, Spike?" Xander asked.

The vampire turned on his heel. "I'm going to get my shirt," he mumbled, and then spun back toward Xander, pointing an accusatory finger. "But don't expect me to be a bloody model prisoner."

Axtius sat in the cool darkness of a trailer that had once belonged to a television starlet. It had all the comforts of home: an entertainment center, a full kitchen, and an exercise room. It both amazed and enraged him how humans chose to pamper celebrities. This was a system he would gladly crush beneath his boot when the pure demon races again dominated the world.

The Brachen demon casually reached up and grabbed hold of one of the many quills protruding from his face—and pulled. The pain was sharp and invigorating as the quill tore loose from the muscle beneath the blue flesh. It was a nervous habit he'd had since he was young, and one he had yet to break himself of. Axtius studied the quill before flicking it off into the darkness. He could already feel a new one rising up through the muscle, growing through the skin. This too was painful, but it did not distract him from his troubles.

Axtius sat behind the desk in the trailer's business office and contemplated the many ways in which he might kill the vampire with a soul, Angel. He had wanted the vampire to experience the most excruciating demise possible. Yes, decapitation or tearing his undead heart from his chest would have been quick, but altogether unsatisfying. He had wanted Angel to suffer.

Axtius reached up and grabbed hold of another quill. He had put his own desires before what was best for the mission, but he had been unable to help himself. And now he had received word from one of his spies on the street that Angel had been seen this very night, alive.

I should have used the Pristagrix to turn the vampire to bloody paste right there in the alley. He tugged the quill from his face. Now Angel was free—the creature responsible for the death of his son was out there in the night—a loose end Axtius could not afford. *This is war.* There was no place for the personal vengeance he had been pursuing. And yet he could not help himself. Angel would be made to suffer.

He was preparing to rip another of the spines from his face when there came a faint knocking at the trailer door. "Enter," he growled, moving his hand away from the pleasuring pain.

His back was to the door, but he knew that Guhl-iban and Haborym, his two most trusted lieutenants, had entered the trailer. Axtius's senses were sharp. The stench of a recently consumed meal of human flesh followed Guhl-iban like a dark cloud, and he could hear the faint snap and crackle of living flame emitted by Haborym's eyes.

"What is it?" he asked, hearing the door slam behind them. He knew they were standing before the desk, waiting for him to face them.

"Great Axtius . . . ," Guhl-iban began, but floundered.

"I am well aware of who I am," he barked, turning the leather chair around. He scowled at them, showing his displeasure. "Now tell me why you have disturbed my meditations."

The diminutive flesh-eater turned to Haborym. This did not bode well, and Axtius felt his ire begin to rise. "You do not need your companion's permission to speak, Guhl-iban. She does not command you. Speak up, or perhaps the next skull I crush will be yours."

Guhl-iban still hesitated.

Haborym lifted her chin defiantly and responded when the flesh-eater seemed unable to do so. Flames shot from her mouth with each disturbing word. "It is the ship, Lord Axtius— we've just received word that it has been sunk."

Axtius surged up from his seat, riding atop the crest of pure, undiluted rage. "What?" he screamed as he flipped the mahogany desk onto its side with a crash. "How is that possible?"

"A vampire. The local talent tells us his name is Angel. Supposedly he has a soul," Guhl-iban said quickly, as if to purge himself of the distressing information. "And the word is that . . . well, he wasn't alone. The Slayer was with him."

Axtius only stared at them, a hollow feeling spreading through his chest. Angel. And the Slayer. If not for his own whimsy, his desire to torture the vampire instead of killing him outright, all of this could have been avoided. It was daunting enough that he still had the vampire to deal with, but now the Slayer had been added to the potent mix as well.

"They found their way onto the ship, killed many of our soldiers, and planted explosives," Haborym explained as Guhliban nodded in agreement.

Axtius stood before the overturned desk, flexing his clawed hands. He wanted something to destroy, but he knew that the satisfaction he might receive from such a violent act would only be short-lived. He needed to calm himself, to think clearly, efficiently—and then he remembered the weapons.

"The Mahkesh cache?" he asked, anticipating the worst.

Guhl-iban smiled. It was a nauseating sight, strings of flesh dangling from yellowed, sharklike teeth. "That is one piece of good news that I can bring you, General," he said, rubbing his hands together eagerly. "We hadn't finalized the deal with the arms merchant. The Mahkesh weaponry had not yet made it to the freighter. They are safe."

Axtius nodded, fresh venom filling that hollow in his chest. This was probably the first true piece of good news he'd heard in weeks. "For once, your incompetence has actually served a purpose," the general said with a rumbling chuckle. "If those ancient weapons had been lost, I would have taken your heads."

Crafted during a time before the rise of Babylon, the Mahkesh cache was created for a similar war against impurity long, long ago. It was a symbol of everything he believed in, and he saw it as a sign that it had been spared.

"Leave me," the demon general ordered with a dismissive wave of his hand.

"As you wish, Lord Axtius," Guhl-iban said as he and the fire deity quickly backed away from the general's quarters, carefully closing the door behind them.

Axtius stood, hands clasped behind his back. With the freighter destroyed, they would need to move quickly to maintain their schedule. He began to analyze the situation, to formulate a course of action.

His thoughts were interrupted by an intrusion upon his mind, words whispered inside his head.

General Axtius, came the voice in his head. *We need to speak with you at once.*

The demon commander sighed heavily and made his way from the office to the space within the trailer that had been designated as the entertainment center. Where once stood a large screen television and state-of-the-art audio system, there was now an undulating pool of dark burgundy liquid upon the floor, the blood of a Vertazzi Seer, a most excellent conduit for communication.

Axtius approached the rippling puddle and bowed his spiny head. "I am here," the general said in obeisance.

The wine-dark fluid began to bubble and seethe, and three shapes began to form.

"We have been hearing whispers, Axtius," the liquid-figure in the shape of Chancellor Dejardom said, seven tentacles waving in the air as he spoke.

"Whispers of what?" Axtius asked, raising his head to gaze at the images of the Coalition's three demon chancellors forged in blood.

"Your ship has been destroyed," Chancellor Tee-Kal gurgled, wings of crimson unfurling upon his back.

"Ah, that," Axtius said with a nod of his head. "I've just heard of this myself. A minor setback," he assured his masters. "I will begin the process of obtaining a new troop transport at once and—"

"Of course you will, General Axtius," Chancellor Dejardom said, arms waving as if caught in a pleasant breeze. "But what is this we have heard about an attack on an archaeological dig in Cambodia?" he asked.

"Yesssssss," Chancellor Shammesh said through multiple mouths, his body of blood changing size and shape as he spoke. "The director of thisssss dig—sssshe wassss attacked and nearly killed by Coalition soldierss. What hass sshe to do with our busssinesss at hand, General Axtiusssssss?"

He thought of his son and felt his rage begin to roil. The demonologist who had—revoltingly enough—been his son's wife was another loose end that he should have seen to himself.

"None directly, sirs," he answered, "but she had been known to provide safe haven for those we wish to see destroyed. I thought an example of our power would crush the morale of those who often relied upon her, and she would no longer be a hindrance to our plans."

The demon chancellors went eerily silent, and he hoped that his explanation was sufficient enough to placate their prying curiosity.

"And what of the vampire with a soul?" Tee-Kal belched, his wings fluttering, spraying blood around the room. "Why pray tell have your actions drawn him into the fray?"

Axtius scowled. "Angel is an abomination," the demon general spat, "the antithesis of everything our cause stands for. With him destroyed, we are that much closer to achieving our desires."

"But he hasss not yet been desstroyed, General Axtiussssss," Chancellor Shammesh chimed in. "And the Sssslayer hasss now become involved asss well."

"I am aware of that, sirs," Axtius said in response, a model of cool efficiency, though his mind was awhirl as he tried to determine who among his legions might be spying upon him for the chancellors. "Another small wrinkle in the tapestry of imminent glory."

"Is there anything you wish to share with us, Axtius?" Dejardom asked, swaying in a nonexistent breeze.

Axtius stood tall before the questioning chancellors. "I have no idea what you're suggesting," he said, clasping his clawed hands behind his back.

"You have always been an exemplary officer in our service, Axtius," Chancellor Tee-Kal hissed. "Do not give us cause to believe that you serve a purpose other than our own."

"There is no other," he lied, the memories of his son forcing their way into his thoughts. He was grateful that none of the chancellors present were psychic, or he would have been in dire trouble indeed.

"You are to deal with thessse—how did you put it?" Shammesh asked. "Sssmall wrinklesss?"

"Angel and the Slayer are proving themselves to be quite the nuisances," Tee-Kal added. "We think it would be in your best interest—and the best interests of the Coalition—that they be dealt with as expeditiously as possible."

Chancellor Dejardom pointed all of his bloody tentacles at him. "Do not give us reason to doubt your abilities further, General Axtius."

"Thy will be done," the general said, bowing his head to his masters, just as the bodies of blood began to discorporate, the shapes losing their cohesion, splashing back down into the body of the small scarlet puddle.

CHAPTER THIRTEEN

Though the patchwork village that was the main population center of Questral likely had places where such a meeting might be held, the Assemblage gathered for their public deliberations in an open-air structure built like a Roman forum. There was a central floor that looked as though it had been created with performance in mind, but a carved-stone dais had been constructed at its center, and it was upon this that the Assemblage met.

Wesley glanced around and marveled at the place as Zeke led them inside the circular forum. Willow and Xander hung back, speaking quietly to each other, but Cordelia and Lorne kept a brisk pace, staying close to Wesley.

"Why do I feel like we're about to be thrown to the lions?" Cordelia whispered.

The former Watcher glanced back at her and nodded. It was an apt comparison—enough to make him shudder—but there were differences that gave him comfort. The Assemblage itself was down in the ring with them. There would be no lions, no gladiatorial combat, and no bullfighting, either—for that was the other thing the place reminded him of, a bullring—as long as the rulers of the island were there with them.

Of course, if the Assemblage was to depart, he would begin to grow concerned.

As he followed Zeke across the vast forum, like the town lit by both electric lamps and torches, as well as the illumination of the moon and stars, Wesley studied the audience that already had begun to gather in the galleries around them. The first two rows, all the way around the circle, were occupied by marble-skinned, black-eyed demons that resembled the Sage, Ephraim. Behind them were a great many Yill demons. Other races of great number were staggered behind those, until the last few rows—even though there were nearer empty seats—were packed with a menagerie of various types of demons.

"Zeke," he whispered. "I'm curious. There appears to be a hierarchy in the seating arrangements."

The Miquot demon's fin gleamed in the light as he turned to Wesley without breaking stride. "More than a hierarchy. A caste system. For the most part, it's majority rule. That's how the Assemblage is decided. The five most populous species are represented . . . along with Garth."

"Garth?"

Zeke shrugged and brought the conversation back to the topic at hand. "Beyond sheer numbers, there's also a pecking order that's based more on what you'd call class. Caste system isn't far off. Your vampire wouldn't even be allowed in the forum, but there are species who are only given seats because the law of the island says no one can be turned away. Doesn't mean there aren't demons who'd like to change the law."

Wesley was horrified. "Which would make them little better than Axtius," he whispered as they approached the dais at the center of the forum.

Behind him, Cordelia and Lorne had moved closer and were listening to the conversation.

"Except the islanders may be snobs, but they don't kill over it," Cordelia pointed out.

"But maybe they'd like to," Lorne noted quietly.

Zeke shot them all a warning glance and turned his attention to the dais. Wesley took his cue and postponed any further discussion of the island's cultural dynamics. Willow and Xander were still whispering to each other, and he looked over his shoulder at them. He caught Willow's eye, and she quickly shushed Xander, and then the five of them, with Zeke as ambassador, stood quietly in front of the dais and waited.

The breeze brought tropical island scents as well as a hundred other more exotic aromas; Wesley could not differentiate between the smells of food and flora and the creatures that lived here. Hundreds of demons had filed into the galleries that looked down upon the forum, and more still were coming in. The Assemblage appeared to be waiting for more of them to arrive, and so Wesley took the opportunity to make a closer study of the ruling body of Questral themselves.

The Assemblage had seats upon the dais, but they had foregone them at the moment, clustered together as they hissed and muttered, obviously discussing their strange visitors and the ominous message they had brought. Wesley recognized Ephraim the Sage immediately, his height and skeletal frame making him impossible to miss. Also with him was the sorcerer Dai'shu, with the long torso particular to Yill demons and the circle of spines that jutted back from his skull like a Native American headdress, distending his features.

There was a Bazhripa—one of the six-armed, red-eyed warriors that had first confronted them when they docked—but this one was a female. She wore a crested iron helmet and a bronze breastplate. Beside her was another female, a green-tinted woman who seemed to be floating. There was something beautiful about her, despite the hue of her skin, and though her long hair seemed to twist Medusa-like around her body, he thought she was naked. Wesley found himself riveted by the sight of her, hardly able to catch his breath. As the breeze blew she seemed to ripple with it and when she turned slightly he realized that he could see through her.

A *Vapor*, he thought, surprised that one of the many disembodied demons—those commonly known to possess human beings—would be accepted by the others and not relegated to the lower castes. She floated there, a stunning, nude woman, nothing but a cloud of greenish mist.

Wesley had to force himself to look away. He glanced around the forum in search of other Vapors. There were none visible, but he knew that the disembodied demons were only seen when they wanted to be or when they were powerless to prevent it.

"She's something, isn't she? A real angel."

Flushing as though he had been caught at something, Wesley turned to find that Lorne had come up beside him. The Host had whispered, but Wesley was still embarrassed. He frowned to cover up his reaction and fiddled with his glasses.

"I'm not sure 'angel' is the word I'd choose."

Zeke shot them a cautionary look, and Wesley nodded back at him.

"There were supposed to be five," he said to Lorne, dropping his voice even further. "I count four."

"Take another look, my friend," the Host replied. He nodded his head toward the dais. "He's the only one already seated."

Wesley stared for a moment at the seats up on the dais. It took him a moment to realize that Lorne was right. The tall, wooden chair second from the left was turned sideways to face the others as they conferred. At that angle he had missed it at first, for the final member of the Assemblage was a demon little more than two feet tall, a savage-looking beast with a back covered in quills. He'd seen these things when they had first arrived, like porcupines carrying swords, and thought they looked almost comical.

But one glimpse of this thing with its upward jutting needle teeth and a cruel sneer on its features, and he was no longer ready to dismiss them.

"Ixwik demon. Blacksmiths and armorers, usually. Vicious little buddies," Lorne whispered.

Cordelia whapped Wesley on the arm. "Would you two please shut up!" she hissed.

Wesley wanted to protest—after all, Lorne had been doing most of the talking—but Cordelia was right. Zeke obviously thought they should be silent out of respect for the Assemblage. But it was difficult for him to suppress his fascination by the different species and the mixed cultures that they had discovered on Questral.

At Cordelia's words, the sorcerer, Dai'shu, glanced up sharply. A moment later Ephraim the Sage nodded to the others, and they began to take their seats. The crowd had been muttering to one another, the combined effect creating a drone of voices all around them, but now it ceased completely, and silence fell over the forum. Wesley had a moment to wonder how many demons lived here, how large Questral was overall, and how long the island had been a sanctuary. Then Ephraim slapped a palm on the table in front of him and all other thoughts were driven from the former Watcher's mind.

The palm-slap seemed to be ritual, a way to call the gathering to order. The other four members of the Assemblage gave Ephraim their attention.

The old demon cleared his throat, wide black eyes scanning the surrounding audience. Then he frowned and looked down at Zeke. "Ambassador," Ephraim said. "We will hear you now."

"That's big of him," Xander muttered.

Alarmed, Wesley glanced back at him, ready to silence him if necessary, but Willow had already done so with a stomp of her foot on Xander's and a withering glare.

A tiny smile touched the edges of Wesley's lips. There were times when, despite the smashing failure it had been, he missed his tenure in Sunnydale.

Zeke stepped forward. Though he had been wearing a cable knit sweater, inexplicably he pulled it over his head, snagging it for a moment on the fin atop his skull. He tied it around his waist, and Wesley stared a moment at the pale yellow complexion of his flesh. Clearly this was more ritual, but a ritual of the Assemblage or of the Miquot he did not know. He hoped it was a Miquot thing, because he doubted Cordelia and Willow were going to be stripping to the waist, no matter what the stakes.

"Venerable Ephraim," Zeke began, bowing his head. "Honored Assemblage. These individuals, human and demon alike, have traveled from Los Angeles to offer their assistance to us in what may well be our darkest hour, though we do not know it yet. Others are on the way, including the vampire with a soul, Angel—who helped save the lives of a large number of those who live here on the island—and Buffy Summers, the Slayer."

A ripple of murmured comments went through the crowd at this revelation.

"Unthinkable!" Dai'shu barked.

Zeke paused only a moment before continuing. "May I then present Wesley Wyndam-Pryce, Xander Harris, Krevlornswath of the Deathwok Clan, the sorceress Willow Rosenberg, and Cordelia Chase, the Princess of Pylea."

As they were named, Wesley and the others each gave some gesture of respect, from Lorne's deep bow to Willow's tiny wave. When Cordelia was named there was even a small smattering of applause from the crowd.

"I have served as Questral's ambassador to the world outside for twenty-seven years," Zeke added. "Never in that time have I brought a human being to these shores. I would not have begun now if the situation were not grave. You have heard the warning these people bring already, but now I must lend it my support. Events have begun to unfold in Los Angeles that make me believe wholly that they speak the truth.

"The Brachen demon Axtius is gathering an army of pure-bloods. This is part of a much larger plan to eliminate those of us they call half-breeds, and any pureblood who might ally themselves with so-called lesser races. There is a larger scheme at work that will reveal itself in time. All that need concern us at the moment is this: Very soon, General Axtius will bring his army here. He intends to eradicate our settlement completely and kill all who reside upon this island."

A roar went through the stands, gasps and shouts and outbursts rippling around the forum. The people of Questral might not believe humans, Wesley mused, and many of them had likely only just heard what news the outsiders had brought, but they would believe Zeke.

Dai'shu stood from his seat upon the dais and raised his hand. A flash of golden light streamed from his fingers. It was silent, but achieved the desired effect of calming the gathered demons and getting them to focus once more.

"And you, venerable Ephraim," Dai'shu said, inclining his head to the Sage, "what do you say?"

But before Ephraim could speak, the Bazhripa female leaned over the dais to glare down at them. "Why should we believe them?" she snarled, red eyes glowing more brightly. "Humans!" she spat.

The Ixwik demon stood on its high chair, quills standing up like a peacock's feathers. "Shikah speaks truth," it growled, its voice difficult to understand. "Humans is vermin. Least of the lesser. Almost as bad as vampires."

Willow took a step forward. For all that she had silenced Xander, it appeared that she could not now remain quiet herself. "We're vermin? But you speak our language. You're speaking English."

Zeke glared at Wesley, obviously wanting him to shut Willow up, but Wesley knew that it was useless. The witch was a gentle soul and always had been. She had a slow fuse, but once it had burned down, it was best to just get out of the way.

The Ixwik raised its nose as if being addressed by a human were beneath the demon. But the Bazhripa, Shikah, was not willing to ignore this affront.

"Most of us on this island lived in your world first. English is the only language many of our races have in common. It is considered the low speech, but at gatherings of the Assemblage it is necessary." The six-armed female sneered at Willow. "Speak up again without being spoken to, and I will have you killed."

Ephraim slapped his palm against the table three times, obviously calling for order. The others relented, though obviously with great reluctance. When the sensual Vapor rippled in the breeze, her hair floating back behind her, and turned to Ephraim, Wesley thought that every creature in the forum held its breath.

"We are being poor hosts, venerable one," she said, her voice a hush like wind through the trees. "If our ambassador gives credence to the claims of these outsiders and they truly have come to offer their aid, the least we ought to offer in return is courtesy."

As the Vapor finished speaking, a tremor shook the ground beneath their feet. Wesley saw on his friends' faces that they were as startled as he was. However when he glanced at Zeke he was surprised to find that the Miquot demon seemed not even to have noticed.

Another tremor, this one more subtle, rumbled through the forum. Cordelia gasped and her eyes widened, and Wesley followed her line of sight to discover what had elicited her astonishment. His mouth opened in a little *O* of surprise. "Good Lord," he muttered.

Beyond the highest wall at the back of the forum, above the last of the galleries, a single bright orange eye stared down at the proceedings. The members of the Assemblage turned toward the Cyclopean monstrosity with curious expressions. The thing rose up higher, revealing that its head consisted of that single eye, a mass of serpentine tentacles that squirmed out from the place a mouth ought to have been, and a skull laden with fissures from which flames jetted in spurts.

"What are we seeing here?" he asked Zeke.

The Miquot shot Wesley a quizzical look. "That? Oh, that's Garth. I thought I'd mentioned him. He's the sixth member of the Assemblage."

"Okay," Xander whispered, coming up behind Wesley. "Why am I getting the feeling that we're going to be fed to that thing now?"

"Too many Japanese monster movies," Willow whispered in reply.

Cordelia tapped him on the arm. "*Wes*. Are we dealing with an Elder God here? Maybe just me, but I don't remember a single reference in all our research to one of the Great Old Ones *not* trying to end the world in fiery apocalypse."

Zeke shushed them again.

Properly chastened, Wesley replied to Cordelia in the lowest whisper from the corner of his mouth, unable to tear his gaze away from the sixth member of the Assemblage.

"First time for everything, I suppose. Though it's possible that . . . *Garth* . . . is not one of the Old Ones at all."

Xander snickered, a bit of hysteria mixed with the sound. "Well, he isn't Mojo Jojo."

With a rumble that sounded like a rockslide, a voice issued from amidst the mass of tentacles upon the Old One's face. The Assemblage and all of the islanders gathered seemed to be listening intently. To Wesley it did not sound like language at all. "What's he saying?" he asked Zeke.

Which was when Lorne stepped up beside Wesley and laid a comforting hand across his shoulders. "Don't get your knickers in a bunch. The Big Ugly's on our side. He thinks they oughta give us the benefit of the doubt."

Wesley glanced at him. "You understood that?"

Lorne shrugged. "Hey, you wanted me to translate. I'm translating."

There was a brief, whispered conference amongst the Assemblage, and then Ephraim stood, his enormous black eyes gleaming.

"Very well. We have decided. You will be given quarters for the night and allowed your freedom while you remain our guests. All save the captive vampire. In the morning we will return our judgment as to whether we will trust this warning and accept your help. Meanwhile, we suggest you look to our ambassador for guidance as to how to conduct yourselves while on the island."

"Of course," Wesley replied, inclining his head in a sort of curt bow. "Thank you."

Cordelia sniffed. "What are we thanking them for again?" she whispered under her breath.

"Not eating us, for starters," Willow replied.

A quartet of Bazhripa warriors approached, and they all fell silent. Zeke and the Bazhripa escorted them from the forum to get them settled in their quarters for the night. Wesley did not want to express his alarm to the others, but it had occurred to him that if the Assemblage decided not to trust them, Xander and Willow's concern about becoming part of the islanders' diet might not be too far from the truth.

He kept a pleasant smile on his face, but only with a tremendous effort.

The island was beautiful. Lorne knew he ought to be more alarmed—things certainly weren't going as according to plan at this point—but he could not help being captivated by his surroundings. The trees and the tropical breeze, the smell of the ocean . . . it was all so wonderful. But he knew there were other reasons the place appealed to him. Despite the obvious racial issues that divided the demon species on Questral, they seemed to live in peace and be relatively accepting of one another. They took their neighbors at face value, not asking them to be anything they were not. It was so different from the way he had been raised, which was half the reason he had left Pylea in the first place. What he had tried to create at Caritas, that kind of environment, seemed to exist here on the island as well. It touched him deeply.

His services as a translator had not been as vital as he had expected, but he was now glad that he had come. This place deserved a chance to survive. Not that he was going to be doing much of the actual defending, but Questral was worth fighting for.

"Lorne?" Wesley prodded.

The Host raised an eyebrow and turned to him. "Huh?"

Wesley sighed in frustration. "What did he say?"

"Oh, sorry Wes. My mind's wandering. Gotta rein it in." Lorne glanced up at the trees again . . . and above the trees, at the Old One called Garth. The ancient demon was huge, perhaps fifty-five feet high, and despite the tentacles on its face it had a body that reminded him mostly of a giant mantis, with its thin insectoid body and limbs. Though its trunk glowed the same orange as its single eye, the fire that leaked out of its head did not seem to spill out anywhere else.

Zeke had arranged for Wesley to have a chat with Garth, and Wes had asked Lorne to translate for him. With a pair of Bazhripa warriors as guides, they had trekked to the cavern where Garth made his home and found the enormous, ominous demon to be very welcoming. Wesley had just asked what it was like on the earth when humanity first appeared. Garth had seemed to hesitate—Lorne guessed he did not want to offend Wesley with the obvious response, which would be that humans were merely a nuisance at the beginning—but in that moment of hesitation, Lorne's mind had begun to wander.

"Garth, my apologies," Lorne said, his voice low and grinding, the language of the Old One much like speaking German with a mouth full of gravel. "Could you repeat that?"

The ancient demon lowered its trunk down, its flaming head sparking, its huge orange eye unblinking. The tentacles at its face really did take the place of a mouth, Lorne had noticed, as each one of them seemed to have a tiny mouth of its own, and they spoke in unison.

"It was as though a new weed had begun to grow in the garden of our world," Garth said. "A weed we could not kill, for everywhere we plucked it from the ground, it spread faster and farther."

Lorne quickly translated for Wesley, but saw that the man was deeply unsettled by Garth's comments. He grew pale and looked as though he might be sick.

"Wes, you all right?"

"Yes, yes," Wesley said with an impatient nod. "It's only that . . . it sounds a great deal like what more advanced human civilizations have been doing to native populations in various parts of the world for millennia."

Lorne offered a reluctant nod in return. "It is in your nature."

Wesley stared at the Old One, the awe he felt plain on his face. "It's so strange being able to talk to him. Who ever thought an opportunity like this would present itself. Strange . . . but also terrifying. It's a chilling perspective on history. I've always known that the world once belonged to demons, but for the first time I really know it. It feels like the truth in a way it never did before. It's most unsettling."

Lorne began to translate.

"Stop!" Wesley snapped. "Don't translate that!"

"Sorry. Any other questions for the big guy?"

Deeply troubled, Wesley shook his head. "No. Just thank him for his time. And for giving us the benefit of the doubt earlier."

Willow stood outside the squat, thatched-roof hut in the Bazhripa village where she and Cordelia were to sleep for the night. The warrior species seemed to be the security force for the entire island under the command of Shikah, the Bazhripa member of the Assemblage. But once all of the tension had gone and the gathering had dispersed, the six-armed demons were more than polite. Despite the claims of Shikah, Willow had found that most of the demons she ran into spoke only a handful of words in English, if at all, but apparently it was the only language the various races had in common.

A short way from the dirt-floored hut, a group of small demon children had gathered around Cordelia. Apparently, they were of the species Cordelia, Angel, and Doyle had saved from pureblood Nazi demons the previous year. The kids looked at Cordy as a hero, gazed at her with open affection, and she indulged them with patience and a kindness that surprised Willow. This image of the woman smiling at demon children did not match her memories of the cynical, superficial girl she'd known in high school. It had been clear to her for ages that Cordy had changed for the better, but those moments watching her play with the kids would stay with Willow for a very long time.

"Okay, evil munchkins," Cordelia said, pushing her hair back away from her face. "Auntie Cordy needs her beauty rest. Maybe we can play some more tomorrow, a little game I like to call stab the nasty invading demon with a sharp, pointy stick."

The kids barely understood her and hesitated.

"Go on," she said, grinning. "Shoo!"

When Cordelia started back toward the hut and noticed Willow watching her, she acted nonchalant, as if embarrassed. Willow turned away and nearly bumped into the sorcerer Dai'shu, who had come up beside her. She let out a tiny gasp, annoyed that she had let him surprise her like that. The Yill demon was not alone either. The leader of the Assemblage, Ephraim, was with him.

"Hi. There." Willow smiled thinly. "Whoa. You guys are pretty stealthy, aren't ya?"

"It was not our intention to startle you, sorceress," Dai'shu said, inclining his head.

"Startled, me? Nah. I'm okay, not easily startled. Not me. Also, sorceress? That isn't entirely accurate." Willow raised a hand and crossed her fingers. "Sure, magick and me, like this. But more of a witch, really."

Cordelia had walked up during her taken-off-guard rambling and now she spoke up. "Don't let her fool you. Willow may seem innocent, but she's quite the sorceress. Oh yeah. Big-time magick."

Ephraim raised an eyebrow, and both he and Dai'shu regarded Willow more closely, as though sizing her up anew. Then Ephraim smiled at Cordelia and extended a skeletal, marble-skinned hand. "Good evening, Princess," he said.

Cordelia took his hand, and Ephraim kissed it, a gesture so chivalric and courtly that Willow could not help but smile. Cordelia herself, as the recipient of this gesture, was practically beaming. Dai'shu, on the other hand, sniffed his disapproval.

"So, to what do we owe the honor?" Willow asked, trying to be as courteous as possible.

Ephraim glanced at Dai'shu, and the sorcerer nodded.

"We are unused to visitors," the Yill demon said, the spikes that jutted from the back of his skull seeming to stretch his face even more tightly. "The Assemblage has not yet reached a joint opinion, but we wanted to extend a more cordial welcome than the one you received upon arrival. We have determined, after speaking with our ambassador, Ezekiel of the Miquot, that your introduction of a vampire onto these shores was not a purposeful slight."

"Thank you," Willow replied, for she could think of no other response that seemed appropriate.

"Yes," Cordelia added, nodding with false sincerity. "That's great of you guys, really."

"We believe that your efforts, regardless of the truth in your warning, are in good faith, and we will try to respond in kind," Ephraim said, glancing at Cordelia. "You have friends here, Princess. Those whose lives you helped to save hold you in high regard." His gaze shifted to Willow. "Sleep well. In the morning you will hear our decision."

Willow smiled. "Great. Thanks for that. Really. You too—the sleeping well part, I mean."

"'Night," Cordelia said simply.

When Ephraim and Dai'shu had departed, Willow and Cordelia stood in front of the hut for several seconds, speechless.

"So what was that about, do you think?" Cordelia said at last, as the two of them turned to go inside the hut.

"Not really sure. Besides freaking me out, I mean. Maybe they just thought it over and realized they hadn't exactly sent out the welcome wagon and wanted to make nice. Or they could be lulling us into a false sense of security before we're executed at dawn."

Cordelia had been about to lie down. Now she shot Willow a withering look. "Were you always this death-obsessed, or is this new?"

"Hello?" Willow replied. "Look around. Monster Island."

Cordy shrugged. "True. Then again, maybe they just started thinking about who they were dealing with—the Slayer, Angel, Witchie-poo, rogue demon hunter, and of course the Princess of an entire demon dimension—and figured they oughta be a little more polite."

• • •

Xander was wired. Twist and turn as he might on the soft earthen floor of the hut, he could not fall asleep. His mind was buzzing with thoughts and questions and with his fears about what the morning might bring. And not merely the morning, but the subsequent hours or days, when at last Axtius's troops struck the island.

He missed Anya. He would have given almost anything in those quiet hours, alone in the hut, to feel her warm breath against his neck, feel her silky, supple skin beneath his hands, even just as they held each other in bed, in the dark. He thought about what she had said when she was disoriented, after she had been injured; what she had said about needing to be okay because she wanted to have his babies someday. The idea thrilled and terrified him at the same time. He loved Anya, but whenever he thought about having children of his own in the future, he thought of his own father. He could not help but wonder if he would repeat the man's mistakes, if he would end up treating his own children the same way. The idea made him feel sick. Xander would rather spend a century in Hell than grow up to be his father. He had never met Doyle, but with a father like Axtius, he figured the Brachen half-breed had to have felt the same way.

Again he thought of Anya. Whatever his fears or reservations, just being with her, laughing with her, having his arms around her, always made him feel better. He needed her now, and he worried for her as well. Though he knew that she would recover quickly enough from her injuries, still he found himself regretting not having stayed with her.

Instead, he was there on the ground on the floor of a hut usually occupied by six-armed battle demons, and the two guys who were supposed to be his roommates for the night—Wesley and the karaoke demon, Lorne—were off on walkabout on the island. Great for them, but Xander did not feel much like sightseeing.

Buffy had been clear about the danger Axtius's plans represented, and though he tended toward self-mockery most of the time, he knew in his heart that he had a lot to offer. Already he had been checking out the island, figuring out which structures could be turned into bunkers, looking for likely places to stage an ambush on invaders. Once upon a time, thanks to a single magick night, he had been temporarily transformed into a U.S. Army soldier. Traces of the training and knowledge he'd had while under the effects of that spell still remained.

It was completely logical for him to have come along. He knew the odds, knew the stakes. But Anya was at home, injured, and all hell was going to break loose here soon. There wasn't anything fun about it for him.

Though his eyes were wide open, his mind abuzz, it was not long before sleep finally began to creep up on him. In the distance he could hear the soothing crash of the waves upon the shore, and a breeze blew through the hut that felt wonderful. His eyelids fluttered, and Xander began to drift off.

"Ohhhh, my," whispered a voice in the darkness inside the hut.

His eyes snapped open. Had he really heard that? Xander glanced around inside the hut but saw nothing. There was only a curtain where the door should have been, and it fluttered in the breeze but there seemed to be nobody in the doorway or just beyond it.

Nerves, he told himself, wishing Wesley and Lorne would come back, even though he'd never been very fond of the one and barely knew the other.

"You're a strapping young man, aren't you?"

Xander sat up straight, staring about the darkness of the hut. It was very warm, and he had been sleeping only in his underwear with a light, raw cotton sheet thrown over him. Now he covered himself with the sheet. The voice had been sensual, filled with insinuation, and unquestionably female.

"Where are you? Who's in here?"

A cloud of mist began to coalesce just a few feet away, a greenish fog that quickly sculpted itself into the form of the stunningly beautiful demon he had been staring at all through their audience with the Assemblage. Her hair still danced around her shoulders as though in some wind he could not feel, but where earlier it had strategically covered her, it no longer did. She was not corporeal, a spirit demon, but her brazen nakedness still had an effect on him.

Xander brought his knees up in front of him and averted his eyes. "Can I help you with something?" he asked in a small voice.

"Oh, I hope so," she said in that same, sultry voice. She floated toward him, her body now hovering above the floor, and her fingers reached out toward his face.

A tremor went through Xander, and he could not be certain if it was fear or excitement or a combination of the two.

"I am Ileana," she said, her voice like a caress on him.

Xander felt compelled to look at her now and could not tear his eyes away.

"I am so pleased that you and your friends have come," the achingly beautiful demon said. "It has been so very long since I have had human contact. I have always believed that all peoples are truly one, all sentient beings belong together. Commingling of races is a wondrous thing, don't you agree?"

Xander edged backward across the floor of the hut. "Oh, absolutely. Sure. Nothing like a little creative commingling, I always say. Well, maybe not it in those words exactly. But, see, I . . . aren't you a Vapor demon? I mean, not of the flesh. Not that, you know, the flesh is all I'm thinking of. But how can you . . . wait, you want to possess me, don't you?"

The sudden realization made him stop moving backward and start to rise to his feet.

Ileana pushed him down again, the most seductive of smiles on her green-hued face. "Don't be ridiculous. If I wanted only to possess you, I could have done that without you ever knowing I was here. I want . . . more than that."

Xander stared at her fingers where they were splayed against his chest. They were solid enough, that was for sure. Solid enough to push him down. Solid enough to now begin to trace across his chest, giving him goose bumps. Solid enough to—

"Hey!" he exclaimed as she drew the sheet away from him. Xander snatched it back and scrambled away from her. His face was flushed, and he forced himself to picture every small detail of Anya's face in his mind.

"Thanks. It was sweet of you to come by. Very neighborly, really. But I'm seriously in need of my beauty sleep. Hard to believe, I know. Plus, y'know, kinda have rules about the commingling. Well, not me, really, but my girlfriend? Did I mention she's a vengeance demon? Wonderful thing, commingling, but the vengeance demon girlfriends can be kinda strict about it."

Ileana drew back, her body suddenly less solid, mist swirling, the outline of her form seeming to blur out of focus. The Vapor demon put a hazy finger to her lips and gave him a coquettish smile the likes of which had never been directed at Xander Harris before in his life. In that moment he nearly forgot all about Anya.

Nearly.

"All right, my young man," the demon whispered. "But when you think of me later . . . when you dream of Ileana . . . remember the pleasure that you might have had."

She blew him a kiss, and then evaporated before his eyes.

Xander swore low, under his breath. After nearly a full minute of simply staring at the darkness of his hut, he lay back down, but he knew there was no way he was going to be able to sleep now.

In a windowless room more like a meat locker than a jail cell, Spike sat up against the stone wall, bored out of his mind. *Bloody hell,* he thought, for perhaps the thousandth time, *a bloke wants to help, and this is the thanks he gets.*

If that wasn't bad enough, he was nearly out of cigarettes.

He took a long drag on the one perched between his lips now, the embers glowing in the darkness, and tapped at the pack. Three left. The vampire wondered if any of the demons on this island of freaks would have cigarettes, or if they were banned. Maybe Zeke. The Miquot spent a lot of time on the streets of L.A. Spike held out hope that Zeke would have some cigarettes.

"Bored now," he muttered to the darkness inside his cell.

The smoke that furled from the end of his cigarette began to blossom and grow, and he noticed that it had taken on a tinge of green. Spike raised an eyebrow.

"What's this, then?"

The smoke continued to grow into a cloud, and then from the cloud, a shape began to take hold. A very lovely shape, indeed.

"Well, well," Spike said, a broad grin stretching across his features. "What have we here? Looks like not everyone on this island thinks vampires're the bottom of the barrel."

Ileana's fingers caressed his healing face, touched his hair, ran down his scarred chest. Spike tossed his lit cigarette onto the stone floor and reached to pull her toward him. She was not the one he wanted, but she was breathtaking, heartbreakingly beautiful. If the one he wanted wouldn't have him, he was more than happy to make due.

The burning ashen ember of the cigarette's tip began to fade. But Spike could see very well in the dark. And he liked what he saw.

CHAPTER FOURTEEN

Sunnydale

The phone jarred Dawn out of a dream that involved school, nudity, humiliation and, oddly enough, bungee-jumping. When her eyes fluttered open and the fog of sleep began to clear from her brain, she was pleased to be rid of the dream. Then the phone rang again, and she raised her head off of the science book she had fallen asleep upon.

Ever since Buffy had left, Giles had been putting so much effort into covering for her that he had let things at the Magic Box go slightly. Anya had taken him to task for the detrimental effect this could have on sales if they did not keep up appearances in the store, not to mention their inventory. Tonight, she had badgered Giles into foregoing any sort of patrol to deal with the store after it had closed for the night.

The truth was, Dawn thought Giles was relieved to take a night off. After he had cleared out the nest of vampires who had been living in a neighborhood over by Miller's Woods and hunting the neighbors, he had slept for nearly fourteen hours straight. The guy deserved a break.

Though with Anya driving him crazy—she worrying about Xander and him worrying about Buffy and the two of them taking it out on each other—Dawn thought Giles might have gotten more rest if he had spent the night patrolling for nasties.

The phone rang again. Anya emerged from the back room and shot Dawn an annoyed glance.

"Hello? Do you hear a strange ringing noise? What on earth could it be?"

Dawn shrugged. "It could be the phone. But I can't be sure, 'cause I'm still half-asleep. I think I drooled on my science book."

Anya sighed in frustration and picked up the phone. "Magic Box. It is so far after hours that this better be Buffy or colorful vengeance will ensue, even if I have to wreak it with my bare, pathetically human hands."

In the midst of this speech, Giles also emerged from the back room. He had left his glasses behind somewhere, but that was all right; Dawn always thought he looked kinder without them.

"Is that Buffy?" the Watcher asked.

Anya glanced at him, listening intently to the voice on the other end of the phone line, and shook her head in his direction. Dawn got up quickly, all traces of sleep banished from her mind, and went over to the counter. Her first thought was that if it was not Buffy, that might mean that something had *happened* to Buffy. "Is everyone all right?" she asked.

Anya ignored her, listening intently.

"Hey. Is Buffy . . . is everyone okay?" Dawn asked again, reaching out to prod Anya on the arm.

Anya turned and seemed about to give her a nasty look, but then surprisingly her expression softened. "Hold on," she said into the phone, then she spoke to Dawn. "Everyone's okay so far. That was the first thing she said."

"Who?" Giles asked. "Who said?"

"Tara," Anya said, holding out the phone to him. "She needs to talk to you. She was asking me about some spells and things, but I'm lost."

Dawn felt a wave of relief pass through her. She wanted to know why it was not Buffy calling, wanted to talk to Tara herself, but she knew that there was a lot going on. Serious business. As long as everyone was all right, she could wait. She was going out of her mind, waiting for word, waiting for everyone to come home, but she could wait.

As if she had any other choice.

"Yes, Tara, what's going on?" Giles asked as he took the phone. Dawn watched his face, his expression grim, as he listened to Tara on the other end of the line. Eventually he began to nod, almost to himself. "Yes, actually, I think I know just the thing. You have to understand, though, that sorcery on that scale . . . war magick . . . it's rarely used these days. Medieval, really. To repel an invasion . . ."

He paused, listening again. *Repel an invasion,* Dawn thought. She bit her lip. It was hard enough to have to worry for Buffy all the time, but she had gotten used to her sister going one-on-one with demons and vamps. One-on-one. Not repelling invasions. Slayer or not, Buffy was only one person.

But she isn't alone, Dawn reminded herself. *Not even close.*

It was cold comfort, but it would have to do.

"Yes, I know," Giles went on. "I'm merely explaining to you why it isn't the sort of thing I'd have in my library. The Council would certainly have the volume you need, though I can't say for certain how quickly . . . hmm? Oh right, sorry. *Medieval War Magick*. No, no, that *is* the title. But I doubt . . . really? Well, I certainly hope so. Call me if there's anything in it that you need help deciphering. And please let us know the instant there's news."

After a few moments spent on good-byes, Giles hung up the phone. Anya and Dawn both watched him, waiting for him to explain the conversation he had just had. When he volunteered nothing, Dawn tapped the counter. "Giles? What's going on?"

"Hmm?" he muttered without looking up. "Oh, Tara needed me to recommend some spells she and Willow might use against . . . against Axtius."

"*Medieval War Magick*?" Anya said. "That sounds a lot bigger than just Axtius."

"Oh, it is," the Watcher replied, speaking quietly. "It is."

Giles was staring at the phone as if he thought it might ring again, or give him some vital piece of information, or promise him that everything was going to be all right.

But the phone remained silent.

Burbank

The warehouse in Burbank was identical to a hundred, even a thousand, others in the greater Los Angeles area. If Gunn's crew had not acquired the precise address there would have been no way for them to track it down. It was located at the rear of an industrial park, set slightly apart from the other buildings in the complex because it had been added as an afterthought to the original development, and apparently no one had wanted to rip up perfectly good trees, landscaping, and pavement when they could throw the warehouse up beside the lot where the trucking company's trailers were parked when not in use.

Except the trucking company had gone belly up a month ago, a victim of shady accounting. The place should have been empty.

Of course it wasn't.

Completely silent, as though he were some stone gargoyle, Angel crouched in the darkened rafters thirty feet above the warehouse floor, a broadsword slung in its scabbard across his back. Below him, in the square portion of the warehouse where the building's current occupants had bothered to turn the lights on, a deal was in the making. Lorne was out of town—thanks to Angel—but there were still whispers on the street. Charlie Nickels had felt as though he had let Angel down—taken one look at the charred spots that still had not completely healed on his skin and decided he was going to make it up to him.

Gunn's crew had pinpointed the time and place where Axtius was supposed to try to acquire some serious hardware for his soldiers. But it had been Charlie Nickels who had discovered the truth of what, exactly, Axtius was trying to buy.

The Mahkesh cache.

As if that damned Pristagrix hadn't been enough, Axtius was bent on getting his hands on an entire armory of cursed weaponry, swords, and axes and arrows that would cut through any hide or armor, that would kill anything or anyone, so long as they found their mark.

All the more reason to ruin Axtius's night, Angel thought grimly.

Perched silently he had watched as Axtius entered. It had taken every ounce of restraint he possessed—and he was not a creature known for his restraint—to prevent himself from descending upon the Brachen demon immediately. Just one look at the blue, spike-faced demon swaggering into the warehouse in his leather armor . . . it brought back in excruciating detail the way Axtius had ambushed him, and images of his torture upon that rooftop, and the pain of his recovery.

His features had shifted into the countenance of the vampire the second he saw Axtius, and he bared his fangs there in the dark.

But he had waited. Buffy and Gunn were outside, watching for the moment they had planned in advance. Two minutes after the weapons merchant entered, they would come in fighting.

Axtius had only two of his lackeys with him—a skeletal demon with jagged-edged limbs, and a tall, imposing female whose eyes poured liquid fire. More than likely there were a handful of others on guard outside, but Buffy and Gunn would make short work of them, he was certain.

The demonic general tapped his foot impatiently, there in the midst of the empty warehouse.

"He's late, Guhl-iban," Axtius grumbled. "I don't like to be kept waiting."

You won't be waiting much longer, Angel thought. He knew Axtius must have been infuriated by the loss of his transport to Questral, but this was another story entirely. The Mahkesh cache was too dangerous to fall into his hands.

The skeletal one, Guhl-iban, went to a small door set into a much larger sliding metal door in the wall of the warehouse. He opened it and glanced out, then turned back toward his general.

"They're here."

Axtius let out a long breath and nodded with satisfaction. Despite his armor, he did not seem to be carrying any weapons. Angel presumed this was a condition of the meeting, but he was pleased because it meant the Pristagrix was not here.

His heart did not beat, but the vampire still felt as though his blood began to flow a little faster. He did not need to breathe, but air hissed in through his lips and he thought he could taste vengeance.

"Haborym, help him with the door," Axtius commanded, standing up to his full height, trying to look as imperious as possible to his guests. The Brachen demon was huge and broad-shouldered, much bigger than his half-human son had been.

The fiery-eyed female, Haborym, went to aid Guhl-iban. Together they unlatched the larger door, a sliding patch of corrugated metal twenty feet square. As it opened, Angel could hear an engine beyond, and headlights flooded the interior of the warehouse. Fortunately the illumination did not extend into the rafters.

A pair of pickup trucks, their beds laden with long wooden boxes, rolled into the warehouse one after the other. The lead truck pulled up right in front of Axtius, the demon grinning in the splash of its headlights, and then the driver killed the engine. The second pickup stopped behind the first and followed suit. The passenger door of the lead vehicle opened and a diminutive, rotund, ebony-skinned Vosqash demon stepped out. Despite its bulk it moved swiftly toward Axtius and offered its hand in greeting.

"General. Trox Caniff. We spoke on the phone. A pleasure to make your acquaintance."

Reluctantly Axtius shook the Vosqash's hand. The weapons merchant might be a pureblood demon, but Axtius obviously did not think much of Trox Caniff, or his species. "Let's see what you've brought me," Axtius told him.

Angel tensed, hands gripping the steel beam upon which he crouched. The clock was ticking.

The demons who climbed out of the pickups after Caniff were not Vosqash at all but a much larger breed Angel did not at first recognize. There were dozens of species of demons that had offered themselves as mercenaries in ages past; powerfully built, durable, and none too bright. He stared at Caniff's three associates—copper-hued creatures with vicious-looking claws, vaguely feline features, and black tiger stripes on their faces.

A ripple of unease went through him, puzzle pieces snapping into place in his mind, and then he realized what he was looking at.

Mahkesh, he thought. *They're Mahkesh.* It should have been impossible. All of the records about the Mahkesh Wars indicated that the entire tribe had been wiped out. But here was evidence to the contrary right in front of his eyes.

Thirty seconds had passed, and the Mahkesh warriors were uncrating the weapons. It made no sense to Angel. Why would Mahkesh warriors be willing to sell—or allow Caniff to sell—the weapons that were their tribe's greatest legacy? As he turned the question over in his head he watched the merchant and his guards display several gorgeous cutlass-style swords that gleamed in the small square of light in the warehouse. Angel felt at once the inferiority of the blade he himself had brought along.

Axtius muttered his praises of the weapons, looking genuinely pleased. Other crates were opened to reveal a pair of war-axes with long, curved handles.

"Oh, well done, Trox. I'm very pleased. The Coalition will reward you handsomely."

Angel frowned. There was something hollow about Axtius's words, something too forced about the way he was speaking, as though he knew he had an audience and was playing to the rafters. That was ridiculous, of course. If Axtius had known Angel was there watching he never would have gone through with the trade without dealing with the intrusion first. *He never would have—*

Alarm bells went off in Angel's head. Even as he was pulling his suspicions together, there came a scraping, scuffling noise at the back of the warehouse. There was motion deep in the shadows there. Angel peered into the darkness, eyes sorting shapes out of the shadows, as they moved forward toward the light.

A phalanx of demons of various breeds dragged Gunn into the light, hands tied behind his back, silver duct tape over his mouth. Axtius glanced over at the new arrivals and at Gunn, who struggled against his captors, but the Brachen demon said nothing. This was no surprise to him at all.

Angel's hand went swiftly to the hilt of his sword, fingers closing around the grip. Unconsciously his lips curled back from his teeth, and he bared his fangs.

"General," said the fire-eyed demon woman, Haborym. "We have more visitors."

On the warehouse floor, Axtius glanced quickly over at the wide entrance. In the rafters, Angel did the same. Shadows outside in the night quickly resolved themselves into eight more Mahkesh warriors, all of them armed with the extraordinary weapons of their tribe.

The last puzzle piece clicked into place. Not only had Axtius known they were coming, not only had he set the entire thing up as a trap, but the weapons deal had already gone down. The rotund merchant, Trox, probably wasn't even a merchant at all, but one of Axtius's men.

The Mahkesh were working for him. They weren't selling their tribal heritage, but were helping Axtius buy it back.

In the fraction of a second that elapsed as the circuitry of all this logic connected in Angel's mind, he saw Guhl-iban, Haborym, and the Mahkesh warriors below spread out as they walked around the pickup trucks toward their general.

The last of the Mahkesh was dragging Buffy by the hair, unconscious and bleeding from several wounds that had blossomed red
stains in her clothes. Angel could smell the copper tang of her
blood in the air, blood with which he was so familiar.

The roar of fury that burst from his throat at that moment
was so feral, so primitive, that he could not have held it back
even if he had desired to do so. With a chime of metal he drew
his sword and tensed to leap down into the fray, unmindful of
the odds or of whatever other preparations Axtius might have
made.

In his peripheral vision he barely saw the slithering, clinging,
spiderlike things that scurried along the rafters toward him with
horrifying speed. Then they were upon him, teeth sinking
deeply into his still-tender flesh, talons tearing the sword from
his hand, and Angel and his two attackers tumbled out into the
open air, fell end over end, and struck the concrete floor with a
crunch of bone.

As he had fallen, Angel had snapped the neck of one of the
hideous things and had used it to break his fall. Still, he was
disoriented, images swirling in his head, a collection of sights
on his way down, of Axtius, Gunn being forced to his knees,
Buffy bleeding on the concrete. Angel rose and kicked the
second of his attackers—they were sleek beasts, a strange
combination of mongoose and lizard, but wrought in the fires
of some Hell or other—his boot striking it hard enough to
send it flailing into the collection of demons that now began to
gather around him.

Guhl-iban. Haborym. At least half a dozen more of Axtius's
soldiers, taken from various breeds. Nearly a dozen Mahkesh,
all now wielding the cutlasses and waraxes of their tribe save
one, who held a golden bow, already nocked with an arrow the
color of rust. They moved quickly to encircle him.

Angel's hands flexed as if only now realizing there was no weapon for them to grasp. He bared his fangs again and turned to Axtius.

"What's incredible to me," Axtius snarled, hatred blazing in his eyes, shuddering slightly so that the spines that jutted from his face shook, "is that you survived my vengeance, and yet still you set yourself against me. Don't you see that this city is already mine? Somehow you have developed the illusion that you are more than a nuisance."

Angel took a single step toward Axtius. The Mahkesh and the other demons closed the circle more tightly, blades now thrusting toward the vampire. Flames flickered around Haborym's hands. Gunn was forced facedown on the ground, and a Vahrall planted a heavy boot on the back of his neck. Unconscious, Buffy was left to bleed.

"You think we're the only ones who are going to stand against you?" Angel asked, the threat implicit in his tone.

Axtius laughed. "You prove my point about your delusions of self-importance, vampire. Nothing can stand in my way."

The Brachen demon waved his hand, a gesture of command. Angel whirled in time to see the Mahkesh bowman release his arrow. It whistled as it sliced through the air toward Angel's chest. He tried to evade the arrow.

He simply wasn't fast enough.

Los Angeles

The hotel was eerily quiet. Tara could not imagine how anyone could stand to be alone inside the enormous old building. It echoed with the ghosts of the lives that had been touched as employees and guests passed through the place. It wasn't meant to be empty. Calvin was crashed out asleep in one of the rooms upstairs, but Tara sat with Fred in Wesley's office. No way was she going anywhere in this old place by herself.

Not that there was anything to be afraid of; not really. It was just so very lonely. The feeling was only exacerbated by the story Fred had been telling.

"You poor thing," Tara said, gazing at the pale, fragile-looking girl. "All that time in such a savage place. Living in a cave by yourself. You must have been so lonesome."

Fred glanced away. Tara felt badly, worried that her words had struck too close to home, had brought back difficult memories for the brilliant young woman about her years lost in the demon dimension of Pylea.

"That was one of the worst parts of it, yes," Fred agreed with a small nod. She smiled shyly. "I'd say spending that much time alone could drive a person crazy, but I don't think it would be just hyperbole. I think I did go a little crazy. And then Angel came along. He saved me."

Tara smiled back, pushing her hair away from her eyes. "He does that a lot, I hear." She yawned, covering her mouth. "It's hard, isn't it? Finding out there's so much darkness in the world. But you've got some good people to face it with."

"Seems like you do too," Fred replied.

"Oh, I do," Tara agreed wistfully. "I do." Her mind went to Willow, and she wondered what was happening out on that island, what kind of reception her girlfriend and the others had received.

"You miss her, huh? Even though it's only been a little while?" Fred asked.

Tara blushed slightly and glanced away. "I . . . I miss her whenever she's not with me. Even . . . even for a minute."

"Gosh, I hope someday I find someone who'll miss me that

much," Fred said with earnest admiration. "Of course, I wouldn't want them to miss me, so I probably wouldn't go anywhere unless I had to."

"Sometimes the choice gets taken away from us. There are just things we have to do," Tara said.

"Yeah," Fred replied, almost dreamily. "Still, it's really something."

From the tone of her voice and the faraway look in her eyes, Tara wondered if there was someone Fred already felt that way about, or hoped to, and though she normally was not one to intrude, she was about to ask when she heard footsteps on the stairs.

"Calvin's awake," she said, hating to state the obvious but feeling as though in a spooky old place like this that it might be for the best.

"In here!" Fred called, and then she seemed to start, as though frightened by her own raised voice.

A moment later, Calvin appeared in the doorway to the office. He wore the same T-shirt and torn jeans he had had on earlier, but he was barefoot. He stretched and yawned as he stepped into the office, a line still creased on his face where he had lain on a pillowcase seam. "Hey," he said. "I just wanted to come down and see how things went. Gunn and the others aren't back yet?"

"Not yet," Tara confirmed.

"When was the last time they called in?" Calvin asked.

"Right before they were going to enter the warehouse," Fred confirmed. "They're supposed to check in every hour, but it's only been . . ." She glanced up at the clock on the wall and her eyes went wide, alarm sketching an almost cartoon expression on her face.

Tara looked at the time. "Oh no," she said, getting up, glancing quickly at Calvin. "We were just talking and lost track of the time."

"Well, when were they supposed to check in?" the young man asked.

Fred had gotten up immediately after noticing the time and had gone to a heavy bookcase at the back of Wesley's office. The glass doors were locked, but she fished around on top of it for the key and opened it up.

"Forty-five minutes ago," she said as she pulled a book from the shelf and began flipping through it.

Calvin swore low, under his breath. "That ain't good, ladies. You don't think they're—"

"Don't even say it," Fred snapped. "And no. They can't be."

Tara's mouth had gone dry, and her heart was beating too loudly in her chest. She was trying to imagine in her mind that Buffy, Angel, and Gunn could be dead, was testing it out in her head, and she could not.

"We've got to go there. Right now," she said, mind whirling, pulse speeding as she tried to figure out how she, Fred, and Calvin might be able to do any harm to demons who had been able to stop Angel, Buffy, and Gunn from checking in.

"Not right now," Fred said curtly.

Tara glanced up at her. Calvin stared at her also. Suddenly Fred did not look nearly as sweet and demure as she had a few moments earlier. A frown creased her forehead, and she was all business as she held out the ancient tome she had drawn from Wesley's bookcase.

"Can you learn this?" she asked, sliding the book into Tara's hands.

"Maybe?" Tara replied hesitantly, studying the Latin text on the page.

Fred glanced down as though she herself were responsible for what had happened to the others. "Maybe isn't going to be good enough."

With a short, sharp intake of breath, Tara nodded. "Then yes. I'll work it out."

"All right," Fred said gravely. "Now we just need a plan." She glanced over at Calvin. "Charles would want you to stay behind, but we could use you."

Calvin grinned. "Then use me, I'm all yours."

Burbank

As consciousness seeped into her mind, Buffy groaned. Before she even opened her eyes she felt the iron cuffs around her wrists and the sensation of dangling from them. Her wrists were chafed badly, but when she put weight on her feet to take the burden off her hands, a sliver of pain shot through her. The Slayer hissed air through her teeth and winced, her eyes at last fluttering open.

Angel's voice floated out of the dimness around her. "Buffy."

Her vision still focusing, she looked around. She was inside a warehouse—presumably the same one where Axtius had turned the tables on their planned ambush—which was lit just enough so that she could see Angel chained to a support beam twenty feet away. "Hey," she rasped, her throat dry.

"Hey." The relief was obvious in his voice. "You had me worried there."

"Take more than the Thundercats to do me in," Buffy replied, though the pain in her lower abdomen and her rib cage beneath her left arm throbbed with an urgent reminder that the demons she had thought of immediately as Thundercats had done a pretty good job of it. If they had wanted her dead, she would be.

Already she had begun to heal. Of all the so-called gifts that came along with being Chosen to be the Slayer, superhuman healing was pretty much number one.

"Are you all right?" she asked Angel.

In the gloom of the warehouse she saw him stand a bit straighter.

"I'll be fine."

Which meant that he wasn't fine now, but that he would be. Buffy might have given him a hard time over the semantics, but since she was in roughly the same condition, she figured she would let it go. A Mahkesh arrow jutted from Angel's chest, just inches from his heart. Word was the Mahkesh weapons never failed to find their mark. That meant that, for now at least, Axtius wanted Angel alive. The arrow had even been removed before Angel was chained up. She knew that probably meant Axtius had far worse in store for them later, but Buffy did not care about that. As far as she was concerned, they weren't going to give Axtius a later.

Should've killed us when you had the chance, moron, she thought. "Gunn?" she asked.

"He's still out," Angel replied.

Buffy glanced around the warehouse. The place was enormous and almost completely empty. It took her only a moment to spot Gunn, chained to another support beam across the floor from her—the three of them in a kind of triangle. Gunn was bound the same way she and Angel had been, but he was seated on the ground, slumped back against the steel beam. A surge of concern swept through her. Gunn looked dead.

"You're sure he's all right?" she asked.

A strange, chuffing sound whispered through the warehouse and it took Buffy a moment to realize it was quiet laughter coming from Angel.

"He's fine. Bruised, maybe, but fine. They didn't knock him out. He's taking a nap. He got bored waiting for you to wake up."

The Slayer gaped across the dimness at Gunn, astonished at the idea that the guy could fall asleep in a situation like this. It had to be some kind of defense mechanism, or sheer exhaustion, or . . . she thought about it and realized that with the life Gunn had led, being able to catch an hour's sleep in almost any circumstance would be considered a survival skill.

"Do you think we should wake him up now?" she asked, lowering her voice.

"He's fine. Give him a little while," Angel said.

They had been speaking quietly, and in the vast warehouse with Gunn asleep and no one else to hear them, there was a kind of intimacy in the air. For a moment Buffy hesitated to continue, relishing all that remained unspoken between them. *This is how it ought to have been,* she thought. *How it could have been.* The two of them, facing the darkness together.

A smile edged up at the corners of her mouth, and she rolled her eyes. *Oh yeah, real romantic, Buffy,* she thought. *Isn't this sweet, we get to be tortured and possibly die together.* Not that she thought that was going to happen—she was confident they would get out of their predicament—but there was certainly something perverse about her idea of romance.

Forget it, she told herself. *That's yesterday.*

She could not tell in the gloom, but she thought Angel might be staring at her.

"Buffy," he said, his voice a low rasp, a familiar, suggestive tone.

"Yeah," she replied. "Fancy meeting you here."

The feelings they had for each other created a tension between them, but now it broke. They both began to laugh softly.

"So what now?" she asked. "Axtius has a major mad-on for you. Why aren't we all dead?"

Angel tugged forward, testing his bonds, using his feet against the support beam to try to get leverage enough to break the chains. This went on only for a few seconds before he paused and turned back to Buffy. She wished she could see his face better in the dark, that she could make out his expression.

"I think we have you to thank for that," he told her. "After they dragged you in here he thanked me for bringing you along. We know that Axtius isn't the top of the totem pole; he has someone he answers to. Something tells me he wants to put on a little show for them."

A chill went through Buffy. The Thundercats had known who she was, called her "Slayer," and though she had managed to kill two of them with one of their own weapons, they had overwhelmed her with their speed and really crappy odds. It had to have been ten or twelve to one.

"Great," she said, sighing. "Nothing like a little public execution to make my day." With a frown, she glanced around again, peering into the darkness. "So why no guards? He doesn't really think we'll just wait for him to come back, does he?"

Once more, with a grunt of effort, Angel lodged his feet against the support beam and tried to snap his chains to no avail.

"Apparently he does. Though I'm guessing there are guards. Probably outside. The Mahkesh. Maybe a few of the others."

"Mahkesh?" Buffy asked.

"Thundercats."

"Ah." She nodded.

For long seconds they stood in silence. Buffy began to test her own bonds. Whatever else he was, Axtius was not a fool. The chains and the iron cuffs that were around her wrists were very thick, very solid. She remembered her little sister Dawn telling her once in very gory detail about a Stephen King novel in which a woman handcuffed to a bed practically tore off her own hands getting out, how her skin started to slide off like she was wearing gloves. Buffy shuddered. Not really an option for her.

Not yet, at least.

"You know what I don't get?" she said, turning to Angel again, peering at him through the gloom. "Axtius was so disgusted with himself, with his own behavior, after doing the wild thing with Doyle's mom, that he went off and joined the Nazi Demon Jamboree or whatever. So he despised what his son was, but he still scoured the world looking for magick that could drain the human out of Doyle, make him more like Axtius. He could have just had more children. A demon as nasty as Axtius . . . why would he care?"

This time the silence that hung suspended between them was heavy with something other than intimacy, a bittersweet thing not unlike regret.

"Very few creatures are pure evil," Angel replied, voice low. "Doyle was his son. I understand why Axtius wants to kill me. It isn't because he blames me for Doyle's death. It's because he blames me for stealing away the possibility that he could finally have made Doyle the son he always wanted him to be. Never mind what Doyle would have wanted. That never matters.

"Lots of fathers are disappointed with their children; it's not unusual for them to want their kids to be more like them. Especially their sons. Fathers want their sons to share their morals and beliefs."

More than ever, Buffy wished that she could see his face, that she could reach out and take his hand. "We're not just talking about Doyle anymore, are we?"

Angel glanced up, his face bathed in shadows. "No. I guess we're not. His father wanted him to be more vicious, more brutal, to kill. It's easy to shake your head at that. Axtius is a demon. He's evil. But lots of fathers just want their sons to grow up to be responsible and decent."

"Like your father," Buffy offered gently.

At first Angel did not reply. At length, though, he chuckled softly. "He was a bastard, my father."

Buffy felt her jaw tighten. Images of her own father flickered through her mind, of this man who had divorced her mother and then become a casual drifter in her life, there when it suited him and gone when it did not, cavalier with her affections, with her heart. She still loved him, of course. He was her father. But there was no intimacy between them; Hank Summers made no effort to understand who his daughter was.

On the other hand, Buffy was more fortunate than many other people in similar circumstances. Her father might have to be reminded he had a daughter, but Buffy had Giles. Certainly the Watcher wasn't her father, but Buffy had a bond with him that went deeper than blood. In life, she had learned, there was the family you were born with and the family you chose. In that sense, Giles was a better father to her than she ever could have hoped. Buffy knew he would always be there for her.

She thought again about Angel's father and her own, and then her mind automatically went to Xander's father, and to Tara's as well.

"Some people aren't meant to be parents," she said, her words echoing through the warehouse. She had spoken more loudly than she'd intended.

"That's a hard truth to learn," he replied. "But was my father any different from other men of his era? Would any of them have behaved differently if they'd had a son like . . . a son like me?"

Buffy wanted to argue with him, but she could not. They had

spoken several times before about what Angel had been like in the days before he had become a vampire. A drunken brawler, an irresponsible layabout. And *after* he had become undead . . . but no, that was something else entirely.

"You turned out all right," Buffy offered. "You're one of the good guys, Angel."

Again, it took him a moment to respond. "I've wondered a million times if he was always a bastard, or if having me for a son made him that way."

Buffy gazed at him, knowing that vampires could see very well in the dark, that he could probably see the expression on her face.

"We all have regrets," she said. "Axtius is a monster, pure and simple. But I'm sure there was a part of Doyle that wondered why it had to be like it was. Once upon a time all of our mothers saw something in all of our fathers that was good. Kinda scary to think about, but true.

"Even if you hated your father then, even if you feel terrible about it now, all of that went into making you who you are now. So I'm grateful for him, just for being your father."

The sound of someone clearing his throat echoed around the empty warehouse. Buffy and Angel both turned to find that the source of the sound was Charles Gunn. He was little more than a silhouette in the dim light, set against that steel beam. Gunn was still seated, but his head was up now. Buffy could not help wondering how long he had been awake; how much he had heard.

"Sorry to interrupt," Gunn said, and she believed that he meant it, that he was as uncomfortable with whatever he had heard of their conversation as she was. "But maybe we should get out of here now. No way to tell how long it'll be before Axtius comes back."

Buffy arched an eyebrow and stared at him a moment. "Easy for you to say, Sleepyhead." She spun around, ducking under her own arms, crossing the chains at her wrists. Then she planted her feet against the beam, just as Angel had done, and with all her strength, hauled against her bonds. The chains scraped the beam, sending sparks flying, and gave a kind of creak that made her think they might snap.

They did not.

"You know," Buffy said as she stopped trying, ignoring the pain in her wrists, "I'm starting to think there's some spell on these or something."

"Makes sense," Gunn replied. "But whoever cast it wasn't exactly thorough."

Something in his tone made her turn toward him. Buffy was stunned when she saw Gunn standing several feet from the beam with a long chain dangling from the cuff on one wrist, and the other wrist completely free.

"You've been busy," Angel observed dryly.

"Didn't mean to eavesdrop," Gunn replied. "But I wasn't sleeping. If Axtius did some hoodoo on these chains, it was only to keep them from breaking. Doesn't stop 'em from being picked."

He raised his hands to display them. Something glinted silver in his right fist, catching the diffuse light, and then Gunn went to work on the other cuff that had been holding him. It had taken him ages to get the first one off, but then he had been bound. The second one took under three minutes.

"You're an expert lockpick?" Buffy asked incredulously.

"Not an expert. Trust me. I know experts," Gunn replied, rubbing at his unmanacled wrists. "Wasn't that hard, actually. Most cuffs aren't. Growing up in my neighborhood, you pick certain things up is all. And there are some tools you always have handy. With my crew, a stake, and one of these." He held up the sliver of steel again.

"You get a gold star," Angel told him. "Now get us out of here."

"My pleasure," Gunn replied.

Buffy still felt slightly awkward—he had overheard her entire conversation with Angel—but somehow she doubted that Gunn was the type to repeat what he had heard. When he walked over to her she gave him a grateful nod and turned so that he could reach her manacles.

In the darkness of the rafters above her head, something hissed.

"Gunn!" Angel shouted.

Even as Buffy looked up, something lunged at Gunn from above, knocking him to the concrete floor. Its skin seemed wet in the dim light, and it hissed as it gripped its forward talons around Gunn's throat and began to squeeze.

Gunn stabbed it in the eye with his lockpick. The thing shrieked and staggered sideways. Wheezing, clutching his throat, Gunn got to his feet and began kicking the demon, which reminded Buffy of a Gila monster, only without a tail.

The problem was, it wasn't alone.

A chorus of hissing came from above, and Buffy looked around to find that there were other Gila-demons crawling down the walls and down the support beams. They moved so quickly, they almost seemed to be swimming toward the floor instead of crawling, bodies undulating back and forth.

Gunn swore. He bent to pick up the chain he had released himself from, lifted it, and began to swing it. He managed to strike one of them before the others leaped upon him and dragged him into the darkness.

Angel called his name, and Buffy listened for some response, but only a muffled rustling and a clanking of chain came from the shadows on the far side of the warehouse.

She gazed up into the rafters. Axtius had not been as foolish as she had thought. The general was not relying only on enchanted bonds. Buffy peered into the gloom, wishing yet again that she could see Angel's face.

Furious, now, she planted her feet against the steel column again and began to tug. The cuffs chafed her wrists, but even when she began to bleed, she did not stop.

Questral

What a weird world this is, Xander thought, lying in the darkness in his hut not far from a green-skinned karaoke-singing psychic demon with a predilection for pastel suits. The weirdest part of that, though, was that Xander had taken to Lorne almost instantly. Sure, demon, and horns and all, but he was almost impossible not to like.

"Hey, Lorne," he said, continuing the kind of middle-of-the-night-can't-sleep conversation he remembered having during sleepovers when he was a kid. "Did you ever meet this Doyle guy? What was he like?"

The demon's silky voice came to him in the darkness. "Never did, chico. But from what I hear, he was a troubled soul. Haunted by what he was and didn't want to be. I've known a lot of guys like that, actually."

Xander glanced over, and even in the dark he could see the outline of Lorne, lying on his back with his hands under his head, horns protruding from his forehead.

"He didn't want to be like his father," Xander said.

"That's about the size of it."

A deep sadness welled up in Xander, then. A melancholy the likes of which he tried desperately never to indulge in. Echoes of his father's voice—seemingly always raised in anger—drifted around inside his mind. And etched there as if in stone, that *look* his father had, the one that had always made him feel so worthless.

"I know the feeling," Xander admitted. "If my dad ever found a spell that could get rid of all the things he didn't want me to be, I'm sure he'd use it in a heartbeat."

Lorne sat up and looked at him. Xander could just make out the kind expression on his face.

"Trust me, sometimes being a disappointment to your parents is the best thing you can do in life. I'm a planet-size disappointment to my family, and, wow, thank goodness for that."

Xander could not help but smile, though he was somewhat envious that Lorne could be so laid back about his family situation.

Before he could respond, there was a rustling at the door and both of them looked up to see Wesley enter. Xander had been growing concerned that he had been gone so long after Lorne came back, but Wesley was smiling.

"Good news?" Xander asked.

Wesley started. "You're awake?" he said in surprise as he took off his glasses and began to settle down on his own bedroll for a nap. "I thought you'd both be sleeping by now."

"Who can sleep while the jury's still out?" Lorne replied.

Xander knew what he meant. They were all concerned about what might happen if the Assemblage decided they were unwelcome after all.

"Not to worry," Wesley told them, smiling even more broadly. "I've just been to speak to Cordelia. It appears that she and Willow made some headway with Ephraim and the sorcerer, Dai'shu. Also, Zeke tells me that the Vapor, Ileana, is going to speak on our behalf as well. She's even going to ask that they release Spike. It seems we've got at least half the Assemblage willing to give us the benefit of the doubt. I've no idea what prompted Ileana's support, but I'm glad to have it."

Xander shuddered slightly. The Vapor demon—the breath-takingly beautiful wraith—was going to support them, and ask for Spike's release. Wesley had no idea why Ileana would do such a thing, but Xander had a feeling he did.

Spike, he thought. It seemed that his hut had not been the Vapor's only stop of the evening.

To his surprise, and not without a certain flush of guilt, Xander found that he was jealous.

CHAPTER FIFTEEN

Los Angeles

"I need another boat," Axtius said, kneeling down at the edge of the swimming pool, staring at the water's sole occupant with an unwavering gaze.

The merman, a hairless demon covered in scales with the upper body of a humanoid and the lower half of a fish, floated in the water with slow, languid waves of its large, fanned tail. His name was Ricco, and Axtius didn't care for his kind in the least.

"Another boat?" Ricco echoed, a disturbing smile adorning his amphibious features. "What do you think, they grow on trees?" He began to laugh, a gurgling sound that reminded Axtius of something drowning, its lungs filling with fluid.

"I'm well aware of their scarcity, Ricco," he said, removing one of his leather gloves, placing his hand in the water, and swirling it around. It was warm—almost to an extreme. "But it doesn't change the fact that I need one."

Ricco's base of operation was an abandoned health club on Hollywood Boulevard. Axtius had already visited once, during the earliest stages of his plan, and had intended never to return, but cruel fate had deemed otherwise.

The annoying merman swam in circles, an irritating clucking sound coming from his mouth. "I need one, I need one," he repeated in a mocking tone. "Just because you need one doesn't mean that I have one," Ricco said, lying back in water and using powerful flips of his tail to propel himself the length of the Olympic-size pool.

Axtius fumed as he waited for the aquatic demon to swim back toward him. But no matter how much Ricco vexed him, he would not allow the creature to blemish his good mood. He thought of Angel and the Slayer imprisoned back at the warehouse, and elation coursed through him. Their deaths would provide the proof his masters needed; proof that he was indeed the correct choice to spearhead this glorious mission to purify the demon race. He mused briefly on the notoriety he would gain with the elimination of the half-breed nest—and how bittersweet the victory would be without his son by his side to share it.

The Brachen's good mood quickly began to evaporate, and he watched with a predator's eye as the merman swam toward him.

"I do have an old ship," Ricco said, swimming closer to the edge. "Not the top of the fleet, but it's the best I can do on such short notice."

"How much?" Axtius asked, his hand moving through the tepid water.

Ricco swam in a circle, his muscular tail splashing the water as he moved about. "Ten million," he replied. "Five now, five on delivery."

Axtius removed his hand from the water, flicking the moisture from it onto the tiles at the pool's edge. "What was that?" he asked, placing the hand to his ear. "With all your splashing about, I couldn't quite hear you."

The merman surged forward with a powerful wave of his tail, a cruel smile on his swollen, fishlike lips. "By all means, let me repeat myself, General. Twenty million," the merman spat defiantly. "Ten million now—"

Axtius shot out his arm and grabbed the aquatic demon by the throat, cutting his words of defiance short. The demon general watched amused as the gills on the side of the supplier's neck began to flap nervously, suddenly eager for the flow of water across them.

"It must be the acoustics here," Axtius said with a rumbling chuckle, pulling Ricco up from the water by the neck. "But I could have sworn you said twenty million dollars."

A strange, fishy odor that could only have been the scent of a merman's fear emanated from Ricco's scaled skin in pungent waves. "I'm the only game in town, Axtius," he stammered, his eyes bulging more than usual. "You don't want to draw attention to yourself yet by slaughtering the crew of some oil tanker. That leaves me. Hurt me and you'll have nothing."

Axtius pulled him closer so their faces nearly touched. "Now who said anything about hurting you?" he growled. "I just want to be certain that I heard the right price—wouldn't want you to think I'd pay anything but fair market value." He increased his grip upon the fish man's throat, enjoying the fact that he held the pathetic creature's life in his hand. "Business is business and fair is fair," Axtius said with a slow, knowledgeable nod of his head. "And I'd hate to have to go to a *human* vendor for my purposes."

"Eight million," Ricco gasped, squirming in the demon's clutches. His tail nervously slapped at the water beneath him.

"Eight million?" Axtius asked, tightening his grip just a bit, to show who was indeed the master.

"Eight million on delivery," Ricco blurted out.

Axtius released the merman, allowing him to fall back into the pool where he quickly submerged himself, diving to the bottom. The general stood, grinning, a bit of his pleasant mood having been revived.

"You'll have your money in a matter of hours," he said as he flexed the muscles in his hand, "and I will expect my ship in the same."

Ricco had returned to the surface and had swum to the center of the pool, rubbing at his throat with a webbed hand. He nodded silently in agreement.

"A pleasure doing business with you again, Ricco," Axtius said with a slight bow before turning his back and striding from the abandoned health spa to his waiting limousine.

There was still much to be done, and time was at a premium.

Burbank

The ancient spell of mistrust floated around in Tara's head, and she had to make a conscious effort to prevent the arcane words from becoming nothing more than an incoherent jumble inside her brain. She had to stay focused. If Buffy, Angel, and Gunn were still alive, and she certainly hoped they were, it was up to Fred, Calvin, and her to free them. Everyone else was occupied elsewhere, on that vacation getaway called Monster Island.

Tara squatted with Fred and Calvin in the cover of high grass and weeds along the edge of the warehouse parking lot. They weren't much, the three of them, but Tara had begun to think that perhaps they each had more to offer than any of them had assumed. Fred had survived years in a demon dimension. Petite and unassuming as she was, she was brilliant and courageous.

And Calvin . . . Tara had only learned a portion of Calvin's story, but what she did know made her shudder. The kid's parents had been slaughtered by vampires years earlier and only recently had he learned that his own father was one of them, and had come back to town in search of his son.

A lot like Axtius, in fact. A nasty, sadistic son of a bitch who wanted his boy to be just like him.

The big difference was that Calvin was still alive. Gunn and his crew . . . and now Tara herself and all of Angel's and Buffy's friends . . . were determined to keep him that way. She felt almost guilty for bringing him into this, not that he would have stood for being left out. But at the same time, there was something comforting in having him around. With the hell some of them had gone through with their own fathers—Tara herself included—this teenage boy was an example to live up to, a reminder that one didn't have to become what your parents expected of you, didn't have to be driven down by the ugliness heaped on you.

Even though Fred apparently had wonderful parents, Tara thought that she admired Calvin's fortitude as well. Fred might not be able to relate, but she saw the kid's big heart.

"All right," Calvin said, grinning, his eyes sparkling. "Let's go kick some demon ass."

"There are two of them guarding the front entrance," Fred said, looking through a compact pair of night-vision goggles that she had found in the hotel weapons chest. "Catlike—in the eat-you-in-one-gulp kind, not the here-kitty-kitty. Very formidable looking, and oh, did I mention sharp weaponry?" Fred brought the goggles down from her eyes and stared at Tara.

Calvin was staring as well.

"You up for this?" Fred asked.

There was a tension in her voice that Tara found a bit disconcerting, but under these circumstances how could they not all be tense? It was up to them to save the day, and with her being a major ingredient in whether the plan would be successful or not, she was feeling a bit stressed.

"I-I'm okay," Tara answered with a nervous nod of her head.

The spell of mistrust spun round and round inside her head. She tried an old trick she had used to help her memorize things in high school—setting the words to music. The old song "Locomotion" and the ancient Latin words seemed to go together quite nicely.

"No time like the here and now," Calvin said, clutching the short sword, also from the weapons chest back at the hotel. He was sounding more and more like a veteran in the battle against the forces of darkness.

"Now?" Tara asked Fred as she positioned the spell in her mind.

Fred held a weapon as well, a nasty-looking mace with a spiked head. *Wouldn't want to be on the receiving end of that,* Tara thought as she prepared to unleash her magick.

"Let'er rip," Fred said, standing up, Calvin at her heels.

Tara stood as well. She had to have some eye contact with the area she was hoping to affect. The ancient spell, to the tune of "Locomotion," spilled from her lips—and she doubted that she had ever been so scared. So much was riding on her performance—but one thing, one happy constant in her life kept her lack of confidence from spinning out of control. Tara thought of Willow—her Willow, and all the magick they had done together, both supernatural and otherwise—and suddenly things didn't seem quite so bad.

I can do this, Tara thought. *Willow would tell me I can do this. She'd believe in me, so I've got to believe in myself.*

The spell had been building up inside her slowly, gradually, and when it felt as though it were going to explode out of her body, Tara extended her arms and let the magick flow from her fingertips at the looming structure before her. It glided through the air and formed a writhing, bluish cloud that drifted down from the sky to envelop the warehouse.

Tara held her breath as she watched the two feline sentries catch sight of the approaching Fred and Calvin. She was about to cast another spell, something a bit more destructive, when she saw that the glamour she had woven had begun to kick in.

Savagely and without provocation, one of the tigerlike demons turned on the other. It raised its gold sword above its head and brought the blade down to slice through the thick, muscular shoulder of its compatriot. The other beast shrieked in a combination of surprise and pain. It turned to face its assailant, pulling a knife from a scabbard at its side, plunging it deep into the attacker's belly.

Tara flinched with each new act of violence. The spell was a complete success, but it made her want to throw up. Calvin turned and gave her the thumbs-up, but she only smiled weakly. She did not want to accept praise for something so violent and bloody.

She and Calvin joined Fred at the warehouse door, but as Tara passed the two cat demons lying one atop the other in a bloody heap, one opened its gore-flecked eyes and glared at her. Its body began to thrash as it tried to pull itself to its feet and attack her. She drew back, fingers contorting as she prepared a spell to fend it off, but that turned out to be unnecessary. A moment later it succumbed to its injuries, a whistling exhalation of death escaping its fanged mouth.

"What was that all about?" Calvin asked her, tensed as he stood near the door. "You said they'd only be going after each other."

"I . . . I don't know," Tara stammered, quickly moving by the demon corpses to join Fred by the warehouse door. "It's supposed to make supernatural beasts turn on one another. It shouldn't even have noticed us."

Tara was shaken, but the question would have to wait until after they had taken care of business inside. Still, she could not shake the sense that something might be wrong.

"Here we go," Fred said, turning the knob and swinging the door wide. The sounds of ferocious battle greeted them as they prepared to enter. "Oh my," Fred whispered.

Tara peered over her shoulder to get a look at what had garnered such a response. Her mouth gaped open in shock as she stared at the melee she saw unfolding before her—the results of her spell of mistrust.

The horrors she had wrought.

The smell of his former lover's blood filled his nostrils—and Angel wanted nothing more than to slip his bonds, go to the Slayer, and beat her within an inch of her life for the pain she had caused him.

He recoiled from the disturbing, alien emotions roiling around inside him and tried to decipher their source, but when the first of the reptilian creatures guarding them had sunk its sharp, needle teeth into the face of another, Angel knew something was amiss. Within seconds all the lizard creatures were tearing at one another, the ferocity of their fighting almost too much to watch.

"Buffy," he called across the darkened room, suppressing the feeling that she had somehow betrayed him, "Buffy, something's happening."

He heard her grunt and then the rattle of chains as she struggled to free herself. "Shut up," she hissed. "I think I've heard more than enough from you the past couple of days."

There was venom in her tone, and he suspected that whatever was affecting him and their reptilian guards was having a similar effect on her as well. *Stupid bitch,* he thought. *Not even listening to me. I should rip out her throat . . . drink her down . . .*

No.

"Listen," he said to her, watching as one of the tailless lizard demons tore the head off one of its brethren in a spray of gore, "I . . . damn it . . . I know how you're feeling right now. I'm feeling pretty much the same."

The smell of her blood was stronger as she continued to work on the chains. It made him want to howl with rage, but he held it in check. "It isn't right. Look . . . look around, Buffy. Something's affecting us—them." He motioned with his chin to the fighting guards, trying to tune out the tearing of flesh and gnashing of fangs.

"It's sorcery, Buffy. Look at . . . look at the guards. I think the cavalry has arrived."

The lizard demons' numbers had dwindled to nearly half, the dead torn asunder, limbs scattered around the room, blood pooling on the concrete. The way they were fighting, Angel guessed that the remainder would be dead in no time at all.

He was returning to his disturbing ruminations on how long it would take for him to beat his former lover to death, when the front door opened and Fred stepped inside followed by Calvin, and then Tara.

"Would you look at that?" he heard Buffy say. "You were actually right about something—for once."

Angel suppressed the overwhelming urge to gnaw off his own hands and leap across the room to shove his bloody stumps down her throat, shutting her up for good. The sight of Tara made him certain they had fallen prey to some kind of magickal spell. He watched as they hurriedly crossed the warehouse, avoiding what remained of the battle-frenzied lizard demons and the puddles of lime green blood and sundered body parts that littered the floor. A pair of the reptilian monstrosities lunged for Tara but she rattled off a spell that froze them in place long enough for Fred and Calvin to finish them off.

"Hey," Fred said as she reached Angel, wearing a big smile filled with relief. "Nice to see that you're still in one piece."

A sense of calm eddied through Angel's tormented mind. The chaos, the rage, and the murderous edge were still there, but Fred's presence seemed to have interrupted it momentarily. He frowned. Whatever made him want to rip Buffy apart did not seem to be affecting how he felt toward Fred.

Calvin came up beside Fred, eyes darting around, searching the darkness of the warehouse. "Hey," the kid said. "Where's Gunn?"

Angel twitched. The urge deep in him to slaughter Buffy, to massacre the reptilian guards, did not seem to apply to Calvin, either. The vampire nodded toward the shadows on the other side of the warehouse.

"They . . . dragged him over there. Check on him."

Immediately, alarm lighting up his eyes, Calvin ran to search for Gunn. Angel glanced around the warehouse and quickly established that the last of the swift, wall-crawling demons that had been left to watch over them was dead. They had massacred one another.

Then Tara stepped up beside Fred, and Angel felt his fury begin to boil all over again. That made him certain.

"What did you use?" he asked the shy witch in an angry hiss. Tara seemed confused by his question, and he couldn't hold back his inexplicable anger.

"What the hell did you use, you stupid cow?" He strained against his bonds, his scarred features transforming into the hideous countenance of the vampire.

Tara stumbled back, eyes flashing with anger. Her mouth began to move, a spell upon her lips—and the tips of her fingers crackled with blue light.

"Hey!" Fred exclaimed, shocked by their actions. "Save it for the bad guys."

Angel shook his head violently, trying to clear the homicidal rage from it. "The spell," he said in a strained whisper. "To make the demons turn on one another—what was it?"

"Get me the hell out of these!" Buffy suddenly shrieked from across the room, pulling on her chains like a madwoman. Blood poured down her forearms, little crimson rivulets where she had torn the flesh at her wrists trying to escape. "I've got business to take care of!"

She was glaring at Angel, and he felt certain she was thinking of how she would love to kill him—it was the same kind of feeling he was experiencing at the moment as well. He suppressed a particularly colorful burst of profanity and returned his attention to Fred. The expression on her face told him that she had just now realized something was seriously amiss.

Tara grunted and put a hand to her face, overtly struggling with her emotions. Angel could tell from the way her lips twisted into a scowl, her teeth grinding together, that she was being affected just as he was. Perhaps not as strongly, but affected just the same.

"It was a spell of mistrust," she blurted out, obviously fighting the magick. "It was supposed to make supernatural beings distrust one another, but I . . . something went wrong."

Angel shook his head, finally understanding what had gone wrong. "No, you didn't screw up . . . spell worked just fine." He found that he was snarling at her, and it took every ounce of willpower to stop.

"I don't . . . ," Tara began, and then the realization of what had happened began to sink in. "Oh," she said, her hand going to her mouth. "How could I have been so stupid?"

"What's goin' on?" Calvin asked, distracting them.

Angel glanced over and saw that Calvin had found Gunn after all. He was bleeding from a gash on his cheek, and his face was bruised and puffy. He favored his right leg when he walked, and winced every time he took a step with the left. But he was alive. Gunn was all right.

Despite the primal, violent feelings that overwhelmed him, relief washed through Angel. But then Gunn moved toward Buffy, and he stiffened. Gunn had somehow retrieved his lockpick and was in the process of setting her free.

"No," Angel spat, straining against his bonds. "Gunn . . . don't. Not until the spell is lifted."

Buffy went crazy, thrashing against the chains like a wild animal. "You set me free right now," she screamed, as both Gunn and Calvin slowly backed away from her. "What's the matter, Angel?" she said with a snarl. "Afraid I'll get to you before you can get to me?"

"Would somebody please tell me what is going on here?" Fred demanded, confused and annoyed.

Tara piped up. "They're . . ." She winced as if speaking caused her pain. "They're supernatural creatures. I'm . . . I'm a supernatural creature, in a way, from the contact I've had with . . . with magick," she said, obviously disgusted by her lack of insight. "I should have put two and two together when that demon tried to attack me outside. The spell can't differentiate between who's good and who's not."

Visibly struggling against the violent urges that must even then have been surging up within her, Tara began to recite another spell. A crackling energy leaped from her outstretched fingertips, permeating the air and dispelling the magick that lingered there. It was as if a gigantic fan had been turned on, blowing away the poisonous glamour. In a matter of seconds, Angel felt the weight of his anger lifted away and breathed a sigh of relief. He had not cared for the feeling in the least; it reminded him a little too much of times past, when he went by the name of Angelus.

Tara lowered her arms and offered a nervous, apologetic smile. "How's that?"

Angel returned the smile, thankful that the madness had passed. "It's safe now," he said to Gunn, who went to work on Buffy's manacles with the long, thin piece of metal.

"Have you out of these in a second," Gunn said, manipulating the metal pick within the locking mechanism of Buffy's bonds.

"And I promise not to kill any of you once you do," the Slayer said as the first of the manacles sprang open.

Buffy glanced around sheepishly, as though she had just pranced naked out into her living room with all her friends around. Angel wanted to laugh or hug her; he could not decide which.

Los Angeles

Guhl-iban sensed opportunity in the air. It was a unique talent of his demonic species to be able to read and exploit an opponent's weakness. Now, for the first time since pledging his allegiance to the Coalition's holy cause, the marrow-eater had the nagging impression that something was amiss, something he could use to his own advantage.

Axtius drove a balled fist down into the center of his desktop, splintering the wood surrounding the point of impact. "Damn him and all who stand with him!" the demon general raged, bringing down the other fist with equal force.

Haborym had just informed Axtius of Angel's escape and, not surprisingly, the Brachen demon was not at all pleased. But there was something in the general's behavior that Guhl-iban had never witnessed before: a raw emotional recklessness that hinted of weakness—a chink in the mighty Axtius's armor. *A vulnerability to be exploited, perhaps?* Guhl-iban wondered. It seemed unlikely that the escape of one captive would be all that was needed to set the fierce Brachen warrior on edge. Perhaps there was something more to Axtius's rage, something yet to be revealed.

"Angel did not escape by himself, General," Guhl-iban said as his commanding officer continued to vent his anger on the office furniture; a far more appealing choice, he mused, than either one of his lieutenants. "From what the survivors of the incident say, powerful magicks were used to support their escape."

"The vampire has already taken so much from me," Axtius hissed, "now he attempts to steal my honor—my glory." The demon's fury was abating, his blows upon the wreckage of the desk slowing. "This is something I will not allow," Axtius said with an emphatic shake of his spiny head.

The general gazed at them—truly looked at them—and it was as if he had just realized that he was not alone. Axtius stood up straighter, suspicion glazing his eyes as he studied them. Clearly, the general was agitated by his irrational display. "We are so close to accomplishing our mission that any setback—no matter how minor—upsets me greatly."

Guhl-iban smiled. "Not to worry, General. We are all on edge now that the most holy of crusades is finally upon us."

It had something to do with Angel—of this, Guhl-iban was certain. The vampire had taken something from the Brachen general—*but what?* he wondered. The demon's thoughts were in a frenzy, reaching back in the past to when they had first became involved with the vampire. It had begun with the questioning of that Jashak demon they had dragged in. Something that Axtius had learned from the Jashak had led the general to search for the vampire with a soul. Guhl-iban pictured the Jashak in his mind—a filthy half-breed with a head shaped like a crescent moon—and wondered what the thing had told the general that had driven Axtius to pursue Angel with such ferocity. To know this, Guhl-iban realized, would be to know the general's weakness.

A weakness he himself was certain to profit from.

Questral

Buffy picked her way carefully along the winding path through the jungle on the island of Questral, her stomach rumbling with hunger. Hobbs, the captain of the boat that had run her, Gunn, and Angel out to the island, had offered her a peanut butter sandwich before they had reached good old Monster Island, and Buffy had been too jacked up on adrenaline to want to eat. Now she wished she had.

Tara, Fred, and Calvin were still back in L.A., taking care of a bit of last-minute business. *And probably feasting on cheeseburgers, fries, and milk shakes at this very moment,* she thought, her stomach growling again.

With a sigh, Buffy picked up her pace. She, Angel, and Gunn were following a quartet of four-armed warrior demons that Angel had identified as Bazhripa demons. They seemed to be security on the island, even though it appeared they did the job with nothing more than spears and sneers.

The demons ahead began to chatter excitedly amongst themselves, and the end of the path came into view. The Bazhripa immediately in front of Buffy turned and spoke to them in its guttural tongue. She stood very still and listened very carefully. Its multiple arms gestured wildly as it spoke.

"What's it saying?" she asked Angel.

"I don't have a clue," he said, watching the demon closely. "I've never had the patience to learn Bazhripa."

"And now don't you feel foolish," Gunn noted dryly.

The demon stopped gesticulating and stared at them with its deep, dark eyes. It appeared to be thinking, wondering how it could bridge the language barrier between them. Suddenly it brought one of its multiple hands up to its mouth and simply hushed them, as though they were boisterous children.

"I think he wants us to be quiet," Buffy whispered.

She made a motion as if she were zipping her lips closed, and the demon smiled, nodding his head wildly and imitating the motion. Then he turned back to the others in their party and they moved toward the end of the path.

The group emerged from the jungle into what seemed like a vast town square. As Buffy gazed about, she was struck by the vastly different structures that seemed to meld from one odd architectural design to the next, with none seeming out of place. There was a harmony here, a balance—as if this was exactly how it was supposed to look. She could see signs of the buildings' inhabitants, and began to suspect why the Bazhripa wanted them to come into the square silently. The residents seemed frightened; peeking out from windows and around corners, some clutching their children—others huddled in mass, giving credence to the phrase "safety in numbers." Buffy was amazed by the variety of demon races standing side by side; some she recognized from past encounters, but many she did not. Obviously the harmony here extended far beyond mere architecture.

Buffy glanced at Angel and Gunn and saw that she wasn't the only one caught up in the exotic beauty of the place, and its overwhelming sense of unity. It made her think of her friends— the so-called Scoobies—and she was certain that Angel was thinking of his adopted family as well. It just went to show that no matter how screwed up you were, there was always some-place you could belong.

"I bid you welcome to the isle of Questral," said a rich, dig-nified voice.

They turned as one to find a regal demon, draped in robes of scarlet, emerging from a structure that appeared to be carved from the bones of some gigantic beast. The Bazhripa bowed their heads as the red-robed demon glided across the town square toward them. Other demons followed, but they, too, kept their distance.

"I am Ephraim," said the demon, whose flesh seemed to be carved from marble. "The voice of the Assemblage."

He gestured toward the small group of demons behind him. Buffy stared at them a moment: a sexy Vapor demon; a female Bazhripa, who looked like she was prepping for some serious ass-kicking; a porcupine on two legs with shining, intelligent eyes; and a thing with what looked like knitting needles jutting backward from the edges of his face, the overall effect of which was to make him look like he'd had seventeen too many plastic surgeries.

Buffy took note of the many rings that adorned Ephraim's unusually long fingers. She wondered if they got the Home Shopping Network on Questral.

"Let me take a wild guess," she said, pointing to the demons behind him. "The Assemblage?"

Ephraim nodded, his dark eyes fixing upon her and her friends, his stare almost hypnotic in its intensity. "And you are . . ."

"Buffy," she said with a smile.

"The Slayer," he finished with a snarl.

"Yes," she said slowly, taken aback by the overt hostility. "That going to be a problem?"

Angel and Gunn moved up to stand beside her.

"I'm Angel," he said, and gestured with his thumb to the man beside him. "And this is Gunn."

Gunn gave the demon a casual nod. "'S'up?"

Ephraim continued to stare at them with eyes like large, black marbles.

Buffy's mind raced. She knew she should say something, but had no real idea what it should be. She could feel hostility in the air, and began to fear for the safety of her friends who had come before her. She was just about to ask after the others, when Ephraim's regal tones broke the ominous stillness.

"Many of our kind are frightened of you, Slayer," he said, pointing with a long, clawed finger, its length bedecked with jewelry. "You, and all of your companions. Demon hunters," he said, spitting the last two words.

"But you, especially. And why should they not be? You are the terror we use to encourage our children to behave—if they do not, they are told, the Slayer will get them. I cannot begin to tell you how often I have heard these words spoken."

She wasn't sure how to react. This was nothing she had not heard before. And yet in the past it had always pleased her, the idea that she could be the bogeyman for the night tribes, the forces of darkness. But this was different. These folks were demons, but they weren't exactly the front lines in the war against humanity. She wanted demons to fear her, of course. But to scare little monsters into eating their broccoli? She wasn't quite sure she was up for the honor.

"Since establishing our retreat, we have always known that the peace and solitude we work so hard for is a fragile one, that there is always a chance that you—or someone like you—will come to take away what we try so hard to maintain."

Behind Ephraim the other demons of the Assemblage nodded their misshapen heads in agreement.

"Now something extraordinary has happened. Our ambassador has broken a cardinal rule, bringing to these shores vampires and humans and demon hunters. And yet we are told that you are all here on Questral to protect us from an even greater threat."

Buffy nodded. "Yep, that's why we're here. Not wanting to scare anybody. Just wanting to help."

"And that is perhaps even more terrifying a happenstance than we could have imagined," Ephraim said as he motioned toward the Assemblage behind him and the other residents peering out from the safety of shadows.

"I don't understand," she said.

"Your helping us goes against all that we have been taught. And it fills us with fear. For we realize that it means that the enemy we face must then be even worse than the nightmares our children have had about *you*. The Assemblage has deliberated, Slayer, and our seers have peered into the fractured future and the minds of your friends. We know that you all speak true."

Ephraim lowered his gaze. "We are left with no choice but to accept your help."

"Great," Buffy said, stepping forward. "Now that we've got that out of the way, where are the others?" she asked, looking around. The demons were slowly emerging from their hiding places for a better look at the personification of their worst nightmares. "I would have thought they'd be here to greet us," she said, seeing only demons.

"Your friends are preparing," Ephraim said, gesturing with a broad sweep of his hand for them to follow. "I will take you to them."

"Preparing?" Buffy asked as they followed the demon spokesman and the Assemblage from the town square. "Preparing for what?"

Ephraim stopped short and turned to gaze at her. She could see her reflection in his enormous, ebony eyes.

"For war, Slayer," he whispered. "They are helping us to prepare for war."

CHAPTER SIXTEEN

Los Angeles

"Feel better now, big man?" Charlie Nickels asked as he picked himself up off the floor of the Ninth Level, righting his overturned chair and sitting down across from the nasty-looking demon that had just struck him.

He reached into his mouth with gnarled fingers to remove a tooth that had been knocked loose by the blow. "So much for getting it capped," he said smugly, dropping the yellowed molar on the table and wiping the bloody saliva from his injured face.

"You are a funny little thing, aren't you?" Guhl-iban asked, nodding in agreement with his own words. He had a beer in front of him, one that he had taken from a now empty table, and Charlie wasn't about to argue with him. The last time he tried, he'd ended up with a fist in his face.

"You have already had dealings with some of my soldiers," the demon said, eyeing the still oozing cigarette burn on the twisted little man's hand. "They said that you were quite impertinent, but informative. 'The answer man,' they called you."

Guhl-iban smiled, and Charlie was reminded of a visit to a zoo in Peru, before he'd been cursed, where'd they kept a tank full of piranha fish on display.

"Oh, were those your friends?" Charlie asked, reaching for his glass of Merlot. "I never would have known."

As he sipped his wine he chanced a look to the ground, where Sol lay bruised and unmoving at his feet. When all hell had broken loose within the Ninth Level, the bartender had heroically come to Charlie's aid, only to be beaten unconscious by the demon soldier. Charlie certainly hoped that Sol was all right; the prospect of having to find yet another Harold Hill for his production filled him with dread. *This project must be cursed,* he thought, swishing some wine around in his mouth to wash away the taste of blood.

Guhl-iban reached out and snatched up Charlie's tooth to study it. "So tell me, answer man, what do you know of Angel and Axtius?"

Charlie brought his glass away from his swelling lip. "Vampire with a soul—demon-Nazi, next question."

The demon moved with lightning quickness, swatting the wineglass out of Charlie's hand. The booth was spattered with purple as the glass shattered against the wall.

"I take it that wasn't the answer you were looking for?"

"Do not mock me," the demon soldier said as he tossed the tooth into his maw and began to chew. Charlie listened with disgust as the molar was ground to dust between powerful jaws. "It would not be healthy for you—or for your friend," Guhl-iban continued, kicking Sol's unconscious form.

Charlie knew what Guhl-iban wanted. The connection between Angel and Axtius was Doyle; the half-breed son of a demon racist who died fighting the good fight for the Powers That Be. He guessed that the leading general for the Coalition for Purity hadn't been very forthcoming about the skeletons rattling in his closet.

Then it hit like a lightning bolt of divine inspiration, and a large smile began to spread across his wide, disfigured face. What would *that* kind of information do to the general's standing with his men—never mind the Coalition?

"Do I amuse you, answer man?" Guhl-iban asked, and again brought his fist down, knocking Charlie from his chair. "It's funny, most people don't find me amusing at all."

Charlie lay on the floor, more blood filling his mouth and dribbling over his split lip to puddle beneath his face. He so wanted to see these Coalition bastards suffer for what they'd done—for what they intended to do—and he believed he had the information that could throw a pretty big monkey wrench into their schemes. It wasn't too often that the little guy got to piddle in the big guy's pool, and here was the perfect opportunity.

Charlie lifted his bloody face to see that the demon had returned to his seat and was finishing what remained of his borrowed beer.

"You should be more careful, answer man," Guhl-iban said, placing the empty mug on the tabletop. "Not everything is a big joke. Talk to me, or I will eat your fingers."

Careful what you wish for, halitosis-boy, Charlie thought. *You've got the questions and maybe you'll even like the answers. But something tells me, the end result is gonna be nasty.*

He figured if the Coalition SOBs were fighting amongst themselves, that could only be helpful to Angel. And here Charlie'd gotten himself whacked around for nothing.

Guhl-iban reached out, grabbed one of Charlie's hands, yanking him up onto the table, and slowly brought the fingers toward his horrible maw.

"Ya'know what?" Charlie said with a nervous grin. "I just recalled some interesting dirt I heard a few days back. It might be what you're lookin' for."

The flesh-eater released his hand, and Charlie began to talk—and talk some more—all the while thinking of his friend Angel. Charlie hoped this was the right thing to do. If anything should happen to the vampire as a result of his flapping gums, Charlie would have to do something special to make it up to him.

Maybe a fruit basket, Charlie thought as he continued to spill his guts, not scrimping on the details. *Fruit is always nice.*

Elijah Carnegie was fighting the urge.

The old magician unlocked yet another door at the back of Cobwebs Antiquarian & Used Bookstore, this one hidden behind an old, moth-eaten curtain the color of dried blood.

"What we're looking for is behind here," he said as much to himself as to his visitors—Tara, Fred, and the kid, Calvin—who were waiting patiently behind him. Elijah could hear the seductive song of power as the objects behind the metal door became aware of his presence. His hands began to tremble, and his memory faltered as he tried to recall the spell that would unlock the door.

A demon child, no more than five, peered out from the storage room across from them, where Elijah was harboring five half-breed families. The little girl stifled a giggle with a webbed hand. They all turned to look at her, and the child waved, bathing them in the beauty of a cherubic smile.

"Cute kid," Calvin said, waving back.

"She's adorable," Tara agreed.

Elijah turned from the door and placed his hands on his hips. "Cute and adorable," he said in a stern voice, "but also very naughty."

"This little angel?" Fred asked. "Naw, you've got to be mistaken."

The old magician strode toward the storeroom door and gazed down at the demon youngling. "Victoria here has been told to go to sleep at least three times tonight," he said. "Haven't you, Victoria?"

The little girl hung on to the doorframe for dear life and looked up at him with wide, emotion-filled eyes. "I want a drink of water," she said in a voice no louder than the squeak of a mouse.

Elijah couldn't hold back any longer, and his angry demeanor cracked. He grinned at the child as he squatted down in front of her, his old knees cracking in protest. "And if I give you a glass of water—will you then go to sleep?"

Victoria nodded her head and tiny antennae, which had been hidden beneath the verdant curls of blond hair, bobbed free, bouncing with the movement of her head.

He held out his hand, palm up, and searched his brain for a spell of transference. He was actually grateful for the child's interruption. It gave him a few more minutes to steel himself, to gather up the strength and courage to face what he had hidden away over ten years ago.

Elijah completed the transference spell, and a pink cup filled to the brim with water appeared in his hand, much to the delight of little Victoria. The demon child clapped happily, then snatched the cup from his hand and began to greedily slurp its contents.

The magician stood up slowly, using the wall to steady himself, exaggerating the pain of his stiffness with a languid stretch.

"A word to the wise, my friends," he said as he placed a hand to the crook of his back. "Never grow old."

Victoria burped, and they all began to laugh. She handed the cup back to Elijah with a soft whisper of thanks. He patted her head, wished her sweet dreams, and gently closed the door behind her.

"Now, forgoing any more interruptions . . . ," he said, clapping his hands together and returning to the door across from him. He felt better, stronger. Performing constructive magick always seemed to bolster his confidence and resolve against temptation.

Elijah noticed Calvin looking at his watch and rolling his eyes. "This shouldn't take but a minute," the magician said, placing the palm of his hand against the cool metal of the door. "I wouldn't want you to miss your boat."

The custom enchantment, designed for him by a necromancer in Prague who specialized in locking spells, took form in his head, and he began to speak it aloud. He heard the sounds of gears beginning to turn and bolts sliding back. Elijah uttered the final words of the elaborate enchantment and stepped back as the last of the magickal locks was tripped, and the heavy metal door swung open.

"Is that it?" Calvin asked as he peered into the closet. "Angel has more than this back at the hotel."

"Calvin, behave yourself," Fred scolded. "Elijah was nice enough to offer us the use of his priceless magickal texts and weaponry and—"

"It's all right, Fred," Elijah said, turning his attention to the closet's contents. "I know it doesn't look like much, but looks can be deceptive. In fact, that's what got me into trouble long ago. It never looked like it was more than I could handle—but I was wrong."

Tara moved closer to stand beside him, gazing at the old volumes and scrolls that littered the shelves inside the compartment. "What are they exactly?"

It had been quite some time since Elijah last considered the contents of the storage closet. But even still, after all these years, their power called to him. He resisted, keeping in the forefront of his mind the ruin his life had become when last he was trapped within their seductive embrace.

"Various hexes, spells, and enchantments—all of an offensive nature," he answered. "Several books, including the one about which you had inquired, *Medieval War Magick*." Elijah stepped back and gestured for them to help themselves. "Take it all," he said. "That devil Axtius must be stopped, no matter the cost."

As he watched the young people filling their arms with books and weapons, he imagined what it would be like once they left to continue their mission. How long the days and nights would seem as he went about the day-to-day running of his shop, watching out for the demon people and families in his care. He knew it would be unbearable, knowing he could have helped but instead sat idly by while others fought the battle.

He was speaking the words aloud before he even realized he had made up his mind.

"I'm going with you."

Tara looked up from a duffel bag she was packing full of bladed weaponry. "What's that?"

He was certain she had heard him the first time, but obliged her with his proclamation again. "I said that I will be going with you—to Questral."

Fred looked to Tara and then back to him. Her arms were filled with ancient texts and scrolls. "You don't have to do that, Elijah," she said gently, placing the items into a box. "You've done enough by letting the demon families stay here and allowing us to take these things. You've helped more than you know. We don't have any right to ask you to jeopardize everything you've worked so hard to achieve."

Elijah smiled, at peace with his decision and feeling the beginning of excitement. It would be good to get out of the musty old store and breathe in the air of adventure. "Your concern for me is unwarranted," he said with confidence. "I'm well aware of my foibles, but I also have much to offer and would be an asset to your team."

Calvin backed from the closet, a sword decorated with red rubies in hand. "An asset? No offense, Mr. Carnegie, but how's that, exactly? You won't use magick to attack the demon army we're gonna be facing. How're you gonna help otherwise?" He looked to Tara and Fred for support. The girls just looked embarrassed. For Calvin, and for Elijah.

Elijah smiled widely and reached behind the red curtain. "Tara and Willow might benefit from my knowledge of these scrolls and I'll be able to help defend all of you during the battle. And if I'm attacked, well, I'll fight back all right," he said, withdrawing a wooden baseball bat and taking a powerful swing at some imaginary foe. "Just not with magick."

Axtius stood in the dank, dark belly of his new transport ship and pondered his impending victory.

How many of his loyal soldiers would die in battle, he wondered as he walked amongst the crates of supplies and weaponry that had been hastily loaded aboard the *Sea Bat*. How many would give their lives willingly to purge the world of the half-breed scum? It really didn't matter, as long as victory was his. He hoped that casualties would be low, that the enemy would fall like wheat beneath the scythe, but he knew that was simply a dream.

There were puddles of water on the floor of the hold, but Ricco had assured him the ship was seaworthy. He thought of his first ship, sunk in the harbor by Angel and his cohorts, and his ire began to bubble to the surface. He would need to deal with the interlopers swiftly to avoid any further delay in the conquest of Questral.

The demon general laid his hands gently upon the weapons crates as he walked amongst them. He could feel the raw power emanating from Mahkesh weaponry, and it gave him confidence.

There was an annoying, tickling sensation at the base of his brain but Axtius ignored it. The Chancellors of the Coalition had been attempting to communicate with him telepathically for hours, but he chose not to answer, the bowels of the ship providing him a certain amount of sanctuary. Axtius did not need to be reminded of his failures yet again. The guilt he felt was eating him up inside like a powerful acid. He would deal with his enemies on Questral, saving the most venomous part of his rage for the vampire with a soul. Angel would feel the wrath of a father whose son's life had been carelessly stolen away—and in Angel's death, he would prove the love of a father for his child.

"Axtius," said a voice from somewhere in the hold.

The Brachen demon turned, curious as to who would dare address him in so familiar a manner. Guhl-iban had descended the metal steps into the hold with the fire deity Haborym at his back.

"I am your commanding officer, Guhl-iban. *General* Axtius, or I'll have your head." He snarled, unwilling to tolerate even the tiniest insolence from his lieutenant.

Axtius watched as Guhl-iban strolled casually toward him and he knew something was amiss. There was no fawning, no apology for the insult. Guhl-iban was smiling, and that felt very wrong indeed.

"Do you understand me, Lieutenant?" Axtius barked, glaring at his subordinate.

The flesh-eater nodded his bald head slowly. "Of course, General Axtius," he hissed, his gaze unwavering. "So sorry to have offended you." Again he smiled, his insincerity blinding.

Haborym stood silently by Guhl-iban's side, a flaming spear in her powerful hands. He had seen her use the mystical weapon in the past, its fiery blade passing through flesh and armor with frightening ease. It was a weapon to fear, almost as much as the warrior woman who wielded it.

"What do you want?" Axtius demanded. "Why do you disturb me?"

Guhl-iban bowed his head slowly, averting his eyes. "I bring you troublesome news, my general," he said. "It has been brought to our attention that there is a traitor in our midst." Guhl-iban looked up into Axtius's eyes. "One of our own—one who serves the cause—has betrayed us."

Axtius looked from one to the other, clenching and unclenching his powerful hands.

"He has lain with a human woman and produced a son," Guhl-iban continued. "Neither demon nor human, a blight upon the world whose sole purpose for existing was achieved when his pathetic life was taken in service to the most hated Powers That Be."

The general's thoughts were awhirl with fury, shame, and confusion. He had no idea how his lieutenant had learned about his indiscretions—about his murdered son—but it was information that could not be allowed to leave the hold. Axtius went for the blade that he kept beneath his leather tunic, close to his heart.

Before he could move, Haborym's burning spear was at his throat.

"Do you know of whom I speak, *General* Axtius?" Guhl-iban asked, sadistic pleasure in his gravelly voice. "Does my information fill you with such rage that you feel the need to dispatch the traitor yourself?" The lieutenant gestured toward his knife. "Drop the blade, General Axtius," Guhl-iban said. "Haborym and I will deal with the betrayer."

Axtius let the dagger fall from his hand. The heat from the spear tip was intense, and he could feel the flesh at his throat begin to blister. "You shall be made to suffer for this insubordination," Axtius spat, looking into the fire deity's blazing eyes. "Both of you."

"Insubordination?" Guhl-iban asked with mock surprise. "Surely you jest, my general. We are performing a heroic act for the good of the Coalition." The demon lieutenant began to pace before him. "Imagine my surprise when I learned of your duplicity," he continued. "How could I ever allow Coalition troops to be commanded in battle by one as deeply tainted as yourself. For all we know, you are in league with the vampire Angel. Or even worse, the Slayer."

Guhl-iban stared at him defiantly, the curl of a snarl upon his lips. "For revealing your hypocrisy, the Chancellors will surely make me general, and then it will be I who is remembered for purging this dimension of the accursed, half-breed blight."

The smell of his own burning flesh filled Axtius's nostrils, but he did not cry out, using the pain as a focus for his hate. If it were within his power, he would propel this hate like a javelin into the traitorous heart of his lieutenant, killing him dead for exposing his past weakness to the world.

"Kill me," he said suddenly, turning his eyes to Haborym. "If you're going to do it, be done with it so I need no longer listen to your partner's jeers. I believe I have at least earned a quick death for my service to the Coalition and their jihad."

He felt the spear tip waver at his throat.

"He . . . he is not my partner," she said, her voice a throaty crackle.

"Do as he asks," Guhl-iban said with a casual wave of his hand. "Then I will contact the Chancellors and inform them of what I have learned—and what I have done as a result."

Axtius was prepared for death; it was an inevitable part of life that he had never feared. He had always hoped to die in battle, the blood of his enemy coating the blade of his weapon. It would have been a good death. He could have fought back, but the fire deity's blade would pierce his throat, cooking him from the inside out, before he even had a chance to act.

"Is it true?" Haborym asked him, tapping the tip of the burning blade against a fresh piece of flesh with a sizzle.

"Kill him," Guhl-iban ordered, the command rolling off his tongue as if practiced many a time.

Axtius looked into the warrior woman's gaze and answered her question. "He whom you wish to punish was destroyed many years ago," he growled as he waited for his life to be brought to an end. "I burned that weakness out of me. The offspring of that moment of degradation is dead. I serve only the vision of purity and the reclamation of this entire plane of existence for the pureblood tribes of a thousand hells.

"Do as you must, Haborym."

"Did you not hear what I said?" Guhl-iban ordered, striding forward. "I said to end the traitor's life—*now!*"

"And so I shall."

Haborym's burning blade cut through the air, easily passing through the flesh, tendons, muscle, and bone of Guhl-iban's neck, severing the lieutenant's head from his body. Axtius watched with a perverse amusement as Guhl-iban's head hit the floor with a bounce. Then the flesh-eater's body collapsed in a broken heap, like a marionette with its strings cruelly cut.

"And he so wanted to be general," Axtius growled, placing his booted foot upon the decapitated head to keep it from rolling. Guhl-iban's face wore an expression of complete surprise. The general turned his attention to Haborym. "Why?" he asked.

"I dislike treachery," she said, tongues of flame shooting from her mouth, as if a fiery anger were growing inside her.

"And what of my own?"

Haborym turned her back upon him and proceeded toward the stairs. "Weakness, not treachery. And, as you said, burned from you long ago."

"Don't expect me to thank you," Axtius said as he watched her begin to ascend the metal steps.

She stopped and watched him with blazing eyes. "I do not want your thanks, my general. All I want is for you to lead well."

"It shall be done," he vowed. In that moment he found the fire deity quite alluring. Perhaps when victory was achieved, he mused, the two of them would celebrate—or maybe he would have her killed. He wasn't quite sure yet.

"Prepare the troops, Lieutenant," he ordered, his powerful voice—the voice of a general—echoing throughout the hold.

Haborym snapped to attention.

"We sail at first light."

Questral

The plaintive wails of the seers shattered the early morning calm, their screeching harbinger of the horrors that would soon be visited upon their home.

Ephraim awoke from a fitful slumber, quickly dressed, and strode across the promenade to the dwelling of the seers. He had been waiting for this moment, but it still filled him with creeping dread. Now was not the time to dwell on defeat. The battle was yet to be fought. But he could not help thinking that no matter what the aftermath, something was about to be lost to Questral forever.

Ephraim reached the seers' dwelling and pulled aside the flap that would take him inside their quarters. The tent was made from the skins of seers past. To be surrounded by the flesh of their brethren was believed to be a great comfort and benefit to the ancient species, heightening their prescience.

As Ephraim entered the darkened quarters, lit only by a single brazier of white-hot coals, he was taken aback by the intensity of the seers' reaction to their latest vision of the future. The three ancient beings sat upon colorful mats, also made from the skin of ancestors, immersed in the horrors of what was to come. Their hooded and cloaked bodies huddled close in the gloom, whimpering and moaning before crying out their mournful lament.

"What do you see?" Ephraim asked, knowing full well what the answer would be, but fearing it nonetheless.

"A ship now crosses the sea," said one of the seers from within the darkened folds of its hood.

"Its belly filled with hate," added another of the precognitives. "Oh, how they revile us for what we are—for what we have," it moaned sadly.

The last of the seers to speak hugged its body and trembled as if cold. "So many different species—all sizes and shapes—unified by dreams of death and destruction. A dark mirror of what has been founded here on Questral."

"So it is true," Ephraim said. The tiny, misguided sliver of hope that it was all a mistake evaporated away to nothing, replaced by a terrible, overpowering foreboding. "The enemy comes."

The seers began to writhe and sway to some inaudible music of the future. Then, as one, they slumped forward and grew still. Tentatively, Ephraim moved closer.

"And what of the outcome? What can you tell me of that?"

"All is darkness," whispered one, its voice tired and weak. "Blood and fire and tears. But to the end . . . who shall survive . . . we are blind."

With those words, the seers went quiet, and Ephraim knew there would be nothing else. He bowed to each and left them to rest. As he strode from the tent of demon flesh, he prayed to the dark gods of creation that there would be a future for them to dream of, not just the cold embrace of death.

Ephraim emerged from the tent, his mind racing with what still needed to be done to prepare the people of Questral for the coming conflict. The Sage was shaken from his ruminations as he beheld a gathering that had formed in front of the seers' dwelling.

"Heard the caterwauling and decided that we should check things out," the Slayer said, hefting an enormous battle-ax that bore the mark of the Ixwik demon Fasjhaol, the chief armorer of Questral.

The others of her band had joined her as well, each sporting some form of lethal weaponry—also forged by the Ixwik and his weaponsmiths—but what truly amazed the Sage was the sheer number of Questral's residents that had gathered around them.

Demons of every tribe had amassed around these outsiders, who up until a few short days ago would have been looked upon as the enemy, loathsome reminders of a world the islanders had left behind. Each of them carried weapons clutched in hands, claws, and tentacles—any appendage that would allow them to take up arms in defense of their home. Ephraim swelled with pride at the overpowering show of unity.

"So what's the word?" Buffy asked, hefting the ax as if it weighed nothing.

As he gazed at the hundreds that had gathered, and the others who continued to gather still, a strange feeling began to grow stronger within him. It was a feeling that he had not experienced at all since the outsiders had come to the island and told of the impending attack. It was a sensation that he had not dared to allow himself, for to experience it and have it torn away would be the most terrible loss of all.

Ephraim felt the stirring of hope within him.

"They come," he croaked, the weight of his words resonating through all that had amassed there.

The Slayer nodded slowly, her eyes connecting with those of her friends and companions who surrounded her. Her gaze then traveled beyond her people, to the residents of Questral, seemingly touching each and every one of them, before returning her attention to him. "We're ready," she said with a powerful certainty.

And Ephraim believed her.

CHAPTER SEVENTEEN

As the denizens of Questral marshaled their forces and prepared their defense of their island home, the word that kept popping up in Angel's mind was "chaos." But every time it did, he had to force it back down again. For this was not chaos, far from it. Simply because it was difficult for his senses to record and his mind to decipher all that was going on simultaneously there on the island did not mean it was anarchy. Rather, he realized, it was the highest form of order, not unlike the feverish work inside a beehive.

The chaos is still to come.

Willow and Dai'shu had gathered the handful of magick-users on the island and were discussing strategy with them. Cordelia, Xander, and Lorne were working with a group of shambling Zhredics to corral the children of the various tribes and gather them in the forum, whose gates would be magickally reinforced and guarded. Wesley and Gunn were in conference with Shikah and Fasjhaol, the leaders of Bazhripa and Ixwik troops that were gathered at the center of the patchwork village. The village of huts had been abandoned, and Zeke was rounding up other non-combatants and trying to get them to the forum.

Morning was only hours away.

Whatever was going to happen, it was going to happen fast.

"I wish we had gotten here sooner," Buffy said, staring out at the dark surface of the ocean, alert for any sign of a ship.

Angel stood beside her on the shore. They were just a short way from the village in case they were needed, but amazingly, they seemed to be needed very little. They had provided all of the strategic advice they could, but the truth of the matter was that their greatest significance in this battle would be as leaders and warriors on the field of combat.

"If we hadn't stayed behind and given Axtius the trouble we did, this would all have been over by now," Angel reminded her. "We bought them the time they needed. Cordelia, Wesley, and Willow and the others have done everything that was possible."

For a long moment the Slayer's gaze drifted across the waves. At length she turned to him, and her eyes locked with his. Angel smiled softly, a sweet melancholy ache in his cold heart. Several minutes passed as the two of them stared at each other in silence. The words had all been said ages ago. Now there was no need for words.

Angel reached out, his fingers grazing Buffy's cheek, and then he bent and kissed her forehead lightly. Buffy smiled and grabbed his hand. Their fingers twined together and hung in the air between them.

"If this is how it ends . . . ," she began.

He nodded. "I've lived a long time. If this is how it ends, that would be all right."

Her smile was gone, but there was a light in her eyes. "Yeah. Yeah, it would. But first we have to make sure the island is safe." Buffy squeezed his hand and then let it go, and the two of them turned to stride back toward the village.

As they approached they saw Wesley in the street in front of a large stone building talking to Ephraim. The leader of the Assemblage was so tall, he had to bend his thin frame and lean down to speak with Wesley. There was something awkward and yet inspired about this odd scene, at the way it communicated what they were all trying to do here, and Angel nodded solemnly to himself.

Ephraim spotted them first. Or, rather, from the way he lifted his head quickly, it seemed that he had sensed them. He said something to Wesley, and then the two of them looked up to watch as Angel and the Slayer strode back into the village. Wesley was grim and dark-eyed, his expression severe. This was the man at the heart of him, Angel knew. Whatever anyone wanted to say about Wesley, he had a ferocity beneath the cultured sheen that was usually in evidence around him. When it came out, it could be startling.

"Any word from the lookouts?" Buffy asked.

Ephraim shook his head. "Nothing yet. And the seers are silent. It seems all that remains is to lie in wait."

"We're about to deploy the warriors," Wesley said, gaze ticking from Buffy to Angel and back to Buffy again. "I was hoping you'd come back before we did that. I think you should talk to them."

Buffy looked alarmed. "Me? And say what?"

Wesley rubbed the back of his hand across his unshaven chin with a rasp. "Something inspirational. This isn't something they were ever prepared for. Certainly there are a great many among them who have been in combat before, and there are a lot of dangerous individuals. But for them to have to draw together like this . . . though they live in harmony, it's been a tenuous one. Many of the tribes don't particularly like one another. They need to feel like an army, like they're in this together."

"Yeah, but why me? Can't Angel do it?"

She glanced at him. Angel felt just as reluctant as Buffy seemed to be, but he understood the point.

"I think it should be you," Wesley prodded.

"He's right," Angel agreed.

Baffled, Buffy shook her head. "Why?"

It was Ephraim who at last answered the question. He raised his hands, spindly fingers pointing toward her. "It should be you, Slayer, because you are the one thing they can all agree on. You are the one thing they all fear."

Her mouth opened as if she were going to argue, but then she closed it again. "All right. But I want Spike with me."

Ephraim's eyes narrowed. If it was at all possible, his skin grew even paler. At length, he nodded.

Angel clenched his jaws tightly together and said nothing. The idea that Buffy would want Spike on the stage with her made him almost nauseated. If he had had any idea just how involved his old ally, his old enemy, had become in the life of the Slayer . . . but no, that was a ridiculous line of thinking. Angel would not have done anything, save perhaps stew over it. Buffy was a big girl. She could take care of herself. Still, no matter what destiny had in store for him and Buffy, envy and hatred seethed inside Angel when he thought of Spike fighting along-side Buffy in what he would always think of as his place.

He pushed all that aside today, however. This was different. He was fairly certain he knew where Buffy was going with this, and Spike belonged beside her this time. Much as he hated to admit it, even to himself.

So Angel kept silent, and within minutes he and Buffy were walking toward the main building at the center of the village. It had high stone steps in front, like some sort of monstrous city hall, and a large crowd of armored demon warriors had gathered in front of it, a low current of mutterings running amongst them. At the base of the steps they passed Gunn, Xander, Cordelia, Lorne, and Willow, who stood in a cluster at the front of the gathered warriors. Together, Buffy and Angel climbed the steps. Ephraim and Wesley were already at the top, in front of a set of tall doors that swung open as they approached. Zeke appeared through the open door, and a moment later Spike emerged from inside that building. The chatter of the crowd ceased completely.

Angel could feel the tension amongst them, the anxiety and the horror that it had come to this . . . these proud demons standing at the base of the steps and looking *up* at a vampire who had been placed above them in their own home. Anger and resentment emanated from them in waves.

Several steps below Ephraim and Xander, Buffy stopped. Angel paused only a moment before continuing on, allowing her to take the forefront, the spotlight, and thus bear the brunt of the ugly emotions surging up from the crowd. Zeke and Spike stood behind Ephraim, but now Buffy turned to gesture toward Spike, who raised an eyebrow in surprise.

"Me?" He glanced at Wesley. "Some kinda ritual sacrifice, then?"

"Sadly, no," Wesley replied.

"Go, Spike," Angel snarled. "She needs you."

A change then swept over the blond vampire. He stood up a bit straighter, his chin lifted high, and he nodded once and walked down the few steps to where Buffy waited with such dignity that he might have been at his own wedding. Angel wanted to throttle him. And yet, there was a part of him that could not help but approve of the way Spike had risen to the occasion.

In the moonlight, Buffy and Spike stood side by side and gazed out over the gathering of demons. Swords and axes and armor plating gleamed in that light, while in the shadows of the night, monstrous eyes burned red and gold and green. Beautiful, hideously angelic Vapors swirled and danced in the darkness above the warriors, come to witness the spectacle. Their job would be to possess as many of the invading demons as they could, turning Axtius's men against one another. But the Vapors were mercurial, unpredictable, and thus far fewer than twenty had sworn their aid in the coming war.

Angel felt it was a good sign that they had come here to listen.

"You all know me," Buffy began.

The crowd was absolutely still. Her voice echoed out over the village square. To Angel's gaze, the petite girl on the steps had never looked more stunning, and never looked more like the warrior she was.

"My name is Buffy Summers. I'm the Slayer. Chances are I've killed someone you knew," she began. Another ripple of anger went through them and several snarled and started for the steps. Buffy continued on. "I'm not here to apologize. I'm not here to make it all right. If they died at my hands—or the hands of any of my friends—they deserved what they got, and probably more."

A few of the bravest warriors began to hiss. A Bazhripa started up the stairs, but his general, Shikah, stopped him with two of her powerful arms.

Angel tensed to spring down the stairs if need be.

"Maybe taunting them is a bad idea," Zeke suggested.

Before Angel could come to her defense, Wesley did it for him.

"She knows what she's doing," the former Watcher said.

"I'm the Slayer," Buffy repeated. "But I'm not a hunter. I'm not a predator. I don't do what I do for fun. I do it to protect my people. Just as you want to protect yours. I defend humanity from demonic threats. If you're not a threat, then I've got no issue with you."

Now she turned toward Spike, slowly and obviously, so that all of them could see her. Silhouetted in the moonlight, Angel could see Buffy scowl in profile.

"You hate vampires. So do I. Spike, here, has tried to kill me . . . how many times, would you say, Spike?"

Like a well-behaved schoolboy, Spike had his hands behind his back and his shoulders straight. "Couple of dozen, I'd say. Give or take. If you count the times I sent blokes after you, as well as the times I tried to kill you myself."

The audience was riveted.

Buffy stared at him. "You're a twisted, sadistic freak."

"Music to my ears, pet."

The Slayer returned her focus to the crowd. "Spike's got no conscience. Vampires never do. But he's got this chip in his brain that prevents him from harming human beings. I've got him helpless. I should just dust him and do us all a favor. There are a lot of reasons I don't. One of them is that I hate the idea of killing something defenseless, something harmless. But the other is this: He may not have a conscience, but with this chip inhibiting his homicidal instincts, I'm wondering if he can *grow* one.

"Given the times he's helped when he didn't have to, I'm starting to think maybe he can. The jury's still out. Call him my little experimental lab rat."

"You've cut me to the quick, Slayer," Spike said, one hand over his heart.

Buffy ignored him, her attention fully upon her audience now.

"My point is this: He wants me dead. I feel the same about him. But I know there's worse out there than him. I know there are evils, the true forces of darkness, that threaten us both. No matter what our differences, fate has thrown us together, made us allies. The same could be said of all of you, living here together on this island, so many varied races. Despite your differences and whatever attitudes and resentments may drive you apart, you share this home together. To protect it, you've got to pull together."

At the base of the steps, Angel saw Willow and Xander—members of Buffy's chosen family—exchange glances with Cordelia, Gunn, and Lorne—members of his own. The vampire understood the looks they gave one another, a moment of recognition that Buffy might as well be talking about them as about the demons of Questral. Something happened for all of them in that moment, a kind of bond forming.

"It isn't just Questral, you must understand that," Buffy went on. "It's this world. This whole plane of existence. The really unnerving thing is that what they've done is a funhouse mirror image of what you've done here. They've gathered together all different breeds as well . . . different full-blooded breeds, at least. But their goals and beliefs are the polar opposite of yours. You want peace. They want blood. If Axtius and his masters have it their way, there won't be anywhere you can hide . . . and there won't be anywhere you can call home."

For a long moment, her words echoed out across the village square. Angel searched the faces in the crowd, and they had all changed. Though still grim, they were no longer focused on

Buffy but were heavy with the burden of shared purpose. The Slayer was the one thing they could all agree on, the one thing they all feared.

And yet she had just given them something else upon which they could all agree.

Angel had never been more proud of her.

The silence was pierced by the noise of a horn sounding, carrying across the island from the south, where the Zhredics had their underground warrens. Angel glanced at Wesley and Ephraim. The old Sage nodded.

"A ship has been sighted."

The cliffs that overlooked the ocean near the village made it difficult to run along the shore. Instead, they were forced to cut through a portion of the jungle, the path snaked with vines and mined with stone outcroppings. In the darkness there were hundreds of things that might have tripped Buffy up, but she felt an adrenaline surging through her unlike anything she had ever felt before. She sprinted along the path, unmindful of the rest of Questral's defenders. Wesley had worked out strategy with their military commanders, and she was not going to question it. Like Willow, Xander, Cordelia, and the others, she was just going to do what she did best.

Of course, it didn't hurt that she had Gunn and Angel and fifty Yill demons armed with swords pounding along the jungle path behind her.

The horn continued to sound, but it mattered little. The moment Buffy emerged from the trees she could see down the hill toward the ocean and the dock where Captain Hobbs had let Wesley and Willow and the others off days earlier. And beyond the dock, out on the water, a single ship appeared through the fogbank that shrouded Questral from the outside world and knifed across the water toward Monster Island, its white sail ghostly against the night sky.

Halfway between the edge of the jungle and the shore, Buffy slowed to a jog and then she halted completely, staring at the boat. She listened intently to hear if there were any other horns being blown, but there were not. Angel and Gunn and the platoon of Yill stopped behind her.

"A sailboat?" Gunn asked, incredulously. "The big bad demon general got himself a sailboat? Couldn't fit more'n ten, twelve people on there. Maybe another half dozen below."

"There must be others," Angel said, starting toward the dock, taking the lead.

"I don't think so," Buffy replied, a smile spreading across her face. "We were worried that Tara and Fred wouldn't make it back with those books before the fighting started. I think we can stop worrying."

Angel glanced back at her, then out at the boat again. It was more a yacht than a sailboat, but Buffy wasn't sure exactly what to call something like that. A schooner? Hobbs had been supposed to pick them up and come back, but obviously they had realized that time was of the essence and somehow had gotten other transport.

"Those girls know how to do it up in style," Gunn said admiringly.

Buffy waved a hand at the Yill to indicate that they should be at ease for the moment. The demons were wary, however, and followed at a respectful distance as she, Gunn, and Angel made their way down to the dock. They watched as the sail was dropped and the boat made its way up to the deepwater dock at the island's edge by motor power.

There were several figures on the deck of the boat, and Buffy could make out Tara's hair whipping in the breeze. Fred had hers tied back from her face. But the two women weren't alone. Calvin was with them.

"Damn, Cal," Gunn groaned. "Fool kid."

The owner of the yacht was a deeply tanned, white-haired man in his sixties who looked as though he had just walked off a Brentwood golf course. None of them had ever seen him before, but he just smiled and shook his head in amazement as the others helped him moor the boat. Tara tossed a leather satchel down to Buffy that was heavy with the books that were inside. Angel and Gunn helped the three of them down to the dock.

"So we made it, I guess," Fred ventured tentatively.

"Barely," Gunn told her. "It's gonna hit the fan pretty quick. We oughta get you to cover." Then he turned to Calvin, brows knitted with anger. Calvin's expression was proud, but it became wounded when Gunn shook a finger at him. "And you and me need to have a talk."

"Hey! I'm in this, Gunn. You think I'm gonna just sit back in the neighborhood, watch TV while this goes down?"

Gunn stared at him. "I told you not to—" He cut off his own words and shook his head. "Not here. But we are going to talk."

Buffy watched as Fred spoke briefly, quietly to Angel. For her part, Tara scanned the shore with hope in her eyes, not even seeming to notice the Yill demons or the jungle. It was obvious who she was looking for.

"She's at the forum," Buffy said. "I'm sure she'll come as soon as she finds out it's you and not the bad guys."

Tara smiled shyly. Buffy could not be certain in the moonlight, but she thought the witch was blushing.

The moment was broken when a voice came to them from the deck of the boat. "What, no one's got a hand for an old man? I could magick myself down, but I want to save my energy. A little courtesy would be appreciated."

All of them looked up. Buffy expected it to be the owner of the boat, but instead found herself gazing at a man with a ruddy complexion and hair and beard so white, he might have been Santa Claus if he gained fifty pounds.

"Elijah?" Angel said, his surprise evident in his voice. Then he snapped his head around to stare at Tara. "You brought Elijah?"

Buffy saw the hurt in Tara's eyes, the protest that she would never put voice to, that she was not responsible for the old man's presence. She tried to get Tara to look at her so that she could offer a nod or a smile or reassurance, but the witch would only look at the ground. Tara frowned, obviously troubled, but then she took the satchel of books back from Buffy and started off up the dock.

As soon as the aging magician was off the boat, the owner laughed, shook his head again in amazement, and started the motor. The boat began to slip away from the island and, in just a few minutes, it was lost again in the fog bank.

"Who the hell was that?" Angel asked.

Elijah arched an eyebrow and glanced at him. "You've got your friends, Angel, and I've got mine. We didn't want to wait for your Captain Hobbs to return, and it seems we made the right choice. Now, shall we get on with it? I hardly think we all ought to be standing here when the forces of Hell come thundering down upon our shores."

Buffy smiled. She had only heard about Elijah, had not met him, but already she liked him a great deal. Angel, however, was obviously very unhappy with the old man's presence.

"You shouldn't have come," the vampire told the old magician.

Elijah's eyes narrowed. "And who are you to decide?"

Gunn and Calvin had gone off a ways down the dock, toward the shore. Tara was standing amidst the silent, gruesome Yill demons as if they were tropical shrubbery. Buffy felt awkward and out of place in the face of the intensity with which Angel regarded Elijah now, but it would have been even more awkward for her to excuse herself, and Angel gave her no opening to do so.

"This is going to be a war, Elijah. Demons and magick. Sorcery. What part of that don't you understand? People are going to be killing one another here in a little while."

"All the more reason for me to come. I can help save lives, Angel."

"Of course you can," Angel replied, scowling. "But can you do that and nothing more? Can you watch the islanders die, maybe watch some of my friends die, and not attack those who are doing the killing?"

Then it all came back to Buffy. When Tara had told her about Elijah, she had said that the old man only did defensive spells, never destructive magick, that once upon a time he had become a power junkie, addicted to sorcery. Angel knew that, and he was afraid Elijah would rip himself apart by being involved in something like this. Buffy could see the pain in Angel's eyes, the concern for this old man, and she understood that at some point in the past, Elijah had been to Angel what Giles represented in her own life. She wondered how it could be that Elijah mattered so very much to Angel, and she had never heard of the old magician before this week. It was yet another reminder that there was so much more to Angel's long life than she had ever learned.

"You're afraid I'll succumb to temptation," Elijah said, sighing. "As well you should be. And perhaps you're right. But if I locked myself in my shop and closed my eyes and pretended none of this was happening, I'd never be able to live with myself. Besides, I'm here now. It's too late to send me back. Get on with it."

For a long time Angel stared at him, but all of the vampire's anger was gone. At length, Angel only reached out to place a hand on Elijah's shoulder. There was only sadness in his eyes, and love for Elijah Carnegie. In that moment it was as though she were seeing Angel face-to-face with the father that fate *should* have given him. It seemed to her that Angel felt that as well. If he and his father had cared for each other a fraction as much as Elijah and Angel did, the whole long, sordid history of terror and murder that was Angel's life might have ended far more pleasantly almost two hundred years earlier.

But there was no room in Buffy's world, no time in her life, for thoughts that began with "if."

Gunn felt a kind of panic take hold of his heart that was entirely unfamiliar to him. The moment he had seen Calvin up on the deck of the yacht his mind had begun to spin, casting about for some way to get the kid off the island. If he could have been one hundred percent certain that the yacht was not going to run into the demon invasion on the way back to Los Angeles and end up at the bottom of the Pacific, or worse, he would have forced the Hollywood type manning the boat to take the kid back with him. But he could not be sure of that.

Hell, he couldn't really be sure of anything anymore.

He cared about Wes and Cordy and Fred, sure. And back in the day, when he had yet to meet Angel and was hunting vampires, running with his crew, he had cared for them as well. When things got down and dirty and it looked like the nasties were gonna win—even when members of his crew died—Gunn had soldiered on. His old crew and the people at Angel Investigations, they all knew the score, knew what they were getting into.

Truth was, Gunn understood that Calvin knew the score just as well as they did. Maybe better than some, after all he'd gone through.

But since what had happened to his parents, Gunn had vowed to himself to look out for Calvin. The kid had never been one of the soldiers, he'd been one of the citizens, no matter what he wanted to think. He was Gunn's responsibility. All along, the only reason he had let Calvin hang around was that he figured the kid was safer with him and Angel and Fred and Tara than he would be back in the neighborhood, especially with his vampire daddy still sniffing around.

Now, though—

"Look, just let it go, Gunn. We got more important things to—"

"Not we. Me. I've got things. You don't . . ."

Gunn fell silent as Angel, Buffy, and Elijah passed them on the dock. Calvin eyed them as they passed. When they had gone on by, Gunn lowered his voice some and gazed intently at Calvin, trying to get through to him.

"How'm I supposed to take care of you here, Cal? Huh? Tell me that."

The teenager looked as if he'd been slapped. "I don't need to be taken care of, *Charles*. I've been doin' pretty well so far. You think I'm a kid. I get that. But I'm fifteen. What were you doin' in the neighborhood when you were my age? I know the answer.

"Listen, back there, most kids got a choice of one gang or

another, beating one another down, climbing into cars and shootin' people for no good reason 'cept they come from a different block of the same crappy tenements." Calvin shook his head and spread his arms out wide. "What you got here, Gunn? 'S'just another gang war. The difference is, right here, right now? There's something *worth* fighting for. Dangerous? Hell, yeah. But no more so than at home. And if I'm gonna cash in at fifteen, I'd rather it be fighting for something than for nothing."

Gunn stared at him a long time. At length, he sucked in a breath and let it out long and slow. "There's a place inland, like an arena. We gathered up the children and the old folks, some of the demons who can't fend for themselves. There's a whole tribe lives underground here, slowest things you ever saw."

Calvin swore. "You ain't gonna put me in there with them!"

"No," Gunn agreed. "I'm not. But someone's gotta defend them. Cordelia's over there now. Willow's working on some protection spells. We've got a ton of demon soldiers guarding the place. I have you on the front lines with me, I'm never gonna be able to focus. Probably get me killed just worrying about you. But if you wanna help, really do some good, that's the place to be."

Calvin stared at him for several long seconds, and then he put out his hand. Gunn took it and they shook, then he pulled Calvin into his arms and hugged him.

"You stay alive," Gunn whispered in a raspy voice into the kid's ear. "Or I'll never be able to go home again."

"Yeah. I wouldn't want to get you in trouble with your boys."

"What do you mean he won't fight?"

Wesley ran along the jungle path with Lorne right behind him. The Host was trying desperately to keep his suit from getting ruined, but the jungle was not being kind to his couture.

"Do I stutter?" Lorne said curtly. "I went to check in with our friendly neighborhood Great Old One, wondering why he hadn't shown his face yet. Ephraim told me to leave him to his business, but I didn't realize that meant the gigantic old softy wasn't gonna fight."

No, no, no, no, this is not happening, Wesley thought. Lorne had tracked him down at the village square only moments after word had come that the first ship was a false alarm, bringing Tara and Fred rather than Axtius's invasion force. Now they had passed the forum and were running deeper into the jungle. There was reportedly an enormous cave in the side of the small mountain at the island's center where Garth, the Old One, kept his lair. Wesley hoped they did not have to go too deep to find him. There was no time for this.

But without him . . . Wesley did not want to think about it.

"Think, Lorne, what did he say exactly?"

"You know," the Host replied, huffing as he ducked beneath some low branches, "you're truly unpleasant when you get into this everyone's-a-moron-except-me mood."

"Lorne!"

"He said it wouldn't be fair."

Wesley stumbled and practically tripped over his own legs as he stopped short on the path. The ground had started to rise under their feet and the hill sloped up even more steeply ahead. He spun on Lorne and stared at the demon's eyes, which were wide and almost eerily white, set into his mottled green skin.

"Did you tell him we don't *want* it to be fair?" Wesley demanded, baffled.

Lorne crossed his arms. "All right, Mr. Pushy. Tell him yourself."

"Tell him—"

Then Wesley noticed that Lorne was not staring at him, but

above him. The former Watcher turned and saw the Old One looming over them, as high as the highest trees. Wesley was at once grateful they did not have to search the caves for him, and terrified that they had found him at all. The Medusa-like mass of serpentine tendrils where the Elder Demon's mouth ought to have been slithered and swayed in upon themselves, and Garth lowered his massive upper body to the path. Wesley recoiled from the stench that came from its face and from the chilling sight of those tendrils, each of which ended with a mouth of its own, snapping and hissing.

"Wesley," the Old One said. *"I understand why you have come, but you should not have. The others will need you now."*

Side by side now, Wesley and Lorne stared at the enormous, antediluvian demon.

"Umm, didn't you have a question for the big guy?" Lorne prompted.

For a moment, Wesley did not respond at all, his mind filled with images of a world before the world of man, a world of pre-prehistory, when beings like Garth roamed the planet. Millions of years ago, Hell on Earth had been a reality. It had always been hard for him to accept that as fact rather than myth. But he knew it was true. It also meant that Garth himself was millions of years old. He had seen death on a scale that reduced full-on war to the significance of a light spring rain. To a human, such a rain shower meant nothing, but to the ants in a flooded anthill, everything.

We're the ants, Wesley thought, staring at Garth.

But still he pulled himself up to his full height and glared at the Old One. "Coward," he snapped.

All of the serpentine tendrils on the Elder Demon's face flinched back at the two syllables as though they had been a physical attack. Then, as one, they hissed. Wesley felt as though his stomach were filled with ice, and he bit his lip on the inside to keep from screaming.

"Way to go, Chief," Lorne whispered beside him. "Wish you'd told me I was gonna be eaten tonight. I would've worn my Sunday best."

Wesley did not take his eyes off of Garth's.

"You dare much, Wesley Wyndam-Pryce," the Old One thundered. *"Explain yourself."*

"I'm not the one who needs to explain. You are. Questral's your home, Garth. You chose not to return to your own dimension, chose to settle here in the company of the other demons on the island."

"That is true," Garth replied, all of those serpentine tendrils speaking in unison, all of them shaking up and down as though they were all nodding. *"I chose to remain here. Ever and always, this is my home. I want no more of destruction, no more of Hell. I will never be what once I was. And so I will not interfere."*

The Old One shuddered as he slid closer to Wesley on the path. It might have been meant as intimidation, but Wesley did not think so; rather, he presumed the ancient demon was fascinated at his defiance and wanted a better look. Wesley gave it to him. He himself moved closer to the Old One, and Garth blinked twice.

Lorne stayed where he was. "Wesleyyyy," he sang in a small, high voice.

Wesley stared. "Coward," he said again.

Once more, the serpent mouths began to hiss.

"You are a part of this community. You have become that, allowed it to be so. This is your home. The other demons on this island might mean little to you, their lives so fleeting and ephemeral. But to them, you are one of them. If you will not fight for them, think on this: Without you, they'll likely die. If Axtius should win, his eventual goal is to return this world to the hellish place it once was. Thousands, likely millions, of demons will trod upon the soil of the earth. It will burn. Blood will run. Others of the Old Ones will return. It will become again the very thing you came here to seek refuge from.

"And all because you chose not to act."

• • •

Tara felt lost. After all she had been through back in Los Angeles, the idea of coming to Questral loomed large in her mind as the end of a journey. She had savored the thought of it, not caring at all that the island was populated by demons or that there was a slaughterhouse in the offing sometime in the next hour or so.

Willow was here. Somewhere. And wherever Willow was, that was home.

But as she stood there on the shore amidst dozens of hideous demons whose faces were grotesquely stretched by spines that jutted backward from their skulls, she felt cast adrift. The others were all in motion already, Buffy, Angel, and Gunn hurrying off to wherever they needed to be now for the fight. Tara had the books from Cobwebs, and she knew there was work for her to do. Elijah and Calvin were waiting for her.

But Tara could not leave yet. She was waiting too.

Waiting for Willow.

She began to feel more and more insignificant, standing there on the shore with the Yill not noticing her at all and Elijah and Calvin deep in conversation, politely ignoring her as a courtesy while she waited. The weight of what was going on around her began to grow heavier, as did the books in the leather satchel. Tara glanced around at Elijah and realized she should just get on with it. She should take out *Medieval War Magick* and ask him to help her figure out how to do the Monstrous Sea spell on her own. Willow was probably involved in something more important. The islanders would need her desperately right about now.

But so do I, Tara thought.

Then she glanced up at the opening in the veil of jungle at the top of the path and she saw an answered prayer. Willow had just stepped out of the trees and now she froze, staring down at Tara there on the shore.

Tara dropped the satchel.

She started toward Willow, her pace picking up, and soon she was running. Willow began to run down toward her as well, and to Tara it looked almost as though her girlfriend, this woman who was her very heart, was flying. Sparks of magick crackled around Willow's hands and face, and Tara figured she wouldn't even notice.

They met halfway between ocean and jungle, their bodies nearly colliding, and instead at the last minute simply folding into each other. Tara's fingers slipped into Willow's hair and tangled themselves there as though they had a mind of their own.

Willow pressed her forehead against Tara's, her eyes sparkling, a small, sweet smile on her lips. "Hey."

Tara's throat was dry. She licked her lips. "Hey."

"How's my girl?" Willow whispered.

Tara had no words to respond. Instead she brushed her fingers through Willow's hair again and then she kissed her, lips brushing against Willow's so lightly, it stole her breath away. Then their mouths met again, this time with a fervor that Tara had longed for, and into which she put all of the fear for Willow and for herself that she had been holding in all this time.

Then she just held Willow tight until she could breathe

again.

"I was so afraid for you," Willow whispered.

Tara laughed and pulled away from her, staring at her in amazement. "The feeling's been very mutual," Tara replied. She sighed lightly and then tried to focus on the world around them again. "So what now?"

Willow began to speak, but her response was cut off by the peal of a horn that cut through the night, echoing from the surf and the jungle. It was joined by another, and then another. Tara saw the alarm in Willow's eyes and she turned to look back out at the ocean just in time to see a massive, rusted freight ship pushing its way through the fog bank that encircled the island. There were already other boats in the water, motorboats that had been lowered over the side, lifeboat style, and were even now buzzing toward several destinations on the shores of Questral.

"Tara!" Elijah shouted as he ran with Calvin up the shore. "The books!"

She saw the satchel where she had dropped it. Her gaze ticked toward the incoming motorboats and the huge freighter, and she wondered how many demons it was carrying. Tara's fingers twined with Willow's and, hand in hand, the two witches ran toward the ocean, toward the leather satchel and the volumes of perilous sorcery contained within.

Tara prayed that it was not too late.

CHAPTER EIGHTEEN

Xander stood in the village square with Gunn, Spike, and Zeke, the four of them waiting to confirm the location of the spearhead of Axtius's attack so that they could lend their help where they were needed most. From what Xander had heard so far, the freighter and motorboats off the eastern shore were the sum total of the onslaught. He was growing impatient. The battle was here, and they were still just standing around.

"Not that I'm a big fan of assault rifles or anything," Gunn said, bouncing on his feet, obviously filled with energy and ready to go, "but this would be a whole lot easier if we had some serious weapons."

He had a double-edged battle-ax draped casually across his shoulder as though it were a baseball bat. Xander had a sword in a heavy scabbard hanging from his belt. Spike had a sword as well, but it was a curved scimitar, the sort of thing that was made just for decapitation. Zeke needed no weapons, of course. The Miquot grew daggers from their own flesh and bone and were able to pluck them from their forearms when they were needed. At the moment, Xander could see the outlines of fresh marrow-blades, as Zeke called them, bulging beneath the Miquot's yellow skin. It was both kind of cool and nauseating at the same time.

"The locals aren't in favor of guns," Xander reminded them. "Zeke made that clear when we were organizing this."

"It is our custom to eschew such modern weapons," Zeke explained. "Some tribes despise them, and for others it is a matter of ritual, of faith. Still other demon races simply cannot use such weaponry without it failing on them, as though they have a kind of hex upon them that causes them to malfunction. Not to worry, however. You will find the same is true of Axtius's troops. Some have this same hex problem, and others simply mistrust such weapons, preferring a more visceral approach."

Spike snorted in amusement. "And hallelujah to that. Besides, s'not as if we'd've been able to find enough assault rifles to equip everyone on the island."

Xander shrugged. "You'd be surprised what you can pick up from the local military base with a little stealth and the right attitude."

Gunn shifted the ax to his other shoulder and glanced around the square. "This is taking too *long*, man. Things are going down and they're going down without us."

He was right. Xander looked up to the steps where Buffy had addressed the troops earlier. Ephraim, Dai'shu, and one of those creepy-looking seers were the only ones still here besides the four of them, and he had to wonder what the hell the sorcerer was standing around for. He exchanged a look with Gunn and then nodded. "Screw this."

With one hand on the pommel of his sword, he ran up the steps. Zeke called out to him to try to discourage him, but Xander was past being patient. A moment later he heard the others trudging up the stairs behind him.

Ephraim glanced up at him, breaking off whatever conversation he was having with Dai'shu. The skeletal Sage had those huge black eyes that made Xander think of alien invaders and gave him the creeps, but he tried to ignore them. Dai'shu was uglier, but Xander had seen ugly plenty of times. *Better that than those staring eyes.*

"Excuse me, boys, but we're just hanging out here. Don't you think we oughta get moving?"

For a long moment the two regarded him. Behind them, several steps farther up, the seer gazed off at nothing, its eyes wide and white.

"The seers are in communication," Ephraim explained. "They have been placed in strategic locations around the island to monitor all angles of approach."

Xander rolled his eyes. "Yeah, I know, it was my idea—remember? Look, have they spotted anything yet? Other than the action we know about?"

Dai'shu grimaced. When he did, the flesh around his mouth pulled even more tightly, and the spikes that jutted back from the sides of his face twitched. "Nothing yet."

"Nothing?" Xander asked. "Nothing. At all."

"No."

Xander slapped his forehead. "Then there isn't anything else. After what Buffy, Angel, and Gunn did to the last boat, we were pretty sure Axtius wouldn't be able to get more than one, anyway. If your seers haven't seen anything more yet, there's nothing else coming. Axtius would've launched it all at once."

"Definitely," Gunn intoned behind him.

"Listen," Xander went on, pointing at Dai'shu, "you can do that translocation thing. This was part of the plan. Leave the seers there, just in case, but go and get all the troops we deployed around the edges of the island. Whip up the doorways or whatever you do and get them to *this* coast. Right now."

Dai'shu's lips curled back from fanged teeth, and he hissed. "Who are you to—"

"He is right," Zeke interrupted. "They are throwing all their forces at the eastern shore. We must repel them here or not at all."

Ephraim hesitated. He glanced past them, down toward the village square. "Where is your leader, Wesley?"

"He's not my leader," Xander replied tersely.

"He has gone to speak with the Old One, who was reluctant to do battle," Zeke explained.

"Gonna be a bloodbath, we don't start making better decisions round here," Spike muttered.

Gunn shot him a hard look. "Good. You could use a bath."

"Look, Wesley's busy, but so what? It doesn't take a tea drinker to figure this out," Xander argued. "There's nobody else coming. Axtius doesn't think he's going to have any problem slaughtering the lot of us, and frankly, if you don't get your full force down there right now, he's probably going to be right."

Several seconds ticked by before Ephraim nodded. He turned to Dai'shu. "Retrieve the warriors from the rest of the island. All of them. Concentrate on the east."

The sorcerer's eyes flashed with a crackle of dark blue energy, but then he made a gesture of obeisance with his hands. "It shall be done."

"Thank you," Xander said. Then he turned to Gunn, Spike, and Zeke. "Let's go!"

He ran down the steps, and the others kept pace with him.

Buffy and Angel had gone back toward the dock with reinforcements for the Yill demons who were guarding it and to back up Willow and Tara, so Xander and the others took another path away from the village, one that would bring them to the coast faster. There would already be a phalanx of half-breed islanders down there, mostly Ixwik and Bazhripa, all of them ready for battle. From that vantage point it would be simple to determine where the full-bloods were going to make landfall, and the islanders would do their best to repel the invaders.

Horns still sounded, echoing out across the island and the ocean waves. Xander was surprised when Spike overtook him on the path. Of course he should not have been; vampires could move far more swiftly than humans. But Spike had a tendency to hang back and jump in when he could be most effective. It might have been cowardice, or simply that he liked to be sneaky, to fight dirty. Not this time. When Spike ran past, his newly-healed face had already changed into the ferocious visage of the vampire, and he wore a wide, hideous grin.

He's loving every minute of this, Xander thought. With the chip in his head, Spike could not harm humans but he could slaughter as many demons as he liked. It looked like he was going to take advantage of the opportunity. Though he was disturbed by the glee in Spike's face, Xander had to admit to himself that he was glad. *Glad, at least, that Spike is on our side.*

The vampire was first to emerge from the trees onto the shore. Xander, Gunn, and Zeke followed quickly after. The dock where Captain Hobbs had dropped them off was perhaps a quarter mile along the coast, but the moonlight was bright and the night over the island was clear and he could see the defenders gathered near the dock. Buffy and Angel were among them, and Willow and Tara as well. The freighter was getting closer to the island. Motorboats buzzed toward shore, spread out across the island's eastern coast, and Xander nodded once to himself.

"Here they come," he said, focusing on a long Boston whaler with at least a dozen of those tiger-demons Gunn had told him about on board. *The Mahkesh,* he thought. *That's what they're called.* The whaler was going to beach itself about twenty yards from where they stood.

Xander drew his sword. Its blade rang against the metal scabbard. "Here, kitty, kitty, kitty," he whispered.

Then he ran forward amongst the half-breeds gathered there and he, Spike, Gunn, and Zeke merged into and became a part of Questral's defending army.

It's all or nothing, now, Xander thought. *All or nothing.*

"Damn it!" Willow snapped. "We're blowing it!"

She crouched on the shore with Tara on one side of her and Elijah on the other. Calvin hung back slightly, staring around with wide eyes, obviously wanting very badly to join the fight. But Tara had the kid's number and she was not going to let him go anywhere. Willow realized that the two had bonded while they were working together the past day or so. They weren't exactly brother and sister, but Calvin seemed to listen to her. Which was good, in the keeping-the-kid-alive department.

Now Tara reached out and covered Willow's hand with her own. "We can start again. But this time stop focusing on the fighting. Tune it all out and focus just on me."

Elijah nodded his encouragement. "Precisely. Clear your mind, Willow. Look at Tara. Find peace. You must be calm to cast such a tumultuous spell."

The old magician was obviously tense. Beads of sweat were running down his forehead. A lot of Willow's frustration came from having Elijah right there with her. Here was a guy who could do this spell himself, probably from memory. He had done it before. But he refused. Okay, she understood the magick junkie thing, at least intellectually. She knew about alcoholics and gambling addicts and, yeah, smokers . . . but if someone told a recovering alcoholic to have one drink and save a thousand lives . . .

"Willow, come on, baby," Tara pleaded.

Willow shook her head to clear her mind. *Gotta focus.*

Not that it was as simple as all that. They had not been fast enough. The first transport boat had hit the shore while they were digging through the book and Elijah was finding the right page. As the Yill demons had defended them against a group of Fyarl and a couple of Brachen—as swords clashed and soldiers died—Elijah had explained the procedure to them, sounding out the German words they could not pronounce.

Buffy and Angel had arrived with reinforcements. Even now Willow could hear the voice of her best friend shouting over the sounds of combat, calling to Angel to watch out for its stinger . . . and Willow did not want to think about what *it* was. Now there were Bazhripa and Ixwik and other island dwellers spread along the coast. More transports came from the freighter.

In the sky, winged demons in the service of General Axtius prowled, picking off half-breeds like seagulls diving for fish swimming too near the surface. The things were scaled like dragons but smaller, with two heads and two tails apiece, and all she could think about was King Ghidorah from the old *Godzilla* movies, except Ghidorah had three heads. Already she and Tara had been forced to use magick to turn one of those things to stone as it lunged from the sky at them, eyes burning in the night. Then they'd had to duck out of the way before the newly fashioned statue had fallen on top of them.

Some of the things in service to Axtius did not need boats at all. They swam or crawled along the ocean bottom, and soon enough more full-blood monsters were on the beach. The Bazhripa commander, Shikah, barked orders to the warriors of Questral. The seductive Vapor Ileana had taken on a more terrifying aspect, and half a dozen others swept down from the sky, shimmering like apparitions—because they *were*—and Ileana commanded them to possess the invading demons. The Vapors obeyed, and soon several of the most hideous, vicious-looking of Axtius's warriors were turning on their comrades, their bodies controlled by the Vapors.

Boots thundered on dirt.

"Willow, look out!" Calvin shouted.

She turned to see a Polgara rushing up toward them, having somehow slipped away from the melee on the shore. The long spike that jutted from its forearm was glistening in the moonlight. Tara uttered a tiny cry of alarm. Willow threw herself in front of her lover and brought up both hands, words already forming on her lips that would incinerate the demon.

Elijah Carnegie moved in front of her. With a quick sketch of his hands in front of his face, he cast a spell that surrounded them in a dome of golden light. The Polgara struck the barrier, and it seemed to leap out at him, sizzling magickal power sparking all over his body. The demon went down but began to stir almost immediately.

"Willow," Calvin snapped.

She looked up at the kid, saw the intensity in his gaze, and she nodded. "Right." Willow reached out and took Tara's hands. Their eyes locked. The book was spread open on the ground between them, but she did not think either one of them needed it anymore. They had done the spell, unsuccessfully, twice already and had been practicing magick long enough that they rarely had trouble memorizing the words quickly, even in another language.

Tara licked her dry lips and nodded.

Together they began to speak. The name of the spell in English was the Monstrous Sea, but according to Elijah it had often been mistranslated to the point where sorcerers expected to use it to conjure sea monsters. That wasn't the point of it at all, however.

"Ozean aufsteig und stossen meine Feinde ab!"

Just to speak the guttural German words hurt her throat, but Willow ignored it. She focused on Tara and she could feel a kind of calm sweeping through her, enveloping her. It was extraordinary to her that even in this chaos, she could find peace in Tara's eyes.

Willow squeezed her girlfriend's hands even more tightly as they spoke the last of the spell. With the final word the two young witches grunted simultaneously, and Willow felt as though someone had punched her in the gut. The magick was torn from them—or thrown from them—and a dark wind swirled around the four of them, there in that protective dome.

"Well done, girls," Elijah muttered.

Calvin swore colorfully.

The witches turned toward the ocean. An invisible wave of power blew along the shore, knocking over invaders and defenders alike. And then it struck the water. A longboat rowed by demons—probably an actual lifeboat from the old freighter—was shattered, and several of the demons on board were literally torn apart by the spell.

The water off the eastern coast of Questral began to churn, the surf exploding upward as if a volcano were erupting beneath the ocean. Waves reached toward the sky like living things, twisting into water funnels, crashing down upon themselves. Whirlpools formed. The Monstrous Sea had come to life, and it battered the freighter's transport boats. Willow saw one of them sucked down into a whirlpool, broken in two, even as another was thrown into the air and then clapped between two enormous waves. A water demon—a beast unfamiliar to her with fins and tendril stingers that seemed to feel the water ahead of it as it swam—was suddenly boiled alive, its blood mixing with the ocean in a pinkish-green geyser that shot upward.

The freighter rolled atop the wild surf. The waves and the wind slammed against it. But much to Willow's dismay, it did not sink. She had so hoped that it would. A much faster end to things would have been in the offing then. Also, the spell did not extend the length of the island's coast, but only a hundred yards or so in either direction.

"It wasn't enough," Willow said gravely.

Tara put a hand on her shoulder. "It will have to be. For now."

"It's a start," Elijah replied. "And there's more to do."

Which made Willow snap to attention. He was right, of course. There was a lot more to do. They had slowed the attack, done some real damage to the invasion force, but there were preparations left incomplete . . . vital ones . . . and they had to be done as quickly as possible.

She reached out and grabbed Tara's hand, then glanced at Elijah and Calvin. "Follow me. And hurry!"

They were ashore.

Gunn was ankle deep in the surf as Axtius's warriors rushed from their boats or crawled from the water. There were more than a dozen Mahkesh nearby, brandishing the engraved weapons from the cache Axtius had bought for them. Each blade seemed to glow with its own interior light. A Fyarl rushed at Gunn swinging a morningstar mace around on its chain, distracting him, and he ducked out of the way of the spiked ball on the end of the chain. His momentum twisted him around and he went with it, letting his hands slide down the grip of his ax so that when he completed his spin he leaned into it and the ax blade hacked right through the Fyarl's neck before the demon could get control of its weapon again.

Its corpse fell at his feet in the water as the waves grew more violent from the witches' spell, but Gunn ignored it. There wasn't time to think about anything but offense and defense. He had seen the tumultuous results of Willow and Tara's magick—those witches were something individually, but get 'em together and they were just amazing—and he had shouted in triumph. But that was only the opening salvo in this battle.

Fasjhaol, the Ixwik member of the Assemblage, appeared suddenly amidst the chaos to Gunn's left. He was hacking at the legs of a Mahkesh with a short sword. Though injured, the feline demon raised a massive broadsword and swung it down at the quill-backed, porcupine-like Ixwik. Gunn shouted—his words lost in the roar of battle—and lunged to defend Fasjhaol, but too late. The Mahkesh blade struck the little demon's armor . . . and was turned aside. Sparks flew.

While the Mahkesh was busy staring in astonishment at the little demon, Gunn swung his ax and buried it in the ancient warrior's chest. It staggered backward and fell into the surf. Gunn tried to tug his ax out but it was lodged in the full-blood demon's rib cage. He put a foot on the corpse, glancing around in a frenzy, on the lookout for other attackers.

A scaly thing with no eyes and too many teeth exploded from the water beside the dead Mahkesh, gnashing its jaws. It obviously didn't need eyes to see him. Gunn cursed and staggered backward.

"Human!" a small voice said.

He glanced beside him to see Fasjhaol proffering the dead Mahkesh's gleaming sword. Gunn snatched it from the Ixwik's hand, fell to his knees in the water, and thrust the blade up into the scaly, eyeless demon's abdomen as it fell upon him. Whatever it bled burned where it spattered his hands and forearms. Gunn slipped out from beneath it and rinsed his arms off, but the sting remained.

"Thank you," he told Fasjhaol, even as he stood up to defend himself again, eyeing several Mahkesh and a couple of Brachen who were closing in. "But how did you survive that? The blades in the Mahkesh cache, they're supposed to kill anything they strike."

Fasjhaol laughed like a little girl. "Indeed. But they's not striking me. I makes this armor, human. Magick in the Mahkesh cache, and magick in my armor, too. We all wants to live, better get those blades away from the Mahkesh."

Gunn glanced around, saw the way the battle was going, and knew Fasjhaol was right. A Bazhripa was still fighting, though three of his arms had been severed. Too many dead half-breeds were in the water and on the shore. Most of it was due to the Mahkesh weapons. The islanders outnumbered Axtius's warriors, but they couldn't defend properly against those things.

He had lost track of Spike and Xander, but now he spotted Zeke. The Miquot had one of his marrow-blades in each hand and was darting around a couple of Axtius's warriors like some kind of freakin' ninja. Every time he passed the full-bloods, Zeke's hands would flash out and he'd cut them, badly. A few passes and the invaders were ripped open, dead before they even knew they'd been hurt.

Gunn was not going to worry about Zeke. Miquot could take care of themselves.

A moment later he caught sight of Xander amongst a few Bazhripa. The kid was always fast and loose with the humor, usually picking the worst possible time to be funny. Not tonight. Tonight Xander was silent and brutal. As Gunn watched, he dove into the water to get away from a Brachen that was after him with a long whip made of metal links, like some ancient warrior's version of a bicycle chain. The Brachen bent over and tried to follow Xander's progress in the shallow water, with the waves rushing past. It even whipped at the water with that heavy metal chain.

From beneath the water, Xander stabbed it in the face with his sword, the point of the blade bursting out the back of the Brachen's spiny head.

"Damn," Gunn whispered. He hadn't given Xander much credit, not even with the stories about him magickally having the memories of military training. The truth was he'd figured Xander wouldn't be worth much in a fight. But it looked like when the chips were down and every fist counted, Xander was ready to surprise everyone.

"Gunn!" a voice erupted from his right.

He turned, but not in time. A Mahkesh was right behind him, sword thrusting for his gut. Gunn just had time to hold his breath and think of his sister, killed by vampires, whom he hoped to see again in the afterlife. Then Spike slammed into the Mahkesh from the side, latching onto it. Gunn realized it was the vampire who had warned him.

Feral, face smeared with blood, and without any weapon at all, Spike grabbed at the hair of the staggered Mahkesh, hauled back its head, and tore out its throat in a single motion. A gout of demon blood splashed his face, and then he sprang away from the feline monster as it fell into the water. Spike bent and pried its sword from his hand. "Lost my other blade," he said happily, drawing a hand across his lips and smearing the Mahkesh's blood farther. "This'll do."

Gunn stared at him. "You saved my life."

Spike gave him a look of regret. "Did I? Bloody hell. Got to be more careful about that. Got my reputation to see to, you know?"

"Don't do it again," Gunn snapped.

The vampire gave him a gruesome smile and drew an X across his chest. "Cross my heart. Just a slipup." Then Spike nodded in Xander's direction. "Boy's got spunk, don't he? This is the first time I've been glad I never got round to killing him in the good old bad days. 'Course I'll likely change my mind tomorrow, but for now—"

"The Mahkesh. The ones that look like tigers," Gunn interrupted. "We need to work together, a little bait and switch, tag-team the mothers and get their weapons from them. Take away their advantage."

"Right," Spike nodded reasonably. "Let's go to it, then."

Gunn stared at him.

Spike chuckled. "Look, street punk, fighting together like this doesn't mean we like each other. You still want to kill me. I get it. I'd like to tear your heart out right about now. But I can't do that. And we've got bigger problems at the mo', yeah?"

"Yeah."

That was one thing they could both agree on. Out on the water, several more boats were headed for shore, the next wave of Axtius's invasion. Gunn and Spike turned and, side by side, waded back into the battle.

Cordelia stared up into the night sky and tried to count the two-headed, winged demons circling above the forum, their shapes silhouetted in the moonlight. "We are so screwed," she muttered.

Her heart pounded and her throat was dry. This was not part of the bargain. Nobody had said anything about winged demons, and she had not had a single vision this entire time. It was as though the Powers That Be were too busy hanging back and watching the show to give her the first clue as to how things were going to turn out.

Maybe that's better, she thought. *Maybe I don't want to know.*

The Zhredics, the underground burrowers who were stashed in the forum along with the demon children—and an uglier bunch of cuties she never did see—were useless in a fight that didn't take place underground. They were up in the stands right now as if they were watching a ball game, and Cordelia wanted to scream at them to do something. But there was nothing they could have done. Just too damn slow.

That left her, Fred, and a bunch of really ancient Yill and Bazhripa, as well as two or three other species she wasn't familiar with. They had weapons—the rustiest, dullest weapons on the island, the only ones that could have been spared—but there weren't even enough of those to go around.

"Don't say that, Cordelia," Fred reassured her. "It's going to be all right. We'll be all right."

Cordy glanced up at the mousy physicist, whose moist eyes were just loaded with sincerity. She wanted to punch Fred in the nose or hug her, she could not decide which.

"I faced way worse odds a few times on Pylea, and I always survived. By hiding." Fred glanced around. "Never out in the open like this, though." She laughed nervously. "That would've been suicide."

"We didn't know they had fliers!" Cordelia protested. "It isn't fair!"

"No," Fred shook her head. "It really isn't."

A chorus of screeching noises erupted in the sky above them and as Cordelia glanced up she saw the two-headed demons diving toward the forum, wings tight against their bodies. They were coming in for the kill. Cordelia raised her rusty sword, and the aged demons around her did the same.

"Oh, we are *so* dead," Fred muttered.

So much for the power of positive thinking, Cordelia thought.

Suddenly a wave of ghostly lights flashed across the sky above the open forum. Several of the winged abominations paused, hesitating, and this time when they went on the attack again they weren't aiming at the forum, but at the other two-headed monsters.

"The Vapors!" Cordelia said excitedly. "I thought they weren't going to help!"

Fred smiled. "Most of them said the outcome of a battle between fleshly creatures didn't matter to them. I guess to some of them it did."

The hope that was sparked in Cordelia did not last long, however. As she gazed up at the heavens she saw that the odds were decidedly against the Vapors. There were only a handful of the winged, hideous demons possessed, and far too many others that were not. The Vapors had bought them a few minutes, no more.

Then Fred tugged on her arm, and Cordelia glanced where she was pointing, at the main entrance to the forum, and hope blossomed once more in her heart. Willow and Tara had arrived with Calvin and, much to Cordelia's surprise, Elijah Carnegie. With a wide grin, Cordelia ran to the old man, dropping her old sword in the dust, and threw her arms around him.

"Oh my *God,* Elijah, you have no idea how glad I am to see you."

The old man offered a sheepish grin. "Had I known I would have engendered that sort of response, Cordelia, I would have joined the cavalry long ago."

Calvin was anxiously watching the entrances on both sides of the forum while Willow and Tara converged with Cordelia, Fred, and Elijah.

"Hey," Cordelia said, "get with the magick, will you? We need something that's going to protect the kids and the fogeys, and we need it now."

Tara smiled, books under her arm as though she were going to class. She set them on the ground and glanced up at Cordelia. "We can do that."

As Fred kept an eye on the demons tearing one another apart above them—bits of demon flesh raining down like bird droppings—Cordelia watched the witches and the sorcerer at work. With Elijah overseeing the whole operation, Willow and Tara drew a huge circle and a lot of sigils in the dirt, hurrying and sweating as they worked as fast as they could. Cordelia felt helpless because she knew if she tried to aid them she would only be in the way.

But at least she had gotten the children here and had helped defend them. At least she had been able to do that much.

When they were finished drawing in the ground, Elijah had the witches hold his hands, Willow on one side of him and Tara on the other. Together they rattled off a spell in Latin. Elijah had said he would be drawing on their innate magickal power, that he would need it for something so large, but he had never explained exactly what that something would be.

Then the wind kicked up, and all of the sigils drawn in the dirt began to glow a golden yellow. A flash of power blasted from that circle as though a bomb had gone off, but an explosion of light and wind only. It sizzled loudly like oil in a frying pan, and then the entire interior of the forum was lit up as though it were daytime.

All around the forum was a dome of shimmering, crackling magickal power, a barrier to keep the demons at bay and protect all of those inside. Willow and Tara shuddered, the strength drained from them, but both of them smiled at the old man.

"You did it," Willow told him.

"Damn skippy!" Cordelia cried.

"We did it," Elijah said, his voice a rasp. For a moment he stumbled, and a hand fluttered to his chest.

"Elijah?" Tara ventured, even as Cordelia rushed to his side.

He waved them away, pale but smiling. The golden light emanated from his hands as though he were the filament inside the world's largest lightbulb, but in that moment . . . just for that moment . . . the dome flickered. Then it was glowing stronger than ever.

Cordelia hesitated, watching Elijah's face, hoping that her fears were unfounded and that the strain of this magick would not be too much for him. He was here to do exactly what he had dedicated himself to . . . he was here to defend them.

She said a silent prayer.

"That ought to keep them out," Willow said warily, also watching Elijah for signs that the stress was too much for him.

"Yeah!" Calvin said, rushing up beside Fred, staring up into the sky. "The ones who weren't already inside the bubble!"

Cordelia saw Fred raise her own rusty blade as she gazed upward. Then she, too, looked up. Three of the winged horrors were on the *inside* of the protective dome.

Wonderful, Cordelia thought, glancing frantically around for the blade she had dropped. *And me empty-handed.*

The demon children began to scream.

CHAPTER NINETEEN

In a haze of pain and rage, the Slayer pirouetted between a pair of Fyarl demons. In her hands was an ax she had picked up somewhere along the way—the sword she had begun the battle with long since lodged in the chest of one attacker or another—and as she spun she scythed the blade through the necks of the demons on either side of her with a splinter of bone.

The haft of the ax broke halfway down, and the head—with several inches of jagged handle—fell to the ground with the dead monsters.

Buffy did not even slow. She ducked to retrieve what remained of her weapon, thinking only of the sharp edge of the ax blade. Then she was off again, moving through the chaos on the eastern shore of Questral. When the war had begun adrenaline had been surging through her, her heart thundering in her chest. Now, though, it had slowed to an almost normal rate as if all of this . . . the blood and death . . . was as natural to her as breathing.

It frightened her to think so, but only in those slivers of time when she gave any thought to it. At the moment Buffy was doing very little thinking. There had been times in the past when she had been in the midst of combat and all of her that was Buffy seemed to slip away, leaving only the Slayer, the primal thing inside her, the warrior. It was like that now.

Primitive. Feral. And yet graceful. She felt herself merging with the first Slayer, as though the ages between the present day and that ancient time had been erased. A whisper of death, she slipped across the battlefield, always with an eye out for Axtius himself. In that tiny place in her mind where rationality was still functioning, Buffy knew that killing him might turn the tide, but thus far she had not spotted him.

The sorcerer Dai'shu had been gathering the half-breed warriors from their defensive positions around the island and returning them to the eastern shore. Had the spell Willow and Tara had cast been permanent this might already have won the day for them, but the effects of that magick had dissipated within minutes, and Axtius's invasion force kept coming. Buffy and Angel had known there were a lot of warriors at the general's disposal, but even they had underestimated. The horrors serving this terrible dream of Hellish reign over Earth continued to come in with each new wave, some in boats, some swimming, some flying.

The battle had been focused on several different spots along the coast at first, but now the three fronts had merged. As she moved through the field of death, blood staining the shore and bubbling in the surf, she caught glimpses of the others—of Angel and Xander, of Spike and Gunn, of Zeke and members of the Assemblage. Several times she had been weaponless, only to have a blade or an ax thrust into her hand by the little quill-backed Ixwik commander, whose name she would have to remember in time to thank him properly. *If we both survive . . .*

Buffy found herself abruptly back to back with Shikah, the warrior queen of the Bazhripa. The four-armed woman had a spear in one hand, a sword in a second, and with one of her remaining arms she was strangling a female Brachen who had been foolish enough to come close to her. The part of Buffy that was still the girl from Sunnydale wanted to flinch away from this terrible visage of death and destruction, like the goddess Kali come to life, but the primal heart of the Slayer recognized in Shikah a kinship, and Buffy was proud to stand and fight at her side.

There was a sound like flesh tearing open, and Buffy whipped around only to find that the noise heralded good tidings rather than bad. Dai'shu, the Yill sorcerer, had returned once more. A hole in reality opened as though it had been sliced into the fabric of the world. It gaped, and from her position Buffy could see through that opening to a shoreline somewhere else on Questral. Dai'shu was there, along with Bazhripa and Ixwik warriors who had been stationed there. With a battle cry, this fresh wave of defenders swarmed through the portal Dai'shu had opened and entered the fray without hesitation.

Buffy nodded with satisfaction, even as a Mahkesh rushed toward her. It carried an ax as well, but its weapon shimmered with unnatural light and Buffy grinned. When she had glimpsed Xander, Gunn, Spike, and Zeke at various intervals, she had noticed they all now wielded bloodstained Mahkesh weapons. *And why not?* Forged in magick, the weapons were deadly.

She wanted one.

The swift and massive feline demon lunged at her. Buffy crouched and sprang toward him, surprising the demon. He tried to bring his weapon down, but she had closed in too quickly. Her momentum and strength threw the Mahkesh backward. She hung on to its torso, shattered haft of her ax in her right hand. When she landed on top of the Mahkesh, the blade was trapped between the demon and the ground and she heard its spine break, the ax cutting flesh and snapping bone.

The glint of life in its eyes was snuffed out.

Buffy tore the gleaming Mahkesh ax from its hand, leaving her broken weapon behind.

"Thanks for the upgrade," she muttered at the demon's corpse. She was drenched in blood, some of which belonged to her enemies and some of which was her own. Her jeans and shirt were torn, long claw marks on her legs and more she could feel on her back. Her hair was a wild mess, matted with blood. But it was just beginning.

Hundreds of demons massed on the shore, slaughtering one another. Buffy knew that unless something was done, most of them would be dead before it was over.

Instinct made her glance toward the ocean. Another motorboat was coming in, whipping toward the shore, and it was obvious that its skipper had no intention of slowing. The boat was going to beach. There were a handful of figures on board, one of whom was a woman whose eyes and hair were on fire, and whose upraised hands lit the way for the boat with flickering flames.

"Incoming!" Buffy shouted.

She evaded an attacker, knocked the thing backward with the butt of the Mahkesh ax blade, and scanned the shore for Angel. She spotted him a short way away . . . noticed him noticing the boat. The way his eyes narrowed and his lips curled back from his fangs confirmed that he'd come to the same conclusion as she had.

Axtius, she thought.

A trio of Yill warriors rushed knee deep into the water to meet the boat. The Miquot, Zeke, was just behind them. Shikah of the Bazhripa ran for the water. A moment later, Ephraim was there as well. Buffy had been astonished by the Sage's speed. His skeletal body seemed so delicate, but he moved swiftly indeed.

Buffy tensed and glanced around. They had been waiting for this moment. The fifth member of the Assemblage, the seductive Ileana, who was leader of the Vapors on Questral, was supposed to make her play now. Buffy beat down a Fyarl that attacked her and looked around again. There was no sign of Ileana, but that was all right. The Vapors could be invisible if they wished.

The boat came in, engine whining. Its prow hit the sand. There were five demons on board: Axtius, the flame-monster Haborym, a pair of Mahkesh, and in front, a deadly looking hulk Buffy did not recognize. It was a massive, ugly beast, a powerfully built monstrosity whose red flesh was knotted with corded muscles and whose mouth was a mass of needle-thin fangs.

She glanced around and saw amongst the melee Spike and Xander to the north and Gunn to the south, all far too busy staying alive, fighting off their own attackers, to help repel Axtius. Buffy thought perhaps that was for the best, since she was certain Axtius would have kept his deadliest warriors by his side.

The Yill waded at the boat to attack. One of Axtius's Makhesh guards was killed almost instantly. But fortunes were reversed far too quickly. Axtius held a gleaming, brutal-looking warhammer that could only have been the Pristagrix, the weapon with which he had defeated Angel the first time. *The only time,* she amended.

The Brachen general barked orders in a guttural tongue that Buffy did not understand, but which echoed up and down the shore. Axtius stood up in the back of the boat, swung the Pristagrix, and shattered the head of a Yill demon as though it were nothing more than rotten fruit.

Ephraim had no fear. As the massive, red-skinned warrior demon jumped from the prow to the shore, revealing that it had hooves instead of feet, the leader of the Assemblage darted in and hacked at its flesh with his blade. With a spark and a clang of metal, the sword was turned away by the needle-fanged warrior's own flesh.

The second of the Mahkesh leaped from the boat toward Zeke as the Miquot approached wielding one of its marrow-daggers in each hand. The Mahkesh had one of the long, cursed swords of its tribe, and the marrow-daggers were short weapons, made for hand-to-hand fighting, up-close nastiness. The feline demon brought its blade down, but Zeke dodged, then darted forward and stabbed the Mahkesh in the gut with both marrow-daggers, ripping upward, eviscerating the enemy where he stood.

Even as this unfolded, Buffy tried to fight her way to the shore to lend her support. Nearby Shikah of the Bazhripa roared as she made her way to the water. A sideways glance revealed that Angel was attempting the same, snapping the neck of a Polgara that tried to block his progress.

The delay was costly.

Haborym, the fire-demon at Axtius's side, stepped to the front of the beached boat and vomited flames onto Zeke. The Miquot screamed as the blaze engulfed him, greasy black fire licking up into the night sky as he was immolated on the spot.

"No!" Angel shouted, all his fury locked inside that one syllable.

The defenders of Questral were still many . . . outnumbering the invaders . . . but all of them paused in that moment. Even at a distance Buffy could see the hesitation in expressions of the Ixwik, Bazhripa, and Yill, as well as the familiar faces of Xander, Spike, and Gunn amongst the mass of bloodied warriors. Hope had been dealt a terrible blow.

The ram-horned demon who had been recruiting for the Coalition up in Sunnydale stepped in front of Buffy, blocking her way. With a scream of fury and frustration she brought the ax over her head as though she were chopping wood. It split the demon in two from skull to navel, stuck there, and then she had to tear the ax away from the thing's stinking remains.

A roar snapped her attention back around to the boat that had brought Axtius to Questral. Ephraim had been distracted by Zeke's death, and now the monstrosity with its impenetrable red skin reached out and grabbed the Sage by the throat. As Ephraim's huge black eyes became impossibly wider and he began to choke, the cloven-hooved creature opened its mouth, hundreds of needle teeth like slivers of glass glistening in the moonlight. There was a pop and a crack and its jaws unhinged, so that it looked as though the top of its skull might simply fall off.

Then it ate Ephraim's head.

This time it was Buffy's turn to scream. The tide had turned and she knew it, but she was unwilling to allow it. The warriors of Questral had seen their leader and their ambassador die within seconds of Axtius's landfall, and she would not allow them to surrender now, not even in their hearts.

She rushed forward, reaching the shore almost in the same instant as Angel and Shikah. The warrior queen of the Bazhripa launched herself at the cloven-hooved thing even as it dropped Ephraim's corpse into the surf. It batted her away with one powerful hand. Shikah hit the ground, rolled, and came up again right between Buffy and Angel.

While the rest of the battle raged around them, the Slayer, Angel, and Shikah faced off against Axtius, Haborym, and the red-skinned devil.

Axtius grinned hideously, the spines that jutted from his face twitching with the expression.

"So now it comes down to this, Angel," the general said, hefting the Pristagrix and feeling its weight in both hands. "I hoped you would live long enough for me to destroy you. I thank you for surviving this long. You owed me that much, at least."

This is bad, Buffy thought. *This is very bad.*

Once again, the air was filled with a ripping sound, but this time it was much louder, close behind her. Buffy did not dare turn to see the portal open and the last of the warriors of Questral spill through. She started forward, sword gripped in her hand so tightly, it hurt, ready to hack at the cloven-hooved demon's neck over and over until she beheaded it.

A hand gripped her shoulder and held her back. It was Shikah. The Bazhripa glanced at her with eyes that glowed a misty green. Buffy had never noticed that little detail before.

"Wait," Shikah said.

Buffy paused.

A lance of blue lightning struck the red-hooved beast, blowing a hole through its chest, and sent it crashing backward with such force that when its corpse struck the prow of the motorboat, it turned the vessel to shattered timber. Axtius and Haborym leaped into the surf, the water steaming where the fire-demon waded into it.

"That's more like it," Angel muttered.

Buffy glanced at him, knowing full well that he had also felt the tide turn against them. Now, though, things might be changing again. With a crackle of power, the sorcerer Dai'shu floated over their heads and hovered there, midway between invader and defender. Tendrils of blue fire arced around him, sparking from his eyes, forging a web of magickal energy that danced along the tips of the spines that jutted like a headdress back from his skull.

Though she knew that they were needed farther inland—that the winged demons that had passed overhead must have been headed for the forum—Buffy wished Willow and Tara were with her as well. Much as she preferred an old-fashioned ass-kicking session, Buffy figured right now they could use all the magick they could get.

"You and your soldiers are not welcome here, General Axtius," Dai'shu sneered, blue fire crackling around his hands.

Axtius shook his head, a malevolent glee in his eyes. "You've made a mistake, sorcerer. I am not your enemy. Think of the future."

"That *is* what I am thinking of," Dai'shu countered.

Slowly the sorcerer descended until his feet hung only inches above the place where the surf washed in tiny waves upon the shore.

Kick his spiny ass, Buffy thought.

Beside her, Shikah laughed softly. "I've been waiting for this a long time," the Bazhripa commander muttered.

So caught up was she in the tension of that moment, that face-off, that it took a second for Shikah's words to sink in. By then, the Bazhripa was already in motion. Buffy shouted and reached to stop her, but one of Shikah's extra arms batted the Slayer's hand away.

Shikah drove her spear through the back of Dai'shu's skull with a pop, the point erupting from the Yill demon's face. The blue light around Dai'shu winked out, the magick dying, and he fell dead into the shallow ocean water.

The Slayer gaped at the dead sorcerer and his murderer. "Oh, crap."

Angel and Buffy lunged at her. Ax and sword came down swiftly, but Shikah was fast. Metal clanged upon metal as Axtius laughed softly.

"Well done, Ileana," the Brachen general said.

And then Buffy understood. The green glow of Shikah's eyes. The mysterious absence of the leader of Questral's Vapor population. Ileana, a member of the Assemblage, had betrayed the island. She was in league with Axtius.

"It isn't her, Angel," Buffy said as she brought her ax up to parry Shikah's sword. "Ileana's possessing her."

"I know what you're thinking, Buffy," the vampire replied, fangs protruding as he snarled with each word. "You think we have to stop her without killing her. But we don't have time to do things the honorable way."

The possessed Bazhripa commander had a dagger in her upper left hand and she waved it at Buffy to keep the Slayer at bay, while with the pair of swords she held in her upper and lower right hands she attacked Angel. The vampire parried as best he could. There was an opening, and Angel hacked off Shikah's lower right arm at the elbow, but Ileana—the demon possessing the Bazhripa—drove her remaining sword through Angel's chest.

Buffy shouted his name as she watched him stagger backward, the sword coming out of the wound with a wet, sucking noise.

We don't have time to do things the honorable way, Angel had said.

"You're right," Buffy told him. "We don't."

Axtius strode through the surf toward shore, Pristagrix in hand. The warhammer seemed to glow ever more brightly. The clang of weapons and shouts of pain and fury rang across the beach as the battle raged on, but Axtius ignored it all. He had eyes only for Angel.

Haborym followed her general, the fire-demon's eyes and hair like one huge torch searing the darkness. When she saw Buffy glancing at her, Haborym grinned, and liquid flame leaked out of her mouth.

Shikah was a warrior. The Bazhripa commander would have understood, would have demanded that Buffy take her life when to do otherwise might cost the lives of everyone on the island. Still, Buffy hesitated. How could she murder her ally, no matter what hung in the balance?

With a roar, a lithe, pale figure lunged past her. Spike ran right into the Bazhripa's dagger thrust, taking the blade in his chest with a grunt, and brought his own Mahkesh sword whistling through the air. The blond vampire beheaded Shikah, then clutched his bleeding abdomen and stood beside Angel on the shore, an instant before the demon woman's head thunked to the ground.

"You hesitate like that again, Slayer, you're gonna get us all killed," Spike grunted painfully.

Buffy could think of no reply. She was grateful to Spike for saving her from having to make a terrible decision, but she would never tell him that.

Green mist spilled from the corpse, quickly coalescing into the floating form of Ileana. The Vapor demon was still nude, but there was nothing at all seductive about her nakedness now. Her face was contorted into an expression of pure hatred.

"Hello, love. Miss me?" Spike asked the Vapor.

"You bastard," she snarled at him.

"What, I ruined everything?" Spike said with a dry, humorless laugh. "You expected me to throw in with you just 'cause we had a little fun? I'm not that easy. You're the traitor, Casper. Deal with the consequences."

Buffy glanced at Angel, but he and Axtius had locked gazes and neither was willing to look away. The Slayer expected the Brachen to shout out a command, to have his warriors descend on her, Angel, and Spike. When he didn't, she had to wonder if it was because they were otherwise occupied, if they were struggling to win this war even with the slaughter of the last few moments, or if Axtius simply no longer cared about the island or the Coalition for Purity, and in that moment only desired to tear apart the one he held responsible for the death of his only child.

She suspected the latter.

Haborym raised her right hand, tendrils of fire licking up from her fingers. She beckoned to Buffy. "Come on, little girl," she hissed. "Looks like you get to dance with me."

"No thanks," Buffy replied. "I'm not really in the mood."

But even as Haborym started toward her, Buffy faced a different enemy. A green fog enveloped her body, and she began to choke as Ileana forced herself into the Slayer's throat and up her nostrils. The mist burned as the Vapor demon slid inside her. Buffy tried not to breathe, but she could not stop Ileana from invading her body.

She could still think, could still hear with her own ears and see with her own eyes, but Buffy was now only a passenger inside a prison of flesh and bone. There was a metallic taste in her mouth.

Her lips moved. Her voice spoke. "Angel."

Yet it was not Buffy who uttered that name. It was Ileana. And when Angel began to turn toward her, it was Ileana, wearing Buffy's body like a suit of armor, who raised the Mahkesh battle-ax in her hand.

• • •

Tara had seen Elijah's eyes glaze over in that moment when the protective spell had been cast, had seen his pallor go white, almost alabaster in the moonlight, and she knew he was not well. Even now as she shot him another inquisitive glance, she saw the strain it cost him to smile at her.

She ran to him again. "You need help. Let me in. We can create a circuit, you can siphon magick from me. You don't have to do this all by yourself."

"I'm fine, my dear," Elijah said, a flourish in his ragged voice that made her think he spoke to her now the same way he had spoken to his audience decades ago when he had been a stage magician. Either way, the confidence in his tone was a sham.

"Elijah—," she began to protest.

Then Willow cried out her name.

Tara turned and saw the first of the two-headed demons— Corvig Draconis—pin its wings back and swoop down toward a clutch of screaming children. Zhredic demons tried to shuffle the young Yill and Ixwik toward the bleacher seats around the forum, but there was no time. Cordelia, Fred, and several elderly islanders brandished grimy blades and moved to intercept the Corvig as it dove, two sets of fangs gnashing, drool slipping from its maws, toward the children.

No one was going to be able to get to them in time.

Willow had her back to Tara. Both hands were up and she was stabbing at nothing with her fingers as though she could carve the air into a weapon. No, no one could reach the children in time.

But magick can.

Tara stood beside Willow. They did not join hands. Their sides did not even touch. But no contact was necessary for them to feel the connection, the bond that they shared. An electric crackle like static electricity sizzled in the air between them, and Tara raised her hands as well, duplicating Willow's gestures.

A single sidelong glance passed between them. Tara held her breath and felt her heart race and her throat go dry. But there was not a shred of doubt in her. Alone, she was capable of minor sorcery, of a certain amount of magick, but when she and Willow were together they were so much more than the sum of their parts. This was the big witchy mojo. Together, Tara felt they could do anything.

A breeze from nowhere blew her hair around her face, and an electrical, burning smell filled her nostrils. Her teeth stung with a metallic flavor, as if she had been chewing aluminum foil. Then the power erupted out of her and Willow simultaneously, the spell complete. Instinctively, Tara had understood what her girlfriend was doing. The Corvig were an unknown; there was no way to predict if a spell to burn or freeze them would work, and turning them to stone might kill people beneath them when they fell.

They had to be destroyed.

The spell the witches completed in that moment was a killer. The power lanced from Willow's and Tara's fingers with a putrid yellow glow, appropriate for the darkness of the magick they were performing. The Corvig that was diving for the children was seized in midair. The eyes on both of its heads went wide, and in a panic it tried to fly away. It twitched and shuddered, locked there in stasis in the air, as the spell boiled all the liquid inside the demon. Its wings flapped once more, but they were tissue-thin now and that motion alone was enough to tear them to ribbons.

The beast fell to the ground, but it was dead before it struck the earth, the impact enough to tear it apart. Its remains spilled all around the point of impact, little more than bones and dried skin now.

Tara felt a wound open in her heart and soul. There was nothing good, no victory at all in this. Still, the children were screaming. It must be done. She reached out and clasped Willow's hand, and the circuit continued to crackle. The spell did not need to be cast again. All they needed to do this time was to turn their attention on the other two Corvig Draconis, the monsters who circled above, preparing to attack.

The winged demons died just as hideously as the first had.

When it was done, Tara let go of Willow's hand and dropped to her knees on the ground, exhausted in body and spirit.

Cordelia and Fred came running over.

"That was amazing!" Cordelia said. "You two are your own army!"

Willow staggered and leaned on Cordelia for support. "Except I'm ready to sleep for about a year now. Takes a lot out of you."

For her part, Fred slipped quietly up beside Tara and waited for the witch to meet her gaze before speaking. "Are you all right?" she asked.

Tara shook her head.

"It had to be done," Fred assured her.

A hundred thoughts went through her mind then. *Was it inevitable? Had there been no other way? Shouldn't there be some other solution to all of this hatred?* She knew she was being unrealistic, but Tara had no interest in rationality at the moment. She watched Willow catching her breath, and a tremor went through her as she wondered how Willow felt about what they had just done. It had felt wrong to Tara, but Willow seemed more exhilarated than anything else.

"Hey," Fred said softly, nudging her. Tara met her gaze and was grateful for the gentle kindness there. "The kids are safe. That's what matters."

Calvin's profanity was becoming familiar to them all by now, but this time when he rattled off a string of curses, Tara could hear the terror in them. She and Fred glanced at him simultaneously and immediately saw what had upset him.

With a spark and crackle, the dome was fading.

"Elijah," Fred whispered.

Cordelia had corralled a bunch of the kids, and the wizened old demons were helping her get them up into the gallery seats, where the roof that hung out to cover that portion of the stands would keep them out of sight from above. Now, though, the woman who held Angel Investigations together stopped and looked down at Tara, Willow, and Fred with sorrow and fear etched in her features.

"Do something!" Cordelia shouted.

For a long moment they all stared at Elijah, cognizant of their magickal protection collapsing around them and of the children whose lives they had vowed to save. As Tara turned to look at him, Elijah fell to his knees. All pretense was gone from his expression. His cheeks were flushed a deep, unhealthy red, and sweat ran with tears down his face. One of his arms was contorted slightly, held against his side as though he wanted desperately to clasp one hand across his chest but did not dare.

Heart attack, Tara thought. *Or a stroke.* But the words barely registered in her mind. They were only a substitute for the other thought, the one that overrode everything else in her head.

He's dying.

Tara ran to him then, this sweet old man who had been kind to her and who had risked everything for a bunch of creatures most people would have called monsters. When she reached him she put a hand on his arm and found that his skin was clammy. His eyes were glazed when he looked at her.

"Elijah?" she ventured.

Fred and Calvin were beside her then.

"Got to protect these kids," Elijah said.

"No!" Calvin snapped. "Just let it fall," the kid told the old magician, raising his blade. "We'll fight them off."

"We can if we have to," Fred said, her words heavy.

Tara glanced upward again. The protective dome flickered and crackled, gaps tearing into it where the magickal field evaporated. Those gaps grew larger. One of the Corvig slipped through, singing its tails on the edge of the hole as it entered the forum. It made a sound that was like a bark, but to Tara it sounded like laughter.

Willow, Tara thought. Confused, she glanced around, wondering where her girlfriend had gone. Willow had been standing with her only moments before, until they had seen Elijah beginning to collapse.

A scream tore through the darkness, echoing across the forum. Zhredic demons turned slowly, children cried out and peered anxiously into the middle of the open ground inside that structure. Cordelia shouted Willow's name from the stands.

Tara gasped and felt her chest tighten as though she, too, were having a heart attack.

Willow stood in the midst of the forum alone. Her hands were raised, and both of them glowed with a brilliant green light that the winged demon could not miss. It was circling vulturelike above them, but all of its attention now was on Willow. She screamed at the Corvig. "Down here, ugly! I'll give you a meal you'll never forget!"

The Corvig dove at her.

Tara screamed, but she was paralyzed with horror and indecision. Elijah was going to die. She had to take his place, reinforce the dome . . . *but Willow* . . .

Without summoning it at all, she felt the magick surge up inside her. Fred was cradling Elijah, but Calvin was standing right next to Tara and he jumped backward as her arms lashed out. A painful spasm racked her body. Instinct had taken over. Her fear for Willow and her hatred of the demons that were trying to kill her had combined with her anguish over Elijah's condition.

The magick flashed from her hands in the very same moment that Willow attacked the Corvig that was swooping down at her. The thing's gaping mouths were open, and both seemed to sneer with pleasure. Willow was an eyeblink from being swallowed whole or torn apart.

The two witches baked the Corvig in midair just as they had done the other three. It fell to the ground as little more than a husk. Willow had to run to get out of the way of its falling remains, and she sprinted over to where the rest of them stood around Elijah. The children were sobbing in the seats around the forum.

Tara glanced up at the dome and saw that it was failing fast. Other Corvig Draconis were flying past its outer edge, surveying the openings, looking for a way in.

"Elijah!" Willow cried as she came over to them. Her eyes flashed with anger. "Stop. Drop the spell. We can protect them. Tara and I can. Let it go. It's going to kill you."

"She's right," Calvin pleaded, "you've got to drop it."

A look of alarm passed across Fred's features. "Can you be sure you can stop them all? What about the kids?"

"We'll protect them," Willow insisted.

Tara could see the adrenaline surging through her and she knew that Willow believed it wholeheartedly. But how could they be sure? They had come here to take part in a war and now they had. Their magick had launched the opening attack in the battle, and Tara was afraid that was not enough for Willow, that her girlfriend would rather take the demons on face-to-face than simply block them out.

"Yeah," Tara agreed, gazing lovingly at Willow. "We will. We've got to protect them because now there's no one else who can."

Willow began to nod, but then Tara crouched beside Elijah and Willow faltered.

"Repeat the spell," Tara told the old magician, "and I'll say the words with you. I'll restore the dome. You've done enough, Elijah. You've saved lives."

The old man grimaced with pain. "I could've done so much more if I wasn't so afraid to give in to it."

Tara laid a hand over his. Elijah was stretched out on the ground now, his head on Fred's lap. The sorceror's power still emanated from him, spreading out to create the dome around the forum, but it faded more and more with each shuddering breath. Elijah winced at the pain in his chest, and his body stiffened.

"We don't need to do it this way," Willow said gently, laying a hand on Tara's shoulder. "He can rest now."

Tara glanced up at her. "This is the better way," she said. Then she urged Elijah on. "The spell," she said.

The magician began to recite the words, and Tara repeated after him. After a moment, Willow's voice joined hers, and Tara felt a kind of grace and peace suffuse her. That was how it was meant to be, the two of them joined.

Gradually the light that emanated from Elijah faded from his agonized body and began to shower upward from Willow and Tara instead, even more brightly than before. When Tara looked up she saw that the dome was completely restored. Corvigs slammed against it and were shocked by the impact and thrown back.

Cordelia came running across the forum, the children having been ensconced in the gallery seats, hidden from an aerial view. Her concern for the old man was obvious, and she fell to her knees in the dirt beside him, taking up a place beside Calvin and across from Fred. "Elijah? Talk to me!" she commanded.

There was no response.

Calvin cleared his throat, but his voice shook when he spoke. "Is he dead?"

"Unconscious but still breathing," Fred replied.

Cordelia looked up at the witches. "They've got to end this fast or he's not going to make it."

The ground began to rumble beneath their feet.

"Man, you gotta be kidding!" Calvin snapped. "What the hell is this now?"

Tara nearly lost her balance and fell against Willow. The witches held one another up.

"I don't think I can take much more of this," Tara whispered in her girlfriend's ear.

Willow clutched her tightly. "I'm here, baby. I'm here."

Then, over Willow's shoulder, Tara saw Fred staring off to the southern end of the forum. She turned . . . they all turned . . . and over the wall of the enormous structure they saw the towering, mantislike Old One as it passed by, the nest of tentacles weaving where its mouth should have been, that one orange eye glowing brightly in the blue-black, predawn darkness. The fissures in its massive, oversized skull shot flames into the air as if each were fed by a giant bellow. Tara had seen the creature before, but still, she held her breath—and her girlfriend—as it passed, making the ground quake. The Old One, one of the Elder Demons who had walked the earth since before the first man.

"All right!" Calvin shouted. "Dude looks pissed."

And it was true.

When the ground had ceased its trembling—though Tara had not—all the children began to come back down onto the open expanse of the forum, the Zhredics and the aged demons gathering there as well. Willow and Tara kept up the magick that powered the protective dome, but the winged demons above were gone, perhaps frightened off by the passing of the Old One.

"Are you familiar with the expression 'deus ex machina'?" Fred asked quietly.

"Intimately," Willow replied.

Fred stared off in the direction the Old One had gone. "Well, baby, here it comes in spades."

CHAPTER TWENTY

All of the rage, all of that primal fury inside Buffy, evaporated in an instant. The ancient power of the Slayer seemed to withdraw, leaving only the ordinary human woman behind, the girl who had once wanted nothing more than what every other girl wanted: a cute boyfriend, cool clothes, parents who didn't fight all the time. That was never to be. Not for Buffy Summers. Fate had other things in store for her. But even as the Slayer, in the midst of all of that, the girl had fallen in love, grown into a woman, and lost that love.

All of that she could survive. But this? No, not this.

The demon Ileana was *inside* her. Buffy felt the Vapor invading her, burning down her throat like a shot of whiskey, which she had tried once and never again. Yet she had not felt the moment when the thing possessing her had taken over, had disconnected Buffy from control of her own body. All of her senses remained. She could hear Angel say her name and see his eyes go wide as he stared at her. Did he see her eyes glowing green as Shikah's had?

Buffy could *feel* the handle of the Mahkesh ax in her hands, but it was not her will that moved the muscles in her arms, that swung the ax toward Angel. With every fiber of her soul, Buffy tried to stop Ileana, to stop the ax from swinging. Perhaps she slowed the possessing demon down just the slightest bit, for Angel spun away from her, the ax passing harmlessly by him.

Trapped inside her own body, Buffy heard the demon Axtius shouting in triumph, exhorting Ileana to batter Angel, to cut him, to break him—but not to kill him. Axtius wanted the Vapor to save that for him alone.

Spike wrapped an arm around the Slayer's throat from behind and began to choke her. Buffy's thoughts churned. *We don't have time to do things the honorable way,* Angel had said before, and Buffy had agreed. She herself had been unwilling to kill Shikah, but she was privately relieved that Spike had not had any such compunctions. Now, though, it was she who was possessed. Spike and Angel should just kill her. Any delay might mean the death of them all. And, besides, she had been dead twice already. What was that saying? *Third time's the charm.*

Instead, Spike was trying to choke her into unconsciousness.

"Never an exorcist around when you need one," the vampire muttered.

Buffy's elbow shot backward into Spike's stomach, her fist crashed up into his face. He was staggered, and then, using the Slayer's body, Ileana leaped into a roundhouse kick that knocked him to the ground. Spike sprawled amidst a violent clash of weapons in which a pair of Mahkesh were trying to prevent Gunn and Xander from joining the fray.

None of them would be in time to change the course of events.

The Slayer's body was faster and stronger than any of them, and Ileana was in control.

"Yes!" Axtius roared from his position on the shore, slaughtering a pair of Ixwik demons who were attacking him. "Drive him down. Make him bleed!"

Buffy wanted to cry, but Ileana would not allow her even that.

She felt every movement as she turned on Angel once again. He brought his sword up, but Buffy knew he would not be able to bring himself to use it. Her mouth opened and, using Buffy's voice, Ileana began to laugh. With the Slayer's speed, she attacked, bringing the ax down. Angel parried the first attack, but the Mahkesh weapon would not be denied blood. Ileana used Buffy's hands to swing the ax around again.

Despite Axtius's orders to the contrary, it was clear to Buffy that the thing possessing her meant to kill Angel. The ax would split his skull. He would die, and the blood would be on Buffy's hands. Ileana cared not at all that Axtius had other plans for Angel.

Buffy's back was to the ocean.

A roar came from behind her, but it was not Spike this time, nor Xander or Gunn, all of whom were too far away. Buffy was a passenger in her own body, staring out through the windows of her eyes as Ileana turned to see Axtius screaming in a fury, bearing down on her with the Pristagrix high over his head, ready to deliver a killing blow with the warhammer.

"Noooo!" the Brachen general shouted.

Buffy felt Ileana's control over her loosen. That moment of panic had shaken her free. The Vapor was still inside her, but for just those seconds, Ileana's uncertainty had given Buffy her body back.

The glowing warhammer crashed down toward her skull.

Buffy stepped in closer to Axtius, sidestepped, and rammed the butt of the ax handle into his side. The Brachen general grunted in pain, tried to turn the heavy warhammer toward her, but its weight and momentum were too great. He let go of it with his right hand and punched her in the side of the face, a blow that sent her to her knees on the shore, head ringing, cheek numb.

The Slayer glanced up and saw Haborym still standing in the surf, water steaming around her ankles, observing the proceedings with great curiosity. Her posturing had disappeared once Ileana had possessed Buffy, and now she seemed more fascinated than homicidal.

Axtius, however, was more enraged than ever.

"How dare you?" the Brachen screamed at Buffy. Or, more accurately, at Ileana. "Break him, I said. Bleed him. But he'll die by *my* hands."

But Buffy wasn't really listening. She was waging another battle, this one inside of her. Her stomach churned now, and there was a sting in her throat. Ileana was trying to get control of her again, but Buffy was not going to allow that. Summoning every ounce of her will, Buffy fought her.

Nausea surged up in her. With a great gasp that wracked her body, Buffy vomited onto the shore, but all that came out was a spray of green mist.

Even as she coalesced again, the Vapor was hissing at Axtius.

"So be it, General!" Ileana sneered. "Stand or fall on your own, then." And the naked form of that woman dispersed into nothing more than a light green fog that was swirled away by the breeze and then disappeared completely.

Angel had risen slowly to his feet, cautious, ready for battle, taking it all in. None of Axtius's warriors would approach him now, though there was blood on his face and he swayed slightly as he regained his bearings.

Axtius saw him and started toward him. Several Bazhripa tried to bar his way, but the Brachen would not be stopped. Inexorably, he began to cut through them, his focus entirely on Angel now.

Wiping the back of her hand across her mouth, Buffy stood, shakily. Spike rushed to her, raising his sword, and the two of them were back to back, waiting for the next attacker. As Buffy glanced over at them, Gunn and Xander ran their swords through a Mahkesh that was blocking their progress. It slid off their blades, and then they rushed to Buffy's side as well.

"What the hell was that all about?" Gunn asked the Slayer, glancing nervously at Haborym, who remained motionless in the water.

Buffy frowned. "Tell you later." She looked at Xander. He was sweating and spattered with blood. There was a long cut on his left cheek and a scrape on his right temple from which a small line of blood trickled. His eyes seemed hollow. "You all right?" she asked, her heart breaking to see him like this.

Their eyes met. Xander nodded. "I will be. When this is over."

Up and down the beach, the battle still raged. The shore and the shallow surf were littered with corpses. Blood tinted the water and stained the island soil. There were far fewer warriors now, and what had been a massive battlefield had split apart into several dozen smaller battles.

Here, though, on the stretch of shoreline where Axtius had beached his motorboat, there were just those seven. Haborym in the water. Buffy, Spike, Gunn, and Xander on the shore. And thirty feet farther inland, Axtius marched toward Angel, who stood waiting with his sword in hand.

"Oy!" Spike shouted.

Buffy whipped around, realizing instantly that he was talking to Haborym.

"What're you waiting for, then, hot stuff? An invitation?" Spike taunted.

Buffy stared at him. She was not exactly sure why, but Haborym had been having second thoughts, obviously hesitant to attack them. Or perhaps she was content to leave them alone as long as they did not try to prevent Axtius from fighting Angel.

Now, though, gouts of flame shot from Haborym's eyes as she took a step toward Spike, the tiniest of waves washing over her feet. Amidst the clash of weapons and the shouts of war, her voice was quiet, and yet Buffy heard every word.

"You will address me with respect, vampire."

"Spike—," Buffy warned.

"What, a fiery little bint like you?" He sneered at Haborym. "Give me an hour, pet, and I'll show you all kinds of respect."

Haborym snarled and raised her hands. Tendrils of fire licked at her fingers.

"Xander! Don't let Axtius have any help!" Buffy snapped.

Then she clapped a hand on Spike's back and propelled him alongside her as she rushed Haborym. Fire leaped from the demon's fingers, and Buffy felt it searing her shoulder and upper arm, but fortunately most of the attack was focused on Spike. He snarled in pain as flames scorched his chest and legs.

But Buffy and Spike were running directly at Haborym. The fire-demon took a step back into the water, and then Buffy careened into her, knocking her off balance, and the three of them fell in a tangle of limbs and a matrix of fire into the ocean. Buffy felt her mouth fill with sea water and she spat it out, then held her breath as she got hold of Haborym's arms.

The Slayer's palms were seared but she held on, hoping Spike had caught on, hoping he would work with her to keep the fire-demon under the water long enough for her to fall unconscious.

Buffy prayed Haborym would run out of air before she did.

With the copper tang of blood in the air and the heat of combat in his cold heart, Angel had stalked across the shore of Questral wearing the visage of the vampire, the face that had terrorized all of Europe in days gone by. Now, in the predawn light, as the war was reduced to desperate duels amongst those warriors left alive, he took in a lungful of tropical air, a breath his undead body did not need. As he let it out, he shuddered and his features changed once more.

When he confronted Axtius, he wore the face of the man he had become.

The general stood a dozen feet away, the two of them circling each other warily on a stretch of beach that seemed to have been staked out as the arena for their final confrontation. The Brachen was a full-blood demon, taller than Angel and broader in the chest. His chest heaved beneath his leather body armor, and he gripped the Pristagrix tightly in both hands as though he planned to hit a home run with Angel's skull.

"Are you remembering, Angel?" Axtius snarled. "Are you recalling the last time we met in battle, and the way the Pristagrix crushed your bones?"

Angel felt vulnerable in his torn shirt and black pants—he *did* remember the feel of his bones breaking—but he wasn't about to let Axtius know that. The vampire shook his head, a bit of pity creeping into his heart to join the disgust that had coagulated there. He raised the sword he had liberated from a Mahkesh demon—

—and then he tossed it away. It landed with a thunk on the shore.

He caught a glimpse of Buffy, Spike, and Haborym fighting beneath the water—of Spike's fist rising up from the waves and falling again and again—but he had to rely on the Slayer to take care of herself. He had faith.

"You're a fool, vampire," Axtius scowled. "You don't honestly think I'll follow suit? That out of some sense of honor I'll toss *this* weapon aside?"

Angel stood a little straighter. A wave of hatred passed through him and his face nearly morphed again, but he fought it back. When the hate was gone, only the pity and disgust remained.

"Never occurred to me," Angel replied with a bitter smile. "It's obvious honor's a foreign concept to you, *General*. Look at you. High and mighty with the hammer. The Pristagrix is dangerous, sure. You could kill me with it, grind my bones to chalk dust."

He let his upper lip curl in revulsion. "But last time, you had the jump on me, *pinhead*. This time I'm looking you right in the eye. I'll lay odds that hammer doesn't touch me. But I am very definitely going to touch you."

They continued to circle. Axtius's heavy boots kicked up sand. His blue skin gleamed in the strained moonlight that remained in this hour before dawn. The hate that burned in his eyes was akin to madness.

"My son died because of you, filth," Axtius said, biting each word off with a snap of his jaws.

Angel froze, glaring at him. "Your son died a hero. He died fighting for people who couldn't fight for themselves. He was a good *man*, Axtius. You would've been so ashamed. But not nearly as ashamed as he would have been had he survived to see what you've done, what *you've* become."

Axtius stopped circling as well. His fingers tensed on the Pristagrix. He shuddered with fury, and then he launched himself at Angel.

The vampire waited for him. Axtius brought the Pristagrix around with inhuman speed and a demon's ferocity. Angel felt it all rising up in him; his disgust, his sadness over all this needless slaughter, and his lingering grief over Doyle's death. A strength immune to fatigue rushed through his body, and he launched a single blow at Axtius. His fist pummeled into the Brachen demon's face, the spines that jutted from Axtius's flesh puncturing Angel fingers. Blood and spittle flew from Axtius's mouth as his head snapped back.

The Pristagrix came down, but the swing was off now and Angel dodged it.

He backed off, letting Axtius catch his breath. A small clutch of demons nearby—invaders and defenders both—had stopped their own combat to witness this.

"Look at you," Angel taunted him. "The big bad demon general . . . whatever you believe now about wiping them all out, about only pure-blood demons having a right to live . . . it's all talk.

"You loved a human woman once, Axtius. You fathered a half-breed. But you wanted all these demons to follow you? You teach them to hate and hate and hate . . . and kill . . . 'cause it's okay for *you* to feel something, but not for them."

"Liar!" Axtius roared. He rushed at Angel again, swinging the Pristagrix.

Angel had another flash of memory of Axtius ambushing him, of the way that hammer felt as it turned his bones to powder. He sidestepped, slipped back in, and grabbed the handle of the warhammer. The Pristagrix burned in his hand, but he held on. With a grunt, Angel kicked Axtius in the abdomen, the air echoing with the impact of his boot on leather.

He held on tight to the hammer and kicked the Brachen again as Axtius tried to pull his weapon from Angel's grasp.

"Hypocrite," Angel sneered. "Your motives are so twisted, you can't even see straight. You hate half-breeds and humans now because you see them as a reflection of the weakness in yourself."

Now Angel grabbed the Pristagrix with both hands, leaped into the air, and snapped a kick at the Brachen's head. Several of the spines in the general's face stuck in Angel's boot, and when Axtius staggered backward, they tore from his skin.

Axtius released the Pristagrix.

Angel dropped the warhammer to the ground.

Fury and shame burned in Axtius's eyes, and when he shouted to his troops now there was a shrill desperation in his voice.

"Kill him!" Axtius cried, glancing around at his warriors. Some of them were simply watching, but others were in the midst of fights of their own. "Kill the vampire!"

"What's the matter?" Angel asked. "Change your mind? Can't kill one vampire on your own?"

"Kill him!" Axtius yelled, then bared a mouthful of deadly sharp teeth and rushed at Angel.

Buffy had swallowed too much water. Haborym had fought back, struck her in the throat with a hard elbow, causing Buffy to gasp underwater, sucking in ocean. Now the Slayer choked as she got her feet under her. She rose from the waves, coughing, hoping she wouldn't throw up a second time.

A hissing sound came from right beside her, and the stench of burning flesh filled her nostrils.

"Bu—Buffy!" a rasping voice called.

The Slayer turned to see that a staggering, weakened Haborym was throttling Spike. Her hands were still on fire . . . and so was the vampire's throat. Once again his skin blackened and charred, and flames licked up Spike's cheeks. His hair had only just begun to burn, the fact that it was damp with ocean water not doing anything to douse the supernatural flames of the fire-deity.

The most bizarre part of all of this was that Haborym was not paying attention to Spike at all. Not anymore. Her focus was on the face-off between Angel and Axtius taking place on the shore. Buffy heard Angel speaking, heard the things he was saying to Axtius, but she could barely make sense of them as she sucked in air, her throat and chest aching from nearly drowning.

The waves lapped against her hips.

"Put him down," Buffy snapped.

Spike looked at her with grateful eyes and then squinted away from the demon's blazing fingers.

Haborym glanced at Buffy and offered a tiny shrug.

"Fine," said the fire-demon.

She dropped Spike into the ocean. He rose to his knees but kept his head underwater, letting the cold sea wash over his burns. Buffy stepped toward Haborym. The Slayer had no weapon and little hope of avoiding a fiery death without the element of surprise. In her mind she prepared to lunge, to try to get her arms around Haborym's neck and break it before the demon could immolate her completely.

But Haborym ignored her.

Up on the island, Axtius began to yell. "Kill him!" the general roared. Some of his warriors continued with their own struggles, and others seemed paralyzed. Many of them, however, fought off their opponents long enough to rush along the beach toward Angel.

Haborym did nothing.

"Damn," Buffy whispered. She gave a thought to Spike, who would heal as long as Haborym did not try to finish the job. Angel needed her more. She started to wade toward shore.

Then the ground began to shake. Buffy glanced at Haborym and saw that the fire-demon was just as surprised as she was, flames gouting from her eyes. Even the ocean trembled. On the shore, all the demons paused in their fighting, some of them thrown to the ground by the earth tremor. Over the noise of the rumbling ground, Axtius screamed again.

"Kill the vampire now!"

"Kill me yourself, you coward," Angel replied.

But then the ground stopped shaking and another voice carried along the shore.

"I think there's been enough killing."

The voice belonged to Wesley. Every being upon the eastern shore of Questral who still lived stared up at the tree line farther inland, at the opening of the path where Wesley had emerged with Lorne, whose green skin looked far too yellow in the predawn light and whose tattered clothes seemed more out of place than ever.

But nobody was paying very much attention to Lorne's fashion sense.

Behind Wesley and Lorne was the cause of the earth tremor. The Old One rested on its hind legs now, its spindly insectoid body partially blending with the trees in a way that its hideous face and that single, massive, orange eye never could. The fire from the fissures in its skull sent up whorls of smoke into the air.

No one moved. Not even Axtius.

Then the Old One began to speak in that low, guttural tongue, the language of the Elder Demons. It was the only sound other than the surf. As the tentacles on the ancient creature's face slithered, its voice coming from those many mouths, Lorne took three steps forward. Despite his attire, there was a quiet dignity about the Host as he began to translate.

"Gar'thraxus the Elder begs your indulgence, fine warriors," Lorne shouted, his voice carrying along the shore. Full-bloods and half-breeds alike gave the Host and the Old One their full attention.

Spike rose from the ocean, spitting salt water and clutching his scorched throat. He glared at Haborym with murder in his eyes. Buffy was about to tell him to hold back when Spike noticed the extraordinary tableau on the shore and then he, too, paused to listen to Krevlornswath of the Deathwok Clan as he translated the language of Hell on Earth.

Once more, Garth—Gar'thraxus the Elder—spoke in that guttural tongue.

"There are those among you who are nearly immortal," Lorne translated as Garth's huge, single orange eye scanned the bloodied combatants. "Yet when your children's children are dust, thousands of years hence, still shall I walk this earth. I was here when the world was young, when the ground shifted and ran molten hot, and I will be here when the sun has died as the world is cold and dead. The age between monkey and man and the end of such things is only a fraction of the life of this world, and of my time here.

"You are all fragile, ephemeral things. I do not understand how you can shatter one another, extinguishing the spark of life. Every death carries you farther along the path to the end of things.

"And yet you follow the will of this child, Axtius? Very well, then. Those among you who are truly pure, who are true demons, kin of my ancient blood, step forward."

Every warrior was still.

"I am eternal," Gar'thraxus said, and Lorne translated. "Yet I do not place myself above even the least of you. Think on this. If there is to be more death here, more blood spilled, then step forward and spill *my* blood. Take *my* life. If this battle is to continue, I demand that I be the next to die. Come for me, then, righteous soldiers. Erase *my* blight from the universe."

The massive mantis body of the Old One shifted. Wesley and Lorne moved aside as Gar'thraxus lumbered from the jungle onto the shore and lowered his head so that it would be vulnerable to the warriors' weapons. Fire leaked from the fissures in his skull, and the tentacles on his face twined around one another. The glowing orange eye of the Elder Demon dimmed somewhat.

When he spoke again it was still guttural, but somehow he managed to form three words in English.

"Or go home."

One by one, and then in groups, the dozens of warriors who remained of Axtius's invasion force began to drop their weapons. Only the surviving Mahkesh kept hold of theirs, but swords were sheathed and axes were lowered. They began to drift back toward the transport vessels that had carried them to Questral, obviously intent upon returning to the freighter out on the water.

The spell was broken. The silence ended. Axtius had been frozen along with all the rest during the Old One's speech, but now the Brachen demon shrieked almost unintelligibly. Buffy could make out only a few words. One of them was "no." The others were a stream of epithets directed toward Haborym, the intent of which was obviously to command her to help him destroy Angel.

The fire that flickered in her eyes leaped a bit higher. Buffy thought that the expression on Haborym's face was more disappointment than anything else.

"You're a disgrace," Haborym said.

Buffy went to see to Spike's burns, turning her back on the fire-demon without concern.

• • •

Angel knew it wasn't over. The madness in Axtius's eyes had only deepened with the Old One's arrival and the withdrawal of the general's soldiers. He faced the Brachen demon in a defensive posture, waiting for the attack he knew was coming, but his heart was calm. He was thinking mostly of Doyle, missing his friend, both sad for him and proud of him at the same time.

Doyle had been living proof that what mattered was not where you began the journey of your life, but the path you chose to travel on the way to its conclusion. Angel thought of all of the people he had surrounded himself with, and the friends Buffy had gathered around her as well, and he knew they would all understand. All save Spike, and though he was reluctant to let himself imagine it, Angel wondered if there might not be a glimmer of hope for him as well. It seemed impossible, yet if there was anything he had learned in his long life, it was that nothing was impossible. Not really.

Axtius was shrieking at Haborym, but she ignored him.

"Come on, then, General," Angel said quietly. "Let's finish it."

All the desperation went out of Axtius's face then. The spines that jutted from his blue skin quivered and he nodded slowly, lowering himself into a predatory crouch. The Pristagrix lay on the ground half a dozen feet away, still glowing. Axtius's gaze ticked toward it, then back to Angel.

The Brachen demon lunged. Angel tried to block the attack, but Axtius was too fast for him. The general's leather armor creaked as he moved in and his massive fists were in motion. Axtius struck Angel in the side of the head with such a blow that Angel felt his cheekbone crack, and he staggered sideways several feet. He lashed out and caught Axtius in the chest, but the demon's armor absorbed most of the blow.

Axtius hit him again with such speed and power that Angel felt two ribs pop. The demon kept coming, striking him twice more before Angel could retaliate. Axtius tried to head-butt him, but Angel punched him in the throat. The Brachen demon staggered, and Angel shot a roundhouse kick at his abdomen, then another kick at Axtius's knee, hoping to break it. He succeeded only in knocking the demon down.

Axtius snarled, wordless and feral, and dove for the Pristagrix. The demon's hands curled around the handle. Angel stomped a boot down on the warhammer, then kicked Axtius in the face again. The Brachen was down and Angel kicked him again and again with every ounce of strength he could muster. Blood began to leak from Axtius's lips. His eyes were no longer mad, but disoriented as he tried to get to his feet again.

"You relied too much on weapons," Angel told him. "You were fast enough. You had the edge. But you thought you needed the hammer, and that slowed you down."

"I'll kill you," the Brachen rasped.

"Maybe. But not today. And not here."

The sky had turned a shining blue, and the eastern horizon glowed golden. The sun would rise soon. Angel looked around for his friends. Wesley and Lorne stood with the Old One. Gunn and Xander were with the little Ixwik armorer and several Bazhripa warriors. He caught sight of Buffy and Spike, knee deep in the ocean. They started in toward shore.

But Haborym was already approaching. The fire-demon's hands were blazing, and her eyes seemed to dance with flames. She smiled.

Angel tensed, exhausted but ready to combat her if need be.

"You're not going to kill him?" Haborym asked as she approached.

"Not today," Angel repeated, looking back with revulsion at the Brachen demon. Then he glanced up at Gar'thraxus. "And not here."

The Old One nodded silently.

"You are merciful," Haborym said.

Axtius struggled to stand and finally managed it, swaying, looking around at those he had tried so furiously to destroy. His own warriors had all turned their backs to him, all save Haborym, and it was to her that he turned now with grateful eyes.

"I am not," the fire-demon said.

She burned Axtius to death, there on the shore.

EPILOGUE

They burned the dead at dusk that night. There were so many corpses, both of islanders and of their attackers—whose comrades had left their remains behind—that four pyres had to be built. Bonfires of the dead burned so brightly and so high in the sky that if not for the magicks that protected Questral from discovery they would have been visible from the Santa Monica pier.

Buffy cried.

They had saved so many lives and yet somehow that seemed little consolation. Haborym and the other demons who had been under Axtius's command had retreated to their vessel; neither they nor the islanders wanted any more dying that day. But despite Garth's example, Buffy knew that it wasn't over. Some of the others might disappear back into the fabric of the world, but Buffy felt certain that Haborym would report the events of the day to whatever evil things were behind the Coalition for Purity. Axtius hadn't been the top of that totem pole. Who or whatever *was* at the top, they weren't going to like what had happened on Questral.

On the other hand, after the casualties they had suffered in the assault, Buffy had a feeling it would be a while before they tried another. Maybe they never would. It was possible the casualties were so great that it would cripple their efforts for the foreseeable future.

Possible.

But she and Angel and all the others—and the islanders—would have to be always on their guard. Just in case.

Her friends gathered around her. Willow laid her head on Tara's shoulder and watched the blaze in silence. Xander's wounds had been tended to, but he still looked grim, impatient to be home. Spike had fought as valiantly for the islanders as anyone, but he held back from the spectacle of the burning of the dead, keeping to the shadows beyond the glow of the pyres.

The people from Angel Investigations stood in a familial cluster near the water. Fred, Cordelia, and Wesley all watched the proceedings gravely, and Gunn kept a paternal hand on Calvin's shoulder as if to reassure the young man that it was over.

Only Angel was missing. But none of them could fault him. As soon as the sun had fallen below the horizon and it was safe for him to emerge into the darkness, he had gone off to bury Elijah.

The news of the magician's death had struck Angel particularly hard. Buffy ached for him. None of them, herself included, had known how much the man had meant to him, the role that Elijah had filled in Angel's life. The sweet, funny old magician had been like a fond uncle. The closest thing to a father Angel had had since regaining his soul, despite the fact that in truth Angel was far older than Elijah could ever have lived to be.

And now Elijah was dead.

It had taken hours for a new Assemblage to be convened. Ephraim, Shikah, and Dai'shu had been replaced by others of their tribes; it turned out that when a Yill sorcerer died, the youngest of that tribe inherited his power, so the Yill representative to the Assemblage was merely a child. The Vapor Ileana had fled after her betrayal, and no other of her breed was invited to sit with the ruling council. As the senior member, then, it fell to the Ixwik armorer, Fashjaol, to lead the Assemblage. Among the first rulings of the new Assemblage was that the Pristagrix, that terrible weapon that Axtius had wielded in battle against them, would be buried there, upon the island. It, and the other Mahkesh weapons that had been captured, would be kept on Questral, never to be used in war again.

Angel asked the permission of the Assemblage to bury Elijah on the island. Though it was Questral's custom to burn the dead and it was unprecedented for a human to be honored on the island, they agreed unanimously to that request.

When they had remained at the pyres long enough to pay their respects, Buffy and the other visitors to the island all made their way somberly through the jungle to the forum. Angel had chosen a spot just outside the massive structure's entry to bury Elijah. When they arrived there, he had completed the interment and was gathering stones and building a cairn on top of the grave.

No one offered to help. Angel had made it clear that he wanted to do this alone.

When he had finished, Buffy hesitated a moment. She was not really a part of his life now. Cordelia and Wesley were probably closer to him than anyone else. Yet when she glanced over at them, she saw that they expected her to be the first to speak with him. She found herself feeling incredibly grateful. No matter how much time they spent apart, she thought that she would never be as close to anyone as she was to Angel, and she knew he felt the same. The others seemed to understand that.

Buffy strode to him, leaving the others behind.

Angel stood quietly over Elijah's grave, staring down at the cairn of stones as though he was wondering if there was anything more he could do. Buffy slipped her hand into his and just stood there, with him, sharing in his sadness.

At length, Angel spoke. "They're going to build a monument here to everyone who's died defending the island. Elijah's name is going to be on it. They're going to put Doyle's on it too."

"That'll be good. I think Elijah would've liked that."

"Yeah," Angel agreed. He didn't have any family. Just his shop. The books. I'm . . . he left it all to me."

"You're going to run the bookstore?"

Angel smiled softly and glanced down at her. "Can't you picture it?" He chuckled. "No, we had a long-standing arrangement. The occult books I'll keep. Everything else will be donated to charity, including whatever I get for selling the store."

"There are too few like him in the world," Buffy said.

"One in a million," Angel agreed, squeezing her hand. "And you know what the worst, most ironic part of it all is? A monster like Axtius fathers a son, and someone like Elijah never gets a chance to have children."

Buffy understood this. Giles had such wisdom, humor, and dignity that he would have made an extraordinary father, but time and fate had not conspired to give him children of his own. Buffy was the closest he might ever come to a daughter. Time and again since all of this had begun she had thought of Giles, but also of her father, Hank Summers. Her mind returned to him again now.

"Parents are just people. Imperfect, just like the rest of us. They bring us into this world, Angel. And maybe the way they behave, and what they expect from us, is partly responsible for what we become. But only partly."

Angel nodded. "Doyle knew what his father was, what his father wanted him to be." He chuckled softly. "He wasn't exactly perfect either, Doyle. But he wanted something more for himself, something better."

"It's what we all want," Buffy whispered.

They stood there, hand in hand, for several minutes longer before turning from the fresh grave and rejoining the others, these friends who had become their families.

Los Angeles

In a condemned tenement building only two blocks from where he grew up, Calvin Symms stared into the face of his father and felt hollow inside. This thing, this grotesque shell, wasn't his father. He stared into the vampire's eyes and he saw no trace of Raymond Symms there.

"Oh, Pop," Calvin muttered through trembling lips.

"Yeah boy, it's me. You don't want to let this happen, Cal," the vampire wheedled, straining against the hold Gunn and Angel had on him.

But Calvin's words had not been recognition. They had been a sigh of mourning, of good-bye.

With help from Gunn's crew—*my crew,* Calvin thought—they had tracked Raymond and his little nest of vampires. During the time they had all been out on Monster Island, Raymond and his leeches had been worming their way back into the neighborhood.

The other vampires were all dust now. All except for Raymond.

"Cal?" Raymond urged, yellow eyes wide.

Calvin took one last look just to confirm it, just so he would always remember. His father wasn't inside those eyes. His father had been dead for years.

He turned his back and left the filthy room, stepped into the corridor, and closed the door behind him. The other members of the crew had retreated to the front of the building to guard the place, and Wesley was with them. Cordelia and Fred waited for him in the hall, and Calvin went to Fred, who put her arms around him.

Calvin let himself cry, and the tears came hard and fast. Fred hushed him and touched his hair and held him close. In the room he had just left, Angel and Gunn would be dusting the vampire that used to be his father.

Cordelia laid a hand on his shoulder. Calvin wiped at his eyes as he glanced at her.

"What's in there, that's the past," she said. "You're free now. Free to figure out what the future's gonna be."

Sunnydale

Business had been dismal all day. Anya had claimed to be recovered enough from her injuries to come in to work, but Giles had told her to wait until tomorrow. She could use the rest, and it was very quiet at the Magic Box. Giles had relished the quiet, actually, in spite of the lack of sales. It gave him the opportunity to tidy up properly, to do some orders he had been unable to get to, and to enjoy the jazz CDs he had bought the day before. But even with the music filtering through the store and the busy work he assigned himself, he could not focus entirely.

With a sigh he went to the hot plate he kept in back and put on a kettle for tea. Then he returned to the counter. While he was attempting to decide whether to order a full or only half a dozen Tantalus crystals, the bell rang over the door of the Magic Box.

Giles glanced up to find Buffy standing just inside the door. She was a bit worse for wear, scratched and bruised here and there, but all in one piece.

"Well, hello there. Look what the cat's dragged in," the Watcher said, smiling softly, one eyebrow raised. "I've just put a pot on for tea. Would you like a cup?"

Buffy sighed and returned his smile. "I'd love one," she said as she marched across the store and boosted herself up onto the counter beside the register.

Giles nodded and turned to fetch the cups. He paused and glanced back at her. "Welcome home."

ABOUT THE AUTHORS

CHRISTOPHER GOLDEN is the award-winning, *L.A. Times* best-selling author of such novels as *The Ferryman*, *Strangewood*, *The Gathering Dark*, *Of Saints and Shadows*, *Prowlers*, and the Body of Evidence series of teen thrillers, which was honored with an award from the American Library Association as one of its Best Books for Young Readers.

Golden has also written or cowritten a great many books and comic books related to the TV series *Buffy the Vampire Slayer* and *Angel*, as well as the script for the *Buffy the Vampire Slayer* video game for Microsoft Xbox, which he cowrote with frequent collaborator Tom Sniegoski. His other comic book work includes stories featuring such characters as Batman, Wolverine, Spider-Man, The Crow, and Hellboy, among many others.

As a pop culture journalist, he was the editor of the Bram Stoker Award–winning book of criticism, *CUT!: Horror Writers* on *Horror Film*, and coauthor of both *Buffy the Vampire Slayer: The Watcher's Guide* and *The Stephen King Universe*.

Golden was born and raised in Massachusetts, where he still lives with his family. He graduated from Tufts University. There are more than six million copies of his books in print. At present he is at work on *The Boys Are Back in Town,* a new novel for Bantam Books. Please visit him at www.christophergolden.com.

THOMAS E. SNIEGOSKI is best known as a comic-book writer who has worked for every major company in the comics industry, including DC, Marvel, Image, and Dark Horse. Some of his more recent works include *Batman: The Real World* for DC, and the Hellboy miniseries for Dark Horse, *B.P.R.D.: The Hollow Earth.* Sniegoski has recently expanded into other areas that showcase his interests and talents. He was one of the writers on Pocket Book's *Buffy the Vampire Slayer: The Monster Book* and coscripted the *Buffy the Vampire Slayer* video game for Xbox with frequent collaborator Christopher Golden. His first Angel novel, *Soul Trade,* was released in the summer of 2001. He and Golden also worked on the Simon Pulse thriller *Force Majeure*. Sniegoski is currently working on an original series for Simon Pulse called The Fallen. He lives in Massachusetts with wife, LeeAnne, and five-year-old Labrador retriever, Mulder. Please visit Tom and Mulder at www.sniegoski.com.